The Plot Thickens
Meadowfiled Mysteries
Book 2

Agatha Frost

Published by Pink Tree Publishing Limited in 2024

All characters and events in this publication, other than those clearly in the public domain, are fictitious and any resemblance to real persons, living or dead, is purely coincidental.

Copyright © Pink Tree Publishing Limited.

The moral right of the author has been asserted.

All rights reserved. This book or any portion thereof may not be reproduced or used in any manner whatsoever without the express written permission of the publisher except for the use of brief quotations in a book review.

For questions and comments about this book, please contact pinktreepublishing@gmail.com

www.pinktreepublishing.com
www.agathafrost.com

WANT TO BE KEPT UP TO DATE WITH AGATHA FROST RELEASES? ***SIGN UP THE FREE NEWSLETTER!***

www.AgathaFrost.com

You can also follow **Agatha Frost** across social media. Search 'Agatha Frost' on:

Facebook
Twitter
Goodreads
Instagram

Also by Agatha Frost

Meadowfield Mysteries (NEW!)

3. The Fatal First Edition

2. The Plot Thickens

1. The Last Draft

Peridale Cafe

33. Cruffins and Confessions (coming soon)

32. Lemon Drizzle and Loathing

31. Sangria and Secrets

30. Mince Pies and Madness

29. Pumpkins and Peril

28. Eton Mess and Enemies

27. Banana Bread and Betrayal

26. Carrot Cake and Concern

25. Marshmallows and Memories

24. Popcorn and Panic

23. Raspberry Lemonade and Ruin

22. Scones and Scandal

21. Profiteroles and Poison

20. Cocktails and Cowardice

19. Brownies and Bloodshed
18. Cheesecake and Confusion
17. Vegetables and Vengeance
16. Red Velvet and Revenge
15. Wedding Cake and Woes
14. Champagne and Catastrophes
13. Ice Cream and Incidents
12. Blueberry Muffins and Misfortune
11. Cupcakes and Casualties
10. Gingerbread and Ghosts
9. Birthday Cake and Bodies
8. Fruit Cake and Fear
7. Macarons and Mayhem
6. Espresso and Evil
5. Shortbread and Sorrow
4. Chocolate Cake and Chaos
3. Doughnuts and Deception
2. Lemonade and Lies
1. Pancakes and Corpses

Claire's Candles
1. Vanilla Bean Vengeance
2. Black Cherry Betrayal
3. Coconut Milk Casualty

4. Rose Petal Revenge

5. Fresh Linen Fraud

6. Toffee Apple Torment

7. Candy Cane Conspiracies

8. Wildflower Worries

9. Frosted Plum Fears

10. Double Espresso Deception

11. Spiced Orange Suspicion

Other

The Agatha Frost Winter Anthology

Peridale Cafe Book 1-10

Peridale Cafe Book 11-20

Claire's Candles Book 1-3

Chapter 1
The Wallpaper Whispers

Ellie Swan wrestled with the vintage wallpaper in her gran's bookshop, Meadowfield Books, gripping the peeling edges and tugging with all her might. Each strip she peeled away brought a satisfying sense of progress—until a hefty section suddenly broke free. It cascaded down in a dusty avalanche, burying her under layers of timeworn paper.

"Lovely," she muttered, blinking away plaster flakes clinging to her lashes. "Do It Yourself? More like *Destroy It Yourself*."

Dragging her brunette hair into a ponytail, she stepped back, her heart pounding as she took in the mess around her. The shop was a patchwork of torn wallpaper, exposed warped floorboards, and half-finished repairs. She couldn't help but wonder how she'd ended up renovating a building this old with no actual skills.

"And there's still so much to do..."

"Talking to yourself again? They'll start calling you mad," Granny Maggie announced as she emerged from the back room, pulling her winter coat over her cardigan. "Blueberry or chocolate?"

"For the new wallpaper colours?"

"Muffins from The Giggling Goat café," she said, laughing at the suggestion while winding a scarf around her neck. "If you took off your DIY hat and pulled yourself away from that wall for a break every so often, you'd have noticed it was lunchtime."

"Blueberry," Ellie said as she picked at the layers of gloopy paper stuck like casts around her fingertips. "And I *am* mad if I thought I had any idea what I was doing."

"*We*'re mad," Maggie corrected, dragging the heavy front door open. "But it's all under control—"

Maggie tripped over the rotting doorframe—the one responsible for breaking her hip during a burglary gone wrong months earlier—catching herself just in time with a quick grab at the door.

"I'm fine! Everything's fine!"

Ellie pushed 'replace that chunk of rotting wood' to the top of her cluttered mental to-do list as Maggie brushed off the trip with a wave and a slam of the door.

"Everything's fine," Ellie echoed, taking in the rundown shop they had spent months tearing apart. "Or it will be... *eventually*... I hope..."

Alone with the constant creaks and groans of the centuries-old bookshop, Ellie kicked aside the fallen wallpaper strip and nudged the metal edge of her scraper under the next piece. Unlike the one that had dropped on her, this strip clung to the powdery lime plaster like a second skin, refusing to budge. She laughed, still baffled by how she'd become *this* person.

In her twenties, she'd worked as a continuity expert for a production company in Wales, meticulously ensuring historical accuracy for television and film. She'd been good at it, too—until the studio was swallowed by a media titan, leaving her redundant.

"You know how it is these days," Simon, the production manager, had said as he handed her a 'Good Luck!' card signed by seven people—two of whom Ellie wasn't even sure she'd met. "It's not that we don't value what you do. But, well, you know how it is."

Ellie understood all too well. The authentic historical dramas she'd thrown herself into fresh out of college, lending her detail-oriented eye to every scene, weren't making enough money to justify keeping a continuity specialist. She loved history, loved the intricate world of television, and would have happily kept plugging away on low pay and tight budgets—if only they hadn't forced her out.

Unemployment at twenty-nine hadn't been part of the plan, and neither had trying to channel that same detail-oriented eye into becoming a decorator at thirty.

"If people enjoy pointing out wrong hems and bad wigs online, why not let them? Best marketing we've got at this late stage. Ellie... listen... I'm..." The apology she'd sensed on the tip of Simon's tongue didn't come. "This isn't easy for me either. We'll keep you in mind if anything comes up, yeah?"

"Yeah," she'd said, and she still couldn't believe she'd forced a smile for his benefit, clutching the card to her chest like it might contain a 'What Happens for Eleanor Swan Next' guide. "It's not like there aren't other studios, right?"

Simon's pitiful upper-management smile should have warned her that the next six months would be spent working in a coffee shop, grinding through job applications and facing rejections hurled at her like scalding milk.

It had taken Granny Maggie's broken hip to pull Ellie back across the bridge from Wales to England, trading Cardiff's bustling modern city centre for the cosy charm of her home village, Meadowfield in Wiltshire. She'd arrived in summer, but now winter was knocking at the door. Crispy leaves, dried from a cold autumn, skittered along the cobbles of South Street outside.

Breathing life back into the old family bookshop had given her the purpose she craved, even if her DIY skills were as lacking as her ability to make a decent salted caramel macchiato.

She flicked off a chunk of wallpaper the size of a hardback book, wondering if the job might be easier without six stubborn layers, each slathered over the last. The top three patterns were familiar. The green-and-white floral design, in particular, pulled her back to being ten years old, spreading paste with a wide brush in one

The Plot Thickens

hand and holding an Agatha Christie paperback in the other.

She'd pass the gloopy piece up to her gran perched high on the ladder, barely looking away from her page, while Maggie hung the paper, just as distracted by her own open novel. It was no wonder the shop had ended up in its current state—Granny Maggie had always cared more about the stories on the shelves than the building that held them.

But Ellie's former career wasn't the only industry where the customer's expectations had changed. Even in a small Wiltshire village like Meadowfield, a tatty, rundown bookshop with a whiff of decay in the air wouldn't cut it. Her beloved granny might have been pretending everything would be 'fine', but Ellie had pored over the details of the shop's accounts. The longer it took them to get the shop ready for its grand reopening, the louder the death rattle wheezed through the empty shelves.

She flipped to the last page of her list, her pen hovering over the square next to 'Curl up with a good book by the fire at the end of opening day—you've done it!', but instead of marking it off, she flipped back nine pages to 'Remove all wallpaper', something she'd hoped to have ticked and finished so they could patch up the plaster. They were on the seventh day of wallpaper and there was still upstairs to do.

Ellie was used to the 'hurry up and wait' culture of working in film studios. She used to spend months researching the sets and costumes for a period piece in pre-production before being expected to adapt to the director changing the year because he 'thought the 1860s sounded cooler than the 1830s' four days before shooting was to commence.

She could have crumbled under the pressure—or got on with it. Like back then, she chose the latter.

Brushing away the fallen wallpaper, she found her phone. With a tap, she resumed the video she'd paused moments before tugging away the perfect piece that had tried to bury her.

"And *that's* when Debbie left me," Handy Steve's tight voice crackled through the phone's tiny speakers, his sigh so deep that Ellie couldn't help but join in.

They were on video 18 of 293 in his 'Decorating for Beginners' playlist—also known as Episode 18 of the *Steve and Debbie Divorce Show*.

"You can't smooth over some cracks, can you?" He sighed again, dunking his trowel into the plaster mix he'd prepared in the previous video using lime, sand, and horsehair. "But if you used the correct ratio, those surface cracks should disappear." Another deeper sigh. "Be careful of those structural cracks, though—the ones you don't realise are there until it's too late. Then suddenly, they're telling you it's 'not working', and the yoga instructor you weren't supposed to worry about? You should have been worrying about them. I should have seen it coming when—"

"*Eleanor Swan!*" Granny Maggie gasped as she

The Plot Thickens

opened the door. Ellie might have heard her coming if they hadn't taken down the bell. "Did you skip ahead from papering to plastering without me? Steve has never mentioned a yoga instructor before..."

"New character," she said, pausing the video with a tap. "Sorry, I couldn't resist."

"Hmm," she grumbled, rounding the shelves with paper bags from the café. "Well, has poor Steve at least explained why Debbie left him yet?"

"Not yet," Ellie groaned as she rose, her lower back protesting after spending much of the morning hovering in a squat. "But his talent for shoehorning divorce details into every DIY video has captivated me—and about twelve hundred other people—since he first posted the videos eight years ago."

"And I can't wait to hear how it ends," Maggie said over her shoulder, her limp from the broken hip noticeable as she powered through to the back room. "Still, you are skipping ahead. We can't plaster until we've stripped all the wallpaper, and you'll only want to rush to see if Steve gets Mr Bean in the divorce. Given what his solicitor said, it sounds like Debbie will take the cat when she moves to Kettering." She spoke as if the cat's fate was to be decided now and not almost a decade ago. "Back to it. You keep peeling, and I'll plate up lunch." Still, she wasn't finished. "Oh, Oliver asked if we wanted any of his old Christmas decorations for our window display. I told him we'd probably be open by then, so I told him to put them aside for us."

Unsure whether to laugh or cry, Ellie glanced around the near-derelict bookshop, which was only recognisable as such because of the shelves. Her gran had always been stubborn, but she'd never been as blind to anything as she was to the shop's state.

"Christmas?" Ellie stabbed at a section clinging like it didn't want to reveal the wall underneath. "A festive window display would be nice, but I'm not sure if we'll be—"

"We will!" Maggie called above the clatter of plates. "It was nice of your brother to remind me. I never notice Christmas is happening until it hits me in the face."

"You've always been in your own world."

"Other people's worlds. Who cares what the season is when you're five hundred pages deep into *Wuthering Heights*?"

As she continued attacking the wallpaper, Ellie almost wanted to fact-check her gran, sure the book was closer to four hundred pages. A fact she knew from working on a low-budget adaptation one critic had described as reaching new 'Wuthering Lows'. At least they'd highlighted the accuracy of the sets and costumes —a win Ellie had clung to after fighting the set designer's impulse to buy everything from IKEA. If only a quick visit to a flatpack warehouse could fix the bookshop's problems.

She froze mid-scrape, her breath catching as a dark patch emerged beneath the paper. Her nerves tingled

The Plot Thickens

with unease as the dark stain grew with each pull of the wallpaper.

"Don't be mould," she begged, the air around her growing thicker. "*Please.*"

She moved in, nostrils flaring, sniffing for the sweet scent of musty decay Handy Steve had warned about. She could only smell the familiar aroma of reactivated wallpaper paste. Despite the issues with the gutters at the back of the shop, the plaster was bone dry.

Her caked fingertips brushed over the surface like sandpaper. Some black flecks crumbled away from the plaster dust, but it was too smooth to be alive. On camera, it might have passed for mould from a distance, but up close, the splatter marks gave it away as something else: spray paint.

"For a moment," she whispered to the patch, "you almost ruined my day."

"*Muffins!*" Maggie called from the back room as she emerged with two plates. "Oliver didn't have blueberry, but he suggested lemon drizzle, and your brother never steers us wrong, so I grabbed that instead..."

But the black spray paint had Ellie too fixated to hear the rest of her gran's café-chat. She forced more of the paper away, and the dark splodge formed an arrow—or maybe a mountain? Another grating scrape of metal against plaster, and the shape morphed into something more deliberate. Her breath caught again as the sharp lines of a letter appeared: W.

She scraped away the wallpaper in the vigorous

manner Steve had warned against, but she wasn't thinking about pulling a muscle or 'protecting the plaster's integrity' at that moment. She was uncovering words...

"*Saw*," she read aloud. "*Saw it...*"

"Are you going to eat this, or are you content waffling to yourself all afternoon on an empty stomach? I'm sure even Michelangelo took a lunch break."

Ellie stepped back, her breath quivering as the words pulsed on the wall, seeping from the lime plaster as though they were trying to grab her. She tripped over Handy Steve, still paused on the phone screen, unable to tear her eyes away from the chilling phrase.

"Forget the muffins, Gran. Look at this."

"*Forget* the muffins?" Maggie mumbled through a mouthful, her back to Ellie as she fussed with the plates at the counter. "I'll tell your brother you said..." Her voice trailed off as she turned to see the words on the wall. She swallowed, her crumb-coated lips tightening. "'*We saw it all*,'" she read aloud. "Saw what?"

"You've never seen this before," Ellie stated with a confident nod. "That answers my first question."

"No, I haven't. The shop was my sister's before mine, and our mother's before hers... but I do remember Lindsay putting up that bottom blue layer with the white daisies. She used to talk about stripping it back for a fresh start."

"Did you help?"

She shook her head. "I did offer, but Lindsay told me

The Plot Thickens

in no uncertain terms that our mother left the shop to her, so she'd be taking care of it... until she couldn't, of course."

"Year?"

She hummed for a moment. "Your mother had already had you, still dragging herself to auditions with a pram and I... I'm sorry, love. I don't know where this came from."

As much as Ellie wanted a quick and easy explanation for the hidden message, she believed her gran had never seen the words before. She looked as confused as she was scared.

"I wish I knew," Maggie continued, hugging her knitted beige cardigan tight. "Do you think it could be builder's slang?"

Ellie shrugged, turning back to the wall. She wasn't an expert on trade terms, but Steve had never said anything so ominous when weaving his tips and tricks through his divorce saga.

"It sounds incomplete," Maggie pointed out.

"There's more paper."

Picking up the scraper she didn't recall dropping, Ellie forced off the next chunk underneath the writing, revealing more black spray.

"Why go to the trouble of telling us they saw something," Ellie said, letting the paper fall with the tool, "without telling us what they saw? *We saw it all. Meredith Fenton killed Tim Baker.*"

"Oh, dear."

Ellie turned to find her gran backing away until she bumped into the counter, rattling the plates of their untouched lunch.

"You know these names. Meredith and Tim?"

Maggie nodded as the colour drained from her cheeks. "It's... a cruel joke."

"You said this wall hasn't seen the light of day since I was in a pram. Did Tim Baker die in the 1990s?"

In her smallest voice, she said, "1994. And if you don't know Meredith Fenton, you know her husband. Mr Fenton?"

"The *other* history teacher." Ellie's eyes widened at the memory of a man she hadn't thought about in years. "People groaned when they got him instead of you. His lessons were... monotonous."

"I'm flattered, but George Fenton was a skilled educator, achieved fine exam results despite his delivery, and *is* a dear friend." She paused, tucking her arms tight. "As was Meredith. She suffered horribly from those vicious rumours the first time around, but I will say this once and only once: Meredith Fenton is *not* a murderer." Her wide eyes flicked from the wall to Ellie. "She was a sweet woman, a little on the kooky side. But being odd doesn't make you a murderer, no matter what people thought around here in 1994."

Ellie barely registered her grandmother's mix of present and past tense, her gaze already sweeping across the rest of the shop. What other secrets might lurk beneath the remaining wallpaper?

The Plot Thickens

"What do we do?"

Granny Maggie shook her head, her brow furrowing deeper. "Nothing. It is incorrect gossip left over from thirty years ago. Someone's idea of a joke."

"But who? And why?" Ellie insisted, unable to accept the speculation. "This isn't casual graffiti. It's an accusation of murder, Gran."

"*Eleanor.*" Maggie exhaled. "This isn't like what happened with the Blackwood family and *The Last Draft* manuscript riddle. There's no mystery for you to dig into."

"But how can you be so sure?"

"What happened in 1994... the frenzy that took over the village after the hauntings..."

"*Hauntings?*"

Maggie sighed, rubbing her temples as if warding off a headache. "I'd rather not dredge all that up. Paint over the wall, leave it alone..."

"But Gran," she pressed, unwilling to let the accusation slide, "if there's a chance this is true, shouldn't we check? For Tim Baker's sake?"

"Ellie..." Maggie exhaled again, letting whatever she'd meant to say float away. "Tim was a lovely photographer in his early twenties, and people needed someone to blame for his death. His fall was nothing more than an accident."

Ellie squirmed at the dismissal, but the pain thick in her gran's voice couldn't be ignored. She wished they could return to talking about Handy Steve and Oliver's low stocks of blueberry muffins at The Giggling Goat, but how could Ellie ignore what she'd found?

"What do we do?" she asked again.

"You can call the police," Maggie said, glancing at the wall one last time before setting off to the back room. "Or forget you ever saw it. Some ghosts are best left undisturbed."

As the door to the back room clicked shut, Ellie stared at the black words. Something within the phrase seemed to stare back, like dark eyes peering from a dense, daunting forest. They pulled at her to uncover the history of how these words had remained hidden beneath the wallpaper at Meadowfield Books for so long.

But more than that, she needed to understand why her gran was comfortable sweeping something as serious as an accusation of murder under the rug.

Chapter 2
They Saw It All

Ellie knew she should have called the police right away—anyone else would have after uncovering a thirty-year-old accusation of murder. But, as her gran kept reminding her, it wasn't a new accusation. And besides, there was still so much wallpaper to strip.

Her hands were raw from hours of scraping, her wrists aching with every desperate movement. The wallpaper clung stubbornly to the walls as if taunting her, mocking her search for more hidden messages. Despite her efforts, she had barely made a dent. She'd ignored Handy Steve's constant advice to 'clean as you go' and instead buried the shop beneath a growing mountain of mush.

She could hear her frustrated grunts as she dug, and dug, and dug... but still, there was no second message, no *just kidding!*—nothing.

Maggie had yet to leave the back room, the door still shut—a rarity. Ellie could have used the extra pair of hands, and her gran had been all up for helping during breakfast at the cottage that morning. But Ellie knew her gran feared what she might find. Ellie wasn't thrilled about the idea either, though she wasn't sure what she was looking for other than more details.

The front door creaked open, and Ellie's mind raced. She pictured the police storming in, led by Detective Sergeant Angela Cookson. Surely someone had seen through the window and called them. She should have called them herself.

But it wasn't the police. It was worse—the last person Ellie wanted to see.

Her mother, Carolyn Swan, swept into the shop, trailing a cloud of dust as she strode through in a sparkly evening gown, wildly out of place in the bookshop's gloom. Close behind her, wielding a battered camcorder perched on her shoulder, was Carolyn's biggest fan, shadow, and sister: Auntie Penny, as Ellie had always called her.

"And... *action!*" Penny announced, grinning with a thumbs up as she swung the camera straight at Ellie.

"Now isn't the best time for..." Ellie scanned her mother's dress, more suited to an award show than a bookshop in distress, and added, "...whatever *this* is."

"*Your* brilliant idea, that's what!" Carolyn struck a pose, one eye on the lens. "We're filming the pilot for my reality show! Don't you remember our pre-

The Plot Thickens

production meeting in my greenhouse a few months ago?"

That wasn't quite how Ellie remembered it. "I told you not to try getting yourself 'cancelled for attention,' Mother... while we were having a heart-to-heart."

"And what a lovely chat it was. You know, we could re-enact it for—"

"I said that your real life is dramatic enough."

"And *then* you said if only there were cameras to capture it!"

Ellie parted her lips to protest, but she *had* said that—and she should have known her mother would take the throwaway comment literally. Not that Carolyn Swan ever needed much encouragement to dive headfirst into a new media project. She'd been chasing a comeback ever since *Heatherwood Haven,* a short-lived 1970s soap, filmed in the village, plucked her from obscurity, and turned her into Meadowfield's answer to Meryl Streep—or so her website claimed the last time Ellie checked. To Ellie, she was far closer to Faye Dunaway.

"Which is why I bought this!" Carolyn gestured at the camera before fluffing her bouncy hair as if Ellie had just proved her point. "Oh, don't look like that, dear. You *never* support me. And I was economical, wasn't I, Penny?"

The lens and Penny both nodded up and down. "We recycled something for it from the local exchange shop up by the post office. One of your bracelets, wasn't it, Carolyn?"

"Thank you, Penny," Carolyn said, silencing her sister with a glare and holding up her hand in a T-shape. "We'll cut that bit out. And how many times do I need to remind you? The person behind the camera shouldn't talk—it confuses the viewer. When you talk, I can't use the footage."

Ellie's stomach twisted. She knew the pearl-shaped jewellery box on her mother's mirrored dressing table containing her 'break-the-glass-if-needed' valuables wasn't as full as it used to be—the shiny lid could now close, for one thing. Carolyn's ex-husband had bought most of them. Mr David Swan, the big-time TV producer, was out of the picture years before Ellie was born. Despite him not being her father, Ellie had inherited his surname.

When Ellie first noticed most of the other children in her class had their father's surname—Cookson, in her case—her mother had explained, very proudly, that a name like *Eleanor Swan* was the name of a future award-winning actress. On the other hand, *Eleanor Cookson* was destined to end up a 'sad librarian, or something.' Unluckily for her mother, Ellie had avoided the red carpets and headed straight for the 'or something' category.

After thinking up a comeback, Auntie Penny muttered, "You *did* say I was the Executive Producer."

"And are you not executive producing this scene?" Carolyn asked, fanning her hands around the shop. She froze in place at the sight of the wall, holding up her

The Plot Thickens

hands as though she were under arrest. "Penny... are you getting this?"

"You said I wasn't supposed to speak."

"You already have." Carolyn clambered over the piles of discarded wallpaper, eyes fixed on the writing like it was drawing her in. "What *is* this?"

"It's scary," Penny whispered.

"It's TV gold, that's what." Carolyn positioned herself in front of the graffiti, licking her teeth before checking for lipstick in a compact that appeared from nowhere. After a few dabs of powder on the bridge of her nose, she asked, "Do I mention this is my daughter's father's mother's bookshop? There was never any chance of me marrying Peter Cookson, so I'm *not* calling her my mother-in-law. Could you imagine?"

"I heard that!" Maggie's voice rang out from the back room, clear as a bell.

Carolyn's camera-ready smile faltered, and in a smaller voice, she added, "Perhaps I meant you to." She tucked the compact into her bra strap through the neckline, glancing at the writing again. "So, what's this in aid of? Modern art? Like that fella who is always on the news, but nobody knows who he is."

"Jack the Ripper?" Penny suggested.

"Banksy," Ellie corrected. "And it's not in aid of anything. It's just... there."

"Well, a strange topic to dig up," Carolyn said, "but I suppose everyone will remember what happened to Tim. Shock marketing. I like it. Perhaps we could do something similar for when we launch the pilot. Penny, write that down."

"But I'm holding the camera—"

"Don't write that down, Penny," Ellie said, fixing her mother with a well-trained hard stare. It had always been like this—every conversation a sparring match. "It's been hidden under the wallpaper for three decades." She glanced at the door to the back room, still unusually closed. "Gran says it's nothing."

"She *would* say that." Carolyn rolled her eyes. "Meredith was her best friend."

"Was?"

Carolyn waved her hand as if to rush Ellie along, already bored with the topic.

"You were a baby, and I was too busy trying to get back out there, proving I still had it, to pay attention to the mother of my daughter's—"

Maggie emerged from the back room with plates in hand.

"You can call me Maggie, Carolyn. Or Margaret. Or Mags. And I'd prefer you didn't mention my shop in whatever you're filming, thank you. There's no telling where this might end up—I still haven't forgiven you for the front of my cottage ending up in that low-budget horror film as 'the murder house.'"

"It was only released in Croatia," Carolyn replied with a defiant glare. "And you should have been *grateful* for the exposure."

"Some of us don't share that sentiment," Maggie

replied through tight lips, her eyes darting at the graffiti without lingering. "So, a reality television show? I'd say I'm surprised you've stooped so low, but..."

"Reality is a *very* popular, valid genre. I once thought it was a little beneath me, but... there are no small shows, only big actors, or whatever the saying is. But if you think about it—"

"I'd rather not," Maggie interjected, still trying to entice Ellie with the muffins. "If you're not going to pick up tools, you can see we're busy."

"We're here to show the world what a natural star I am by letting the cameras go where they've never gone before. This is about capturing what's real and raw, and..." She clapped her hands, ushering Penny towards the front door, and added, "... and let's do that entrance again. I *know* I can do better. Film me from inside this time and get my good side. And can we do something about the light? I don't know how I'm expected to work in these..."

Maggie thrust the plate into Ellie's hands, then covered the camera lens with her palm as Penny tried to zoom in on her. Penny stumbled back but didn't argue, knowing better than to challenge Maggie's authority. She turned to follow Carolyn, who was already planning her second take of reality at the door.

Still stuck on the first take, Ellie set her plate on an empty shelf, her midday appetite long gone. She turned to her gran, who was quietly shifting books from one stack to another.

"You moved them here from there yesterday."

"And now I'm moving them from *there* to *here*," Maggie stated, still moving the books. "Or is it here to there?"

"Gran..."

Maggie exhaled through her nostrils.

"We need to talk about this."

"Must we?"

"About Meredith Fenton."

Maggie glanced at the camera, which Penny had pointed at the front door. Carolyn pranced in and out like she was stuck in a revolving door, giving several variations of the same 'shocked' gasp. None were close to the genuine confusion that had gripped the few who had seen the message so far.

"Gran?" Ellie said, reaching out to rest her hand on *The Wind in the Willows* before it moved to the twin pile. "Please."

"Meredith was my best friend," Maggie stated, relinquishing the book. "I knew George Fenton first, but Meredith and I connected over our love of films. We loved the same old—" She paused, her voice softening. "What happened in 1994 with the Meadowfield Ghost Watch Club destroyed our friendship."

A sudden crash interrupted them as porcelain shattered against the floorboards. The plate Ellie had placed on the shelf had toppled, breaking on impact. Its contents—a ham and cheese sandwich—lay scattered

The Plot Thickens

across the exposed wallpaper, adding to the growing mess.

Before Ellie could react, Carolyn swooped in. "This is great stuff. A real-life haunting event, captured on *my* film!"

"But I wasn't pointing the camera in *that* direction!" Penny fumbled with the equipment before declaring, "We'll fix it in post-production. *Action!*"

Carolyn slipped into what Ellie recognised as her mother's 'ghost hunter' voice. The sound transported her back to the early 2000s when her mother had forced Ellie to pretend to be a ghost for weeks before the audition, stumbling around the house cloaked under a bedsheet while Carolyn improvised her narration. She hadn't got the part, nor had a camera captured the rehearsals. Ellie had been grateful for both.

"Like most things," Ellie said, bending down to pick up the broken pieces of the plate, "there's usually a rational explanation buried in the details." The shelf wobbled beneath her touch. "This was Celebrity Autobiographies, and that's always been a little wobbly. Remember when those Gordon Ramsey books almost broke that girl's big toe?"

"She shouldn't have been leaning on the shelf so hard," Maggie grumbled, just as she had then. "I'm lucky her father didn't sue."

"Okay, so you can explain a falling sandwich," Carolyn said, narrating directly to the camera, "but *this?*" She motioned for Penny to zoom in on the wall until the camera was almost up Carolyn's nostrils. "Dear viewer, what we are seeing here is a clear message from beyond the grave. A message... from *Tim Baker* himself!"

Ellie and Maggie sighed in unison—the theory was so outlandish it hadn't come up.

"I should have done this hours ago," Ellie said, pulling out her phone, the video still paused on Steve's glum face. "I'm calling Angela."

"Oh, it's *Angela* now, is it?" her mother's voice dripped with disdain. "You know she hates you, dear."

"She hates *you*, Carolyn," her gran corrected, shaking her head at Carolyn as she often did. "You did have a baby with her husband, and I still don't know what my son was thinking. No offence, Ellie." Maggie turned to her granddaughter, her expression softening. "Angela was at the café when I nipped in for lunch earlier. No need to make a fuss calling the station. It's been a few hours, but Oliver might know where his mum went."

After one last glance at the accusation on the wall, Ellie brushed away the camera as Penny tried to follow her out of the bookshop.

The chilly air of South Street hit her, and she regretted not grabbing her coat. Hugging her splattered decorating jumper for warmth, she glanced back at the bookshop on the corner—a tiny cottage with a sagging thatched roof at first glance, but so much more to Ellie. It

The Plot Thickens

was everything right now. Her gut twisted with the enormity of the task ahead, a Christmas reopening already a pipe dream without the added pressure of the discovery.

* * *

The bell above the door chimed as Ellie entered The Giggling Goat, where the mouth-watering scents of sugar and spice blended with the gentle hum of village gossip. She basked in the warmth for a moment—it was the most pleasant feeling she'd had all day.

"Blackberry muffin?" her half-brother, Oliver, asked, clicking his fingers as he spun around. "Or was it blueberry? They taste the same, right?"

"Do they?" Ellie laughed, shaking her head. "And if Granny asks, I ate a muffin, a sandwich, and anything else you can think of."

He squinted at her, taking in her messy state. "Or you eat and don't make me an accomplice in whatever you're scheming?" He gasped, resembling Carolyn Swan's second-take reactions to the graffiti. "You're pregnant! I knew it. That's why you're back. That's why—"

"*Shut up!*" Ellie cried, hugging her midsection. "Just... shut up! I'm not pregnant." He lowered his fingertips from his mouth. "Why is that the first place people go? Are *you* pregnant?"

"Not yet." He winked. "So, you don't want a muffin,

I'm an awful person, and you look even paler than usual. Seen a ghost?"

Ellie scratched at the speckled brunette nest piled atop her head, and Oliver abandoned the muffin case and leaned across the counter.

"Sort of?"

"Go on."

"Heard of Tim Baker? Meredith Fenton?"

"Meredith Fenton?" a familiar voice squawked.

Ellie turned to see Sylvia Fortescue, the owner of Bramble & Brie, waving her over to their table. Beside Sylvia sat Amber Matthews, the sweet, pink-haired girl who ran the antique shop, and Zara Williams from the gift shop—a sharp-tongued woman with a laugh that could fill a room.

Ellie had always meant to join them more often. Different combinations of the shopkeepers were regulars at the café, but she'd spent most of her time wolfing down sandwiches while engrossed in the latest courtroom drama between Steve and Debbie.

"I saw Meredith on my rounds," Sylvia said, patting a free chair beside her, though Ellie's nerves were too frayed to sit still. "Poor dear."

"Do not tell me," Zara said, "besides being this village's biggest busybody, you also work in a prison?"

Sylvia laughed, then took a sobering gulp, her bird-like features drooping. "Goodness, no! I volunteer at the hospital once a week. Cheese tasting for the sick. And for the needy. The young. The old. The middle-aged. For the families of the sick, and the families of the—"

"Yes, we understand," Zara said, holding a commanding hand to silence the cheese shop owner. "Meredith is in the hospital, where she sampled your charity cheese."

"Oh, no, she didn't eat any."

"Ah!" Zara replied, slapping a hand down on the wooden table. "A woman of taste!"

"A woman... in a coma."

Sylvia's delivery was so flat that the conversations at the nearby tables skidded to a halt, heads whipping their way. Ellie, unsure whether to laugh or cry, leaned in, perching on the edge of the chair.

"Sylvia," Ellie asked carefully, "are you sure we're discussing the same Meredith?"

"You do have a tendency to make things up," Zara said flatly.

"I *object* to that claim! I pride myself on my honesty, but I am sometimes given... incorrect information." Sylvia clutched the single ring of pearls around her neck at the mere suggestion she'd mix up such a thing. "I spoke with George, her husband. The poor man was rather morose about the whole affair, as you'd expect. A retired science teacher, I believe."

"History," Ellie corrected.

"Regardless, my award-winning Camembert failed to raise a smile." She sighed as if it were the worst news she'd delivered. "Why do you ask? Has something happened to Meredith? Oh, the poor dear! Sometimes death is the *kindest* option—"

"She's not dead," Ellie interrupted, clenching her eyes for strength. "At least, I don't think so. I've found something. A message."

"In a bottle?" Zara asked.

"Don't be daft," Amber giggled, fingers tapping her phone in a steady rhythm, barely paying attention to the conversation. "She meant a text or a DM."

"I meant a message on the wall," Ellie said, opening her eyes with a calming breath. "And it was buried under six layers of wallpaper. I shouldn't say more until I've spoken to the police. Has anyone seen Detective Sergeant Cookson?"

Ellie turned back to Oliver, who was wiping down the counter with a damp cloth. He glanced up, met her eyes, and jerked his head towards the bathroom door.

"She's been slacking off work all afternoon." He tossed his head back and cried, "*Mother*? You're needed."

The door swung open, and Detective Sergeant Angela Cookson emerged, the permanent frown creasing her brows to meet in deep lines that resembled the number eleven.

"The hand dryer is on the fritz again," Angela said, "and you're out of paper towels."

Angela's gaze landed on Ellie, and she froze. Ellie felt the familiar weight of Angela's stare, a mixture of surprise and something else—perhaps resentment—that had lingered for as long as Ellie could remember. She always had that slight snarl in her upper lip, as if there were a bad smell only her flared nostrils could detect.

"Ellie needs you," Oliver said, breaking the tense silence. "She's found something."

"If this is a police matter, call the station like everyone else. I'm on my break."

Ellie took a deep breath. She couldn't fault Angela for her lingering animosity—not after what had unfolded between Carolyn, Peter, and Angela back in '93. The ghost of that ill-fated karaoke finale clung to them like an unspoken curse, her very existence a constant reminder.

But she wasn't here to dredge up that history—she was more interested in 1994.

"Well?" Angela pushed, and Ellie hadn't realised she'd gone silent. "This had better not be another body."

But Ellie stayed silent, her expression grave. Angela's face fell, irritation shifting to a flicker of concern that surprised Ellie. Without another word, Angela tossed the blue paper towel onto the counter and followed Ellie to the message that had waited thirty years to haunt Meadowfield.

Chapter 3
Ghosts of '94

As day faded to night, Ellie locked up the shop, twisting the heavy key in the door until it clicked with a final, solid clunk. When she turned, she noticed PC Finn Walsh hovering near the entrance, his youthful face full of concern.

DS Angela Cookson had left shortly after taking Ellie's statement, not one to linger.

"It's hardly a *new* accusation," the detective sergeant had muttered, glancing at the wall as though she'd rather be in the café. "Unless you find something else, we don't have the resources to open an investigation into this. This rumour was well-documented at the time."

"I told you it was nothing," Maggie had said, handing Ellie a broom. "Let's get cleaned up and go home."

But PC Walsh had returned hours later to take pictures and had been hanging around since Maggie decided she was done for the day around three in the afternoon. It was almost as if he sensed Ellie was too unsettled to be left alone.

"Don't worry too much about the graffiti," he said, trying to sound reassuring as he attempted a smile. "If they ruled it an accident in 1994, that's probably what happened."

"I hope you're right."

"How about a drink at The Old Bell?" he suggested in a friendly tone. "I'm clocking off now. I think Sammie has some new food on the menu for Christmas."

"Thanks, but I need to go home. I think my gran knows more than she's letting on."

"Another time," he offered as he walked away, his boots crunching on the gravel.

Ellie glanced back at the shop and spotted a familiar figure approaching. She smiled as Daniel Clark, a local schoolteacher—and former classmate of Ellie's—raised a hand in greeting.

"Ellie! I'm glad I caught you," Daniel called out, his face warmed by the street lights, his cheeks rosy. "I've been meaning to ask you something."

"Is this about the graffiti?"

"G-graffiti?"

"I suppose you'll hear all about it soon enough," she said, surprised news hadn't spread around the village. "I found something at the shop."

"I tend to stay out of that stuff, but I'm sure my nan

will have all the details waiting for me at home." He paused, then looked at her with concern. "Do you want to talk about it?"

Ellie considered telling him about the strange words on the wall and the unfamiliar names from the past reappearing in her present. But she shook her head.

"It's probably nothing," she lied, though her gut told her otherwise. "So, what did you want to ask me?"

Daniel shifted nervously. "Ah. It's... about Luke."

Ellie's stomach flipped at the mention of her former fiancé. She forced a smile, hoping to mask her shock, but her brows betrayed her, tightening into a worried knot.

"Oh?"

"Do you remember me telling you about the road safety assembly we put on at the school?" Daniel asked, pausing expectantly. Ellie nodded—too quickly, too enthusiastically, and her hair slipped loose from its bobble. She already wanted the conversation to end. As she moved to fix it, he continued, "Every year, we tell the kids Luke's story. With him being so local and his motorbike accident happening so close, it makes it real for them."

He pushed up his glasses, his confidence waning with every word. "It's the week after next. Usually, his sister, Willow, helps with it, but..." He trailed off, his cheeks blotchy as he scratched his head. "I'm sorry, Ellie. I think I misjudged how this was going to go."

Ellie's heart sank.

"You just caught me off-guard," she said softly. "It's been a strange day, and I... I don't think I can, Daniel. I'm sorry."

His face fell, and her heart sank further.

"No, I'm sorry," he said quickly. "I didn't mean to pry... It's just, you mentioned you were coming to terms with what happened before you left the village, and I thought... I shouldn't have asked."

"Can I take some time to think about it?" she asked, almost choking out the words in a high-pitched voice.

Daniel brightened up and nodded, and she hated herself for even suggesting it. The answer was no, but now she could see the hope in his eyes.

"Thank you," he said.

"I can't promise—"

"Just think about it," he urged. "It could be good for you."

She swallowed hard, feeling the weight of her words. Desperate to change the subject, she forced a smile.

"Do you want to grab a drink? The Old Bell?"

He hesitated. "I've got too much marking to do," he said quickly, the excuse awkward but sincere. "Another night?"

"Yeah, sure," Ellie replied, though she wasn't sure at all. "Another night."

As Daniel turned to leave, Ellie watched him go, certain things couldn't have gone much worse. She wished she knew where they stood—whether all their

The Plot Thickens

almost-dates since her return meant something more than two friends reconnecting. She sighed.

Another worry for another night.

Tonight, Granny Maggie had some explaining to do.

* * *

At her gran's picturesque cottage on the quiet outskirts of the village, Ellie blinked back tears as she chopped onions into uneven chunks. Each thud of the knife felt heavier, burdened by the day's shocks pressing down harder than she cared to admit.

One of those worries was now with the police, though that brought little comfort—she doubted they'd do much about it. The other... well, she didn't want to think about that.

Across the kitchen, Maggie hummed along to an old Dusty Springfield song, her timing just slightly behind the beat as she chopped carrots with careful precision. The husky tones of *You Don't Have to Say You Love Me* filled the room, but they weren't sweet enough to cut through the tension, which hung as thick as the steam clouding the windows from the simmering soup.

"You know," Maggie said chirpily as she wafted the knife in Ellie's direction, "we could use an extra pair of hands for the makeover. I know a lad. Joey. He helped me fix those roof leaks a few years back. Such a pleasant boy. I suppose he'll be all grown up now. I tutored him a few years ago. After I'd retired, mind you."

Ellie paused, her blade hovering above the cutting board. She knew her grandmother well enough to recognise the distraction.

"Are we going to address the elephant in the room?"

"Why does it need to be an elephant?" Maggie sighed, still avoiding eye contact as she sliced three carrots at a time. "It's more the size of a church mouse. Or a fruit fly. It's old nonsense—"

"Someone wrote that message for a reason."

"To throw suspicion onto an innocent woman."

"That's *still* a reason," Ellie said firmly. "If Meredith is as innocent as you're convinced and someone is trying to frame her, who are they? And why?"

Maggie finally set her knife down, her shoulders tensing up as she turned to face Ellie.

"Some things are better left buried, and you'll have to trust me when I say this is one of them. Meredith has suffered enough."

"So, you know she's in a coma."

Maggie shot her a withering look that made Ellie shrink back. Her gran was the last person she wanted to be at odds with.

"Gotcha, I suppose?" Maggie said.

"You know that's not what I meant." Ellie reached for another onion, her hand hovering in hesitation before the knife sliced through its silvery skin. "I want to know the truth."

Maggie grabbed more carrots. Chop. Chop. Chop. There were enough now to feed the whole village.

The Plot Thickens

"I told you the truth," Maggie continued. "Meredith is suffering. If there's even a chance she did kill Tim, isn't that enough?" Her knife moved faster, the rhythmic chop growing sharper. "I visit when I can, but those are dark, difficult days. I don't know how George manages to stay by her side every day, but that's love—and their love is real."

Ellie pictured Mr Fenton at the front of a classroom, tall and broad, droning on in his monotone voice from behind a thick black beard. She didn't know what Meredith looked like, but it wasn't hard to imagine tubes and beeping machines keeping her alive. In high school, Granny Maggie—Mrs Cookson—had taught most of Ellie's history lessons, but Mr Fenton had covered her first year. Though boring and prone to tangents few could follow, he'd always been fair and patient. Her classmates had always been too harsh on him.

"Meredith fell ill around the time you moved back," Maggie admitted, pushing the carrots into the boiling water and adding more salt, even though she'd already salted it twice. "I didn't mention it because it wasn't your burden to carry. Nobody knows what happened. George found his wife unconscious by the bird feeder in her garden, and she hasn't been responsive since. He said she's had fits before, but never like this."

Ellie's heart ached for this woman she'd never met, but before she could voice her concerns, Maggie hurried out of the kitchen, her face tight as though holding back tears.

Ellie added the onions to the frying pan, but no sizzle came.

Why were they pretending everything was normal? Maggie had insisted on cooking—it was their routine—but they didn't usually attempt a full roast dinner on a Saturday evening after a long day of DIY at the bookshop.

She craned her neck, half-expecting to find her gran had slipped away. But then Maggie reappeared, hurrying down the hall with a battered cardboard box in her arms. She set it on the kitchen table with a thud and began spreading out yellowed newspaper clippings.

Ellie turned the boiling carrots down to a simmer and joined her gran at the table. The smell of cold onions and oil lingered in the air.

"The summer of 1994," Maggie began, her voice low and tinged with reluctance, "was when everything changed in Meadowfield."

Ellie leaned in, her eyes scanning the headlines of the old articles:

Strange Lights Spotted Over Village Green

Unexplained War Memorial Sounds Baffle Locals

Cold Spots: Natural Phenomenon or Supernatural Occurrence?

"It started with little things nobody could explain," she continued. "I hoped it would fizzle out, like when all the students started stomping around in those heavy Doc Martens one year." She laughed at the memory, but the shadow of something else removed the smile. "The

The Plot Thickens

hauntings became a fire that something always seemed to fuel. By autumn, everyone and their dog had a Meadowfield ghost story. Noises, lights... I'll never forget one student claiming an 'entity' threw her mother across the room, only to confront the woman to find out the family had already performed the exorcism, and it *only* cost them £99. And all that was before Meredith formed the Ghost Watch Club."

A sad smile crossed her face as she glanced over the newspapers, though she wasn't concentrating.

"She *really* believed," Maggie said. "There was this experience she couldn't explain from when she was a girl. Meredith brought it up the first time I met her, and I found it endearing at first. Sweet, even. I've never believed in ghosts, but Meredith had a way of drawing people in. She added a lot of fuel to that fire by being so insistent."

"But the fire did stop," Ellie pointed out, glancing around the cottage as though she could see the rest of the village. "A plate might occasionally fall off a wobbly shelf, but we're hardly a paranormal hotspot. What put an end to the phantasmagoria?"

Maggie sucked air through her teeth. "Delicious word."

"Learned it from a film I nitpicked on—was voted the worst film of 2015 by *Horror Flicks Magazine*."

"Congratulations," Maggie said dryly, sliding a newspaper clipping across the table towards Ellie. It was an excerpt from the *Wiltshire Chronicle*, the headline reading: *Daily Ghost Tours Boost Meadowfield Economy.* "A certain buzz was in the air as the nights grew darker that year. We love our spooky stories here in Wiltshire, but the Halloween spirit possessed the village, and there was a feeling that All Hallows' Eve would be the night that proved everything, once and for all. An expectation, even."

"To prove that ghosts are real?" Ellie asked, glancing at the article's quote from Harold at The Drowsy Duck, proclaiming an increase in beer sales. "Since that's not the village I grew up in, what did happen that night?"

"*Death.*"

Maggie slid another article across the table, this one a front-page spread. Ellie unfolded the *Meadowfield Gazette*, a newspaper that had gone out of circulation long before she'd left. The headline read: *Popular Photographer's Pub Fall Death.*

"Tim fell down the steps into The Drowsy Duck's cellar," Maggie said. "Someone left the door open, and nobody could explain what happened to him."

"And you think he fell?" Ellie asked.

"It makes sense." She frowned, and Ellie wondered if her gran was considering if it still made sense. "We didn't have much to work on. The pub was heaving that night, but even with the crowds, nobody saw what happened. But an open door leading to a cellar in a busy pub... does there need to be any more explanation? Especially on a night like that when people were waiting for something to happen. It's like they willed it into existence, and the next day?" She chuckled, though it was a hollow sound. "Meadowfield woke up from a trance. After Tim's death, it was no longer fashionable to want to be haunted anymore. The tourists kept coming for a while, but the strange lights, cold spots, and exorcisms stopped—as though none of it had happened in the first place."

"So, you all chalked it up to an accident and moved on?" Ellie could hardly believe her ears. "You talk like Tim was a sacrifice to whet a public appetite."

"And you talk as though I could have changed how any of it played out," Maggie replied, her words so sharp and precise that Ellie recoiled, the corner of the counter poking her in the back. "A man died, and this village's obsession with the returning afterlife died with him. And Meredith and I... our friendship did not survive."

"Because of her beliefs?"

Maggie rested her eyes, jerking her head to one side like she wanted to shake it but couldn't bring herself to deny the suggestion.

"I'm not proud of turning my back on her," she said in a small voice. "Meredith broke my heart for the same reason people couldn't stop accusing her of murder."

Ellie gulped. "What did she do?"

Maggie's fingertips brushed against a grainy black-and-white photo in one of the articles. The caption revealed the free-spirited-looking woman to be Meredith Fenton, aged forty-two, posing with her arms wide open in front of the duck pond. Her wild curls, crowned by a bandana, framed a face brimming with unrestrained excitement. Her arms were stretched wide as if embracing the air itself, her expression one of pure awe.

"Meredith wasn't a bad person," Maggie said, running her finger over the hair in the picture as though she could feel it. "*Isn't* a bad person," she corrected, pulling her hand back and stuffing it into her pocket. She pulled a tissue from her cardigan pocket and dabbed at her nose. "Within an hour of Tim's body being found in that cellar, Meredith was blaming an old ghost for pushing him. And nothing I said made a difference. I told her I disagreed. Not just with the statement but her willingness and insistence to keep repeating it to anyone who would listen. I made it clear that I thought the fairy tale hurt his legacy. And it wasn't very kind to Tim's mother. Meredith thought she was helping, but…" She trailed off as though she didn't know what she was trying to say.

"It was counterproductive to the truth?"

Maggie nodded, sighing through a sad smile. "She thought it was the truth. I hoped she'd move on. Get bored. Find another ghost to chase, but she kept banging that drum. In the pub, in the post office, in the street. People said she was projecting, deflecting, but she already wouldn't talk to me by then." She scanned a hand up and down her face like a pane of glass was blocking her. "I wanted to find the Meredith I first met. The sweet, kind, wild woman who believed in everything I didn't, but we still loved each other as friends do. She viewed my rejection of her beliefs as a rejection of her, but I've read far too many historical records of 'ghost sightings' that are easy to explain today." Leaning in, she said, "The way I see it, if it's three in the morning and you're wandering around a Victorian manor by candlelight after your husband died from consumption, there's something wrong if you're *not* seeing ghosts."

"And when cameras came along, suddenly a lot fewer reports of ghosts."

"Not that people didn't try to capture them."

"I'd assume it was a filter today."

"Because it would be," Maggie said with a sobering sigh, "and always was, they just used different methods back then."

She stared at the articles as though she didn't know why she'd brought them out in the first place. Ellie hated to see her gran like this—so withdrawn and conflicted. Maggie gathered the articles, slicing her finger with a neat paper cut in her rush to banish the past back to its cardboard box. She winced, and it took a moment for the blood to rush to the surface.

"Maybe I do believe in ghosts," Maggie said, trying to inject a cheery laugh into her voice as she hurried to the kitchen sink. "It would explain why I feel so off-kilter whenever I'm forced to think about that time period."

She let cold water rush over her finger while Ellie dug for a plaster in one of the many old biscuit tins—some dating back several decades—stacked in the fit-to-bursting cupboards. She secured a plaster around Maggie's finger, then gave it a quick kiss.

"You'll tell me to let it stay buried, but I unearthed something of historical note in your bookshop. I don't think I can let this go until I know more about what happened that night."

Maggie exhaled, checking on the chicken roasting to a leathery crisp through the grease-stained oven door.

"I'll never stop you from doing what you need to do. I only have one request."

"Don't involve Meredith?"

"Don't involve *me*," she said instead, placing the sizzling chicken on the counter next to the mountain of chopped carrots. "I'm too old and tired to go back there."

After the clippings were stuffed back in their box, dinner was quieter-than-usual. They didn't talk about the books they were reading or plans for the shop, and neither attempted to start a game of word association.

Instead, the chill of the conservatory crept into their bones as they ate, and Ellie was expected to eat her dinner in peace and pretend she wasn't shivering to her core.

Before dessert suggestions could be made, Maggie excused herself with mutterings of a headache. Their usual post-dinner ritual of choosing between 'a book or a film' left a void, and it was a comfort Ellie hadn't realised she'd come to rely on until it was gone.

Ellie cleared up alone, drawn to the box of clippings every time she opened a cupboard door. The kitchen layout felt foreign now, something she'd been sure about that morning. She dried her hands and glanced upstairs

The Plot Thickens

as her gran moved about, settling in for the night. This would be her last chance to catch her, to try one last time before sunrise.

But Granny Maggie needed rest. And space.

And so did Ellie.

Curled in an armchair in the cosy sitting room, Ellie hoped for a few hours of peace, free from the accusation that had followed her all day. But the house's silence pressed in, leaving her thoughts too much room to wander. She made a cup of tea—it didn't help. She opened the freezer's bottom drawer, but even the cinnamon ice cream failed to tempt her.

Her gaze fell on the box of articles waiting on the kitchen counter.

She carried it upstairs to her small bedroom above the kitchen, with its window overlooking the garden. Most nights, she'd sit there with a book, losing herself in another world while her thoughts drifted to the next day's tasks at the shop. But tonight, reading felt impossible—not with the articles pulling at her attention.

She dropped the box onto her single bed and sat cross-legged on the festive polar bear-patterned bedspread. Carefully, she spread the yellowed clippings out like pieces of a jigsaw—each one a fragment of Meadowfield's past.

A soft creak down the hallway made Ellie glance up, half-expecting to see her grandmother in the doorway. But the house settled, and she turned back to the articles, picking up the first one.

The reports ranged from earnest to vaguely mocking, depending on the writer, but one thing stayed the consistent: the same names appeared again and again.

Meredith Fenton's name came up most often, a steady presence amid the swirling rumours and supernatural tales.

One that stood out was a declaration from Meredith that The Drowsy Duck pub should be declared a paranormal hotspot:

> *It was absolutely transcendental. Right there, outside the pub, a figure floated across the street. Not just any figure, mind you, but a luminous apparition, clear as the glasses behind the bar. It was a moment of pure connection, a confirmation that there's more to this world than what meets the eye, and the upcoming séance will prove our village's special connection to the other side.*

Despite what Ellie thought, Meredith seemed sincere in her quote, but Ellie still struggled to imagine a ghost zipping down South Street. The strangest thing she'd seen was Oliver crawling out of a taxi after a late night, only to charm everyone at the café the next day without showing any signs of the demon hangover ravaging him.

But an actual ghost?

Like her gran, and unlike Meredith, Ellie hadn't

The Plot Thickens

encountered anything that would make her jump to conclusions about the afterlife.

She grabbed her leather-bound notepad and 'I Love Meadowfield' pen—bought ironically, at first—and started jotting down the key figures, the nib scratching against the paper in the silence.

Alongside Meredith, there was Jack Campbell. A scrawny eighteen-year-old with a bright yellow spiked mohawk running down his shaved scalp. He wore a sleeveless, ripped denim jacket over a t-shirt with so many holes Ellie wasn't sure what was holding it together. Like Tim, he was a keen photographer and was quoted as saying he 'didn't believe, as such,' but that if he captured something on film, he 'might be persuaded to change his mind.' Ellie recalled seeing a man with a mohawk around the village in her younger days, but not since her return.

There was also Cassandra Winters, a seventeen-year-old who claimed she 'just knew ghosts were real because why wouldn't they be?' She featured less heavily, though she stood out in the photographs she was in. She had a facial piercing everywhere that could be pierced, jet black hair with a slightly too-short fringe, and wore platform boots that made her as tall as Jack's hair.

George Fenton popped up too, the dissenting voice in the believers. The articles were often quick to point out the Ghost Watch Club wasn't 'all pro-ghost,' with Mr Fenton taking every opportunity to brand their gatherings as 'poppycock,' never hiding his scepticism.

His quotes often followed Meredith's, presented like a measured counterpoint. George even went as far as to write a full-page letter, demanding the editor stop reporting on the 'ghost farce' because they were feeding into the 'mass hysteria' and the hauntings were becoming 'a disease infecting Meadowfield's once-solid reputation.'

But as Ellie arranged the articles in chronological order, it didn't seem the newspaper listened. Almost every week between the summer of 1994 and Halloween had some coverage—sometimes front pages, often only a few column inches to report the locals' ghostly anecdotes, but always constant updates.

Harold Fletcher, the landlord of The Drowsy Duck, featured a fair amount. The Ghost Watch seemed to use the pub as their clubhouse, given how many articles referenced the place, and Harold took full advantage, using every quote to promote his two-for-one Ghost Ale. He claimed it could 'enhance the drinker's ability to communicate with spirits.' When a journalist asked if he meant it would boost their ability to 'order spirits and make them doubles,' Harold declined further comment.

Dr Christina Marsh, a psychologist and another sceptic, rounded out the club. Her name cropped up in connection with several villagers who sought treatment for sleep disturbances during the height of Ghost Fever, something the local GP couldn't keep up with. He'd put out an appeal for the ghosts to adopt 'more appropriate haunting hours' since his wife didn't appreciate him being on call so late at night.

The Plot Thickens

Ellie was intrigued by the psychological angle behind Meadowfield's madness, but Dr Marsh's name stopped appearing in the issues leading up to Tim's death, and she seemed less willing than George to offer emotional outbursts, sticking to brief factual answers.

Turning to a fresh page in her notebook, Ellie summarised the key figures:

- Jack Campbell (Now 48) Photographer - Undecided

- Cassandra Winters (48) Believer

- George Fenton (70-something) Retired schoolteacher - Sceptic

- Meredith Fenton (72) BELIEVER

- Dr Christina Marsh (Unknown) Psychologist - Sceptic

She tossed the pad and pen onto the well-worn rug.

Yawning, she flicked off the light and let her head sink into the pillow. The moment her eyes shut, the message from 1994 appeared as vivid in her mind as it had on the wall, scrawled in black.

She flipped her pillow to the cool side, but that wouldn't be enough to send her to sleep tonight. Rolling back over, she grabbed her old work laptop from the drawer, still sporting the defunct IronHawk Studios logo.

She was sure she should have returned the computer on her way out, but when nobody asked, she considered it compensation.

Blinded by the brightness, the loading chime rang out around the bedroom at maximum volume. She held her breath and waited for her gran to knock as though Ellie might have been doing something illicit on her stolen device.

"Nothing wrong with a little research," she said to herself, alternating between the buttons to turn the volume and brightness down. Fingers primed, she hovered over the search bar, peering down at the list on the rug. "Start from the bottom and work your way up. Dr Christina Marsh, what ghosts has your digital footprint left behind…"

After a quick search, she found the doctor's ghost with the top result—her first dead-end. She clicked on the link, a 1999 archived obituary from the *Meadowfield Gazette*, and read:

> Dr Christina Marsh, a renowned psychological researcher, has died, according to reports. Dr Marsh, a vocal paranormal sceptic, earned her bachelor's honours degree in Psychological and Behavioural Sciences from the University of Cambridge, where she published her infamous 'No, Your House Isn't Haunted' paper that caused quite a stir during the time of The Enfield Hauntings in London. She dedicated much of her career to travelling to so-called 'hot spots'

The Plot Thickens

and debunking claims of supernatural activity. Dr Marsh, along with several other locals, was once questioned in connection to the death of Tim Baker, a fellow paranormal investigator. No charges were brought, and the death was ruled accidental. According to Dr Marsh's neighbours, the sceptic hadn't been seen publicly for almost five years...

Chapter 4
Detect It Yourself

Sitting on Luke Thompson's memorial bench, which faced both Meadowfield Primary School and St. Mary's Church, Ellie stifled a lip-curling yawn. She'd forgotten to set her alarms the night before—the ones she arranged in five-minute intervals, never quite mastering the art of being a morning person. Another yawn escaped her, and for as early as it felt, it was already past noon.

Inhaling deeply, she patted the moss-covered wood of the old bench and gazed up at the sky, as blue as a spring afternoon. The crisp bite in the air reminded her winter was in full swing.

She often found herself sitting on Luke's bench. It had taken her months to even look at it after returning to the village. Aside from feeling closer to her late fiancé, the bench was secluded enough to give her space to think.

She thought about Daniel's request to help with the road safety assembly. What would she even say to the children?

Luke and she had been from such different worlds—he, the sporty footballer who everyone adored, and she, the quiet loner who'd eaten her packed lunch in the school library. The only reason they'd ever spoken was because of his essay on *To Kill a Mockingbird*. She smiled at the memory. Luke had misunderstood every theme, struggling with the text until she couldn't help but intervene. That first conversation had sparked a connection neither of them had expected.

She'd been endeared by how hard he'd tried to understand, and she'd later found out, he'd appreciated that she'd been patient with him. They'd never said two words to each other before their final year, and might never have if not for that single moment. And then they'd let the same old routine drag them along, neither of them right for each other. She'd let things get too close to the wedding, one of her biggest regrets.

A familiar bark snapped her out of her contemplation, drawing her to the village green just around the corner.

* * *

In the shadow of the clock tower above the church, Duchess the Third trotted ahead, dragging Auntie Penny

The Plot Thickens

along. Both were swaddled in matching orange woolly jumpers. Duchess, a sweet white Maltese, technically belonged to Ellie's mother—though catching Carolyn with a lead in hand was a rare sight.

At the sight of Ellie, Duchess yanked in her direction, kicking up tufts of grass with her hind legs as Penny, ever dutiful, bent to scoop up after her with a green doggie bag.

"Morning, Ellie!" Penny called out, waving the bag like a flag. "I'm glad I caught you! I need your help with something—there's been a terrible, awful emergency."

With Auntie Penny, there was always an emergency, usually terrible, and more often than not, could be traced back to Ellie's mother.

"I'm a little busy," she replied, scratching behind Duchess's ears without letting herself stand too still. If she did, Penny would loop her arm through hers and drag her back to the cottage she shared with Carolyn, just across the green. She glanced at the bedroom window and spotted her mother dragging rollers from her bouncy blow-dry. "What's she done this time?"

"She's blaming me," Penny whispered, exasperated. "But it was working fine before my bath, and now everything's gone black and white, and the lens won't screw on."

"Camera trouble?" Ellie surmised, to which her auntie nodded, nibbling at her bottom lip. "She was probably searching for a soft-focus button."

"So, you'll know how to fix it!" Penny's face brightened. "I told Carolyn you would—you know, with your TV experience."

"I worked in an office. And when I did visit the sets, I didn't operate the cameras."

"Oh. Well, the pilot's *over*. Your mother's going to be *devastated*. This was supposed to be her big comeback."

Comeback number three hundred and two, Ellie thought, though she kept the remark to herself. Despite knowing better than to get drawn into Carolyn's schemes, she couldn't bear to see the look of disappointment on Penny's face. No one was more invested in Carolyn's 'big comeback' than Auntie Penny.

"How about I stop by the cottage after I've ticked off some of my to-do list?" Ellie offered, taking the doggie bag from Penny. "In the meantime, maybe it's best to find someone who actually knows about cameras."

"Do you know anyone?"

Tim Baker's name floated to the edge of Ellie's mind, but they were about thirty years too late for his advice. And if he did miraculously return from the great beyond, there'd be more pressing questions to ask than how to fix a vintage camera. Ellie shrugged as she backed away towards The Old Bell pub.

She tossed the doggie bag into the bin outside the pub, her mind already drifting back to the previous night's to-do list, made just before her heavy eyelids had finally given in. She'd stopped glancing at the clock

The Plot Thickens

around three in the morning, but if it had been summer, she knew she'd have been awake to greet the sunrise.

The first item on her list was a visit to The Drowsy Duck, the village's lesser-liked pub. Dr Christina Marsh's pre-millennium death might have left Ellie chasing a dead end, but there were still plenty of threads left to pull. Jack and Cassandra's whereabouts remained elusive, but the second pub's landlord, Harold Fletcher, was still around.

Next to The Old Bell, Ellie passed by Blackwood House, where young Charles Blackwood—the recent inheritor of the old bell foundry home—was painting the railings. They exchanged a brief nod before she rounded the corner, only to find The Drowsy Duck still locked up. Sighing, she knocked on the thick wooden doors and peered through the dusty window.

"Harold?" she called, cupping her hands against the glass. Behind the bar, she glimpsed a shadowy figure preparing for the day's first customers. "It's Ellie Swan. Maggie's granddaughter? From the bookshop? I was hoping to talk to you about something important. It's about... 1994."

The figure froze for a moment before shuffling down a long corridor, retreating into the back. Ellie let out a frustrated grunt. The one small consolation to waking up late, face down and drooling on her notepad, had been the hope that she'd at least arrive in time for the doors to be open and the first pints to be poured.

"The opening times are more of a suggestion," Charles Blackwood remarked, appearing at the corner with a dripping paintbrush in hand, black gloss splattering onto the pavement. "Depends on whether there was a lock-in the night before. Karaoke was belting out of here well past closing. If you're after a drink, The Old Bell's open."

"Thanks, Charles, but I'm here for something else," Ellie replied, glancing towards the small museum next door, also shut. Not that it bothered with opening hours in quite the same way the other Meadowfield establishments did. "Any tour buses passing through today?"

"Not that I know of. Bit cold for them."

Ellie nodded, her gaze drifting past the duck pond towards South Street, where Meadowfield Books sat on the corner.

Once a vibrant hub drawing people onto the winding shopping street, it was now a shadow. Despite her best efforts, it had never looked more unloved. She could almost feel the sprayed words, as black as the gloss pooling on the pavement, a coldness radiating from the shop and chilling the air. There was a faint light inside, likely Granny Maggie busy with something. She'd left before Ellie was out of bed.

She should have headed straight to the shop, but the prospect of a long day of gruelling repairs wasn't enticing her like it had yesterday morning.

"Anything I can help with?" Charles asked, always so

polite and soft-spoken. "I owe you after everything you did to help put our old housekeeper behind bars."

"You don't owe me a thing, but you might be able to help. Do you still volunteer at the museum?"

Charles nodded, pulling a ring of keys from his pocket. Ellie lingered for a moment, peering once more through the pub window. The shadowy figure had returned behind the bar, moving with purpose. She'd be back.

Once Charles unlocked the several locks guarding the village's history, Ellie stepped into the cramped, overstuffed space, the familiar scent of old books and antiques filling the air. This had been one of her favourite places as a child, and it still brought the same feeling of comfort.

"Remember this?" Charles said, tapping one of the glass displays containing coins from the village's Roman past. "The Penny of King Offa, the final piece of our collection."

"I might never have proved your housekeeper was behind that murder spree if she hadn't dropped the coin so close to the crime scene."

Ellie paused, the memory of the body found at *that* crime scene—aka the bookshop's back room—coming back. Charles's father had been murdered there in a desperate attempt to get hold of Edmund Blackwood's final manuscript.

"How are you, Charles? How's everything at Blackwood House?"

"I'm fine," he said, placing his black brush on a leaflet for a nearby steam railway. He hesitated. "The house is... big. I'm trying my best, but it's more than I can handle. I'm sure I'll grow into it." He cleared his throat, wiping his paint-covered fingers on his trousers. "So, what can I help you with? Looking into the bell foundry's history? Or are you after information about the WWII Meadow Company?"

"Neither," Ellie replied, scanning the displays, mostly centred on those two topics. "I'm after something more recent. It's about the 1994 hauntings and the Ghost Watch Club. Gran has a decent archive of old papers, but my online search isn't turning up much beyond what was written in the press."

"You don't believe in all that, do you?" he asked unsurely. "Ghosts, I mean?"

Ellie almost shook her head but instead asked, "Do you?"

"If any house is haunted, it's Blackwood." His gaze drifted, as though he could see right through the museum walls towards the house. "My sister died there. And my grandfather... and before him, who knows how many generations took their final breaths within those walls?"

"And do they?" Ellie asked, intrigued by the conflicted expression creasing his otherwise soft features. "Haunt the place, I mean?"

"I hear noises. Creaks late at night, like someone's walking the halls."

"Does it frighten you?"

The Plot Thickens

"Sometimes," he admitted, though his worry softened into a smile. "But I always come to the same conclusion."

"Which is?"

"Old houses make noises," he said with a taut shrug. "And like I said, it's far too big for me. No wonder my mind wants to conjure up spirits—makes the place feel less lonely. I should sell it and move on, but... Blackwood is my name. My history."

It was Ellie's turn to stare through the walls, though her gaze was drawn towards the bookshop on the corner of South Street.

"I know the feeling," she said, returning to him. "But no one will blame you if you want to sell it. Your family history won't change, and there doesn't have to be a Blackwood living there for it to remain Blackwood House."

"And those are the things I tell myself every day. I'm sure I'll figure it out."

"I *know* you will. You've got a good head on your shoulders."

His cheeks flushed, and she'd meant it.

"For now, running this museum is plenty," he said. "And I think I can help you with your 1994 research." He studied her for a moment, then motioned for her to follow him around the single row of displays crammed into the tiny room. "If anyone asks, I didn't let you into the private archives—but you'll find my predecessors kept quite detailed records."

Charles led Ellie through a door she'd never noticed before, despite the countless times she'd visited the museum. It was hidden behind a timeline of the weeks the American 501st Infantry Regiment had spent in Meadowfield before heading to Normandy—a story every Meadowling knew well, one that drew in the occasional fair-weather tourists during the warmer months.

The door opened into a cramped room, even smaller than the main exhibition space, with floor-to-ceiling shelves crammed full of labelled archive boxes. She scanned the shelves, noting the neat labels written in various handwriting styles, each marking a different generation of the museum's guardians.

"There are records dating back centuries," Charles said, his finger tracing along the spines of the boxes. "If there's anything on the Ghost Watch Club, it'll be here. 1994 wasn't too long ago, in the grand scheme of things."

"And yet it was almost a lifetime for me," Ellie muttered under her breath. "If only I'd been more aware as a ten-month-old—and able to form lasting memories."

Charles chuckled, drawing her attention to a specific box. Ellie's eyes widened as she spotted a familiar name: *THE BLACKWOOD FAMILY MURDERS - 2024.*

A wave of admiration washed over her at his thoroughness. She wondered who, one day, might open that box to learn the story of her riddle-solving, but today wasn't the time for that.

The Plot Thickens

They continued along the shelves until Charles slid out another heavy box: *THE HAUNTINGS - 1994*.

"I heard you found a message written in blood at the bookshop," Charles said, carrying the box to a small table with a lamp at the back of the room. "A confession of murder, they're saying."

Ellie sighed, unsurprised by the exaggeration. "It wasn't blood—it was spray paint. And it wasn't exactly a confession, more like an admission that someone witnessed the murder."

"And you're trying to verify the accusation?"

"Verify or disprove. The jury's still out."

Charles flicked on a desk lamp and Ellie held her breath, hoping for a treasure trove of information. The box had felt heavy, but when she opened it, disappointment set in.

Inside were only a few items: an envelope full of photographs, a few scraps of paper torn from a notepad, and an old VHS tape in a tatty old cardboard box labelled *Experiment 3 – 12/10/94*.

"Experiment?" Ellie echoed. "Do you have anything that could play this?"

"Sorry."

"Can I borrow it?"

Charles grumbled, and she knew it wasn't an immediate yes. "You shouldn't even really be back here. I—"

"*Anyone in?*" someone called from the front. "The front door was open."

Charles left to deal with the visitor, and Ellie pulled the tape from the sleeve. Aside from the label, there were no other clues. If she could get it out of the museum, she was certain her mother would have a VHS player—the last medium for a *Heatherwood Haven* release. She set the tape aside.

She opened an envelope of photographs, expecting to see the usual blurry images of supposed apparitions. What she found was far more surprising: personal snapshots taken in and around the village. She recognised a few faces—the rebellious-looking Jack and Cassandra, a younger Harold, and George and Meredith, who appeared in multiple photos. But one figure stood out. Dr Christina Marsh appeared only once, captured in a group shot inside The Drowsy Duck. They were gathered, laughing like old friends, as if they'd asked a passer-by to take the photo. They looked happy, almost like a family.

The dates, printed in the orange LED corner of each photo from an old wind-up camera, all pointed to the summer of 1994. None were taken after September. She checked the tape's label again: 12/10/94.

It seemed these items had once belonged to Dr Christina Marsh—the very person Ellie couldn't reach, unless she intended to try through a psychic, something Marsh would have undoubtedly scoffed at.

Gathering the items, Ellie went to find Charles, but as she reached the door, it swung open to reveal DS

Angela Cookson, looking irritated at the contents in Ellie's hands.

"If those are connected to the case, you need to hand them over," Angela insisted. "And why are you here? Shouldn't you be painting a shelf at the shop or something?"

"So, there *is* a case now?" Ellie asked, sidestepping the jab about the shop—her guilt over DIY-dodging already gnawing at her. "I thought you didn't have the resources to investigate?"

Too exasperated for niceties, Angela snatched the tape and photographs from Ellie's grip.

"I don't need to explain my procedures to you, Eleanor Swan. Officially, it's still an accidental death." She paused, her eyes scanning the room as if considering her next words carefully. "After reviewing the old files, something didn't sit right. The DS at the time was about to retire, and he thought the people of Meadowfield were too good to have pushed someone as well-liked as Tim."

"And if it had been your case, you wouldn't have closed it so quickly?" Ellie pressed.

"Items were missing from Tim's person, and a strange chemical was found at the scene."

"What kind of chemical?"

"I've already said too much," Angela snapped, waving her away.

Leaving the archives with little more than frustration, Ellie found Charles at the counter, struggling to peel his dried paintbrush from the railway leaflet.

"I stalled her as long as I could," he explained with an apologetic smile. "Did you find anything useful?"

Ellie hesitated, her thoughts drifting to the tape.

"Maybe. I'm sure that stuff belonged to Dr Christina Marsh. Do you know how it ended up here?"

"People donate things they think are important. Sometimes it's just birth or death notices, or wedding memorabilia. But whoever donated these must've thought they were significant."

"Perhaps they are," she mused, eyeing the door. "Thanks for your help, Charles."

"Keep me in the loop," he called after her, "and watch out for the ghosts."

"Likewise."

Outside, a haze of grey had washed over the blue, the sky mottled with clouds creeping from the direction of the church. She tried her luck at The Drowsy Duck again, but the doors remained locked. Cupping her hands to the window, she was sure she saw two figures inside this time.

"It's Ellie... again," she called, trying to sound patient. "We can talk now, or I'll be back later... your choice."

One figure shuffled away down the long corridor while the other remained motionless behind the bar.

Frustrated, Ellie counted the closed pub as her third dead end of the day. She hadn't expected to get all the answers when she left the cottage, but she'd hoped to

The Plot Thickens

cross at least one thing off her list before returning to the bookshop.

Her gran's laughter echoed from the direction of South Street—a sure sign that Granny Maggie had no plans to pull her head out of the sand.

With a sigh and reluctant steps, Ellie walked to the shop as it began to rain.

Chapter 5
Brick by Brick

Inside Meadowfield Books, a new face greeted Ellie. A young man, perhaps in his mid-twenties, stood chatting with Granny Maggie, his wide, lopsided smile warm and disarming. Ellie lingered in the doorway, watching as her gran, with a broad grin, gestured at the man as if Ellie should know who he was.

He had tanned skin and chestnut hair streaked with sun, neatly tucked behind ears that stuck out at perfect right angles. There was a jolly, almost carefree air about him—and something vaguely familiar that Ellie couldn't quite place.

"Ellie Swan, Joey Harper. Joey, Ellie," Maggie introduced, ushering her into the shop. Ellie tripped over the loose doorframe on her way in before shutting the door against the rain. "I told you about him last night. He was supposed to work on the restoration at Blackwood House, but Charles has cold feet, so..."

"Here's Joey!" the boyish man extended a hand. His big smile reached his doe eyes, which sparkled like Walt Disney had drawn them. "My dad named me after that guy from that sitcom."

"*Friends?*" Ellie asked, still shaking his hand at the end of an arm that seemed to be made of rubber. "Nice to meet you."

"That's the one," he exclaimed, giving her hand a final squeeze before letting go. "Never seen it." He rocked back on his heels and took in the bookshop, whistling as his doe eyes absorbed the scope of the problems. "This place needs some love. Not quite the bookshop I remember, Mrs C."

"But it can be fixed?" Maggie asked, desperation colouring her voice.

"Most things can be. You know me, Mrs C—I love a challenge. Can't sit still for more than five minutes, can I?"

"You were a fidget when I tutored you, and please, Maggie is perfectly fine. I was never actually your teacher."

"But I'd never have got that C in history if you hadn't helped. Lucky that I came in here," he said, slapping the wobbly shelf. "Budget?"

"Ah." Maggie winced. "Well... we..."

"We can't sell books right now," Ellie replied, unsure why her gran thought this was the right time to bring in outside help, "which is, funnily enough, how the shop makes money."

"I know you're good for it. You can pay me when the numbers are up, and I won't hear more about it."

"Oh, you've got a good heart, Joey. Always have." Maggie nodded her head in a definite way. "You keep a record of every hour, every cost, and we'll cover it. Plus interest! And a tip. Won't we, Ellie?"

"Even if we have to go selling books door-to-door."

"Not the worst idea," Maggie agreed, suddenly shaking her head. "I'm dreadful! Where are my manners? Tea, Joey? How do you like it?"

"You know the way to my heart, Mrs—Maggie." He swallowed, as though the name burned in his throat. "Good and proper, please."

"Good and proper, coming up."

"Make that two," Ellie said, curious about the newcomer. "It's nice to have a real professional on set, as it were. Is the shop really that simple to fix?"

Joey kept his jolly smile frozen until Maggie disappeared into the back. When the kettle was boiling, his smile faltered at the corners.

"Listen," he whispered, drawing Ellie in with a beckoning finger. "Anyone else, I'd tell them to cut their losses and not waste their time with the hassle. Old buildings like this usually need sorting out brick by brick. But I couldn't break Mrs C's heart like that." He scratched at his soft chin, and if he could grow stubble, Ellie couldn't see it. "You got ideas?"

"Ideas?"

"Business ideas?" he urged. "To make this place

work. I'm no Alan Sugar, but when you go in and out of businesses as often as I do, you get a sense of what works and what doesn't. And let me tell you this—I haven't been going in and out of many bookshops lately."

Ellie rubbed the faint creases bunching up her forehead, a sobering thought that would keep her up at night, as if she didn't have enough on her mind.

"Coffee?" she suggested.

"Your gran's making tea."

"A coffee machine," she corrected, her mouth dry and needing that tea. "I have some barista experience... sort of. I wasn't very good at it, but I know how to make most things. And people like coffee, don't they?"

"Do you?"

She shook her head.

"Me neither," he admitted in a naughty whisper. "And don't get me started on those Frappuccino milkshake things that cost almost a tenner these days." He gasped, his eyes dancing with an idea. "Oh, you could print little quotes on the paper cups. People like quotes, right? Book quotes, I mean. Silly idea. Probably."

But Ellie was already digging in her bag for her pad and pen.

"That's a great idea," she said, "but we need to get there first. If this is the last gasp for the bookshop, we're doing it with wallpaper on the walls and books on the shelves. Can you help?"

"I'll need to do a full top to bottom, inside out job," he said, slapping the wobbly shelf again. Whatever had been holding it together splintered, and he jumped to catch it. "I'm sure we won't find anything too concerning. Probably."

"Then let's act like it *probably* is fine, but first, please —before anything—can you fix that wobbly doorframe?"

"Easy."

But the graffiti drew him in on his way to the toolboxes piled up by the door. He couldn't seem to stop himself from getting as close as possible, his nose almost touching the words.

"Weird," he whispered, glancing back at Ellie. "My grandad told me all about Tim Baker."

"What did he say?"

"A ghost killed him at The Drowsy Duck."

"Ah."

"Sounds like a cover-up to me," he added quickly, "but he said The Duck was some entrance to the afterlife. Built on top of an ancient graveyard or something."

This was the first Ellie had heard about an ancient graveyard.

"Any proof?"

He laughed, shaking his head. "Grandad also thought they were trying to kill us with toothpaste, so believe what you want. He almost joined some club about ghosts, but he said this Meredith woman, whoever she is, freaked him out." His smile faded as he took a step away from the scrawl. "He went to school with her and said she'd spend all her time sitting on a tree stump, talking to an imaginary friend. Nobody would go near her. Meredith the Mad, they called her. Live and let live, I say, but even that's a bit... odd."

"Meredith Fenton *is* odd," Maggie called as she returned with their steaming cups of tea on a tray, rattling as she walked. "She'd be the first to tell you and never apologised for it. And your grandad missed little by missing the club meetings. I went to a couple to appease Meredith, and it was a lot of much ado about nothing."

Joey accepted the tea in his palm, not caring about the heat. Ellie took the handle, glad to see the dark colour of the 'good and proper' brew.

"Did you see any of the hauntings yourself?" he asked Maggie after a hot slurp while Ellie blew ripples across the surface. "I used to love flicking through this old history book that Gramps had. Full of evidence, it was."

Ellie's ears pricked up.

"History book?" she asked.

"*Prematurely* published," Maggie stated flatly, hugging her tea as she leaned against the counter. "And calling it 'history' is a stretch. *If* I'd sold the book, I'd have categorised it as fiction—nothing more than a record of how far some people went to pull the wool over our eyes for a few pound coins."

Maggie fell silent, and Ellie could feel her gran's reluctance to divulge more.

Undeterred, she turned back to Joey and pulled out the list of names. Her gran sighed as Joey examined the list.

The Plot Thickens

"I think Cassandra goes by Cassie now," he said. "She's a photographer. I see her around all the time with some bloke with a ponytail, and I think they have a studio down the—"

"Aren't we here to work?" Maggie asked with a frustrated laugh. "Get those teas down your necks, and let's get on with it. There's plenty to do here and now without worrying about the events of three decades ago."

Joey gulped down his tea on command, but Ellie took a slow sip, her irritation mounting at her gran's insistence that anything tied to Meredith and Tim be buried as deeply as the message under the wallpaper.

Maggie thrust paint scrapers into their hands before flitting off to the back room with Joey's empty cup. Joey, however, couldn't tear his eyes from the wall.

"What are you going to do about *that*?" he asked.

Ellie took another sip of tea and replied, "I'll let you know when I figure it out."

The afternoon passed in a blur of moving the heavy shelves Ellie and her gran had avoided, peeling off more wallpaper, all backdropped by Joey's constant chatter.

He was talkative in a way Ellie had never mastered, bouncing from cricket scores to supermarket deals on protein powder and then earnestly wondering why daylight savings was 'a thing.' His name suited him perfectly. His sweet, easy-going nature was a welcome distraction from Ellie's frequent glances at the graffiti on the wall.

Maggie, on the other hand, kept herself busy in a different way.

While Ellie and Joey tackled the harder tasks, Maggie gathered the various catalogues they'd collected over the past months. Red pen in hand, she worked her way through them, circling and scribbling like she was back in school marking homework. From the pages she occasionally flipped around to show Ellie, it became clear her gran wasn't as afraid of the past as she'd been acting.

"I think I've found the *exact* wallpaper I used last time," Maggie declared, stamping her finger on a page. She lifted her reading glasses from the chain around her neck and took a closer look. "Perhaps not *quite* the same shade of blue. But I did always love those little owl details in the design." She drew several circles around it. "It'd be nice to get the same one again."

"Don't you want something different, Mags?" Joey asked. "Something new?"

"What do they say? 'If it isn't broke, don't fix it?'"

But it *was* broken.

And Maggie had broken it.

Not intentionally, but through neglect—by pretending the shop's problems weren't problems, just quirks. The damp patches, flickering bulbs, and persistent musty smell that no amount of air freshener could shift didn't seem to matter to her. The thatched roof could've blown off, and she wouldn't have blinked if there were still books to sell.

Ellie should have sensed her gran would snatch back the reins at some point. The deal had been that Ellie would spruce up the shop, make the 'big decisions', and run the place. Maggie was supposed to step back, rest, relax—*retire*. But old habits die hard, and that stubborn history teacher was never too far from the surface.

As the sun began to dip below the horizon and their wallpaper removing slowed, Maggie sent Joey off with a thank-you hug and a promise to see him again tomorrow. She didn't linger—bolting out the back door as if she'd been waiting for hours to escape—leaving Ellie alone in the quiet of the bookshop. The sudden absence of Maggie's constant tweeting and Joey's cheerful chatter was both a relief and a burden.

Ellie climbed the narrow staircase to the long-abandoned upstairs room in the eaves of the roof, her shoe slipping on the worn, thread-born carpet. At the top, she forced the door open and peeked inside.

The room was half the size of the shop below, with sloped walls and low beams. Two small windows let in the yellow glow of the street light outside, its light filtering through the straw ceiling in thin, tight lines.

The upstairs room had never been open to customers in Ellie's lifetime, but it had been her weekend hideaway during school exam revision. The thatched roof had provided a muffled quiet, offering refuge from the chaos of her mother's audition drama and the backseat teaching of her gran.

Boxes crammed with hundreds of books from downstairs sat waiting to be unpacked and rediscovered. Granny Maggie hadn't been able to carry them, leaving Ellie to spend the first week of their project hauling them upstairs, trip after trip. The effort had given her tiny bicep muscles that had lingered for at least the following week.

In Ellie's daydreams, she had envisioned the upstairs space as a cosy reading nook. Like downstairs, it featured another stone fireplace, unused for decades. She pictured flickering flames in the dusty hearth, surrounded by low, comfy armchairs and bean bags where customers could relax and sample books before buying them.

The perfect place for a bookworm.

But after how the day had unfolded, her gran would likely be just as happy to seal the room up for good. That's how things had always been. Meadowfield Books seemed destined to remain a relic, forever pickled in its past form.

A brief surge of motivation spurred Ellie to shift two boxes, clearing enough space to squeeze into a corner. But the day's exhaustion was already seeping into her bones, heavy and unrelenting. She exhaled slowly. This was why she'd wanted to talk to Harold earlier—her body and mind were drained.

Her phone vibrated against her thigh. A notification from a job-hunting app flashed onto the screen:

The Plot Thickens

IMPORTANT! 🔔 New alerts (3) in YOUR (TV/FILM) field...

She'd stopped checking the app months ago, too focused on the shop. But the old urge to run away resurfaced for the first time since deciding to stay in Meadowfield. She imagined being back in a city like Cardiff, lost in a crowd. Head down, keep moving.

Anonymous. No longer a Meadowling, her past a story she revisited on the nights she couldn't sleep.

She hadn't felt the itch to run since after Luke's motorbike accident. As if his death and the funeral hadn't been enough to deal with, someone had painted 'MURDERER!' across her mother's front door. Maggie had packed her onto a train immediately, urging her to escape the suffocating small-village whispers.

Ellie never found out who sprayed the message, though she hadn't wanted to stick around long enough to find out. The guilt had eaten away at her as though it were true. The locals had connected Luke's accident and Ellie calling off the wedding despite three weeks separating those events. Much like Meredith's obsession with blaming a ghost for Tim's death, the truth hadn't mattered to the Meadowlings. The guilty brush had tarred her, and Ellie had rolled in the feathers.

She put her phone away, ignoring the call to run for now.

* * *

Back downstairs in the quiet shop, Sylvia's musical laugh drifted in from the cheese shop as Ellie stood before the big black letters on the wall.

It was an odd place to leave such a heavy accusation—somewhere it could have been uncovered at any moment, yet it might have remained hidden for years. A message that had silently watched every customer who passed through the shop, only to be uncovered by Ellie's naïve belief that she could handle this DIY project. But now, the message had someone staring back.

She tried to imagine what the graffiti artist must have felt when they sprayed those words. Relief, perhaps, at getting something off their chest? Glee at continuing a rumour? And if they had 'seen it all,' did *all* mean they'd witnessed Meredith pushing Tim down the stairs into the pub cellar? Angela had claimed there were no witnesses.

"So, why not tell the police?" Ellie thought aloud.

A cold draught brushed against her neck, sending a prickling wave down her spine. She turned, expecting to see her gran rushing back in for her reading glasses. But she was alone.

It must have been the wind, though she wasn't entirely convinced. The rational part of her mind insisted that old buildings were draughty, especially ones with exposed plaster. But a nagging feeling whispered that she wasn't alone.

She cried out as a loud crash shattered the silence. Glass exploded inwards from the shop's front window, and a brick landed with a dull thud by her feet, rolling inches past her shoes. Her heart thudded in her chest as she darted around the last of the shelves and through the front door.

She scanned South Street in both directions, towards The Drowsy Duck and down to where the shopping street curved away. It stood as calm and still as a pond's surface, as though nothing had happened. The hole in the glass panel was the only sign of disturbance.

Ellie's skin prickled as she peered through the shattered window, replaying where she'd been standing just moments before. From that spot by the wall, she would have been visible to anyone passing by, and the brick had come far too close for its trajectory to be accidental.

Sylvia's head popped out from the cheese shop next door, and she asked, "Did I hear smashing glass?"

Before Ellie could answer, Amber and Zara appeared further down the street, drawn by the commotion. Zara gasped, her eyes locked on the shattered window, while Amber, phone in hand as always, snapped a picture with a blinding flash of light. Ellie blinked, snapping back to her senses.

She was sure the brick had been meant to hit her.

The three women joined Ellie inside the shop, their gazes shifting from the broken glass to the writing on the wall.

"This... this is bad, Ellie," Zara said in a deep,

ominous voice. "That brick—it was an omen. A warning."

"Let's not get carried away," Sylvia said, brushing something off Ellie's jumper. "It was likely bored teenagers causing trouble. You know how it is these days. Don't let it spook you." Still, her eyes gleamed with excitement—Sylvia loved local drama more than anyone. "I must say, hearing about the graffiti is one thing, but *seeing* it..." She reached out, stopping just before her fingers touched the plaster. "Rather eerie."

Amber stood silent, her face paler than usual, eyes fixed on the wall. This time, she didn't lift her phone to take a picture. Ellie sensed Amber's silence meant something more.

"He was my cousin," Amber croaked.

"Tim?" Ellie confirmed.

Amber nodded, stepping closer to the wall.

"He died before I was born," she said, "but my Auntie Carol talked about him all the time."

"Oh, the poor woman!" Sylvia exclaimed, resting a comforting hand on Amber's shoulder. "Let's hope these new developments lead to some answers for Carol."

"Auntie Carol died a few years ago, never knowing what happened to her son, and she hated that people were always speculating. She never believed his death was accidental."

"Did she have a reason to doubt the police?" Ellie asked.

"Just a feeling."

The Plot Thickens

A silence fell over them, twisting Ellie's gut—Tim's mother had died without answers, the uncertainty tugging at her until the end. Staring at the brick, Ellie hated how little she knew.

"Perhaps Sylvia is correct," Zara said, shifting from one foot to the other. "Teenagers."

"On any other day, I might have believed that," Ellie said, bending to pick up the brick, "but I'm certain this was meant for me."

Sylvia gasped. "To chase you off the case?"

"I haven't done much yet," Ellie replied, squinting towards the soft glow of The Drowsy Duck, weighing the brick in her hand. "Though, not for lack of trying."

"But why would someone not want you to prove this?" Sylvia asked. "If they *saw* Meredith push Tim, wouldn't they want people to know? Why leave the message otherwise?"

"To throw suspicion off themselves?" Amber suggested.

"I know a glazier," Sylvia announced, rummaging in her tweed jacket for her phone. "He owes me a favour for catering his mother's divorce party—her ex-husband was lactose intolerant and never allowed cheese in the house, so she wanted to try *everything*, but in the end, she didn't really like..."

Sylvia's voice faded as Ellie stepped onto South Street, the cool breeze stirring her hair. She tucked stray strands behind her ears, glancing once more towards the pub. In her mind's eye, she saw herself as she'd been before: hands cupped to the glass, announcing her presence and intentions.

Had the brick been Harold Fletcher's reply?

"What are you going to do?" Amber asked, appearing behind her.

"Heed the warning, I say!" Zara replied, hurrying out of the shop as though she'd needed no prompting. "It would not be wise to stir up the spirits."

"Not unless you're adding tonic and a wedge of lime," Sylvia added with a chuckle, joining them outside. "Besides, it wasn't a spirit that threw a brick through that window. If you're on the right track, Ellie, I say keep going!"

The three women turned to Ellie, waiting for her choice. She looked back at the bookshop, the new jagged gap in the window only adding to its air of dereliction. She stared up at the sign above the door. The green paint had peeled, but it still gave her the same stirring sense of belonging—this shop was more of a home to her than anywhere else.

The shop needed her to mend it.

But it was also trying to tell her something. She might have found the graffiti by chance, and Tim's death could have been an accident, but someone had sprayed those words with purpose.

"I'll keep going," she said. "History is hidden in the details, and someone tried to define Meredith and Tim's story with that message. They must have known it could take decades, maybe even centuries, for someone to strip

The Plot Thickens

back the paper. My question is: were they leaving a trail back to the truth, or did they mean to solidify the lie?"

"Atta girl!" Sylvia exclaimed, giving her a hearty pat on the back. "And we'll help, won't we, ladies?"

"I'll try," Amber said hesitantly, "but... it's just... a bit strange, the whole cousin thing."

"And leave me out of it," Zara said, stepping back from the shop. "Be careful, Ellie. I've got a bad feeling about all of this."

Ellie shared the feeling, but she was ready to charge at it headfirst.

"I have every faith in you," Sylvia whispered, giving Ellie's shoulders a reassuring rub from behind. "You remind me of the girls back at the boarding school—you'd have made a fantastic croquet captain. So, what will be your first move? Interviewing a suspect? A stake-out?" She gave Ellie's shoulders a little squeeze, shattering the calming effect with her excitement. "Oh, how I'd love to tag along, but I'll stay here and coordinate the glass refitting."

"Sylvia, are you—"

"You'd do the same for me, so don't argue. That's what friends are for." Sylvia straightened out Ellie's jumper, then fussed with her hair until it was to her satisfaction. "Perhaps you should go home and change before tackling whatever it is you're itching to do."

"A visit to The Drowsy Duck."

"On second thought, you'll fit right in." Sylvia's lips pressed into a concerned purse as her gaze drifted towards the pub. "I know we're both fortified women made of strong stuff, but even I get the heebie-jeebies going there. That place has quite the reputation, you know."

Ellie had heard all the warnings about The Drowsy Duck since her return, but if the brick was meant to frighten her, it had only fuelled her resolve to continue down the path she knew she couldn't ignore.

Chapter 6
Spirits in the Cellar

Leaving Sylvia to coordinate the glass refitting, Ellie set off for the place she'd been itching to visit all day. She passed the pond, its still water reflecting the brooding evening sky, and approached The Drowsy Duck. The pub's small, leaded windows glowed with a warm, rosy light against the encroaching shadows.

At some point, the exterior had been painted white, but the paint now peeled and crumbled in places, with black streaks trailing from the gutters. Rowdy sounds spilled into the night, and Ellie had a feeling she was about to discover how the pub had earned its unpleasant reputation.

Taking a steadying breath, she straightened her jumper and stepped inside. The air was heavy with the musty tang of stale beer and damp. The pub felt oppressively cramped, the low-beamed ceiling almost pressing down on her. Dim light from the wall sconces struggled to soften the disarray of scuffed chairs and uneven tables scattered haphazardly across the room.

A loud crash by the fireplace seized her attention. Two burly figures were locked in a fierce struggle, fists flying as they staggered into tables and chairs, sending patrons scurrying out of the way. One man was bald, the other had long black hair, and it quickly became apparent that this was no fair fight. The one with the black hair delivered punch after punch, while the bald man could do little more than shield his face with his arms.

Harold Fletcher, the pub's stocky landlord, stormed through the crowd. His booming voice sliced through the chaos as he bellowed, "That's enough, Cassie!"

"Leave me alone!" the black hair flung back, revealing a woman's face twisted in a rageful grimace. She still had a clenched fist, but at least she'd stopped swinging it. "*He* started it!"

"Because it was *my* turn to use the pool table!" her opponent shot back, licking his lips, blood tinging his teeth. "Everyone knows a pound coin on the corner means it's reserved for the next game. You can't hog it all night."

"Yeah? Says who?" Cassie bellowed, lunging for him again, but Harold locked her arms behind her back. "Let me go!"

"You're barred!" Harold cried. "And I mean it this time. I'm tired of you lashing out every other week."

With a swift shove, he threw Cassie onto the street,

the door slamming shut behind her with a satisfying thud. A light smattering of applause rippled through the room as the man with the bloody mouth chalked his pool cue.

But Ellie's attention lingered on the woman who'd just been ejected. Cassie was in her late forties now, and most of her piercings were gone, leaving only a black lip ring, but there was no mistaking her—she was Cassandra Winters, Jack Campbell's girlfriend from the old Ghost Watch Club.

The pub had changed even less from those old photographs, and Ellie could almost see them all gathered by the pool table back in 1994, smiling at the camera.

How times had changed.

The room soon settled back into its rhythm of drinking and loud conversation. Fights had become part of the norm these days, with many blaming Harold for letting standards slip.

Ellie took a deep breath, steeling herself for the conversation she'd tried to have earlier, back when she'd felt a little fresher.

"What can I get you?" Harold asked, his eyes scanning her. "Someone's been busy. Decorating?"

"Yes, actually," she began, sensing a way in. "At the bookshop, but you might already know that. I was hoping you'd be able to help me with some research."

"You're Maggie's granddaughter," he said, slinging a towel over his shoulder, his flat expression giving nothing away. "She doesn't come in here much anymore."

Ellie nodded, a mix of pride and apprehension swelling at being recognised. She hoped he still held her gran in the same regard as most Meadowlings despite her infrequent visits.

"I take it you've heard about what we found at the shop yesterday?" she asked. "About Meredith and Tim?"

"You hear all sorts in here," he said, shrugging as he got on with collecting the empty glasses on the bar. "I take it all with a grain of salt. Not sure what that's got to do with me."

"Tim died in *this* pub," she said, looking around for an obvious entrance to the cellar, but none jumped out. "And his club spent a lot of time here. I know it's none of my business but those words are in my shop. I can't ignore them."

"You're right. It is none of *your* business," a croaky voice called out, "Stirring up quite the hornet's nest, aren't you, little girl?"

"That's Mother," Harold explained, a hint of apology in his tone. "She's not been well."

As if on cue, an old woman shuffled out from the back room. She moved with deliberate slowness, each step cautious, as though the next might be her last. Beneath a heavy black shawl, her thin frame seemed to bow under its weight, yet her eyes were keen and fixed on Ellie with such piercing intensity that Ellie stepped back from the bar.

The Plot Thickens

"I'm perfectly fine, Harold," the woman declared, her voice surprisingly strong. There was a stubbornness to her tone that reminded Ellie of her gran—though Harold's mother seemed much older than Maggie by quite a margin. "I am Tilly, and you are Eleanor Swan. You're related to that dreadful actress who was trying to film in my private quarters this afternoon."

"Try not to hold that against me."

"In all my one hundred and one years, I've never met anyone so rude." Her words cut across the bar like a challenge, sending a chill through Ellie. "That makes me old enough to tell you this—you haven't the strength of character for what you may uncover. Oh no." She chuckled darkly. "This world isn't one for the likes of *you* to meddle with."

With that, Tilly shuffled off, leaving Ellie unsettled, though that seemed to have been the point. Her request had been simple enough, but Tilly's cryptic attempt to scare her off only raised more questions.

"Sorry about her," Harold whispered, running a hand through his thinning hair and glancing over his shoulder to ensure Tilly had gone. "She can be intense. Comes from a long line of psychics, but she hung up her crystal ball back in her twenties."

"Only because I was too proficient at communing with the spirits!" Tilly's voice rang out from the back room. "My powers terrified people, and you have no idea how it messed with my energies."

"Yes, Mother," Harold called back, then muttered

under his breath, "I should've bought the cheaper hearing aids. Can't even sneak out for a ciggie without her hearing my lighter." Realising he might've said too much, he cleared his throat. "So, why the interest in the hauntings? It's old news."

"The accusation, you mean?"

Harold shrugged. "Everyone was saying that back then. Meredith made a good case for herself, but if it's the hauntings you want to talk about, You've come to the right place, Miss Swan." The sternness in his eyes softened, replaced by a gleam of excitement. His posture relaxed, and a slow, practised smile spread across his face. "The Drowsy Duck is *infamous* for its legendary spiritual activity. I've seen more than a few ghouls here in my time."

"And the hauntings started in 1994?" she asked as she retrieved her pad and pen from her bag.

"Try before 1857," he corrected, leaning in closer, his voice dropping to a cigarette-breath husky whisper. "This old place was built on top of an ancient graveyard."

"1857 is hardly ancient," Ellie replied, unable to help herself. "Any proof? People were keeping thorough records of graves long before that."

"That's what *they* say," Harold replied with another shrug.

"Who?"

He gritted his jaw. "This place *is* haunted. I started working here as a lad when Mother and Father's names were above the door." He glanced towards the bathrooms, and Ellie noticed the door marked 'CELLAR – PRIVATE' between the Gents and the Ladies. "One night, I was down there changing a barrel. Newcastle Brown Ale, it was. My parents were cashing up and kicking out the stragglers. I *know* the cellar was empty, but I heard footsteps coming down the stairs. Thud, thud, thud..." He tapped his fingers on the water-stained bar, bouncing the nearby glasses. "... and then, cold breath on my neck, and I was pushed right into the barrels. I *felt* the hands on my shoulders. Ice cold fingers, pushing with all their strength."

Harold demonstrated the shove, his eyes locked on Ellie, checking she was listening. She was, though if he was trying to suggest the same had happened to Tim Baker, she wasn't buying it.

"When I turned around," he said quietly, "I was alone. No retreating footsteps, nobody in the shadows, just the empty cellar." He folded his arms with a pleased grin. "Explain *that*."

As she jotted down the bullet points, a shiver ran down Ellie's spine—not entirely from the well-rehearsed tale, but from the gleam in Harold's eyes as he relished every word.

"You heard footsteps," Ellie confirmed, reviewing her notes, "and then you felt a breath, but you didn't turn around until *after* you were pushed?"

Without missing a beat, he said, "I thought it was my

father coming to check on me, so I wasn't going to give him the satisfaction. My parents ran down to see what all the fuss was about. Father clipped me around the ear because I'd had a couple of pints, but Mother believed me. That's when she told me about our family's gifts. She says that's why the pub was chosen as the hotspot in the village."

Ellie flipped back a page in her notebook.

"But you said the 'ancient graveyard' caused the paranormal activity."

"The spirits work in mysterious ways," he said, barely concealing the bite in his voice. "Tim Baker found out the hard way, and he wasn't pushed by any old spirit." His voice dropped to a conspiratorial murmur, and the shadows seemed to lean in, eager to hear what he would say next. "Have you ever heard the tale of the *first* landlord?"

"Here we go," one of the old men propped up at the bar muttered into his pint. "This is a good one."

Ellie shook her head, and despite her rational mind, the pub's atmosphere lent itself perfectly to such tales. She couldn't help but be drawn in by Harold's theatrics.

"John Partridge," he said, "spent years building this place from the ground up with his own two hands, pouring his heart and soul into every brick and beam. The night this place opened, there was to be a grand celebration, but poor John never saw the drawing of the first pint. That very night, he tumbled headfirst down those cellar steps. Broke his neck clean in two, and the story goes, he wasn't found until after the party was over... and he was still *alive*. His final words were..." he paused to drew in a staggered breath and groaned, "... *I waited for you*."

Ellie's eyes darted to the cellar door, half expecting it to creak open. She could almost picture the scene: the triumphant landlord descending the steps, only to meet a tragic end before his special opening night had even begun. Ironic, if the tale held any truth.

"And *they* say," Harold's voice dropped lower, but Ellie resisted leaning in any further, "he's been pushing people down ever since—a bitter, jealous soul trapped between realms. He never got to run the pub he built with his own hands. Can't you *feel* him, Miss Swan?"

A log in the fireplace popped loudly, making Ellie jump. She laughed at herself, reminding herself she was here for the facts, not the scares. Still, she had to admit—he was a decent showman.

"So, you're suggesting John pushed Tim?" Ellie confirmed as she scanned her notes. "John Partridge, deceased one hundred and thirty-seven years before murdering Tim?"

"You don't believe me?" Harold flipped up the panel at the end of the bar and stepped out, gesturing for Ellie to follow him. "Go and see the cellar for yourself."

Harold pushed open the door between the bathrooms, and Ellie crept down the narrow stone staircase into the dark, dank cellar. Her hand trailed along the wall for balance, the old plaster cold and rough beneath her fingers. Harold hesitated on the last step, his usual showman's bravado faltering as he gestured to a patch of floor with less of a flourish than usual.

"This very spot is where Tim was found. Cold as ice, he was. Some say you can still hear his final breath on quiet nights."

Ellie couldn't bring herself to stand on that patch. She stepped around it, feeling the weight of Tim's death settle over the cellar, making it feel real, immediate, not just a footnote in the pub's history. The stale scent of old beer hung in the air, mingling with something faintly chemical and a lingering trace of cigarette smoke.

She gulped the lump in her throat. "Harold, as fascinating as these ghost stories are, I'm more curious about what happened that night. You were here. You know the rest of his club were here too, as they often were. What happened in the lead up to the fall?"

Harold's smile faltered, replaced by something else —worry? Guilt? He retreated to a corner and pulled out a box of cigarettes from behind the barrels, sliding one out with his lips. After a few drags, he went to put them away, then doubled back, offering Ellie one. She declined, watching as he lit the tip with a blazing match.

"I need to pick up some lighter fluid," he said, exhaling smoke in the shadows, staring at the walls rather than Ellie as she lingered by the light from the stairwell.

The Plot Thickens

"Tim's death was a long time ago. My memory's a bit foggy on the details, you understand."

"It seems you know more about 1857 than 1994."

He took several deep puffs like a stressed chimney.

"The mind works in mysterious ways," he said.

"But surely you remember *something*?" she asked, stepping closer to him. "It must have been quite an event for the—"

Harold rushed and grabbed Ellie's arm, cutting her off mid-sentence. She froze, startled by the abruptness and firmness of his grip.

"Please," he muttered around his cigarette, nodding to the ground as he gently pulled her back a step. "You're standing on a trapdoor that leads down to an old well. I've no idea how sturdy the wood is—or how deep the well goes."

Ellie glanced down, watching the bright tip of his cigarette cast a faint glow over the worn, uneven planks beneath her feet. The boards creaked as she stepped back, and she couldn't shake the thought that Harold might be playing at another cheap thrill.

"Perhaps we should head back upstairs," he suggested, hopping over Tim's patch once more. Ellie wondered if the move was for her benefit or if he did it every time. "Getting a bit chilly down here, don't you think?"

Without waiting for her response, Harold stubbed out his half-finished cigarette and tossed it into a corner, taking the steps two at a time as he hurried upstairs. But

Ellie lingered in the dim cellar, tasting that faintly sweet, chemical tang in the air.

It triggered a distant memory—her gran's dining room on a hot summer day, the vinyl on the turntable warping in the direct sunlight as the smell of melting plastic filled the room.

Glancing around, she saw nothing particularly unusual. No vinyl player piping in eerie sounds, though the air was growing colder by the second.

Like in the bookshop, she felt an icy breath brushing the nape of her neck. This time, however, it wasn't her imagination. She traced the stream of misty, cool air to its source, that strange vinyl-like scent growing thicker. Following the breeze, she found a small vent hidden within the doorframe, carefully painted to blend with the woodwork.

"Parlour tricks," she muttered with a strained laugh, shaking her head. "Oh, Harold…"

She ascended the cold, stone steps, the penultimate one snagging the tip of her shoe. On closer inspection, she noticed the steps were uneven—the last few misaligned by nearly an inch. If Tim hadn't been pushed, the poor design seemed a more plausible culprit than the ghost of John Partridge, the man who'd built the wonky steps.

Reaching for the handle, she wanted to leave the pub. Harold wasn't going to be straight with her, which only deepened her suspicions. The pub was just a stone's throw from the bookshop; it wouldn't have taken him long to slip out, hurl the brick through the window, and be back behind the bar pulling pints before anyone noticed. She wobbled the handle back and forth, but the door wouldn't budge.

"It's stuck," she called, her voice echoing back to the cellar. "Harold, the door won't open…" She shook the handle again, panic hot in her chest. "Let me out, Harold!"

The door burst open, and she stumbled straight into Harold. He reached out to steady her, but she pulled back instinctively, nearly toppling backwards. Just as her heel teetered over the edge of the top step, with nothing behind her but the cold cellar and its strange, scented draughts, Harold caught her jumper, pulling her to safety.

"Easy there," he said, as he closed the door. "Gets stuck when it's cold," he explained eagerly. "Was it cold? They say you can feel it most when you're down there on your—"

"Nope," she said, pulling down the hem of her jumper with a defiant tug. "In fact, I was starting to feel rather warm."

The amusement drained from Harold's face before he retreated to the bar, wiping down the water-stains and avoiding her gaze. Ellie followed, standing where she had been moments before, sensing she had him on the back foot.

"I just want to know what happened, Harold. Surely you understand that?" Ellie braced herself, expecting

Harold to throw her out like he had done with Cassie earlier. But he continued wiping the bar. "What about the Ghost Watch? They spent a lot of time here. They were all connected to Tim in some—"

"You know, George Fenton *never* believed in this stuff," Harold said, catching Ellie's attention. "He came to all the meetings and joined all their little ghost-hunting expeditions, but he always said it was a load of rubbish."

The sudden mention of George took Ellie aback.

"I already know George doesn't believe," she said, narrowing her eyes. "What are you suggesting?"

"I'm not *suggesting* anything," Harold replied with a huff, any trace of the showman long gone. "But it's odd, don't you think? His wife was such a believer—she talked about her dead brother like he was always by her side. It irritated George no end. They were always bickering. Don't think he liked her much, if I'm honest." He shrugged as though he'd finished, but Ellie waited, arching her brows until Harold huffed again. "*Maybe* George tried to stitch Meredith up? Wanted everyone to blame her so he could get rid of her easily. Quicker and cheaper than a divorce, isn't it?"

"Who said they wanted a divorce?" Ellie asked, surprised by the detail. "My gran said they were in love."

"Like I said earlier, you hear things working behind a bar. People talk about other people, especially Meadowlings, and I *saw* what they were like. He seemed more like her minder than her husband, always watching her... correcting her..."

Reaching for the pen she'd left on the bar, Ellie glanced around and spotted her notepad wedged between a column and a charity tin for the Dogs Trust. She couldn't quite remember where she'd left it before following Harold down to the cellar, but she was certain she hadn't propped it up like that.

Opening it, she found only fresh, blank pages. Her to-do lists for the shop, her research notes—all gone. The jagged edges where the pages had been torn out were the only trace of what had once been there. She looked over at the sleepy man at the bar, but he only gave a nonchalant shrug.

"Do you have cameras in here, Harold?"

"We don't make a habit of spying on our customers," he said, no longer interested in humouring her. "Look, I'll tell you what I told that Ghost Watch lot: I don't mind you hanging around talking about spirits as long as you're buying a drink. Otherwise, get off the pot..."

Flipping through the blank pages of her notepad, Ellie decided to do just that. She left the pub behind, stepping out into the night air, colder than the stale chill Harold had pumped into the cellar. He hadn't ripped the pages from her notebook—maybe his mother had, or someone else she hadn't noticed. Whoever it was, she wouldn't be surprised if they were the same person who'd thrown the brick.

They wanted to scare her off, to send her back to

square one. It should have worked, but it hadn't. She'd woken that afternoon unsure of what answers the day would bring, and now, after the museum, the pub, and everything in between, she had even more burning questions.

Whoever was trying to douse her investigation was only confirming that she was getting warmer.

Chapter 7
Say 'Cheese!'

Ellie awoke late the next morning, having forgotten—yet again—to set her alarms. The night before, after another lavish roast dinner distraction from her gran—beef, this time—she'd spent hours rewriting everything she could remember from her missing notepad. She'd made sure to snap photos on her phone as a backup.

"George *framed* Meredith?" Granny Maggie had laughed when Ellie finally summoned the courage to share Harold's suggestion over bread-and-butter pudding once the beef was done with. "You've said some strange things these past few days, but that is the most bizarre. George loves Meredith like our lungs love air."

"Our lungs need air to survive."

"And they love that they get it!" Granny Maggie had shot her a look as though she'd gone mad before gathering the plates to busy herself with the washing up. "You can play your research games all you want, Ellie, but you won't shift the blame from Meredith to George."

Once again, Maggie wasn't there for breakfast, so Ellie had dry toast with the last butter scrapings, gulped down some tea, and set off to the shop. As much as she knew she'd be busy with work today, she wouldn't let her gran dodge questions any longer. Perhaps she'd be more open when Ellie told her about the brick through the window and the pages torn from her notepad—she hadn't wanted to spoil dinner more than she already had.

After speed-walking through the village, Ellie burst into the shop, greeted by Duchess the Third as the fluffy dog leapt up. A camera swung towards her, but it wasn't being operated by her mother or auntie today, and no renovation work was underway either.

Joey had shown up, as promised, rummaging through a cardboard box mottled with black mould. Carolyn and Penny watched with bated breath while Granny Maggie busied herself in the back room.

"More much ado about nothing!" Maggie called over the clinking of a teaspoon rattling in her cup. "Sometimes a box is simply a box."

"And sometimes," Joey muttered, pulling something from the jumble of shredded paper, "a box you find in a secret fireplace has a..." He held an old wooden object up to the light. "... whatever this is."

"It's a *camera*," Carolyn gasped, waving for their new cameraman to get a closer shot. "An antique camera, no

The Plot Thickens

doubt hidden in the walls of this haunted bookshop by the very spirit who scrawled the warning!"

Ellie tried to get a better look at the man her mother had roped into filming, but the bulky camera on his shoulder blocked his face. He wore a graphic shirt for *Anthrax*, a band Ellie had never heard of, though she guessed they made heavy metal from the flaming skull and sharp silver text. His thinning hair was pulled back into a ponytail. Joey had mentioned Jack—Cassie's partner and Tim's former apprentice—wore his hair like that.

"What now?" Maggie groaned, entering with a tray of tea. She stopped dead at the sight of Ellie, the tray wobbling in her hands. "Ah, Ellie! You're up. I... I was going to wake you, but—" Her eyes dropped to the camera. "That was in the box?"

"Gran, have you seen it before?"

"No." Maggie set the tea down and took a closer look. "We found the box behind the non-fiction shelves. Joey thinks it might have been a fireplace at some point, but as far as I know, there's always been a heavy bookcase blocking it."

"Jack, get up the chimney with that camera!" Carolyn ordered, clicking her fingers. "I've had a brilliant idea for a shot—start in the chimney, pull back to me, and I'll hold this old bit of junk—" She reached out for the old camera, but Maggie took it from Joey and didn't hand it over. "Ellie, tell your grandmother to behave, would you? I *need* this shot."

"I thought *I* was directing?" Penny interjected, sending Carolyn a sideways look. "But yes, Jack, that does sound like a good shot."

Ellie's gaze lingered on the cameraman as he quietly adjusted the lens. Jack Campbell. Another member of the original Ghost Watch Club. He looked almost nothing like the scrawny punk with the spikey mohawk and leathers—now sporting a prominent beer belly—but he was still working in photography.

Ellie cleared her throat. "Jack, do you know anything about this camera?"

Before he could respond, Carolyn swooped in, standing between them.

"Ellie, darling," she said in her sweetest voice, "you know better than to break the fourth wall while we're filming. Jack is here for *my* show, not your little mystery. Please don't address the crew."

Ellie held out her hand, and after a moment of reluctance, her gran passed the camera to her. It had a polished mahogany body, brass fittings that gleamed despite their age, and a leather middle that gave it the look of a musical instrument—if not for the lens. The leather was cracked in places, but the craftsmanship was undeniable.

"Back when photography was an art, not just a quick snap on our phones," Ellie said, her eyes shifting to the cameraman. "Wouldn't you agree, Jack?"

"Ellie! What did I—"

"This is *my* bookshop, Carolyn, not your set,"

Maggie interrupted, hands firmly on her hips. "Ellie can ask any questions she likes." She paused, perhaps realising the irony of her words, given how she'd been dodging Ellie's questions for days. "It's up to Jack if he wants to respond."

After a second, Jack offered, "Not really my area of expertise."

He lowered the camera slightly to take a closer look at the antique, and Ellie finally got a better look at him. His nose was bent to the right, and his deep-set eyes, shadowed by dark circles, gave him the appearance of someone who spent too much time in dark rooms.

"Look, Carolyn, I said I could do a couple of hours today, but I've got a shoot to get to later."

"Ridiculous! I've already paid you for the full day," Carolyn cried, snapping her compact mirror shut after powdering her nose. "Nobody leaves until the star—"

Jack cut her off with a snort, thrusting the heavy camera at Penny before leaving. On his way, he tripped on the doorframe Joey hadn't fixed, shaking his head as he hunched his shoulders against the cold. He jogged down South Street and out of sight.

"Crumbs," Penny whispered, torn between the camera and running after Jack. "That didn't go as planned. We did agree that it was a *full* day rate."

"Where did you find that amateur?" Carolyn hissed.

"You told me to find someone to fix the camera, and I did."

"Well, Back in my day—"

"Let it go, Carolyn." Maggie threw her hands up. "I'll be in the back until some sanity returns around here."

As Carolyn and Penny squabbled over how best to film inside the chimney, Ellie turned the antique camera around in her hands, searching for clues about its origin. But aside from a few scuffs, it was well-preserved and unmarked.

"Your family reminds me of mine at Christmas," Joey said, breaking the tension with a chuckle. "Do you think this old thing is connected to the wall?"

"It would be strange if it wasn't." Ellie chewed her lip before handing the camera to Joey. "Hide this somewhere safe where my mum can't get her hands on it." She took several photos of the camera with her phone and added, "It might be evidence."

"Where are you going?" Joey asked.

"To talk to Jack properly. Do you know where his studio is?"

"I keep seeing them around, just be careful with his girlfriend, yeah?" He glanced around, nodding for her to move closer. "The reason I know them is because they photographed my cousin's dog's wedding. We thought they were cool until it came time to be paid at the end of the night. My cousin lost her bank card—easy mistake—but the way Cassie was carrying on, you'd think she'd lost it on purpose."

"I saw her punch a fully grown man in the face over a game of pool yesterday," Ellie confessed. "Nothing would surprise me."

The Plot Thickens

"She swung for my uncle when he tried to get rid of her, and then she snatched one of the dog's leads from my cousin. She basically held the dog hostage until someone paid her, so we clubbed together all the cash we had to get rid of them. Someone found the bank card in the bathroom ten minutes later, but she'd already ruined the day." He sighed, shaking his head at the memory. "I think their studio is down the street. I keep seeing them both around. I'm sure she recognises me from all the dirty looks."

"I have a feeling she looks at everyone like that," Ellie said. "Thanks, Joey. I'll be careful."

She considered asking Auntie Penny—who must have tracked Jack down to fix the camera—but South Street wasn't so long that she couldn't find it herself, now that she had a lead. She'd never noticed a photography studio before, though she hadn't yet re-explored every nook and cranny of the village. Still, she was determined to find it.

Walking down the cobbled street, she scanned every inch for signs of the studio as the usual bustle of village life carried on like normal. Next door, Sylvia was entertaining a handsome man with a small platter of cheese samples. A few doors down, Amber was lost in her phone in her antique shop, surrounded by old furniture. Ellie almost veered into the Second Chances Emporium to ask about the camera, but just as her hand hovered near the handle, the pull of heavy metal music drew her back.

To her surprise, the noise led Ellie further down the street, past The Giggling Goat, to Zara's shop, Wiltshire Whimsy. The music thundered from above—an assault of crashing guitars and relentless drums. Ellie hesitated, blinking up at the second-floor window. There was no sign or clue that a studio existed above the gift shop, but she opened the door anyway.

Inside, Zara stood on top of her counter, brandishing a broom like a lance, beating it against the ceiling.

"Day and night!" she fumed, each word punctuated with a furious whack of the broom. "It sounds like pots and pans being thrown down the world's longest staircase! I have written to the council, the landlord—I even tried being *nice* to them!"

Raising her voice over the racket, Ellie asked, "Cassie and Jack, by any chance?"

"Please, tell me you know them?" Zara froze mid-swing. "Could you talk to them? They are so hostile towards me."

"I know *of* them," Ellie admitted, spotting a stack of leather notepads identical to her own. She'd bought the first from Zara and she'd need another soon, considering half the pages in hers had vanished. "I'll try to ask."

Zara snorted. "Good luck. *She* slammed the door in my face this morning. The woman is almost fifty and is still throwing tantrums."

Ellie didn't need to ask who 'she' was. With the tale of the hostage situation at Joey's cousin's dog wedding still fresh in her mind and the memory of Cassie getting thrown out of the pub by Harold, a slammed door seemed almost polite.

"Up the metal staircase." Zara nodded towards a narrow door at the back of the shop. "Stomp on the floor if you need me to call the police."

After helping Zara down from the counter and setting a new notepad aside to pay for on her way out, Ellie stepped into the tiny yard. The thick smell of mildew hung in the air, and plant pots filled with brittle, dead stems were scattered across the uneven cobblestones. She placed her foot on the first metal step, wincing at its loud creak—not that they'd hear it over the racket from above. She glanced around, and a piece of history made her catch her breath.

A faded, forgotten sign hung precariously next to a flower basket that had long since dried up. The curled, claw-like stems clung to the edges of the painted words, revealing that she'd found Tim Baker's Studio.

She climbed the rickety staircase, the pounding music growing louder as she neared the door, the frenetic electric guitar twisting her stomach with each vibration. She decided knocking would be a waste of time.

Letting herself in, she found Cassie with her back to the door, directing a photoshoot. A young man with spiked hair clutched a guitar awkwardly under harsh studio lights. He glanced at Ellie as she crept in.

"Stop getting distracted!" Cassie yelled before spinning around. "Jack, is that—"

Cassie lowered the camera, squinting at Ellie as

though she couldn't see her properly through the noise filling the cluttered room. Still, she didn't reach for the remote to turn the music down.

"*What?*" Cassie barked. "I'm busy!"

Ellie smiled as politely as she could.

"I don't mind waiting."

"Whatever."

Turning back to the shoot, she pulled a few pouches from a box and, with a few strategic throws, sent up colourful plumes of smoke that swirled around the young man with the guitar, engulfing him in a black and red haze. Smoke bombs. Ellie knew them from her days on set—cheap and effective for a quick, dramatic effect.

Through the fog, the young punk's gaze lingered on Ellie, his shyness more pronounced under her scrutiny. Cassie noticed and shot Ellie a sharp glare. No words were needed. Ellie shifted her attention to the framed photos on the walls, attempting to ignore the prickling curiosity over Cassie's simmering rage.

The walls were covered with the standard family portraits and wedding pictures Ellie would expect in a photography studio. Tasteful, restrained—nothing like what Cassie was trying to achieve with her current model. Perhaps Jack was behind these more traditional shots. She wondered whether her wedding to Luke would have ended up immortalised on this wall. She could almost see them beaming at the camera, with a future ahead of them, while Cassie and Jack sulked behind the camera.

The Plot Thickens

Ellie shook off the thought and turned away from the pictures, unwilling to pursue it further. As she leaned back against a counter, something hard pressed into her lower back. She glanced down to find a hardback book resting atop a pile of letters, its glossy cover catching the glare of the studio lights. *Famous Photography from World-Changing Events*, the title proclaimed in bold letters.

Curiosity piqued, Ellie opened the book and noticed a bookmark peeking from the pages. It led her to a photograph of what looked like a riot—no, a strike. She recognised it immediately: the 1984 miners' strike. Men in plain clothes clashed with a line of police officers in hard hats. One man held a sign reading COAL NOT DOLE, another THE MINERS' FIGHT IS FOR ALL OF US. Though the strikes had ended nearly a decade before she was born, Ellie had grown up hearing stories about the closing of the mines.

The rest of the book looked pristine, but this page was dog-eared, its corners bent and worn. She turned the page, checking whether the bookmark had been leading her to something else, but the back was blank. Her eyes narrowed on the caption, and the photographer's name confirmed the connection: Kenneth Campbell.

Kenneth must have been related to Jack. Ellie glanced around, looking for signs of the ponytail. A faint red glow shone from a side door, and she poked her head inside a dark room to see if Jack was there. Dried photographs hung on washing lines, but there was no sign of him. As abrupt as his exit had been from the bookshop, she couldn't blame him for not wanting to trail after Carolyn all day.

The blaring music cut off. Ellie spun around, startled by the sudden silence. Her ears rang with a high-pitched whine as she closed the book. The young musician had changed into casual clothes, his spikey hair nothing more than a hairpiece.

"*Poser*," Cassie snarled as she watched him leave.

She turned her scrutinising eye to Ellie, her lip curling in a sneer. She scanned Ellie from head to toe like she was sizing her up. There was a flicker of recognition in her eyes when they locked onto Ellie's face—maybe she'd seen her in the pub, though she'd been too busy throwing punches to make proper eye contact.

Ellie wasn't there to cause trouble, and she needed Cassie to believe that. She kept her polite smile while Cassie scowled, the black rings dragging down the corners of her mouth. Undeterred, Ellie gestured to the book behind her, hoping to find some safe, common ground.

"Photography must run in the family," she said.

"What?" Cassie spat.

"Kenneth Campbell? Your husband's... father?"

"*Not* my husband," she snapped, folding her arms. Despite her gruff exterior, delicate tattoos of ivy wrapped around both arms in soft, swirling patterns starting at her wrists. "We don't believe in all that stuff. But yeah, that's

The Plot Thickens

Jack's dad's work in the history book—the only source of family pride he's got."

The admission caught Ellie off guard. Cassie must have decided Ellie wasn't much of a threat, though she was still squinting at her.

"Are you getting married or something?" she demanded. "Jack handles that stuff."

"Not at all. I'm not sure I believe in 'that stuff' either."

Cassie shrugged, and Ellie believed her—there was no hint that the surly photographer cared in the slightest. Her gaze drifted around the room, clearly waiting for Ellie to leave so the conversation could end.

"I was hoping for some advice," Ellie said, pulling out her phone. She noticed Cassie flinch at the movement, so she slowed down. "What do you make of this?"

She showed her the photograph of the antique camera, and Cassie barely glanced at it.

"Never seen it before."

Ellie nodded, biting her tongue rather than pointing out she hadn't asked if Cassie had seen it. Instead, she slipped her phone back into her pocket and watched as Cassie busied herself with tidying up after the photoshoot.

"Didn't this used to be Tim Baker's studio?"

"That's what the sign says." After a pause, Cassie added, "He collected those old bits of junk. I don't know much more than that."

"So, this camera might've belonged to Tim?" Ellie asked. "Any idea how it ended up hidden in my gran's bookshop?"

"What did I *just* say?"

Cassie spun around, knocking over a box in her haste. More smoke bombs burst into plumes of colourful smoke—pink, green, orange, red, black—all mingling into a murky grey cloud.

"I don't know any more than that, alright?" Cassie cried, wafting the smoke. "Stop bothering me."

At that moment, the door opened, and Jack walked in with a steaming bag from The Golden Sun takeaway.

"Cheeky buggers have put the prices up again," he grumbled before catching sight of Ellie. He stopped abruptly, eyeing her. "You here to cause trouble?" The question came out with a strange drawl as if he were impersonating a Wild West sheriff. "Everything good?"

"She turned up talking rubbish. Look at what she made me do." Cassie grabbed a piece of white cardboard and wafted at the smoke, the colours continuing the swirl to grey. "She can pay for these."

"It's alright, Cass." Jack dumped the food on the table. "She's the daughter of that actress I told you about. Ellie, right? Did she send you here to drag me back? Because you can tell her what I told her sister when she came crying about her broken camera—I can do a few hours a day and no more."

Ellie nodded, noting how Cassie's defensiveness eased knowing that Jack seemed familiar with her.

The Plot Thickens

Despite his bluntness, Jack wasn't as bad-tempered as his girlfriend.

"Sorry, I don't mean to be rude," he said as he glanced at his food, "but if your mum didn't send you, why *are* you here?"

"She's asking questions," Cassie cut in like she was telling tales to the teacher. "About your dad. And some old camera. And Tim."

Jack didn't respond as he unwrapped two large portions of chips soaked in salt and vinegar. The scent hit Ellie's nostrils, and her stomach grumbled in response—her rushed toast with barely any butter already felt like days ago.

"Why do you want to know about my dad?"

Ellie nodded at the book. "I noticed his name in there. He was a photographer like you?"

"Yep." Jack nodded, tossing a soggy chip into his mouth. "Inspired me, didn't he? Gave me something to aim for. And then I met Tim, and the rest is history, as they say. Now we run this studio, don't we, Cass?"

Cassie was busy taking down the city backdrop from the photoshoot. Behind it, a new scene appeared—one of a wintery graveyard.

"Don't we, Cass?" Jack repeated.

"Hmm."

"Are you a sleuth or something?" he asked through a mouthful, spitting bits of mushy potato everywhere. "Like those women who listen to too many podcasts and think they can solve murders?"

"I don't really have much time for podcasts these days," Ellie replied, unsure of where she stood with the cameraman. The atmosphere was hostile, but she couldn't take her eyes off the odd couple. Whatever approach she'd had in mind wasn't working. "How about I level with you? I found that graffiti, and now I've got a bee in my bonnet about what happened. You were both part of the Ghost Watch, and you knew Tim and—"

"*Part* of it?" Cassie interrupted with a dry laugh. "We *ran* it."

"I thought it was Meredith's group?"

"It was," Jack corrected, shooting Cassie a warning look that sent her back to folding the backdrop. "You want to know about that club? There's not much to tell. We came together by accident. Nothing was planned—just people with similar interests."

Ellie nodded. "Which ended with your friend's death."

"That was John Partridge's fault," Cassie cut in. She slapped her hand on the table before tossing it in Ellie's direction. "*She* doesn't believe in ghosts. I can tell. She only came here to mock us. I knew it the second she walked in. Looking down her nose at us, all high and mighty because her mum's that washed-up has-been."

Ellie didn't mean to laugh, but a chuckle slipped out before she could stop it. The rage returned to Cassie's eyes, and Ellie was sure that if there hadn't been a table between them, she might've ended up fighting for her

The Plot Thickens

two front teeth like the poor bloke who'd dared to put his coin down on the pool table.

"Apologise," Jack said, and to Ellie's surprise, the demand wasn't aimed at her. "I can safely say Ellie's nothing like her mother. Apologise, Cass."

"Seriously?" Cassie huffed, snatching a handful of chips before stomping off. "*Sorry!*"

With that, she retreated into the dark room, slamming the door behind her. She was forty-something going on fourteen, but Ellie didn't need to say it—the expression on Jack's face said it all.

"She had a tough upbringing," he explained, pulling the mountain of chips closer as he ate. "Her parents gave her up young and stuff like that leaves scars. You get it. What else do you want to know?" He paused, then added, "Actually, I'll tell you what you *need* to know. Did you know Meredith was faking a bunch of stuff?"

"When you say 'stuff,' do you mean the hauntings?"

"Yep. We found scripts for a séance she planned at The Duck. She was so desperate to prove her spirits were real, she had to fake them. We weren't all waiting for knocks on the wall and floating orbs like her. We wanted to capture something we could put in print. Something *real*."

Ellie's ears pricked up at the mention of print. She asked, "Is this about the 'history book' with the ghost photographs? Do you have a copy I can look at?"

"Yep. But it's at home. This place is just for work stuff." He glanced at the clock on the wall. "We didn't end up taking anything, anyway. Tim never believed in any of it. Is this going to go on much longer? We've got a shoot to get to."

A wave of frustration swept over Ellie—she hadn't managed to ask any of the questions she really needed answers to. What had happened the night Tim died? She wanted to press further, but before she could, Cassie stormed out of the dark room, slamming the door behind her.

"It's George Fenton you should be talking to," she said as she brushed past Ellie, their shoulders bumping as she crossed the studio. "Always was a rubbish teacher. Ask him about how he got fired. Old git pushed a student. Anyone else would have been sent down. Only got away with it because he's a know-it-all. They wouldn't think twice about it if I—"

"Alright, Cassie." Jack grunted a frustrated sigh. "Look, Ellie, I'm sorry, but we've got to get ready for this portrait shoot. The school's had us booked for months, and I don't know what else to tell you. We thought we were onto something back then, but Tim fell into the cellar and... well, all our lives went in different directions. We moved on. The truth is, I try not to think about it much. Things were fun—until they weren't. You're too young to get it, but one day there'll be things you don't want to look back at."

"I understand," Ellie said, the words slipping out before she could stop them, Luke on her mind. "I'm sorry for prying. I know it can't be easy, but before you

The Plot Thickens

go, can you at least tell me about Tim? What was he like?"

"A great guy," Jack began, his tone softening as his cheeks lifted with a weary smile. "The best. He gave me my first job after I dropped out of college. I couldn't stand the tutors talking down to me like they knew everything, but Tim was cool. Chill. Loved photography."

"He was sweet," Cassie said, her voice quieter now.

"Yep," Jack agreed, wrapping a cable around his hands "He taught me everything I know—composition, lighting, how to move with the camera, like it was an extension of you. People liked him. He always had a camera around his neck, taking pictures of anything and anyone. He just... *got* it. Saw the beauty in everyday life, you know? It's cool you're trying to figure out what happened to Tim. That night haunted me for years. It wasn't an accident like the police said."

Surprised by the sudden shift, Ellie raised a brow and gave him a nod to continue. In the background, Cassie busied herself packing up the equipment, her ears tuned to the conversation.

"I think that message in your shop *is* true," Jack said, dropping his voice to a whisper. "Maybe Meredith's state now is justice finally happening. I saw the scripts with my own eyes. She wanted to make Tim believe his dad was coming back to him during that séance. His dad had died two months before, and Meredith was... messed up. Tim didn't believe in ghosts at all, which made him her main target. She wanted to twist his mind, manipulate him. And George wasn't any better. He only joined the club to keep an eye on her, and they were always at each other's throats. She was stubborn, but so is George. If it wasn't her, it was him."

"Enough chat," Cassie interrupted, swinging open the front door. "If you don't mind, we've got stuff to get on with."

Ellie knew better than to linger, and she didn't want to spend any longer in their stuffy studio. She thanked them for their time and walked back down the rickety staircase, her mind swirling with confusion.

Meredith, so convinced of the afterlife, had tried to fake a séance? And given the many reports of supernatural 'events' around the village, what else had she faked? If Meredith truly believed in the afterlife, why the need to stage anything?

As these questions gnawed at her, Ellie wandered back into Wiltshire Whimsy, surprised when Zara threw her arms around her in a tight hug.

"Thank you, Ellie!" she beamed. "I cannot believe it, but you got them to turn that music off. Today, you are my hero. Your next pad is on me."

Ellie didn't have the heart to tell her she hadn't done anything and that the music would likely return. She thanked Zara for the gift and left the shop with her new notepad, still in a daze. She glanced up the street towards the bookshop, but she couldn't bring herself to go back.

The Plot Thickens

She knew where she needed to go. It was time to talk to George Fenton.

Her gran would know where George lived, but Maggie was the last person she wanted to ask if she hoped for a straight answer.

Instead, she followed the sound of the poshest laughter she'd ever heard and found herself at Brie and Bramble, Meadowfield's premier—and only—cheese shop.

Chapter 8
The Fenton Residence

Inside Brie and Bramble, the aroma of tangy cheeses and fresh bread made Ellie's stomach rumble. The shop exuded luxury, with decadent sampling displays garnished with crackers and grapes set beside bottles of wine that could cost a month's rent. It was out of place in Meadowfield—though ideally suited to Sylvia Fortescue,

Sylvia stood behind the counter, as polished as ever, her hair swept up in a stylish twist, her tweed jacket stiff and pristine. She chatted with a man at least half her age, with a jaw so sharp it could slice cheese. Sylvia's soft and teasing laughter floated through the shop as she leaned forward, her hand resting on the counter just close enough to his.

When Sylvia spotted Ellie, she straightened, her attention turning to Ellie as though the man were no longer there.

"Well, if it isn't my favourite fellow businesswoman," she called, handing the man his change before sending him on his way with a wink. "Lovely meeting you!" she called as she watched him leave before turning to Ellie like an excited schoolgirl with a new poster boy to hang up. "Dreamy, wasn't he? I could see him modelling for M&S men's wear. I know the woman who does their booking. *That's* how I could have given him my number." She shook her head, though Ellie could tell she was considering running after him. "Next time."

Ellie chuckled, shaking her head. "Sylvia, I don't know how you do it."

"Flirting, you mean?" Sylvia returned the laugh. "Men are simple creatures, dear. A well-timed look, a bit of attention, even a simple compliment will do the trick. Is this about that lovely teacher who dotes on his nan? Daniel, isn't it?"

Ellie was about to deny the accusation but found she couldn't lie to Sylvia.

"Or perhaps Joey? He's quite the looker, if you can get past the ears." Sylvia leaned across the counter, her eyes twinkling, and in a gossipy whisper said, "From the way he was eyeing you when I passed the shop yesterday, I'd say you're already halfway there. Would you like me to have a word? Get old Sylvia to play Cupid?"

"No!" Ellie held up a hand in protest. "No... please... *no.*"

Sylvia chuckled. "Point taken, dear. Just remember, if all else fails, you can win them through their stomach.

The Plot Thickens

Few men can resist a hearty block of cheese." She gestured to the tray of samples. "Blacksticks Blue. Don't let the 'blue' put you off—it's mild, buttery, and tangy and always hits the spot."

Ellie was about to decline, but her stomach betrayed her with a loud growl. Raising an eyebrow, Sylvia added a dollop of chutney to each cracker and slid the tray across the counter. As Ellie took a bite, Sylvia's gaze shifted towards the wall separating the shop from the bookshop next door.

"I can feel those words staring at me," Sylvia said with a shiver. "That graffiti... it's like it's alive."

Ellie swallowed her mouthful. "It is buttery. Delicious, actually." Licking her lips as she accepted a second sample, she followed Sylvia's eyes. "I'm glad I'm not the only one unsettled by it. My gran's acting like she can't see it."

"Surely the police are doing something?"

"You'd hope so," she said, declining a third sample before dusting the crumbs from her jumper. "DS Cookson didn't seem all that interested when she first saw it, though I did bump into her in the museum's archive room. Maybe she found something I didn't."

"Let's hope they do come up with something." Sylvia narrowed her eyes, dusting her hands on her apron. "So, what brought you in here today? You're one of the few shopkeepers on South Street who doesn't regularly pop in for the freebies. In fact, this might be the first time."

Ellie hesitated, but there was no point beating around the bush with Sylvia.

"I need to find George Fenton."

"And because people call me a nosey busybody, you thought I'd know?"

"That's about the long and short of it."

Sylvia's lips curved into a nifty smile, and she said, "Well, you're in luck. I *do* know where he lives, and I happen to be about to take my lunch break."

Before Ellie could respond, Sylvia darted around the counter, grabbed her keys, and snatched up a basket covered with a red blanket. Looping it over one arm, she hooked the other around Ellie's.

"This way, dear," Sylvia announced, pulling Ellie out of the shop as she flipped the sign to 'Closed'. "The Fenton residence isn't far, but most of the walk is uphill. Brace yourself."

As they passed Meadowfield Books, Ellie saw her gran sat at the counter, her head in her hands. The shop was empty—no customers, no books on display. A pang of guilt twisted inside Ellie. She needed to help her gran, to bring life back to that shop.

But first, George Fenton had some explaining to do about the incident that had cost him his teaching job.

* * *

After navigating the sloping lanes away from the village centre, Ellie and Sylvia arrived at the Fenton residence—

The Plot Thickens

a quaint cottage that had clearly fallen into neglect. The windows were streaked with grime, and the grass hadn't been mown in months. Wind chimes tinkled softly in the breeze above an overgrown garden filled with faded fairy statues, their once-bright colours dulled by time. It must have been Meredith who had kept it all in order—certainly not George, unless he had given up entirely.

"It doesn't appear that anyone is home," Sylvia remarked after peering through the front windows. "I could check around the back?"

"Let's try the old-fashioned way." Ellie balled up her fist and knocked on the wooden door. Before they could even wait for an answer, the door creaked open from the force of her knuckles. "It wasn't shut."

"Mr Fenton?" Without hesitation, Sylvia pushed it further open. "Are you in?"

When no reply came, Sylvia stepped inside. Ellie's eyes widened in alarm.

"We can't just let ourselves in!" she whispered, tugging at Sylvia's arm.

"But this is a murder investigation."

"It's still trespassing."

"Geooorge?" Sylvia called again as she ventured further down the hallway. She stumbled over something—a walking stick. She picked it up, inspecting the handle, and Ellie noticed the sun catching a ghostly pearl embedded deep in the gnarled wood. "Mr Fenton, I've brought you some cheese," she announced, holding up the basket in the empty hallway as if that would make everything right. "Manchego and Stilton? It's rather delicious."

They waited, listening. Still no response.

"Maybe he's in the bath?" Ellie suggested. "Or asleep?"

"The offer of free cheese could raise a man from the dead!" Sylvia insisted, pulling back the blanket and gazing at her travelling samples with an almost wounded expression. "Maybe he isn't home, after all?"

"He probably forgot to pull the door shut," Ellie insisted, wafting Sylvia back towards the front door. "We really need to go. Now. I'll... come back later."

Sylvia's pout deepened. "Well, I'll leave him something, at least. It would be a shame to come all this way for nothing—"

"You might as well leave a calling card."

"Ah, good point," Sylvia muttered as a loud creaking sound echoed upstairs. "Maybe the house is settling?"

They froze, and it wasn't the typical sound of a house settling. The plodding of laboured footsteps could be heard on the landing above. Without a word, Ellie turned on her heels and bolted for the door.

"I thought you wanted to talk to him?" Sylvia hissed as she followed close behind. "This is your chance!"

Ellie did want to talk to him, but certainly not like this.

Out in the overgrown fairy garden, Sylvia meandered along the winding path, seemingly in no rush, despite the urgency of their situation. They'd never make it to the gate before George caught up with them.

Thinking fast, Ellie darted around the side of the house and ducked behind the bins. The stench of rotting food and sour milk hit her, a pungent cocktail of bins that hadn't been collected in a while. Ellie gagged, and the Blacksticks Blue churned in her stomach as she peeked out from behind the bins, just in time to see Sylvia reach the gate.

"Who the hell are you?" George barked, his voice worn and angry—so unlike the calm, monotonous tone Ellie remembered from his days as a history teacher. "Why are you trespassing in my garden? If you're with the press, I've nothing to say. If you're the police, it's the same answer."

Ellie couldn't reconcile this grizzled, abrasive man with the George she'd known. But Sylvia, as always, didn't miss a beat. With her usual unflappable grace, she flashed him a wide smile.

"Mr Fenton, how *lovely* to see you again! We met at the hospital the other day. Remember?" She lifted the basket. "I thought I'd bring you some cheese samples since you didn't get a chance to try any last time."

"Cheese?" he growled. "Why would you do that?"

Sylvia stepped closer, holding out the basket like a peace offering. Her eyes flicked briefly towards Ellie, and she gave a subtle wave, motioning for her to reveal herself. Ellie shook her head from behind the bins. Sticking with Sylvia, she might've been able to style this out too—but popping up from behind George's rubbish would raise suspicions. She edged further back, nudging one of the bulging bags, which toppled over with a soft thud.

Ellie froze as Sylvia began coughing wildly, holding her breath as she waited for George to storm over and catch her. The Mr Fenton she remembered would have simply tutted and calmly asked what she was doing—but with this older version, she couldn't be sure what to expect. Somehow, the cough seemed to work.

"Sorry about that!" Sylvia gasped. "I think I swallowed a fly! Here, you *must* try the Manchego—it's got a lovely nutty flavour. Meredith always adored a good cheese platter, didn't she? That's what you said at the hospital. How is dear Meredith, by the way?"

At the mention of his wife, George fell silent. Taking advantage of the distraction, Ellie gathered the fallen rubbish. Among banana skins and coffee grounds—both fresh enough to have been thrown away that week—she found torn scraps of paper, crumpled and yellowed with age.

She squinted at the scribbled notes, and at first glance, they looked like they could have come from her own pad, but the handwriting, though it wasn't hers, was familiar. Mr Fenton's. Her breath caught as she read the scrawled words. There were mentions of Meredith... and ghosts. The entries were dated throughout 1994.

Her finger hovered over one of the entries, and she

The Plot Thickens

read: *13th September 1994: Meredith is losing whatever grip she has on reality. She's not the woman I—*

"Go away!" George suddenly roared, making Ellie drop the sheets. "I don't want your pity or your sympathy, or whatever this is. Just *leave!*"

"I *do* apologise, I just—would you like me to leave some cheese at—"

"I don't want your stinking cheese!"

The door slammed with a resounding thud, and a moment later, Sylvia popped her head around the side of the house. Before Ellie could emerge from her hiding spot, the garden gate at the end of the path creaked open. Sylvia spun around, blocking Ellie's view.

"Sylvia?" a familiar voice asked uncertainly. "What are you doing here?"

"*Maggie!*" Sylvia exclaimed, leaning against the bin. Ellie realised she was blocking the view on purpose. She almost jumped out to ask why her gran was there, but curiosity kept her rooted, eager to see how this would play out. "I came on a charity cheese mission, but it didn't go as planned. And you?"

"I—" Maggie sighed. "George and I go back a long way. Can I ask a favour of you?"

"Anything! What is it?"

"Don't tell Ellie you saw me here." She sighed, then added, "Please?"

Sylvia gave a casual nod, waving her off as if it were nothing. Then she hurried away, but Ellie remained hidden. Maggie let herself into the house, and Ellie crept closer to an open window leading into the hallway.

"There's no change," George said, his voice cracking with emotion. Ellie could hear the strain—the grief of a man on the edge. This was the George she remembered from school, softer, calmer, not the angry man who had roared at Sylvia moments ago. "At this rate, it's only a matter of time before they talk about switching her off."

"Oh, George, don't say that. I'm sure they won't. The nurse said the signals were good last week. Her fingers were twitching, remember?" Maggie stopped, waiting for George to cheer up, but nothing came. She exhaled and said, "Be careful, George. My Ellie is snooping around, and you know how sharp she is. Just be mindful—if she comes here, the less you tell her, the better."

Ellie's heart pounded as she strained to hear more, daring to peer through the window. She could see George's face, the shadow of the man she once knew. His grey hair was wild and unkempt, his beard thick and wiry, and white.

"I don't care anymore, Mags," he muttered, unable to look away from the floor.

"But *I* care. You can't let her find out what Meredith did that night..." Maggie's voice trailed off as they moved deeper into the house, their words swallowed by the walls.

Before Ellie could fully process what she'd found, Sylvia caught her eye from the garden gate, waving her

The Plot Thickens

over. Ellie scooped up the torn notes and bolted, her mind racing as she stuffed them under her jumper. They walked back down the lane in silence for a while, both seemingly too shocked to speak.

"That was rather close," Sylvia said when the jaunty cottages leading back to the village appeared. "And thrilling. I thought we were goners then, and it's a shame we didn't have a chance to speak with him, though he didn't seem to be in the most receptive mood."

"No, he didn't," Ellie agreed, hugging the paperwork to her t-shirt, not entirely leaving empty-handed. "He's not the man I remember."

"Time can do that to you, but..." Sylvia hesitated, glancing back towards the distant cottage with its wild, overgrown garden before adding, "... please be careful. It takes a lot to scare me, but Mr Fenton reminded me of my second husband—and the less said about him, the better."

Ellie hadn't wanted to admit it, but hearing George's anger had unsettled her too. The more she uncovered, the more she realised she hadn't known him at all. Once, the worst she might have accused him of was being dull. But now? She couldn't wait to dig into George's notes from 1994 to uncover what kind of man he truly was. The Mr Fenton she thought she remembered would never have shouted Sylvia off his doorstep or, as Cassie claimed, been suspended for pushing a student.

And most baffling, what did he know about

Meredith's actions on the night Tim Baker died? The very thing her gran, Maggie, seemed so determined to keep buried?

Chapter 9
Underfloor Secrets

Alone in the bookshop, Ellie drew in a steady breath as she spread the torn notes across the counter, her fingers trembling with a mix of anger and disbelief.

The pages were meticulously detailed, filled with dates, names, and events, all connected to the 1994 hauntings. George's handwriting was neat and precise, mirroring his structured, logical nature—almost clinical.

But these weren't just notes about the supposed hauntings. They were detailed accounts of Meredith's every move, from things as simple as her interactions with people in the village, to comments she'd made during her involvement in the Ghost Watch Club. It was as though George had been following her. His observations about her mental state were detached yet disturbingly insightful, and the tone betrayed a quiet frustration simmering beneath his words. She read:

Meredith believes in things she cannot see, but what worries me is that she's beginning to value them more than the things she can. It's like watching her drift into a world where I can't follow. At first, I thought it was harmless. We all have our quirks. But now... it's like Meredith is slipping through my fingers, chasing shadows. The more I pull her back, the further she goes. And I... I don't know if I want to keep trying. She's ruining our marriage.

Ellie's gut churned as she spread the pages out further, relieved to find some entries that were more scientific and less personal.

July 15th, 1994 - The Drowsy Duck, 22:17. Witness claims glasses flew off the shelf. Possible explanation: Clear fishing wire hanging out of Harold Fletcher's back pocket that he couldn't/wouldn't explain. Meredith claims I'm looking for strings where there are none, yet she is the one claiming to be hearing the voices of the dead.

August 3rd, 1994 - St. Mary's Church, 15:45. Multiple reports of cold spots near the altar. Obvious cause: Faulty heating system and overactive imaginations.

September 8th, 1994 - Village Green, 23:30. Groans are still being heard at the war memorial. Hidden

The Plot Thickens

speaker? Investigate further. Meadowlings continue to disappoint me.

As she turned the next page, a particular note caught her eye. No date, but in George's familiar handwriting.

I hope the nagging voice in my mind is wrong about the hauntings being of Meredith's making.

Another accusation against Meredith, this one dripping with betrayal. Ellie shivered, considering the implications. If George believed Meredith capable of fabricating the hauntings, what else might he have suspected her of?

October 2nd, 1994: Bought vintage camera from Tim (very knowledgeable). Good quality, well-maintained. He assured me it'll do the job.

Ellie paused. It wasn't strange that Tim had sold George a camera, but it made her uneasy, especially since they'd recently found a similar vintage camera hidden in the bookshop's old fireplace. What was 'the job' George wanted it to do? She scanned for more references to the camera but found none. She couldn't be sure if it was the same one, but she could easily picture that Victorian antique in George's hands.

As she stood in the stillness of the shop, staring at the

troubling notes, a noise from upstairs broke her concentration. It was faint but unmistakable—the sound of boxes shifting. Ellie tensed. With her gran presumably having tea with George, she'd assumed the shop was empty. Her heart quickened as she crept up the staircase.

When she reached the top, she paused, holding her breath. She peered around the corner, and relief washed over her.

"Joey," she said. "It's just you."

"Just me," he echoed as he lugged a box of old books across the room. A grin spread across his face. "Sorry, I didn't mean to scare you. I should've called down when I heard someone come back. I thought there might be more hidden spots up here."

"Great minds think alike," Ellie said, flicking back one of the lids. It was filled with horror books, of course. "I almost did the same yesterday. Found anything yet?"

"Not yet. Was just thinking about lunch."

"Tell you what," she said, her mood lifting after the strange afternoon. "Fancy something from The Giggling Goat? My treat."

"Sounds perfect," Joey replied, his smile growing. "Ellie... before you go... fancy grabbing a drink later?"

Ellie blinked, caught off guard by the question. Sylvia's joke about the way Joey had been looking at her echoed in her mind. He was peering at her now, his face half-hidden behind the box, hope lighting up in his eyes.

"Can I think about it?" she asked gently, an unsure smile wobbling her lips. "I've got a lot on my mind."

The Plot Thickens

"Yeah, of course," Joey said quickly, returning to his work, though his voice held a faint note of disappointment. "No pressure, you know?"

As Ellie descended the stairs, she couldn't help but glance over her shoulder. Joey was already absorbed in shifting the books, his back turned to her, and for a brief moment, Ellie felt a pang of something she couldn't quite identify. She'd only known him for a few days, but it already felt like longer. Shaking off the strange feeling, she pushed open the door to the bookshop and stepped out into the fresh air, her mind still buzzing with unanswered questions.

Further down South Street, the café was bustling with its usual mix of locals, but Ellie made a beeline for Oliver, who was busy making coffee behind the counter.

"Cheer me up," she said, staring at the neat rows of sweet loafs of all kinds but unable to focus on the labels. "Please?"

"And hello to you," Oliver replied with a wide grin as he looked up. "What's our gran done now?"

She laughed. "That obvious?"

"Lately? Yes," he teased, but his grin softened when he saw her face. "Is it that serious? You look like our father when you frown like that."

"Gran's sneaking around. And avoiding me. I just overheard her warning someone about *me* like I'm up to no good."

"Are you?"

She sighed. "I don't think so?"

"How boring. I try to be up to no good at least once a day." But when Ellie didn't laugh, concern crept into his expression. "Why would our gran be sneaking around?"

Ellie leaned in, her voice low. "She doesn't want me to find out what happened in 1994. I overheard her saying as much. She's actively trying to keep me from looking into the details, like she's hiding something."

"Maybe you're getting in too deep? You're so distracted, you didn't even notice your boyfriend sitting over there."

Ellie turned to where Oliver was pointing, and at a back table, Daniel sat alone, cutting shapes out of colourful cardboard. He glanced up, offering a small wave and a warm smile. Ellie smiled back, feeling a little uncomfortable and yet relieved. Her shoulders loosened, though her mind was still whirling with questions.

"Daniel isn't my boyfriend," she replied, turning back to Oliver. "And I need something for lunch—a builder's special."

"Ah, the guy with the ears—Joey, right? He's cute. Is he single?"

"How should I know?" Ellie rolled her eyes but couldn't help laughing. "I haven't asked."

"Well, leave lunch with me," he said, whipping at her with a tea towel. "You go schmooze with your non-boyfriend, I'll rustle something up."

After swatting Oliver's toned arm with the back of her hand, Ellie approached Daniel's table. Her heart was still racing but starting to slow as she neared him. He looked up from his cutting as she sat across from him, blushing as he fiddled with his glasses. It reminded her of their school days—the quiet boy with the stutter, who let her be the quiet bookworm that preferred not to talk. A sense of calm washed over her, as it often did around Daniel Clark.

"Hoping for snow?" she asked, nodding at the pile of cardboard flakes he'd been cutting out.

Daniel chuckled. "It's for the school's winter disco. I v-volunteer every year. The other teachers hate it, but the kids love it. I remember how much fun they were when we were their age."

Ellie eased into the conversation.

Something normal, finally.

"I did always enjoy those discos," she admitted. "Even if we'd only sit around the edges, not dancing. It's nice to be part of a group sometimes. You don't have to be yourself as much."

"I quite like you being Ellie," he said with a slight shrug. "Is this about the graffiti?"

She hesitated. "I don't suppose you know anything about George Fenton? I know we went to different high schools, but he taught history at my old place."

"I know George." Daniel nodded, setting down his scissors. "He used to help with the after-school history club. He's a very knowledgeable man. It's a shame what happened."

Ellie gulped. "What did happen?"

"I don't think he joined the club to inspire the children about getting into history," he whispered, looking like he regretted that he was sharing the information. "Some of the other teachers suspected his wife signed him up to give him something to do, but he had no patience. He hated explaining himself, he just wanted to... drone on."

"At least some things don't change."

"Was he a... loud teacher?" he asked, to which Ellie shook her head. "Let's just say you can only raise your voice in a classroom so many times before parents start making formal complaints. He seemed relieved when he was asked to take a step back."

"That's not what I expected to hear after what I heard earlier." Ellie frowned, glancing at Oliver as he whipped up their lunch orders. "I heard he pushed a student and was suspended for it."

"I didn't h-hear about that. Do you think he's behind what happened to that photographer?"

"Perhaps, but something's going on, and he's mixed up in it."

Before Daniel could respond, a sharp whistle caught their attention. Ellie turned to see Oliver standing behind the counter, holding up a hefty brown paper bag.

"I think that's my cue," she said, getting up. She hesitated for a moment, then turned back to Daniel. "Fancy a drink at the pub later?"

The Plot Thickens

Daniel looked apologetic, rubbing the back of his neck. She knew what was coming—she regretted asking.

"I'm swamped with these decorations," he explained, "and I promised to drop my nan off at bingo."

"Of course. No worries. See you around?"

"Definitely."

Ellie made her way back to the counter, and Oliver dumped down the paper bag.

"Can't go wrong with a Ploughman's sandwich and crisps. What pub, by the way? I might be heading to The Drowsy Duck tonight if you want to tag along?"

"You once told me it was filled with big scary men."

"And it is, but this might be the weirdest thing to happen in the village in a while." Oliver picked up his phone from the counter and showed her a social media post. "They're relaunching their Ghost Ale. Isn't that funny?"

She grumbled in her throat. "Funny is one word for it."

"Oh wow. They've *just* posted there's also going to be a *séance*!" He scrolled through the comments under the announcement. "As you can see, people are rather excited. And oh boy—so many of them are saying they've seen ghosts over the past few days."

Ellie groaned, dropping her head back and rolling it around on her neck before she dragged the lunch bag off the counter.

"Here we go again..."

* * *

Ellie opened the door to Meadowfield Books, but Granny Maggie didn't look up. She tightened her cardigan around herself, absorbed in her endless book rearranging—moving titles from one pile to the next, looping around the shop in a well-worn default mode.

"You're back," Maggie stated. "I... I popped home to grab this," she said, holding up the nearest book within reach. *"Persuasion.* I've been searching for it all morning."

Ellie nodded, lingering by the door, wondering how much longer she could go along with the games. Her gran wasn't behaving much differently from recent days, but after overhearing what she had at George's, Ellie now saw her in a more evasive light. She didn't like it, and she couldn't shake the feeling.

"Why, Gran?"

"Oh... erm..." Maggie scratched at her grey hair with the corner of the book. "I just fancied another read—"

"Gran, stop," Ellie said firmly, closing the shop door behind herself, shutting out the noise of South Street. "I know you went to see George earlier."

Maggie sighed, her gaze fixing on the words painted on the wall, though Ellie knew she wasn't really seeing them—she was staring through to the cheese shop next door.

"It wasn't Sylvia," Ellie continued, folding her arms. "She showed me where George lives, and I didn't get the chance to speak to him, but I heard you. You *warned* him about me." She paused, her voice tightening. "Except I'm not the one sneaking around."

"Well, it sounds like you *were* sneaking around." Maggie's eyes narrowed as she exhaled a long breath. "Especially if you didn't make yourself known because I certainly didn't see you."

"Gran... what happened the night Tim died that I'm not allowed to know?"

"I only warned George because he's been through enough." Maggie's voice was low, weary. She stared at the floor. "Meredith falling into that coma turned his world upside down. And no offence, Eleanor, but you're very persistent with your research, and you always have been. It's an admirable quality, but all of this digging is just causing too much—"

"Because there *is* something going on," Ellie interrupted, glancing at the new pane of glass her gran hadn't yet noticed. "I was going to tell you sooner, but... someone threw a brick through the window at me. *And* someone stole my notes. They ripped them right from my pad. Whoever it is, like you, doesn't want me digging." She hesitated, the words hanging on the tip of her tongue. "Unless you're the one throwing bricks and stealing pages?"

Maggie's eyes flashed with hurt. "Ellie..."

But Ellie looked away. "I wouldn't want to think so, but I don't recognise you with how you've been acting. I know you can be stubborn, but you've *never* shut me out like this."

When Maggie spoke again, her voice was soft, almost pleading. "There's a reason I don't want *you* digging, Ellie. This is painful. For George. For me. I've carried so much guilt over what happened in 1994. You don't understand—"

"Of all people, I think I understand guilt," she said quietly, closing her eyes and seeing Luke's cheeky grin, forever frozen in time.

"Ellie, I didn't mean—"

"You're not the only one it's affecting," Ellie cut in. "Unless Meredith is somehow walking around in her coma, she didn't throw that brick or rip out my pages. But *someone* did. Someone who doesn't want me to find out the truth. Someone who's hiding a secret—"

"I know where you're going." Maggie's face fell, her expression drained. She looked down at the copy of *Persuasion* she held, gripping it with white knuckles. "You think George is trying to clean up his wife's mess? Trying to protect Meredith? I just don't think so."

"When I first uncovered that message, you were certain neither of them had anything to do with it."

"I was certain," Maggie replied, still staring at the words with a wide, unflinching stare. It was as though she was seeing them properly for the first time. "Perhaps I was just... hopeful. You're right, Ellie. There's something I need to—"

The Plot Thickens

But before Maggie could get her words out, Joey's footsteps pounded down the stairs.

"I've found something!" he shouted, vanishing as quickly as he'd appeared. "Under the floor!"

Maggie's face paled, so Ellie reached out, squeezing her gran's hand.

"Whatever it is, we have each other," she said, wishing things could go back to how they were. "We don't have to be on opposite sides."

Maggie sighed, patting Ellie's cheek. "We were never on opposite sides, love. Believe it or not, I've been trying to protect you. I didn't want you getting mixed up in all this ancient history. Look what happened to Tim." She glanced at the newly repaired window, her expression grave. "But if someone tried to harm you, this isn't history. Not anymore. This is happening right now. You were right, Ellie. I didn't want to face this. Let's go and see what young Joey has found."

Together, they climbed the stairs to find Joey in the centre of the upstairs room, standing over an old wooden projector, an array of colourful glass slides scattered around him.

"They say things come in threes, so I *knew* there'd be something else hidden," he said, holding up a slide to the light. "I moved those boxes with the sci-fi books, pulled back the rug, and noticed the floorboards didn't have nails. And *ta-da*! This was down there, wrapped in a bag. Looks like an old toy."

"It's an antique projector," Maggie said, tapping her chin. "I've read about these."

"Where's the on switch?" He turned the device over in his hands. "Or the plug, for that matter?"

Ellie leaned in, sniffing the projector. The faint scent of oil tickled her nostrils.

"It's older than electricity," she said. "Looks like it was powered by an oil lamp."

Undeterred, Joey held his phone's flash to a slide, projecting a ghostly skeleton onto the wall. Maggie rummaged through the horror section, pulling out an old volume titled *The Victorian Book of the Dead*.

As Joey continued examining the slides, Ellie's mind raced with questions about the projector's purpose and origin. Maggie flipped through the book's index, finding a passage that shed light on the Victorian obsession with faking ghostly photographs.

"Well, I never knew *this*," Maggie said, pointing to a passage. "Before ghosts started appearing in photographs, they weren't translucent."

Ellie watched as Joey projected a slide of a ghostly woman onto the wall, making her drift along as though she were stalking the room. If it had been a little darker, it might have been enough to make Ellie think twice about what was in front of her.

"The technology of the time shaped the myth?" Ellie pondered.

"Ghosts didn't like cameras, so they went see-

The Plot Thickens

through?" Joey asked, abandoning the slides. "I'm not following."

Maggie's finger traced the lines. "Ellie's right. It says here that people would gather to witness ghosts and ghouls using these projectors. *Phantasmagoria*." She smiled up at Ellie, and it was so nice to see again. "They couldn't project solid shapes, so people began to believe that ghosts were translucent. Before then, there were very few references to see-through ghosts."

"And they really believed in them?" Joey asked. "The Victorians?"

"There are reports of believers in the supernatural dating back to the beginning of the written word," Maggie explained, slipping quickly back into teacher mode, "but these projections were like going to the cinema—you don't believe Freddy Krueger is real, just because you can see him, but you still watch for the thrill that he *might* be." She flipped the page. "They used projectors and various double-exposure techniques to capture images from 'the other side.' These images became fashionable collectables, and quite a profitable industry built up around ghost photography."

Ellie glanced out of the window as the afternoon light began to fade. Across the pond, Harold Fletcher was up a ladder, hanging a banner on the pub, no doubt advertising the relaunch of his Ghost Ale. Was that what all of this was about? Profit?

"So, this is how they made the pictures in that history book?" Joey asked, then corrected himself. "Sorry,

Maggie—the *fictional* history book. If you say it wasn't real, I believe you, but they did look convincing."

"Do you have a copy of the book, Gran?"

Maggie shook her head. "I didn't stock it on principle. It felt exploitative of Tim's memory. And yes, the images *appeared* to be real, but I'm not surprised." She turned the book to show a full-page sepia-toned photograph of a man posing against a dark background, with the ghostly outline of a woman's face beside him. "So far, we've found an old camera and projector. Without the internet, these techniques might have been as convincing in 1994 to anyone who didn't know how these images were made."

"Like filters today, you mean?" Joey said, holding up his phone. He snapped a picture of Maggie and Ellie, then after some fiddling, showed them the result. Just like in the old photographs, a silvery ghostly figure hovered behind them. "She looks more solid, but you can tell it's not real—you can't beat those old pictures. Do you think it's a coincidence all this old stuff's been hidden around the shop?"

"Once, perhaps, but not three times." Maggie sighed, patting the low beam above her head. "Someone used this place as a dumping ground the last time the shop was dismantled." She dropped her gaze, glancing in the direction of The Drowsy Duck. "Not just someone—Tim Baker's *murderer*."

Ellie let out a breath she hadn't realised she was holding. Hearing her gran admit the obvious truth, instead of dancing around by claiming Tim's death was an accident, brought a sense of relief she hadn't known she needed.

"So, what do we do next?" Ellie asked.

"We should telephone Angela," Maggie said, though her tone carried a hint of resignation. "Not that she'll *want* to believe us, but a dinner summons from her former mother-in-law will be enough of a shock that she'll have to listen."

Maggie went downstairs to make the call, leaving Ellie with Joey.

"Let's take this down," Ellie said, gathering the slides. "Where did you put the camera? We'll need to show Angela everything we've found."

Joey nodded and followed Maggie, leaving Ellie alone with the slides. She lingered a moment, holding the ghostly images up to the fading light. They were hand-painted, macabre in that distinctly Victorian way. On any other day, she might have enjoyed the novelty of such a historical find in the bookshop. But now, the items felt tainted—possibly connected to Tim's murder. She bundled the slides into the crinkled bag Joey had found them in. The logo was faded, but she could just make out that it had once belonged to a shoe shop.

Before she could examine it further, Joey sprinted back up the stairs.

"It's not there," he said breathlessly. "You told me to put the camera somewhere safe, so I put it back in the chimney. I'm an *idiot*, Ellie." He thrust a fist into the doorframe. Not enough to hurt himself, but enough to make Ellie take a wary step back. "I thought because nobody had looked there for years, nobody would look, but... it's gone. Someone must've come back for it when I was up here."

"It's not your fault, Joey," she said, though she couldn't help thinking she should have chosen a better hiding place—somewhere the person who had initially put it there wouldn't already know to look. "We'll just have to ensure we don't let things out of sight again. Whoever this is, they're determined to gather the pieces before we can see the full picture." She bundled the projector into the shoe shop bag and secured the handle around her fingers. "But thanks to you, we've beaten them to the next one."

In a small voice, he said, "I was just trying to help... Drink?"

"Not tonight," she replied, patting him on the shoulder. "If my gran has said the right things, I have dinner plans with Detective Sergeant Cookson. Hopefully, she'll want to see the hidden treasure you found. Good work, Joey."

"Anytime," he said, swapping places with her. "I'll get these planks back in place. Don't want someone falling."

No, they didn't, but Ellie kept her thoughts to herself, especially with what was about to take place in the pub across the pond. She wasn't superstitious, but even she had to admit that hosting another séance felt a little too much like tempting fate.

* * *

Ellie, Maggie, and the projector left the bookshop in an uncomfortable silence, which didn't break until they passed The Drowsy Duck, where Harold Fletcher wobbled atop a ladder, hanging a large banner advertising the séance.

"Call it a funny feeling," Maggie said, pulling Ellie close by the arm, her breath misting in the cool air, "but I think we'll end up there tonight."

"Do we have a choice?" Ellie replied, drawing her gran closer as they rounded the corner. It was nice to be back on the same page. "But first—did Angela agree to dinner?"

"Fortunately—or unfortunately—she did. Now we actually have to host her, which might be the scariest thing so far."

"So far today," Ellie murmured, glancing at the pub's upper floor and catching a glimpse of a figure in black at the window. Tilly was watching them head towards the green. "I wish I didn't have such a bad feeling about this."

"The dinner?" Maggie asked.

"The séance."

"Then I'm not alone there." Maggie exhaled, shaking her head. "It's disappointing to see that lessons weren't learned last time. Now we're doing it all over again, hoping for a different result."

Arm in arm, they passed the village green, where a few villagers gathered around the war memorial, leaning in as if listening for something.

"This all feels far too familiar," Maggie said, dabbing her nose. "But first, a painful dinner with Angela. I suppose like with most things, the only way through is forwards. And when we get home, I promise I'll tell you everything I know about Meredith Fenton and the séance of '94."

Chapter 10
The Detective Who Came to Dinner

The sky deepened into twilight as Maggie and Ellie approached their cottage. Angela's car was parked outside, her headlights dimmed, the faint glow of her phone casting sharp shadows over her face. Maggie's steps slowed, her eyes narrowing as she let out a soft, irritated sigh.

"She hasn't given me a chance to cook."

Angela, catching the murmur, swung open her car door and stepped out, the slam reverberating through the stillness. Ellie flinched, her nerves already raw from everything that had unfolded that day. A subtle tremor ran through her body that she tried—and failed—to suppress.

"What?" Angela demanded, the word grating but not unkind. "What's happened to you?"

"Let's all go inside," Maggie suggested with a touch

of forced brightness before Ellie could respond. "I'll whip up something quick. We have a lot to tell you."

"I'm not here to eat, Maggie." Her tone slipped back into its usual clipped rhythm. "I've got to head off to a crime scene—"

"Something to do with all this, I hope?" Maggie asked.

"No. The usual. Road rage turned ugly. Domestic disputes. Nothing as exciting as you lot." She shook her head, muttering under her breath, "Meadowfield isn't my highest priority, you know." For a second, it seemed like she might leave. "Dinner would be... nice. Something quick," she added, eyeing Maggie warily. "If your cooking is as bad as your son's was..."

Maggie chuckled as she shuffled towards the door, keys jingling in her hand. "I tried to teach that boy everything I knew, but Peter never paid attention to anything he didn't care about. Always had his eyes on the sky—more interested in birds than cooking. And people, for that matter."

Under her breath, Angela said, "You don't have to remind me."

As Maggie fumbled with her keys, the tension between Ellie and Angela dragged out, a silence that neither wanted to break.

"What's in the bag?" Angela asked, her tone casual but her eyes sharp. "I recognise the logo. An old shoe shop. It closed down when you and Oliver were kids."

"Where was it?"

"Somewhere on South Street. So, what is it? You're clinging to it for dear life."

"You'll find out."

Angela's sigh hung heavy as Maggie wrestled the stubborn lock into submission, bursting through the door with a triumphant huff.

"Come in, come in. I'll sort some lights." Without pausing, she hurried through the cluttered hallway, flicking on lamps, casting pools of warm, golden light across the cottage's mismatched furniture. "Do you still eat like a rabbit, Angela? Of course you do. You haven't gained a gram since your wedding day."

Left alone in the quiet, Ellie motioned for Angela to follow her into the conservatory, the small room at the back of the house where a faint light still lingered from the fading sky. Angela folded her arms against the chill, glancing around with impatience, her mouth set in a thin line. Ellie gestured for her to sit at the small, round table where she and her gran took their meals, then clicked on the space heater. The coils glowed red, but with Angela's foot tapping impatiently, it was clear she wouldn't be sticking around long enough to feel the warmth.

As they settled, Ellie reached into the bag and carefully pulled out the old projector and slides. She handled the projector like it might fall apart at the slightest touch, and given its age, it might. She set it on the cast iron table and lay the glass slides beside it.

"I didn't come here for a slide show." Angela's eyes darted from the projector to Ellie, her expression more irritated than intrigued. She leaned back in her chair, crossing her arms even tighter across her chest.

"Are you working on the graffiti case?" Ellie asked, keeping her tone calm.

"Do you know how difficult it is to reopen a cold case without new evidence?" Angela's voice rose, revealing frustration beyond Ellie's question. "Just... tell me what you've got, or let me go—I have a glass of red with my name on it waiting at the..."

Her voice trailed off as Maggie bustled in, setting a generous measure of wine in front of Angela before flitting off to the kitchen.

"Go on, Ellie," Maggie called over the sound of a knife chopping. "There is new evidence."

Angela took a deep sip, leaving a red mark on her upper lip as she whipped out her notebook and clicked open a small silver pen, one brow arched as she eyed Ellie expectantly.

"Alright," she demanded. "Let's see what you've got."

"There have been some developments since the museum," Ellie began, pausing to clear her throat. As if on cue, Maggie appeared, setting a glass of water down before returning to her chopping. Ellie took a sip, steadying herself. "Someone threw a brick through the bookshop window while I was inside. Given how close it got, I think they were aiming for me."

Angela huffed. "Why didn't you report it?"

"I had other things on my mind. Sylvia handled the

The Plot Thickens

window, so I went to The Drowsy Duck... only to have my notes ripped out of my pad." Ellie reached into her bag and pulled out the leather notepad, showing the torn edges. Then, she carefully unfolded some yellowed pages from Mr Fenton's old notes. "You look like you recognise these."

"Mr Fenton's handwriting," she said, almost to herself. "I'd know it anywhere. He had this way of writing 'Must do better' on my history coursework—scarred me for life. I never did care for history." Her gaze shifted to Ellie. "He was in that strange club. It didn't make sense to me back then; he was always so... immovable."

"That's George for you," Maggie called from the kitchen. "Nothing exists beyond what history can explain."

Angela's eyes narrowed. "Odd choice of a wife, then. But I can relate—I once married Meadowfield's dullest man. Speaking of Peter Cookson, how's your father, Ellie? Still chasing birds?"

"I think he's in Scotland," Ellie replied.

"Think?" Angela's eyebrow arched further.

"He's gone off the radar again," Maggie interjected, as matter-of-factly as if discussing the weather. "You know what he's like."

Angela and Ellie exchanged a glance, nodding in silent agreement, unseen by Maggie.

"He checked in when he found out I was home," Ellie continued, as Angela scribbled down details about the brick and the missing notes. "I haven't heard anything since."

"Neither has Oliver."

"He can take care of himself," Maggie chimed in again, never missing a beat.

Angela muttered, almost to herself, "Can he? He was always flighty, but I thought he'd settle down by our fifties."

Ellie leaned closer, hearing the genuine worry in Angela's voice.

"What's different this time?" Ellie asked

"He didn't say goodbye before he left." Angela swirled her wine, her expression darkening. "He usually does. Even me."

Maggie returned with two bowls of salad, and quickly retreated to the kitchen again, avoiding the table.

Ellie lowered her voice. "Did something happen between my father and Gran before he left? She clams up whenever I mention him lately."

Angela shrugged. "In her eyes, Peter could do no wrong, so if there is something, it must be serious." She tapped her notebook and refocused on George's notes. "What is all this? It looks like he's tracking someone."

"Meredith," Ellie said, spreading out the pages. "The notes are filled with observations about her, mixed in with details from ghost-watching expeditions. Mostly George's scathing remarks on wandering the graveyard and attempting to commune with John Partridge in the pub cellar."

The Plot Thickens

"Ah, so Harold gave you the grand tour?" Angela smirked, then tugged the notes closer, scanning them quickly.

"Along with the brick and missing notes, we also found an old camera hidden in a fireplace. Someone took it back later. I'd say they stole it, but it's likely they were the ones who hid it in the first place. Only a few of us knew it was there. And today, we uncovered this projector under the floorboards. It's as if someone's been using the shop as a dumping ground. Maybe it's linked to a decorating company or—"

"Oh, I can help with this!" Maggie exclaimed, reappearing with a small notepad usually stuck to the fridge and reserved for shopping lists. "I found the decorating company my sister hired in her old receipts—Wiltshire Interiors. I spoke with the owner's son. Lovely man from Scotland, though he did mention his father was more interested in hobbies than running the business."

Angela rubbed her temples. "Did he know anything about the bookshop?"

"He was quite young at the time, so he doesn't remember the bookshop specifically," Maggie replied, "but he did say his father would hire whoever was cheapest."

"Which means a high turnover of cash-in-hand workers. If his father's gone, there won't be any records. Not a viable lead."

Maggie's voice softened. "The polite chap did

mention that Ken passed away some time ago. He was very apologetic about not being able to help. But I thought it was worth a try." She dabbed at her nose with a tissue, then gestured towards the projector. "Surely this, along with what Ellie told you about her stalker—" She held up a hand to stop Ellie from protesting. "—let's call it what it is. Someone is keeping an eye on you and the shop, Ellie. The brick, the missing notes, and now the camera."

"An old camera, you said?" Angela asked, pulling one of the crinkled pages closer. "How old?"

"Antique?" Ellie guessed. "I'd guess late 1800s."

"1862," Maggie corrected. "There was a sticker with the date on the bottom. I took a proper look at it before Joey put it away. I was... curious."

Hearing that her gran had been quietly hunting for clues made Ellie feel less alone. Even when they'd been at odds, her gran's sharp mind and methodical eye hadn't gone to waste.

"What are you writing down?" Maggie asked.

"Not your concern." Angela's gaze flicked up to Ellie. "Where did you find these?"

"Does that matter?" Maggie answered for her.

"It might if you stole them."

"What if the person had thrown them away?" Ellie countered.

"You'd need to be sure they wanted to get rid of them. Just because it's in a bin doesn't mean it's yours to take. If it's in a private bin, it's still technically their property—or the council's, once it's out for collection... Are you saying you went through George Fenton's bins?"

"I nudged a bag, it fell over, and these slipped out. It wasn't intentional."

Angela sighed. "But it *was* intentional when you took them off his property."

"Oh, give it a rest, Angela," Maggie snapped, turning back to the kitchen. "You're not going to arrest Ellie for bringing you evidence like this. And if you weren't planning to use those notes, you wouldn't be writing down half of what's in them."

Angela's pen scratched to a halt as she glared after Maggie, making it clear Maggie had won that round. Ellie had always appreciated her gran's ability to stand up to Angela—and Carolyn, for that matter. It wasn't that Ellie couldn't hold her own; she'd learned to do that early on, growing up between a distracted actress and a sour police officer. But she had yet to develop her gran's quick wit, a skill Maggie seemed to save for exactly these moments.

"In George's handwriting, there are several mentions of discussing a camera purchase with Tim Baker," Angela stated flatly, her tone reverting to a low, authoritative drone. "This entry here notes that the camera is from 1862, cost him £99 after a 'generous discount' from Tim, and would be 'perfect for Meredith for...'" She frowned at the torn page. "There's nothing more." She snapped her notebook shut and began to push her chair back. "Unless you have anything pertinent to add, I'll thank you for—"

"I do," Ellie interjected, and Angela paused, settling back in her chair. "You think George is involved, don't you? That's why you're in such a rush to leave." She nudged Angela's untouched salad bowl towards her. "I've got a lot to go over, so you might as well eat."

With a sigh, Angela pulled her chair back under the table and reluctantly swapped her notepad for the salad. She speared a piece of limp lettuce and leathery prosciutto, eating as Ellie gathered her thoughts on George Fenton. She began by describing her childhood view of him as a boring but kindly teacher, contrasting that with how he'd treated Sylvia when she'd tried to offer him cheese. Angela didn't ask how Ellie knew that, and Ellie didn't volunteer that they'd technically trespassed just before she'd taken his notes.

"And then there's the idea that George might have wanted to frame Meredith," Ellie said, pausing to wrestle through a tough mouthful of salad. "Harold suggested George was controlling Meredith, and framing her for Tim's murder would've been easier than divorce. His own notes admit he didn't know how much longer he could tolerate Meredith's behaviour."

Angela huffed, stabbing a cherry tomato so hard that red juice splattered across George's notes. With a sigh, she dabbed at the mess with some crumpled napkins left over from Christmas.

"What else?"

"When I spoke to Jack and Cassie at Tim's old studio, they mentioned the same thing, but Cassie went further—she claimed George was suspended for pushing a student."

Ellie waited for her gran to chime in with a correction, but Maggie stayed in the kitchen, and the rhythmic clinking of her knife stopped.

"Yes, I remember that," Angela said. "It was early '95. I was a young PC at the time. I took the kid's statement."

Ellie leaned closer. "What happened?"

Angela took another bite before she continued, "Rumours about Meredith spread around the school like wildfire, and one lad wouldn't let it go. He scrawled it on the chalkboard like it was sprayed on your wall. Mr Fenton caught him in the act and shoved him." She shrugged. "The suspension only lasted until the end of term. Nobody blamed him—the kid was a real bad egg, and everyone knew he'd driven Fenton to it. He's been in prison for years now, locked up after a botched bank robbery." She muttered, almost to herself, "Fenton didn't shove him hard enough if you ask me."

"But the fact that he did push him..." Ellie's heart raced as Cassie's claim was validated. "If Tim was pushed to his death—"

"Anyone for dessert?" Maggie called over the hum of the fridge. "It's leftover bread-and-butter pudding, I'm afraid."

"No," they replied in unison, both sounding slightly irritated.

Angela glanced down at her half-eaten salad, as if suddenly uncertain of what she was doing there. She pushed it away and began gathering up the notes.

"I think it's someone connected to that group," Ellie said quickly. "Dr Christina Marsh is dead, but the rest are still in the village. Cassie has obvious rage issues. Jack seems shifty. Harold and Tilly are in a world of their own. George isn't the same man I knew, and Meredith isn't here to defend herself. You mentioned things in the case notes that didn't make sense—"

"You're more likely to fall on your front if it's an accident," Angela said, slotting the notes into a leather binder. "How many times have you tripped down the stairs and caught yourself? Tim was found on his back. It's not impossible to fall backwards, but—"

"There's a wonky step at the top," Ellie remembered.

Angela looked up, eyebrows raised. "You noticed it too. The autopsy found no evidence of a struggle nor any signs that he fell down any stairs. Those steps are concrete and steep."

"He'd have hit them on the way down."

"Yet the only injuries he sustained were consistent with a fall from a great height onto the stone floor."

Ellie let Angela's words sink in, picturing the force to send someone down the stairs without hitting a single step.

The Plot Thickens

"So, it would've been almost *impossible* for the fall to be an accident?"

Angela exhaled. "I'm not here to speculate, but... yes, Tim was pushed with such force that he didn't connect with anything until the cellar floor. And there was a chemical splashed all over his clothes—a developing liquid," she added abruptly, muttering to herself as she reached for her phone. "You never saw this, and you certainly didn't get it from me," she grumbled, showing Ellie the screen. "What does this look like to you?"

Ellie held out her hand, and Angela reluctantly passed over the phone, turning back to the salad. She stabbed at the lettuce, each jab suggesting she couldn't bear to watch Ellie examine the evidence.

Ellie zoomed in on the image: a light denim shirt, its chest marred by a dark stain that streaked downward in ominous trails.

"It looks like someone threw a drink on him," Ellie said, zooming in, but Angela quickly pulled the phone away.

"The chemical's an uncommon developing liquid used in photography," Angela explained. "It wasn't investigated further, given Tim's profession. But I thought the same as you when I saw it—the splash's concentration, the downward drips. It would be difficult to get those results by accident. Someone threw it at him."

"As difficult as throwing yourself down the stairs backwards," Ellie replied, nodding. "And the liquid couldn't have been splashed on him after the fall—the drips would have run to the sides, not straight down. Maybe there was an altercation at the studio before the séance?"

Angela dabbed her mouth one last time before standing. Without asking any further questions, she gathered the projector and slides, stuffing them into the plastic bag from the old shoe shop. Then, without a word, she headed down the hallway.

It wasn't enough for Ellie. She hurried after her.

"Will you reopen the case?" she asked.

"There was one more thing," Angela said over her shoulder as she paused at the doorway. "His camera. It wasn't on his person when he died, and it was never found."

"I've heard he was never without it," Ellie recalled.

"It was enough for his mother, Carol, to report it missing," Angela continued, stepping down the frosty garden path to her car. A thin layer of ice glittered on the roof under the streetlamp. "Carol said Tim was inseparable from that camera—his thirteenth-birthday gift from his father. An old 1960s model, and he never went anywhere without it." She cupped her hands and blew a hot breath through her cold palms. "If I were as good a photographer as people say Tim was, and someone had just pushed me to my death, I know what my final *killer* shot would be."

After Angela climbed into her car and sped off, Ellie retreated to the warmth of the hallway, though DS

The Plot Thickens

Angela Cookson's parting words had left a chill no space heater could chase away. Her gran lingered in the doorway to the kitchen, wringing a tea towel between her hands.

"You're onto something," Maggie stated, wafting the towel to beckon Ellie into the kitchen. "She wouldn't have shared all of that unless you'd hit the nail on the head. Tough as Angela is, I can't say she's never been fair. Except when it comes to you, of course," she added with a quick glance. "But given the history between Carolyn and my Peter, I can't blame her."

Ellie let out a breath, her head buzzing with everything Angela had revealed.

"Families are complicated, Gran."

"That they are, love."

"Which is why I didn't tell Angela what I overheard," Ellie said as her gran moved to the sink, facing the foggy window. "About what you said to George."

"About me warning him that you might go asking questions?" Her gran twisted the taps on with slow, stiff movements. "Which, I'll remind you, I was *correct* about."

"Not that. I heard you tell George I couldn't find out what Meredith did that night. So, Gran, it's time to tell me. What did Meredith do?"

"Oh, Ellie." She exhaled, bracing herself against the sink as the taps dribbled into the basin. She'd barely turned them on. "I know I said I'd tell you everything when we got home, but I'm not the woman I was earlier. I'm tired, Ellie. It's... it's been a long day. I just want to crawl into bed and..." Her voice trailed off, and Ellie wondered if her gran remembered their earlier promise. "... the séance. Why does it have to be tonight? Or at all, for that—"

The doorbell rang, halting her gran's rising frustration. She twisted off the taps and headed for the door, leaving Ellie to check the conservatory for anything Angela might have left behind, but everything seemed in place. She joined her gran at the door to find Sylvia and Oliver standing side by side.

"We didn't come together," Sylvia laughed, waving past Maggie to Ellie, "but we happened to be heading in the same direction for the same reason. Rather an eerie coincidence, wouldn't you say?"

"Less of that tonight, thank you," Maggie said, tugging her cardigan tighter. "What can we help with?"

"We're here to take you on a night out," Oliver announced, pulling Ellie outside. "We agreed to kidnap one of you each, so you're coming with me."

As Oliver led her down the garden path, Ellie glanced back at her gran, who was already deep in pleasantries with Sylvia, her weariness replaced with a bright smile as she locked up.

Though Maggie had dodged her questions, she seemed more than happy to chat with Sylvia. Her gran always knew how to kick the can down the road, but Ellie wasn't sure she liked where this road was going.

The Plot Thickens

* * *

As they walked down the steep cobbled lane past the old mill—now holiday apartments—Oliver drew Ellie in close, his voice low. "So, I've been hearing a *peculiar* rumour."

"I hope you're not about to fill my head with another ghost story."

"Scarier than that," he replied, his voice dropping to a whisper. "I heard Gran invited my mother to dinner... and she actually showed up." He shot Ellie a sideways look. "Firstly, why wasn't I invited? And was this about Dad?"

"His name came up, but it wasn't the reason," she said, though she was worried about their father. "Any idea where he is?"

"Nope." His casual tone didn't quite hide the concern beneath it. Oliver was used to their father's erratic ways—Peter Cookson, mild-mannered and quiet, seemed to float through life, his mind ever on the birds he loved. "He did leave a little suddenly. He called after the fact."

"You actually spoke to him? I only got a text. Are you sure it was him?"

"I think so..." Oliver's face darkened. "Now you're scaring me. Should I be worried? Is this connected to the case?"

Ellie shook her head. "No, it's not connected. And you shouldn't be scared," she added, trying to convince herself as much as him. She echoed their gran's familiar phrase. "We know what he's like."

Oliver let out a long breath, rubbing the back of his neck, but he didn't take the line of questioning further.

"So, what was dinner about, then?" he asked.

"I'm hoping it was to nudge your mum into reopening the Tim Baker case."

Oliver groaned. "That story's been on repeat at the café all day. It's doing my head. I only have one ghost story, and it's hardly worth telling."

She raised an eyebrow, waiting. "And you're not going to share it?"

"Well..." he began with a grin, "I once saw Cher come to me through the fog in a dark alley—the most beautiful apparition you can imagine. She was in her ice-blonde wig with the beads, floating—"

"Cher's not dead, Oliver."

"No, and she never will be. But for years, I swore I'd seen a ghost. Looking back, it was probably a drag queen on skates, but... the less you know about my early twenties in Brighton, the better." He nodded with mock solemnity. "I won't elaborate."

"So, no real ghost sightings?" she asked, laughing.

"Honestly? I'm not sure I believe in them," he admitted as they approached the village green. Ellie glanced at the shadow of the memorial bench, and Oliver followed her gaze. He took her hand and said, "On second thought, there are ghosts everywhere."

Ellie closed her eyes, wishing she could laugh again

The Plot Thickens

like she had moments ago. She still wasn't sure what she would say to Daniel about the assembly. When she opened her eyes, she saw a blurred mass of people walking towards The Drowsy Duck.

"I know I don't believe in *these* kinds of ghosts," Ellie said, drawing her brother in closer. "The ones that only show up after a few pints of Harold's premium Ghost Ale."

"Premium is one word for it. I heard he's charging six quid a pint. What does he think this is? *London?*"

Ellie smiled, though it didn't quite reach her eyes. She glanced back at her gran, who'd kept a few paces behind the whole walk down, nodding and grumbling in agreement as Sylvia treated her to a whistle-stop tour of the local gossip.

"Can you hear that?" Oliver asked with a disbelieving laugh as ghostly groans echoed into the night. "I don't think I've ever seen this place so packed. But I'll give it to Harold—he's got people talking. It's almost like..."

He paused, searching for the right word. Ellie held her breath, willing him not to say it.

"It's almost like, tonight, people are *expecting* something bad to happen." After a breath, he added, "History isn't likely to repeat itself... is it?"

Bracing herself as they stepped into the glow of the pub, Ellie said, "It's more likely than you'd think."

Chapter 11
The Gathering

Ellie held the door as the crowd flowed into The Drowsy Duck, the dim light from the pub spilling onto the damp cobbles outside. Inside, the air was thick with the scent of melted wax, the scattered candles flickering and casting shadows that danced along the walls. She barely had a moment to take it in before Oliver brushed past her, his eyes gleaming as he headed straight for the bar.

"I'd best get us a table before there's nowhere left," Sylvia called over her shoulder, weaving expertly through the crowd. "This is going to be quite the show!"

Ellie held her breath as her gran shuffled in next. There was a sag in her shoulders, her mouth set in a disapproving line as she surveyed the gathering. But her attention was drawn straight to the corner, where a Ouija board sat on a table draped in a pristine white cloth. A single spotlight hung over it. Villagers clutching pints that glowed an unnatural green hovered nearby, but none dared enter the ring of light. Without a word, her gran shook her head before she followed Sylvia.

After her gran, someone unexpected appeared—the last person Ellie had expected to see at the séance.

George Fenton stepped over the threshold, his clothes rumpled, his face unshaven, as though he hadn't seen a mirror in days. His tired eyes swept the room, scanning for someone. He didn't look in Ellie's direction, and for a fleeting moment, she wondered if he didn't recognise her. Yet, of the two of them, she'd changed the least since her school days.

Ellie almost let go of the door when a woman with glassy eyes followed close behind, one hand clutching a wooden cane, the other resting on George's elbow. He waited for her slow steps, guiding her inside. For a moment, the doorway felt too small for all of them, especially as Ellie realised he was intent on ignoring her presence. Once inside, he led the woman to one of the last empty tables.

Ellie kept her hold on the door, scanning for anyone else who might come in. She'd already spotted Tilly helping Harold serve drinks at the bar and Cassie and Jack playing pool in the corner, the sharp, electric clacks of the billiard balls cutting through the hushed, excited whispers filling the air.

As she turned to step inside, Daniel's fingers brushed against hers, catching the door. She froze, and so did he, their eyes meeting as a faint smile tugged at his lips.

"Hey," he said softly, his hand resting on the door.

"Hi," Ellie replied, her voice quieter than she'd intended.

They both hesitated, a flicker of something unspoken hanging in the air. Then, almost at the same time, they broke into awkward smiles.

"You first," Daniel said, stepping aside to let her pass.

"Thanks," Ellie murmured as she stepped inside.

He followed, glancing at his nan, who stood near the entrance with her arms crossed, looking as annoyed as ever.

"I hope your grandfather doesn't come back tonight," his nan muttered, her voice low and bristling. "I heard enough of his lip when he was alive."

Daniel gave Ellie an apologetic smile before guiding his nan to the last table near the pool table. She lingered by the door, watching him go, a pang of something sharp and unresolved tugging at her. Was he disappointed she hadn't agreed to help with the assembly?

But it wasn't the time to dwell on that when there were more pressing concerns. George Fenton had shown up to the séance with a woman Ellie didn't recognise, yet she recalled Sylvia tripping over a cane like that in George's hallway. Ellie heard the echo of the roar he'd unleashed on Sylvia to get her to go away. She dreaded to think how he'd have reacted to finding her hiding behind his bin. His unexpected arrival, along with Cassie and Jack, and Harold and Tilly, had the room feeling unsettlingly like a reunion of 1994.

She noticed her gran, whose gaze remained fixed on the Ouija board while Sylvia chatted her ear off. Ellie wove through the crowded room, feeling the press of bodies and the thickening heat. Villagers were fanning themselves with beer mats, surrounded by too many candles and pints of Harold's Ghost Ale. Somehow, the beer glowed a spectral green, and judging by the number of pints floating about the room, the steep price hadn't put anyone off.

Ellie had a feeling it was going to be a long night—and something, she wasn't sure what, was waiting in the shadows just beyond the reach of the flickering light.

"It tastes like batteries," Oliver muttered, sipping as he swiped left and right on a dating app. "No wonder there's a giant 'No refunds' sign on the bar. It's just an ordinary pint with a little LED bobbing up and down in it. I think we might've been scammed."

"You think?" Ellie replied, still not brave enough to sip the one he'd put in front of her. "Harold's certainly managed to whip up a storm. I don't think I've ever seen this place so packed. Everyone's here."

"It's the graffiti in Gran's shop that's done it," he corrected, nudging his pint away. "People took a while to remember the story of Tim Baker and start seeing ghosts around every corner, but if you hadn't found those words, none of this would be happening."

The Plot Thickens

Ellie sighed. "Thanks."

"I didn't mean it like that."

"No, I know." She tried to swallow, but her mouth was too dry. She eyed her pint but couldn't bring herself to sip something that allegedly tasted like 'batteries.' She needed something more refreshing. "You're right—I just wish you weren't. Gran warned me this would happen." She glanced over to see her gran, now deep in conversation with George at the bar. "I'm going to get some water. Want anything?"

"Water?" Oliver almost choked on another sip of his pint, barely looking up as he kept swiping. "At least get a glass of wine. You're going to need it tonight. Any idea who they've got to host the—" He cut himself off with a gasp, grabbing her arm as she started to stand. "It's *him*!"

Ellie tugged her arm free and glanced at George by the bar.

"Who?"

"Big ears!" Oliver whispered, flashing his phone to show her a quick picture of Joey as she stood. "I *found* him! Do you know what this means?"

"I... I have no idea," she replied over her shoulder, already squeezing through the crowded seats. "I'll be back in a minute."

Turning from Oliver, Ellie focused on her gran at the bar. She'd hurried over there, despite Sylvia having already bought her a half-pint of regular, non-glowing beer, as soon as George had made his way across the room. Ellie had been itching for a reason to join them, and her dry mouth was as good an excuse as any.

But before she could make it to the bar, a flash of short orange ringlet curls intercepted.

"Emergency!" Auntie Penny said through gritted teeth. "No time to explain!"

Auntie Penny grabbed Ellie's hand and, without a word, dragged her across the pub to the bathroom doors near the cellar. The cellar door stood ajar, and a rush of damp air hit Ellie as they passed, carrying that strange, plastic-like chemical smell. She barely had time to glance inside, where Harold might have been rigging the place for an inevitable tour after the séance.

Whatever emergency Penny was dealing with rendered her speechless, and from the growling noises ahead, Ellie could already guess the drama she was about to walk into.

"I *cannot* do this!" Carolyn wailed, her heavily made-up face twisted in rage as she tried to fasten a silk scarf around her head. "I cannot and *will not* go on!"

Auntie Penny looked at Ellie like a lion tamer on their first day in the enclosure. Ellie knew better than to panic at the first roar. Her mother was still attempting to fasten her headscarf in place for one, which rated low on the pre-show tantrum scale, given the spectacles Ellie had grown up around. She knew just what to say to make the faffing stop.

"It's alright, Mother," Ellie said, joining her in the streaky mirror above the row of cracked sinks. "I'll go and tell Harold to cancel the show. You can't go on like this." Despite her words, Ellie reached out and wafted her mother's hands away from trying to pin the scarf in place. Pinching some hair pins from the tub, she placed a few between her teeth before she started a crisscrossing pattern. "I'm sure people won't be too disappointed to have missed your big comeback."

"How busy is it?" Carolyn asked, looking for Penny's support in the mirror. "If only you hadn't stood on that safety pin, I might not have got worked up into this mess trying to use these tiny pins."

"My foot came off worse," Penny grumbled to herself. She joined on the other side with an enthusiastic grin. "The place is *packed*, Carolyn. It's your biggest audience in years."

"My episode of *Causality* got two million viewers!" she was quick to correct. "Which of course, playing a dead woman in the morgue, was a much more internal performance."

Carolyn glanced to the corner of the mirror. Ellie followed her gaze and noticed the camera in the corner filming them, and she saw Jack poking out of a cubicle stall, focused on capturing the scene. Sighing, Ellie added in the last pin and took a step back, uncomfortable that she'd just given them material for the pilot.

"Perhaps it's the live aspect that I'm nervous about," Carolyn said, her voice already picking up as she tested the strength of Ellie's pinning with a few shakes of her head. "It has been a few years since I've been in front of an audience as big as this."

"Marlborough Panto at the library 2017," Penny recalled instantly. "You were the ugly step—"

"*Cut!*" Carolyn yelled, spinning around to face Jack. "I don't want that in there—why are you dropping the camera?"

"You yelled 'cut,'" Jack replied.

"I meant 'cut it out of the edit later.'"

Jack slipped a cigarette between his lips, setting the camera on the toilet lid.

"I think we've got it," he muttered. "We'll stitch it up with confessionals in the edit."

He nodded at Ellie as he squeezed past her while her mother, already stacking necklaces around her neck, continued primping. Carolyn Swan would, without question, be performing tonight's séance, nerves or not. As much as Ellie disapproved of her mother's choice of gig, she wasn't about to lecture her on the ethics of pretending to channel spirits. If nothing else, her mother's lack of psychic ability might make the night entertaining. She caught the door just before it swung shut.

"Jack?" Ellie called, raising her voice above the renewed chatter in the pub. "Can I have a word?"

He paused. "I'm going out for a smoke."

It wasn't a refusal, so Ellie followed him across the crowded room. Her gran was still deep in conversation with George at the bar, and after all that had surfaced during their earlier dinner with Detective Sergeant Angela Cookson, Ellie was surprised to see her gran willing to trust George so quickly. Ellie needed to talk to him before the night was over, but there was still time.

Jack, however, would likely spend the evening behind a camera, filming the mess. She followed him to the beer garden, nearly as lively as the pub inside.

"Can I ask you something?" Ellie said, hugging herself against the chill as Jack's cigarette smoke wrapped around her. "What do you make of all of this? As someone who was Tim Baker's friend?"

He took a deep drag as he zipped his jacket up to his neck, covering his band t-shirt.

"What's this got to do with Tim?" he muttered, avoiding her gaze. "Because he died at the last séance, you mean?" He shrugged. "Depends how superstitious you are, doesn't it?"

"I suppose it does," she replied, though she wasn't sure what to believe. She'd never thought of herself as superstitious, but tonight, the eerie familiarity unnerved her. "Maybe it's just a feeling of déjà vu."

"You weren't even there the first time," he said, a laugh slipping out, but it sounded forced. "Why are you so interested in the past, anyway? You're young. You should be out there having fun—not messing around in old bookshops."

"Until I found that graffiti, I *was* having fun 'messing around' in that place." She hesitated, choosing her words carefully. "That bookshop's been in my family for years. I want to be proud of it again."

He took another drag. "Waste of time. Nobody reads books anymore."

"I do," she said sharply.

"Yeah? You and how many others? People don't have time for books anymore. There's no point in trying to revive something that's already dead."

Ellie stiffened. Jack's words echoed the doubts she'd tried to ignore, but she forced herself to push back.

"You could say the same about *your* field," she replied, nodding at the camera around his neck. "Everyone has a phone in their pocket now." She watched his face, expecting a reaction, but he only smiled, something dark and amused flitting across his expression. She pressed on. "That bookshop is my family's legacy. My gran practically raised me, and she deserves to see it thriving again. Tim Baker's story is tied to it now, for better or worse. But I can't see a future for the shop while there are still so many questions about what happened that night."

As she spoke, she caught her breath, surprised by her own intensity. Jack ground out his cigarette against the wall, smearing ash in rough streaks before flicking the butt in the direction of the bin. He turned back, his face a shadowed mask.

"What happened that night is that I lost my best friend," he said, his voice low and unsteady. "And I've

The Plot Thickens

never had another. Believe it or not, I've spent thirty years trying to forget. Just... leave it alone."

Without waiting for a reply, he let the heavy door swing shut behind him. Ellie stood there for a moment, the air heavy with the smell of smoke and the damp evening chill. She hugged her arms around herself, but it didn't stave off the hollow feeling Jack's words had left. Was she meddling in something she should leave alone?

As she reached for the door, her gaze landed on Harold, leaning against the wall with a cigarette nearly burnt to the end. He must have been listening from the shadows, the faint glow of his cigarette tracing the tight line of his mouth and the hard glint in his eye. He didn't look away, and his voice came in a low murmur as he approached.

"You heard him, little girl," he said, his tone even, with an edge that cut through the evening's quiet. "Leave it alone."

"So you can keep spinning your fairy tales?" she said, surprised by her own sharpness. "Selling your horrible-tasting pints to go with them?"

A ripple of laughter ran through the onlookers, and someone slurred, "She got you there, Harold! Tastes like old boots, it does!"

Harold's jaw clenched, his face twisting with a flash of anger. For a moment, Ellie felt a stab of unease—his stare was far darker than she'd expected, and it reminded her of the fury she'd braced herself to see in Jack. She didn't have a chance to say anything before his mother popped her head out of a side window, her black shawl dangling towards cobbles.

"Harold, it's almost time," Tilly called. "Mrs Diva has given us the five-minute warning."

"Go on, Harold," the same drunk taunted. "Mummy's calling!"

Harold's composure snapped, and he lunged towards the source of the taunt—a grinning man who took an unsteady step back, hands up, already laughing.

"I was only joking, mate!"

But Harold's glare didn't waver. "You're barred. Sling your hook."

The man held his hands higher and slunk off into the night, muttering as Harold stormed back inside. Ellie followed, slipping in behind him.

Scanning the room, she noticed her gran and George had left the bar and were now seated at her and Oliver's table. Her brother was nowhere to be seen, and Sylvia flitted between tables, chatting like she was at any other social gathering, seemingly knowing everyone.

Then, Ellie caught sight of Cassie striding straight at her, a glowing pint clenched in her tight fist.

Cassie's glare was cold as ice, and though Ellie had never had a drink thrown at her, she knew exactly what was coming. Cassie stopped inches away, raising the pint with a deliberate slowness.

Ellie barely had time to flinch before her gran stepped between them, calm and resolute. The icy splash of beer hit Maggie squarely, soaking her cardigan. She blinked but didn't budge an inch.

The crowd gasped, a wave of muttering spreading through the room as Ellie stared at the mess of beer dripping from Maggie's sleeves. A surprised smile tugged at her gran's lips as she gasped for breath.

"Leave it, Cass!" Jack warned as he pulled her back, though the grip on her shoulder barely seemed enough to contain her. "She's not worth it."

Cassie glared at Ellie over Maggie's shoulder, a savage glint in her eye.

"Stay away from my man!"

Ellie's cheeks flushed as the words settled over the crowd, turning their murmurs to curious stares. She didn't have to look around to know what they were thinking. Cassie's emphasis on 'my man' left little to question—somehow, Cassie thought Ellie had eyes for Jack.

"You all came for a show, didn't you?" Maggie called, her voice booming around the pub like she was back in a classroom. "Well, there you go. Nothing more to see, unless you all want detention."

A few people laughed as George rose and gestured for Maggie to follow him. To Ellie's surprise, he nodded for her to come too, and she wasn't going to miss the opportunity to talk to him. She'd wanted to get him alone, and though this wasn't how she'd imagined it, it was better than nothing.

"Come on, let's get you cleaned up," he said, offering

her an awkward smile. "You can use the gents since the ladies' bathroom is still out of order."

Feeling the heat of curious and disgusted stares as she crossed the pub, Ellie straightened her shoulders and followed her gran and George. Her face grew even hotter when she caught sight of Daniel watching her from his table with his nan, who was scowling more than usual.

He raised his eyebrows, mouthing, "You alright?"

She gave a quick nod and looked away, though his puzzled frown lingered in her mind as she followed George into the bathroom, her thoughts spinning.

Meanwhile, Jack and Cassie had returned to playing pool like nothing had happened.

George held the door as Maggie ducked into a cubicle, casting Ellie a brief, reassuring smile. Ellie shrugged off her jacket, twisting the sleeves to wring out any lingering dampness, and stepped under the hand dryer, letting the warm air blast against her jumper.

"You're not mixed up with those two, are you?" George asked, raising an eyebrow.

Ellie's cheeks burned. "No, not the way it probably looked. I... I honestly don't know what's going on with them. But Cassie seems to have taken a dislike to my very existence. I think..." She hesitated, almost embarrassed. "I think she actually believes there's something between me and Jack."

George snorted softly. "Sounds like Cassandra, alright. Easily the worst student I ever had. They were a couple back then, always circling trouble. Knew they'd end up as wasters." He shook his head, regret shadowing his expression. "She dragged him down, you know. Jack's dad was that Campbell chap—the photographer who took those famous riot pictures. Jack was proud of that and wanted to follow in his footsteps. But then she came along and... well, she poisoned the waters. He could've been something."

Ellie was startled by George's frankness, but before she could respond, he nodded towards the sinks, his gaze sharpening.

"Look under that panel," he instructed, "below the sinks."

Ellie crouched, uncertain of what she'd find. Lifting the panel, she uncovered a small set-up—a smoke machine wired to thin pipes snaking into the floorboards, with a few bottles of chemicals stacked in the shadows.

"The cold spots."

George nodded. "Same trick as last time. Dr Christina Marsh figured it out early on."

"She never published her findings."

"She had her reasons."

Ellie took in the rig, recognising the plastic-chemical scent she'd noticed in the cellar earlier. It now reminded her of childhood school discos, and she understood why. A simple smoke machine. A concrete explanation and George had just handed it to her.

"Why are you showing me this?" she asked.

"Because Harold's never changed. Greedy as ever," George replied, meeting her gaze in the cracked mirror above the sink. She caught a flicker of something—almost a weary understanding—in his expression.

"Why did you come tonight?"

He looked away. "Meeting someone."

Before Ellie could ask who, Harold's voice crackled over a microphone from the main room, announcing Carolyn Swan with all the grandiosity of a ringleader. George opened the door a crack, letting the noise flood in.

"You'd best get back out there," he said.

Ellie glanced towards the cubicle where her gran was still dabbing her cardigan with toilet roll, then back to George.

"I'd rather stay here."

George sighed, letting the door swing shut again. "You don't trust me, do you?" Her silence was answer enough. "Mags filled me in on your theories. You've built quite the case against me."

"That wasn't my intention. Your notes—"

"The ones you stole?" he interrupted. But the outburst Ellie expected didn't come. He shrugged, almost defeated. "Yes, they do look rather incriminating, don't they? I should've shredded them, but I've had a lot on my mind, what with Meredith's condition…"

Ellie softened, catching a flicker of sadness on his face. "I am sorry to hear about what happened to her."

"Yes," he replied, looking away. "Me too."

She took a steadying breath. She couldn't miss this

The Plot Thickens

chance to press him, and one detail from his notes had stuck in her mind, nagging at her.

"George, why did you buy that antique camera from Tim Baker?"

"Did I fake the photographs, you mean?" He shook his head. "No. And neither did Meredith. I bought it out of... love for her."

"What does that mean?"

"It doesn't matter. Someone broke into our home and stole the camera before we had the chance to use it. And I hear it turned up in your shop and the same happened again." He held up a hand, his eyes serious. "Please, Ellie. Don't get more involved in this than you need to."

With that, he pushed open the door, gesturing for her to step through. Ellie hesitated, glancing back at her gran, who was emerging from the cubicle, muttering about the uselessness of toilet roll. Maggie nodded towards the door.

"I'll be right out behind you. Go on, I'll be alright, Ellie. I've known the man longer than you've been alive."

It wasn't enough for Ellie, but it would have to be. She didn't want another terse exchange with her gran. Reluctantly, she walked through the door, surprised when George planted a heavy hand on her shoulder as she passed.

"Please," he urged, his nails digging through her jumper. "Be careful."

Chapter 12
Is Anyone There?

Back in the crowded pub, Ellie's eyes adjusted to the dim lighting, catching sight of her mother bathed in a spotlight near the bathroom door across the room. Carolyn stood frozen, her sequinned costume glittering as she took in the scene. She looked dumbfounded.

Their abandoned table had been claimed, so Ellie leaned against the bar, gripping the brass edge as a strange apprehension crept over her. Jack and Harold had warned her away from the investigation, and Cassie's drink had only strengthened that message. But George's sombre words lingered most, his quiet plea echoing in her mind.

"Ladies and gents," Harold's voice crackled through the speakers, though Ellie couldn't see him. "It seems our special guest is feeling a bit of first-night jitters on this debut evening of her psychic abilities—which, I'm told, she's had since birth. So, why don't we give her a warm round of applause?"

A smattering of hesitant applause rippled through the crowd. For her mother's sake, Ellie clapped a bit more enthusiastically, prompting a few others nearby to join in.

"That's more like it!" Harold boomed. "So, please, raise your Ghost Ale high for the one and only... Meadowfield's very own *Psychic Swan!*"

The applause was all Carolyn needed to come alive. She hunched her shoulders, adopting a solemn expression, and began to move with slow, exaggerated steps, weighed down by the world's burdens.

Ellie squinted into the spotlight and noticed Tilly standing nearby, holding a giant torch taped to a stick. Tilly tracked Carolyn with the beam, casting a focused glow that caught every glimmer of her sequined dress. She followed her with surprising precision, never losing her mark, even as Carolyn wove through the longest route possible, soaking up attention from each person who reached out a hand.

The Psychic Swan finally arrived at the Ouija board set up in the far corner of the room. The dark wooden beams supporting the old building converged at a point in the flaky white plaster walls, forming a twisted, throne-like backdrop behind the stool. Ellie glanced back at Tilly, wondering if that clever staging was her handiwork as well. Aside from Carolyn's initial blank stare when the spotlight hit her, everything else seemed meticulously arranged, as if guided by a seasoned eye.

For once, Ellie had to admit her mother was acting rather well.

Carolyn greeted the board with a bow as if acknowledging an old, familiar friend. Her fingers brushed over its surface, and the wall-mounted lights dimmed to a soft glow. Ellie flinched as the lightbulb closest to her head popped and shattered, followed by another near the pool table. More bulbs burst behind the bar, triggering a mix of choked gasps and nervous laughter from the expectant crowd.

"Cheap tricks," Maggie muttered as she joined Ellie's side, still smelling faintly of beer. "I'm not sure I want to be here for this charade. I can't believe people are falling for it."

"With any luck, they won't," Ellie reassured her. "It won't take much for the wheels to fall off. Tonight could be the night people stop believing this place is actually haunted."

"If anyone's bound to mess this up, your mother's the perfect casting choice."

At that moment, the Psychic Swan sprang to her feet, the squeak of Carolyn's chair slicing through the room. Silence settled as she waited, her head lowered, savouring the attention.

"Please, do not be afraid," she said, forcing her voice

down a few notes, adopting a vague European lilt. "We gather tonight on this sacred ground to pierce the veil between worlds, to seek answers from beyond the grave—truths about what happened in this very pub." She lifted her gaze and swept her eyes across the room, lowering her voice to a hoarse whisper. "Tonight, Meadowlings, we shall contact the other side to uncover what we've all been wondering for thirty years... did John Partridge really kill Tim Baker?"

Genuine gasps rose all around the pub, and Ellie was surprised by how many people were captivated by her mother's performance.

"This is worse than I thought," Maggie muttered.

"I had a chance to talk her out of it earlier," Ellie admitted.

"You think it would have made any difference?"

Carolyn cleared her throat, raising her hands for quiet. "Please, settle down. Yes, it's going to be quite the evening. But first, we must enter the spirit world gently, so I'll start by contacting some of your dear relatives." She swept her hand across the crowd, and Ellie could see people fidgeting in anticipation. "I have someone. A woman... with pink glasses. A... Ada... Ada... *Adaline?*"

"That's my gran!" a woman shouted, her hands clasped over her mouth. "Oh my days, that's *my* gran!"

Maggie groaned, and Ellie squirmed as phones appeared all around, recording Carolyn's performance. With a practised solemnity, Carolyn moved closer to the woman.

The Plot Thickens

"Hello, my child." She laid both hands on the woman's head, accidentally knocking her in the eye with a swinging necklace. "Your name is... Karen?" The woman nodded, transfixed. "Your gran loved gardening, didn't she? And she adored sitting in that chair by her shed... her... *pink* shed."

"It *was* pink!" the woman cried, drawing gasps from the crowd. "How did you know that?"

Carolyn waved a hand, as if it were all beyond explanation. "She loved cats, reading Mills and Boon, and even entered a competition to win a family holiday to Butlins in 2019."

"Oh, I don't know about that last bit..."

"I assure you, she did," Carolyn said quickly. "She shared the po—" She choked out a cough, and Ellie could hear the rest of sentence as 'the post on Facebook', but her mother recovered quickly. "She shared the *thought* with me just now... Hang on!" She gave Karen's head a dramatic shake. "That's it—she meant she would have *wanted* to take you to Butlins, in Skegness, but sadly, she passed on before she could make it happen. She also wants you to know she's doing fine."

The woman blinked, stunned, nodding as though she couldn't process the news, and a ripple of applause spread through the room. Ellie couldn't tell if Carolyn was pulling it off or if the audience was too mesmerised to question her.

"I'm getting a Derick Simms," Carolyn called, scanning the room. "He attended St Augustine's School from 1964 to 1969 and supported Marlborough football team..."

"That's my husband!"

The readings went on, growing so uncannily accurate that Ellie noticed a few others starting to wear the same sceptical expression as her gran. When one man finally challenged Carolyn, demanding to know where she got her information, there was a sudden crack as half a dozen more bulbs burst, and the remaining lights faded before plunging the pub into near-total darkness. Nervous laughter and hushed gasps rippled through the crowd.

"*Meadowlings!*" The Psychic Swan's voice rose above the noise. "It is time to contact the other side. Will we talk to Tim? Will we contact John?" The pub fell silent, Carolyn's words lingering ominously in the air. Her voice rose, theatrical and commanding. "To find out, I need willing volunteers. Please, don't be scared... step this way..."

A shudder of anticipation rippled through the crowd, and excited chatter broke out. But when no one moved forward, an uneasy silence took hold.

"Ellie..." Maggie's warning tone barely registered.

Ellie left the bar and stepped towards the Ouija board. She found herself at the table, sitting across from Cassie, who avoided her gaze. Others joined them, but Carolyn only needed six. Ellie didn't know what she was doing but she needed to see it all up close. Out of the

The Plot Thickens

corner of her eye, she noticed Jack perched on a stool behind the camera, more interested in finishing his pint.

As the volunteers placed their fingers on the planchette, the table began to shake, startling the crowd. Gasps erupted as drinks rattled and the Ouija board trembled beneath their hands. Carolyn's eyes widened like she couldn't believe it was working, while Ellie's scepticism grew with each staged tremor.

Without hesitation, Ellie reached down and yanked back the tablecloth, narrowing her eyes at exactly what she'd suspected—her mother's knees banging hard against the underside of the table. The shaking stopped.

A hard silence filled the room as Carolyn, unfazed, folded her hands serenely in her lap, her smile steady. But before the tension could dissipate, an eerie groan echoed through the pub, sending a fresh wave of murmurs through the crowd.

Ellie leaned across the table, grabbing her mother's wrist. Her fingers brushed against something cold and metallic—a small remote control taped to her mother's skin. Carolyn yanked her hand back, shooting Ellie a venomous look.

"Stop. It. Now. Eleanor," Carolyn muttered through gritted teeth, her accent slipping.

"What was that?" Cassie asked, her eyes widening.

"*Ohhhhhh*," Carolyn groaned dramatically, rolling her head back as if overcome. "The spirits... I can *feel* them..."

Ellie's heart pounded, anger simmering. Once Carolyn's theatrics subsided, she regained her composure.

"Are there any spirits who wish to communicate?" Carolyn called, her hands hovering above the board, palms outstretched. "Now is your time..."

The planchette jerked, and the room fell silent as everyone held their breath. It began to move in a deliberate circle, and Ellie could feel her mother's subtle pressure guiding it. Nobody else seemed to notice.

Slowly, it spelled out: *T... I... M... B... A... K... E... R.*

Ellie clenched her jaw as Carolyn's lips curled into a smug smile. The crowd buzzed with whispers, the onlookers exchanging nervous glances.

Then, out of the corner of her eye, Ellie spotted movement. Glancing up, she saw DS Angela Cookson making her way through the crowd.

"Attention on the board!" Carolyn snapped, and Ellie turned back.

"Yeah, have some respect for the dead," Cassie sneered, seizing the moment to take another jab at Ellie. "*Rude.*"

Ellie took a deep breath, refusing to rise to the bait, and returned her focus to the planchette as it began to move again, slower this time.

L... U... K...

Her heart sank, a cold knot twisting in her stomach. She pulled her fingers away. But the planchette continued without her, spelling out: *L-U-K-E.*

The Plot Thickens

"We mustn't break the chain," Carolyn insisted. "The spirits need us to stay connected!"

But Ellie was done playing along.

"Who did that?" she demanded, her voice cracking.

"The spirits, dear. You must open yourself up to—"

"*No*. This... isn't funny." Ellie's hands curled into balls at her sides, her voice trembling. "It's not—"

Without warning, the pub plunged into darkness again. Lightbulbs shattered, popping in rapid succession, their echoes reverberating through the room. This time, no lights flickered back on to break the gloom.

"What's going on?" Carolyn muttered, her accent vanishing.

The room dissolved into chaos. Chairs scraped and tables knocked over, smashing pints against the floor as people stumbled in the dark.

"Turn them back on," Ellie demanded.

"It wasn't me."

"I saw the remote, Mother."

"Eleanor, it was not *me*. I swear."

Something in her mother's voice sounded almost frightened, and Ellie hesitated. She squinted into the darkness, trying to make sense of the shifting shadows as phones shone, their flashes casting brief, erratic beams around the room.

"Spelling out Luke's name was a low blow."

"That wasn't me either," Carolyn replied, her voice subdued. "But you won't believe me, will you?"

"I... I need to talk to Harold," she said, desperate to

step away from the board. "I need to understand why he thought this was a good idea."

"Maybe he's cut the lights for some big surprise? You know he loves putting on a—"

But then a man's voice cried out, followed by the unmistakable sound of someone tumbling. Ellie's heart leapt into her throat as the room fell into an ominous hush.

Moments later, a woman screamed, "He's *fallen!*"

Ellie spun around, her pulse pounding as she pushed through the crowd, thickest near the cellar stairs. People parted reluctantly, vying to see what had happened. She reached the top of the stairs, peering down. Pulling out her phone, she turned on the flashlight and aimed it into the darkness.

George Fenton lay crumpled at the bottom of the stairs. Shouts erupted around her as people surged forward, some moving closer for a better look, others retreating in shock. A man darted down, shouting that he knew first aid. Ellie was about to follow when a firm hand grasped her shoulder. She turned to see DS Angela Cookson, her expression grim.

"Stay where I can see you," Angela commanded, her voice leaving no room for argument. "Harold, lock those doors! Nobody leaves." The detective sergeant's voice cut through the noise. Pulling Ellie aside, she said, "I called George tonight to question him about the notes you found." Her eyes swept the room with a sharp, wary stare. "George said he'd uncovered some evidence—

something that might explain all this. He asked me to meet him here."

Staring down at George as the man checked for a pulse, Ellie said, "Looks like someone else got there first." She closed her eyes, biting back tears. "Oh, Mr Fenton, *you* should have been more careful."

Chapter 13
Back From the Dead

Wedged into the corner beside the droning slot machine, Ellie rocked on a stool with a wobbly, too-short leg. Eyes closed, she tried to shut out the maddening din of the pub.

As per Angela's orders, no one had been allowed to leave, and the conversation had circled back to the same two questions: had George fallen, or had he been pushed? This time, unlike with Tim Baker, George had been alive—just barely—when the ambulance sped away with its siren wailing.

Harold hadn't budged from behind the bar, as still as stone, his gaze fixed in a thousand-yard stare. Tilly's spotlight hadn't reappeared since the blackout, and Ellie now knew for certain that Harold had been pumping dry ice into the cellar to create those mysterious cold spots.

A Ghost Watch Club and an antique camera connected Tim and George, and Ellie longed for her backpack so she could jot her thoughts down. The pub's garbled din—the oppressive chatter like being submerged in a fishbowl—made it impossible to think. She opened her eyes to the glare of the ceiling lights and scanned the room again. The candles had all burned out. By the pool table, Cassie and Jack sat close together.

From the corner of her eye, Ellie spotted Maggie hurrying back into the pub through the side door, clutching a bag, imitating steam and the sharp tang of salt and vinegar.

"Help yourselves, everyone," she announced, unwrapping several large portions of chips for eager hands to grab. "It's just chips, mind you. I'm not made of money, but I couldn't bear to see you all going hungry."

A few villagers murmured their thanks, subdued but sincere. Maggie lingered for a moment, tearing off a small portion wrapped in a square of chippy paper before finding Ellie hiding next to the slot machine. She set the chips on their table and gestured for Ellie to dig in. She didn't hesitate, grabbing a handful of thick-cut chips, still soggy from the fryer.

"How did you get in and out?" Ellie asked.

"PC Walsh let me sneak out the side door," Maggie said, lowering her voice. "I taught his father at school, and I suppose that still counts for something around here. Besides, we know I didn't push George. Neither did you. Nor anyone on this side of the room, for that matter."

"People have been moving around all night," Ellie

The Plot Thickens

pointed out, her eyes following Angela as she called Cassie and Jack over from the pool table. "And you just slipped in and out during a police lockdown. There's no guarantee the pusher is still here. And if they are, they've made a big mistake by pushing the prime suspect out of the picture."

Maggie's expression tightened. "I *knew* George wasn't behind this," she murmured, almost to herself. Reaching across the table, she clasped Ellie's hand with fingers still warm and salty from the chips. "I'm done burying my head in the sand. It's time to face the truth—whatever that turns out to be. For George's sake. And Tim's. And all of ours, for that matter. There's no knowing what will happen next."

"Sometimes doing the painful thing is the only way through. That's what you told me when you invited Angela to dinner." She squeezed Maggie's hand before letting go. "Any news on George's condition?"

"Finn says he's still touch-and-go. If there are spirits, I hope they're helping him tonight." Maggie sighed, glancing up at the ceiling. "Listen to me—I sound like Meredith. That poor couple. Why George? And why now?"

Ellie leaned in, lowering her voice. "He told me he was here to meet someone. Angela said he came to show her evidence—something that could end all of this." She held Maggie's gaze as she popped another chip into her mouth. "Did he tell you anything about that?"

Maggie shook her head. "He mentioned finding

something in his attic but wouldn't say what. I... I don't think he trusts me anymore." Tears threatened to spill as she looked at Ellie. "When I dried myself off in the bathroom, he said he'd follow me out, but he never did. He kept checking his watch like he was waiting for someone."

Ellie craned her neck towards the bathrooms, flanking the open cellar door. Police officers rushed around the taped-off scene. It wouldn't have been too difficult to turn off the lights and shove George down the stairs.

"Maybe George left the bathroom when it went dark?" Ellie mused aloud. "That would mean someone had to know he was in there." After a moment, she added, "The whole pub watched us walk there after Cassie threw that drink."

"But to know he was still in there after all that time while the séance was going on? What if he arranged to meet whoever he thought the evidence incriminated in there? To give them a chance to explain before going to the police?" Maggie frowned thoughtfully. "George would want to be sure before accusing anyone. Too fastidious for his own good."

Just then, Oliver slid back into his old seat.

"Where'd the chips come from?"

"Gran went on a covert chippy run," Ellie said.

"Don't tell your mother," Maggie warned, dabbing at the tears in her eyes as she pushed the chips towards Oliver. "I've lost my appetite."

The Plot Thickens

"I'll stay here and eat your chips, but it's my mother who wants you. She's waiting by the pool table."

"Why?" Maggie asked.

Mumbling through a mouthful of chips, Oliver replied, "I'm just the messenger. She's been talking to some old woman. Go and find out."

Exchanging glances, Maggie and Ellie wound their way through the pub, navigating crowded tables filled with the restless remnants of the party. They found Angela pacing back and forth by the pool table, her face tight with frustration. Nearby, Jack and Cassie lined up a new game, their cues poised but their focus elsewhere.

Angela spotted them approaching, her eyes narrowing as she jabbed an accusatory finger in their direction.

"You told me she was dead," the detective sergeant hissed, her voice sharp and low. "Earlier tonight, in your statement—you said Doctor Christina Marsh was dead."

"She *is*," Ellie said firmly. "She died in 1999. I read the obituary myself."

Before Angela could respond, an elderly woman rose slowly from a nearby chair. Her silver hair swept into a low, loose bun, shimmered in the light. She gripped a cane adorned with a pearl on its head. When she straightened, her commanding presence silenced the surrounding chatter.

The woman's milky eyes, unfocused and distant, drifted in her direction. Ellie recognised them—and the cane. This woman had followed George into the pub earlier, and she'd seen that pearl-topped cane before. It had been propped in George Fenton's hallway, where Sylvia had knocked it over earlier that day.

The woman's gaze seemed to pass through Ellie as she spoke in a low, deliberate tone.

"*I* am Christina Marsh," she said, her words slicing through the pub like a knife, "and reports of my death have been greatly exaggerated."

The revelation that Dr Christina Marsh had updated her status from 'deceased' to 'very much alive' barely stirred the atmosphere in the pub. Ellie and her gran were so shaken by the news that chairs were offered to them on their reactions alone.

Angela shared their shock, but only the detective sergeant seemed to recognise—or care—who the woman was.

For all the Meadowlings' fascination with ghosts, it appeared Ellie was one of the few who had looked into how they had arrived at this moment. Yet, as she stared into Christina Marsh's clouded eyes—her pupils like faint headlights swallowed by fog—Ellie realised she knew nothing at all.

When Angela and her officers began sending away those already interviewed, the pub emptied as swiftly as water draining from a bath. For Ellie, it felt as if the ground had been yanked from beneath her feet. And

The Plot Thickens

there sat Dr Christina Marsh with a gritted jaw, composed and unmoved, ignoring the commotion around her as though it were beneath her to notice.

"*How* are you here?" Ellie forced out, breaking the suffocating silence. "I don't understand."

"I walked from where I've been staying," Christina replied evenly.

Maggie huffed. "She means, how did you *fake* your death?"

Christina chuckled, the sound humourless. "You're speaking as if that was my plan," she said, her knuckles whitening as her bony fingers tightened around the cane. "The assumption of my death came from a simple misunderstanding."

Angela returned after herding the last of those she deemed innocent enough to leave. Beside her, PC Walsh fumbled to find a fresh page in his notepad.

"You're aware it's an arrestable offence to fake your death?" Angela said, wasting no time. "I could arrest you for fraud."

"Then arrest me," Christina replied, unwavering. "But as I just said, *I* did not fake my death."

Ellie, still grappling with the shock of the doctor's presence, found herself strangely grateful to be seated before her first flesh-and-blood ghost. Her research into Dr Christina Marsh had reached a frustrating dead end, yet here she was—a living key to the mysteries of 1994. There was so much the woman might know, but instead of rushing into confrontation, Ellie decided to take a more measured approach.

"Your obituary claimed you hadn't been seen for five years," Ellie said, steadying her voice as she tried to regain her composure. "That would mean the last time anyone saw you was around the time of Tim Baker's death."

"Hmm," Christina murmured with a slow nod. "I suppose it would."

"But if you didn't fake your death, how did the rumour start?" Ellie pressed.

"How do most delicious rumours begin?" Christina's thin lips curved into a dry smile. "At a party, of course—or so I was told." She cleared her throat, her brows furrowing as she sifted through decades of memories. "The story goes that an old university acquaintance mentioned at a party she hadn't seen me in years—a concern significant enough to share publicly but not pressing enough to prompt her to check on me. Someone else suggested I might have died, and that caught the ear of a journalist who'd been rather critical of my attempts to debunk The Enfield Hauntings in the late '70s. He acquired my home telephone number and called to ask if the rumour was true."

"And you told him you were dead?" Angela asked, shaking her head.

"In a manner of speaking, yes. Though in other ways, my answering the phone was just a well-timed coincidence." Christina's smile curled higher. "You see, I was already retired from public life, preoccupied with my watercolour paintings, when the phone rang. The young man on the other end asked if the 'paranormal-sceptic' Dr Christina Marsh still lived there. I barked back, 'No, and she won't be coming back.' That was enough, I suppose. The rumour must have made the rounds until someone decided to make it official in print."

"But didn't you notice that people thought you were dead?" Maggie asked, her expression incredulous. "Nobody came to check on you?"

"Do you make a habit of visiting old friends after hearing they've passed on?" Christina's icy gaze flicked towards the corner where the séance had fallen apart. "Aside from my landline, I'd long since discarded anything that beeped. Months later, I spotted my obituary in an industry magazine while catching up on back issues."

"And you didn't think to set the record straight?" Angela asked, as PC Walsh scribbled furiously beside her, struggling to keep up. "That's when most people would announce they were alive—not twenty-five years later."

"Detective Sergeant," Christina said, tilting her head slightly as her sharp stare snapped in Angela's direction, "do I strike you as 'most people?' Truthfully, the whole thing amused me, and I needed the laugh. My life at that time had been so devoid of joy, so to hear it was 'over' brought me such relief. Dr Christina Marsh was ready to disappear, and if people wanted to believe I was dead, so be it—let them. Grief can be so indulgent, as is all this." She lifted her cane, sweeping it around the room as if taking aim at everyone still lingering. "Meadowfield never fails to prove me right."

"About what?" Ellie asked.

"That, given the right circumstances, reasonable people will believe just about anything." She thudded her cane against the floor. "Before I died, I was exhausted—of the attention, the scrutiny, constantly defending reason and sense." She inhaled a steadying breath. "Knowing I had a chance at a fresh start, I bought a cottage on a quiet lane in Castle Combe where I was born, not too far from here. I stopped dying my hair and I didn't recognise myself, so nobody else stood a chance. I started going by 'Tina' for those who cared enough to ask my name."

"This is absurd," Angela muttered.

"Detective Sergeant, there comes an age when women can become invisible, whether they like it or not." Her smile returned, softer now. "Becoming invisible was when my life truly began. For a time, it was sweet. Christina had spent too many years being far too serious for her own good. But Tina—Tina took the time to sit still and paint birds in her garden. She sketched flowers as the seasons turned, and she sipped tea to savour the taste in the afternoon, not to chase a caffeine rush."

Ellie could almost hear the birdsong calling to some calm and distant place, but the sharp clack of billiard

The Plot Thickens

balls against a pool table yanked her back to Meadowfield. This was no peaceful garden—this was a pub, yet again at the centre of a crime scene.

"Why leave paradise now?" Ellie pressed.

"Look at my eyes. Look at my hands." Christina lifted her gnarled fingers from the cane, her swollen knuckles a clear sign of arthritis. "I lost the ability to hold a brush long before I stopped seeing the canvas. I used to wish it had been the other way around—so I wouldn't have to witness those final, clumsy attempts to capture beauty on the page. I retreated from life, and then life retreated from me."

Maggie sighed, her expression softening at the story. "But you must realise how strange the timing of your return looks?"

"I never planned to return," Christina said, exhaling deeply as she lowered her head. "But when George telephoned and told me about what had been sprayed on the wall of the bookshop... I knew I couldn't stay hidden any longer. Old curiosities got the better of me."

"George *knew* you weren't dead?" Maggie asked, her voice tinged with disappointment.

"I have always respected George for his pragmatic and logical approach to the so-called phenomena that crop up around this village—especially considering his wife's... excitable disposition." She stopped mid-sentence, hearing her harshness towards a woman lying unresponsive in a hospital bed. She cleared her throat. "George knew the hauntings were nothing more than local chancers stirring up trouble for fame and glory. But the revival of that old rumour about Meredith worried him—just as tonight did."

"You're saying he knew something would happen?" PC Walsh asked, pen poised over his notepad.

"Not factually, no," Christina said. "But he had good reason to be suspicious. With so many of the same elements reappearing thirty years later, his hypothesis proved correct. If only he'd foreseen that he'd be the one to suffer at the hands of this rogue element."

Angela rubbed at her temples, her patience stretched thin. "And do you know who this 'rogue element' is?"

"If I did, I would have told you," Christina replied flatly. "Before the night of the original séance, I made no secret of my disapproval of the club's direction. I joined the Ghost Watch to disprove the outlandish claims splashed across the newspapers. I wanted to restore reason. Instead, I watched hysteria take over, and there was little I could do to stop it. And then... I started receiving threats."

"Threats?" Angela interrupted, her tone sharp. "There was no mention of threats in your original statement back in '94."

"Because they stopped the night Tim Barker died, and I didn't think they were relevant," Christina said without hesitation. "I had collected my evidence and was ready to publish my findings when I had a change of heart. Someone took exception to my refusal to share my conclusions publicly, and they weren't shy about letting

The Plot Thickens

me know. Letters appeared through my letterbox, under my car wiper, crumpled in my shopping bags—all making the same accusation." She drew a long, steadying breath. "According to them, the only reason I kept my findings private was because I'd disproved my own theory. That I'd proven the existence of ghosts but refused to admit it for fear of being called a hypocrite."

She chuckled dryly, but the laughter broke into a rattling cough. PC Walsh fetched her a glass of water, which she took with a nod. After a deliberate pause, she recomposed herself, ignoring Angela's impatient foot-tapping.

"I care about the truth," Christina continued, setting the glass down. "If I'd disproved my theory, I would have happily gone on record as the first person to scientifically prove the existence of a contactable afterlife. Who wouldn't? I'd have collected my flowers, accepted my awards, written a book, and retired all the same. Perhaps I wouldn't have had time for painting, but... that's not what I concluded."

"We'll get to that," Angela said, grabbing the notes from PC Walsh. She scanned the page, squinting at his hasty scribbles. "I'm more interested in how long you've been in Meadowfield."

"George sent a taxi for me a few days ago. I told him I'd take the bus, but he insisted. He's a good man, he..."

Christina's voice trailed off as she tapped her cane around under her chair until it bumped against a black leather bag. With some effort, she slid it out and positioned it between her feet. Reaching inside, she pulled out a padded envelope.

"...George asked me to keep this in my bag tonight," she said, holding up the manila envelope. "At the time, I didn't think much of it, but given how things have unfolded, it may be important."

As Christina extended the envelope, Maggie moved to take it, but Angela was quicker. She snatched it and handed it off to PC Walsh without hesitation.

"What is it?" Ellie asked. "Is this what George found in the attic?"

"Perhaps." Christina tilted her head in thought. "That would explain the rummaging above the guest bedroom that woke me up earlier, just before I heard him shouting at someone at the door. And then..." She paused, pointing her cane in Maggie's direction. "I heard your voice."

Ellie realised Christina was confirming that George had been in the attic when she and Sylvia arrived. No wonder he hadn't heard their calls.

Ellie gulped. "What's inside?"

"He didn't say, but it felt fragile to me."

"This must be the evidence George was pushed for," Maggie murmured, her fingertips pressed against her mouth. "Oh, George..."

"We don't know he was pushed," Angela said, though her tone lacked conviction. She opened the envelope and peered inside but gave no indication of its contents. "Thank you. I'll have this sent in for further analysis. But before that, I still have more questions for you."

"Could they wait until morning?" Christina asked, leaning more heavily on her cane. "I can assure you, Detective Sergeant, that I did not push my dear friend down the stairs. And I've already stayed longer than I intended. I spent a lot of time in this pub, and though I cannot see it, it feels as it always did."

At that moment, Daniel stepped forward from where he'd been quietly watching everything unfold beside his nan. He positioned himself behind Ellie's chair, his hands gripping the backrest for support. The tips of his fingers lightly brushed her shoulder. So much had happened since he'd arrived—barely saying two words to her—that she'd almost forgotten he was there. His presence now felt all the more reassuring. When she leaned into his touch, expecting him to flinch, he surprised her by creeping his fingers closer, giving her shoulder a gentle squeeze.

"DS Cookson," Daniel said, moving his hand away to gesture towards his nan. Ellie missed the brief contact, wishing he'd used the other hand. "This lady was exactly where she is now—"

"Ah, yes!" Christina's expression brightened, and she wagged a finger in his direction. "You're the sweet gentleman who came to check on me when the light vanished."

"*And* he helped you out of the taxi," Daniel's nan added, chiming in with gusto. "He's a schoolteacher, you know—my grandson is no liar. He left my side like a whippet and stayed with the lady until the lights came back on. No doubt shielding her from the stampede of animals charging around this place at the first sign of a power cut. None of you would have survived The Blitz." With that, she rose to her feet, drained her gin and tonic in one decisive gulp, and adjusted her scarf. "I've been questioned twice now. I'm vouching for Daniel, and he's vouching for the blind lady."

"Ma'am," PC Walsh interjected in a low voice, "it's unlikely Dr Marsh ran across the room to push a man down the stairs, given her cane."

"Please, don't call me that." Christina pushed herself upright, shrugging off Daniel's offer of help. Raising her chin in Angela's direction, she said, "Now, I shall bid you good evening, Detective Sergeant, and I expect you'll be paying a visit tomorrow. I believe there's nothing more to be said tonight, other than this: George is a strong man, and when he makes it through," she paused, scanning the room with that foggy stare, "he'll tell us exactly what happened."

Reaching the door Daniel was already holding open, Christina brushed past him without acknowledgement. Silence settled over the pub as Christina shuffled out, her words hanging heavy like a threat. Daniel raised a hand in Ellie's direction, but the door swung shut before she could return the gesture.

She sat frozen, her focus now locked on the room, scanning the faces of those who'd been present at both

The Plot Thickens

events. Cassie and Jack were setting up another game of pool, their expressions blank as though they hadn't been listening to any of it. At the bar, Harold stood stock-still, his shoulders rigid, his blank stare somewhere far away. Behind him, his mother hovered in the shadow of the doorway, drowning in her black shawl, her eyes trained on the police interview as though she could hear every word. The spotlight caught on a ring as Tilly's fingers clenched around Harold's shoulder. Harold's stiff posture contrasted with how Ellie had felt under Daniel's touch—a tension that seemed impossible to ignore.

With the doctor gone and her gran slouched deep in her chair—checked out and long since ready for bed—Ellie found she wasn't quite ready to leave. After the lightbulb-popping display from Harold and Tilly, and the stray pint Cassie had lobbed across the room, she doubted straight answers would surface tonight. But she couldn't walk out without finding something.

When Angela and Finn pulled Tilly aside for questioning, Ellie left her gran and approached the bar. Harold had stopped staring and instead busied himself with tidying up. Like her gran, he moved with little purpose, rearranging bottles and wiping down a spotless counter.

"They've told me I can't serve anyone," Harold

muttered without looking at her. His voice had lost its usual bravado, replaced with something quieter. "Bugger off, alright?"

"I'd love to," Ellie replied, undeterred, "right after you tell me where you were when the lights went out."

"Smoking," he said quickly, almost too quickly.

"You were smoking earlier."

"Never heard of chain-smoking?" he snapped, lining up the gin bottles. "I don't have to tell you anything."

Ellie hadn't expected Harold to be easy to talk to, not after their first meeting. But stripped of his performative confidence, he looked more like a scared boy trapped in a situation he couldn't control.

"Harold, you must know how this looks," Ellie said, slipping onto the stool she'd sat on during her first visit. "Two men were pushed down *your* cellar stairs, and here you are, selling glowing drinks."

"It's not a crime to want your business to succeed."

"It is if you did something you shouldn't have to get there." Ellie's gaze bore into him. "I found your little cold spot machine in the bathroom."

Harold froze, his fingers brushing the neck of a vodka bottle. He dropped it, catching it mid-fall, but his knuckles stayed white as he gripped the glass.

"What else have you been up to, Harold?" Ellie pressed. "Did you fake the Victorian ghost pictures? Did Tim find—"

"*Enough.*"

The voice came from behind her, sharp and

commanding. Ellie turned to see Angela marching over, her finger pointed like a dagger.

"You don't go any further with this, do you understand?" Angela ordered. "Thank you for your statement and information, but this isn't a story from one of those books you're always buried in."

Sliding off the stool, Ellie fired back, "I'd love for a chance to lose myself in a book, Detective, but reality keeps getting in the way—"

"It wasn't a *question*, Eleanor." Angela fixed her with a testing stare. "I won't have you causing more trouble. You might fool everyone else with your quiet mouse act, but your eyes give you away every—"

"Leave the girl alone, Angela," Maggie's voice rang out from across the room, calm but firm. It wasn't a tone to argue with. "Ellie's just trying to help."

Angela straightened, digging her hands into her pockets and rocking back on her heels. Her gaze drifted, avoiding Ellie's. Harold, still hovering by the bar, shifted from foot to foot but didn't speak.

"I don't need help with my case," Angela said, softer this time but no less firm. "And if I hear you've been digging through bins again, Ellie, I'll arrest you for obstruction."

"If it wasn't for Ellie, you wouldn't have a case to—"

Angela strode back to the crime scene, shutting down the conversation.

"Pay Angela no mind," Maggie said, tucking her arm around Ellie's. "She's all bark."

As they passed the spot where they'd spoken with Christina, Maggie's sharp gaze caught on something under a nearby table. Christina's leather bag sat in the shadows, its strap dangling just out of sight.

"Perhaps we should get it back to her?" she suggested.

"And get arrested for obstruction?" Ellie asked, raising an eyebrow.

"Hmm, I'd like to see Angela try." Maggie looped the bag over her free arm, her tone leaving no room for argument. "The last thing she needs is another police officer banging on her door tonight. We'll take it to her first thing in the morning. But for now, it's time for bed."

As Ellie pulled open the pub door, the frosty air rushed in, biting at her cheeks.

"We will, Gran, but there are two things we need to do first. We need to check on George."

Maggie sighed as she stepped into the icy night, and Ellie lingered for a moment, glancing back at The Drowsy Duck. Its windows glowed against the darkness, the banner advertising the séance hanging askew, one corner fluttering in the wind.

The events of the night made her feet drag as they walked away. They passed by the corner where Oliver had asked about history repeating itself. Now, more than anything, Ellie wished she hadn't been right.

"And I need to tell you about what happened with Meredith the night Tim died." Maggie gave Ellie a tired but determined look as they walked. "Let's get home by the fire, and I'll tell you the whole story."

* * *

The wind howled outside the cottage, rattling the windowpanes like a restless intruder. Inside, it was another world—warm, quiet, a cocoon of familiarity. Ellie and Maggie sat close to the fireplace, their usual chairs drawn in as if it were any other night. But tonight, there was no comfort in the silence, no books to distract them, only the crackle of the fire and the burden of the unresolved case hanging between them.

"I should have told you this the moment you uncovered those words." Maggie's voice was barely above a whisper, but the sorrow in it cut through the quiet. "I'm afraid you may have built up my strange behaviour in your mind. I don't know anything that will lead to us figuring this out, which is why I thought I could keep it to myself. The biggest secret I have to reveal is my own shame."

Ellie offered a soft, supportive smile. "Whatever it is, Gran, you can tell me. And you always could."

Maggie hunched forward, her face hollowed by the flames, looking older than Ellie had ever seen her.

"I know, love," she said with a sigh. "But seeing that graffiti brought back feelings I thought I'd buried. It opened an old wound I didn't want to admit still hurt." She sniffed, reaching for a tissue from the box beside her.

"Meredith was already on my mind more than usual after she fell ill this summer. I've been seeing George more—trying to help him not feel so alone—but I failed them both, Ellie. I wasn't the friend I should've been to Meredith."

Ellie stayed quiet as Maggie dabbed at her eyes, sensing that her gran needed space to sift through her memories.

"The night of the séance, back in '94," she continued, her voice growing steadier as she nodded, "I overheard someone—a young man outside the pub—warning Tim Baker about something. They were outside smoking, and I was just on the other side of the door. I was about to leave when I heard the man say that Meredith had been researching Tim's father."

"Who was his father?"

"I never knew him, but I do know he died in early '94." Maggie's gaze grew distant. "I turned around and marched back into the pub to find Meredith. I was furious. I found George first and told him I thought Meredith was about to interfere with the séance to manipulate Tim. She was going to play the role your mother butchered tonight. George didn't have a response for me. All the years I'd known him, and I'd never seen him so speechless. He knew what Meredith was up to."

"What did you do?"

"I found Meredith in Tilly's private readings room at the back of the pub. Meredith was taking tips from the old psychic. George tried to talk her out of going through

The Plot Thickens

with summoning Tim's father. He understood it was too soon, too fragile for Tim... but Meredith was convinced she was doing the right thing."

Ellie's chest tightened. She'd heard this story before, from Jack and Cassie at the studio, but hearing it now—from her gran—made it feel painfully real.

"What did you do next?" Ellie asked.

"I waited until Meredith was alone and challenged her like I never had before." Maggie's voice trembled, but she pressed on. "We were *best* friends—I was closer to her than my own sister—and I thought if anyone could stop her, it was me. I didn't mean to give her an ultimatum, but I told her if she went through with it, I'd never talk to her again." She twisted the tissue around her fingers until it shredded, scattering flecks across her lap. "That's my shame, Ellie. I forced Meredith's hand, and I pushed her away forever."

Ellie's heart broke seeing her gran like this. "But she shouldn't have put you in that situation, Gran. No matter what she believed."

"I was so angry." Maggie drew in a tight breath, her eyes closing. "And then I did something I can never forgive myself for. I ran to the bathroom to splash water on my face—it was like a nightmare I wanted to wake from. But there were women in there giggling about the ghost nonsense. I... I snapped and said something I shouldn't have."

She opened her eyes, meeting Ellie's gaze, though the words caught in her throat.

"What did you say, Gran?"

"Remember what Christina said about good rumours starting at parties?" Maggie let out a brittle laugh. "I should've left them to their evening, but I didn't. I decided to burst their bubble and told them they ought to be ashamed—that if anything happened to Tim Baker that night, it would be on Meredith's head."

Tears spilled down her cheeks, and Ellie handed her a fresh tissue.

"Oh, Granny."

"And that was it." She scrubbed her tears away with dragging motions. "I think *that's* how the vicious rumours started, Ellie. *I* planted the seed and look what it's grown into. That's why I couldn't face it... I didn't want to face myself."

Ellie squeezed her gran's hand. "Given how Meredith was acting, people would've drawn their own conclusions. You said yourself she blamed Tim's fall on John Patridge's ghost. That would make anyone look guilty."

"Maybe... but I said it *first*." Maggie's face crumpled under the weight of her guilt. "I handed them the narrative, and I think Meredith knew that. She never forgave me. We became ghosts to each other, and I... I never got over that."

Ellie hesitated, unsure of what to say to make things better. She hated seeing her gran like this, though she was relieved she was finally opening up to her.

"We don't know for sure that Meredith is innocent."

The Plot Thickens

Maggie sighed. "A woman in a coma didn't push her husband down the stairs."

"Then what if it was George?" Ellie suggested, desperation creeping into her voice. "What if he tried to frame Meredith, and the guilt drove him to this?"

Maggie tossed another log into the fire, jabbing at the flames with a poker. To Ellie's surprise, her gran was considering her outlandish theories.

"You know who you sound like now?" Maggie asked.

"Like everyone else."

"Perhaps," she said, nodding side to side. "Or maybe you're seeing exactly what someone *wants* you to see. If Meredith and George are innocent, someone's going to great lengths to make them *appear* guilty." She glanced at the clock. "But George apparently knew too much. Whatever he found in his attic must have triggered something. Let's hope he pulls through. It's been an hour since I last called the hospital. I'll call, and for you, it's time to rest your eyes. And your mind. I need you alert tomorrow. New day, new perspectives..."

Ellie dragged herself to bed, leaving Maggie on the phone with an unhelpful receptionist. As the wind battered the windowpanes, Ellie reached for her notepad but let it fall back into her bag. Too drained to write, she turned off the lamp and sank into her cold pillow, hoping George could talk and give them the break they needed.

At least now, she had her gran back on her side.

Chapter 14
History Repeats

Knotting her dressing gown, Ellie shuffled into the kitchen, the soft scuff of her slippers barely audible over the radio. A news bulletin offered the first update of the morning.

"... *and* when asked if police were pursuing the same suspect for both attacks, DS Cookson declined to confirm a connection. Next up, the sport—"

Granny Maggie marched across the kitchen with a thunderous expression before she flicked the radio off with a sharp huff.

"Ah, you're up," she said, shaking her head towards the now-silent radio perched on the windowsill. Outside, the storm that had raged through the night still clawed at the trees, dragging them like rag dolls in the wind. "There's toast and jam in the conservatory, and I threw some extra teabags in the pot. I think we're going to need them today."

"I think you're right," Ellie said, stifling a yawn. "Any updates on George?"

"A small one, but get yourself in there and warm up first."

Ellie wandered into the conservatory, where a near-tropical heat greeted her, the space heater humming in the corner. Moments later, Maggie swept in with plates piled high with fried bread, crispy bacon, and a perfectly charred tomato.

With napkins on their knees and strong tea poured, they tucked into the hearty breakfast, exactly what Ellie needed after the events of last night.

After her first sip of tea, Maggie said, "George is alive."

Ellie let out a sigh of relief that quickly turned into a yawn, and Maggie followed suit.

"You too?" Maggie asked, topping up Ellie's tea. "I don't know if it was the weather or the memories of last night that kept me awake. Best not to dwell, though. We must be proactive." She slurped her tea before continuing, "So, this update."

"There's more?" Ellie asked.

"Silver paint," Maggie said, fixing Ellie with a pointed look as if expecting a revelation. Ellie could only shrug. "No, it didn't jog anything for me either."

"Is it important?"

"The nurse I spoke to said it was under his fingernails." Maggie glanced down at her own as if trying to imagine the explanation. "She thought it looked like

The Plot Thickens

the residue you get from a scratchcard, but I don't think George was a gambling man. I thought he might have grabbed something on his fall down."

Ellie considered this for a moment. "Could it be connected to whatever's in that envelope that Christina gave to Angela?"

Maggie's brows shot up in surprise. "I hadn't thought of that, but two brains are better than one. Another question to throw onto the unanswered pile."

"Like what's actually in that envelope," Ellie suggested, finishing her eggy bread, fried to perfection, just like Maggie had made it when she was little. "And whatever it is, how has it been hiding in George's attic all these years?"

"I suppose it's in the right hands with Angela." Maggie dabbed her mouth with a festive napkin. "I tried calling her, but she didn't answer. Hopefully, I'll bump into her at George's cottage when I take Christina her bag."

Ellie's gaze drifted to the leather bag resting in the corner, momentarily forgotten since her gran had scooped it up at the pub the night before. Curiosity tugged at her, tempted to peek inside.

"I'll come with you," Ellie said. "I think I was too in shock last night. We asked about her fake death but barely touched on what happened in 1994."

Maggie held up her hands, palms out. "I'm going to have to insist I go alone. There are no more secrets, I promise, but I want a moment alone with her. We're closer in age, and I might be able to level with her differently. Besides, surely there's something you're itching to do?"

Ellie considered what she wanted to do as she finished her tea. Five people had been present at both séances: Harold and Tilly, Jack and Cassie, and Dr Christina Marsh. Ellie needed to speak to each of them again—alone, if possible. Some would be easier to approach than others. The thought of being alone with Cassie made her stomach churn. She still didn't know how Cassie had connected the dots that led to the drink-throwing, and Ellie prayed it wouldn't spark a fresh rumour.

"There is one silver lining to all of this," Maggie said before pushing her chair against the terracotta tiles. "As unfortunate as it was, Tim's fall was the thing that broke the ghost fever last time. The sightings, the photographs... it all stopped."

"I'm crossing my fingers for that one," Ellie said, tossing back the last of the strong tea before helping load the milk jug and teapot onto the tray. "But I think I'm more intrigued by the ghost sightings from 1994 than ever. George admitted to buying that camera from Tim when we were in the bathroom, and he said he bought it out of 'love' for his wife?"

"He does love Meredith more than anything," Maggie said, lifting her napkin to dab at her eyes. "It breaks my heart to know they're both lying in hospital beds, fighting for their lives, and there's nothing I can do to help them."

"Putting a stop to this will help them," Ellie said, reaching across the table to squeeze her gran's hand. "And heaven forbid, if the worst happens, we'll set the story straight for the legacies they leave behind. What we do next could write their histories." She smiled at her gran until Maggie returned it, faint but genuine. "You heard Christina—George is made of strong stuff. He'll pull through."

Maggie pulled her hand away. "I do hope so."

"Speaking of history, are you sure you don't have a copy of the book Joey mentioned? The one with the pictures from '94?"

"I've never so much as skimmed through it," Maggie said, the shift in topic prompting her to stack the breakfast plates. "You could try the library in Marlborough, or one of the charity shops on South Street might have an old copy."

"Good backup plans," Ellie said, pushing back her chair. "I think I know of a shop on South Street that might have a copy."

"*The Real Ghosts of Wiltshire*, if I recall," Maggie said, rolling her eyes as she carried the plates to the sink. Over her shoulder, she called, "And if you do find one, don't bring it in here. I hate to sound superstitious, but just the thought of that book unsettles me."

"Because of the ghosts?"

"No—the audacity to claim the images show 'real'

anything," Maggie said sharply. "Those pictures that were circulating around the village back then might have looked convincing at first glance, but you don't have to stare at them for long to know they're blatant forgeries." Sighing, she added, "You'll see."

* * *

Passing through the village, Ellie watched as council workers wrestled against the wind to raise a towering pine tree on the green. Colourful lights flickered to life, their glow trembling in the branches as the storm tested their resolve.

Ellie wanted to believe the scene marked the end of the ghost fever, but she couldn't embrace the festive cheer yet. Christmas was too close, the days slipping by too fast. After what had happened to George, who knew what might come next?

And if the police didn't solve it soon, Ellie would have to unravel the mystery herself—while still opening the bookshop before Christmas. It wouldn't be long until festive shoppers would flood the street, and missing the rush wasn't an option—not if they hoped to survive the lean post-New Year months.

Focusing on what she could control, Ellie ducked into Willow's Apothecary, bracing against the wind as she sealed the door behind her. The air inside was thick and spicy, the scent stinging at the back of her throat.

Through the haze of curling incense smoke, Willow appeared through a beaded curtain.

The shop owner's face lit up at the sight of Ellie. Without hesitation, Willow pulled her into a warm hug, damp coat and all. She lingered, as always—a quiet reminder of their shared history. Willow was Luke's sister. He used to joke he was 'the sporty one' and Willow was 'the weird one.' Ellie had always liked her old boyfriend's 'weird' sister—so much that she'd once asked Willow to be her bridesmaid, if things had gone that far.

Ellie hadn't seen much of Willow during her years away, but her hugs hadn't changed. Tight, warm, and oddly energising, they steadied Ellie even when life felt out of control.

"I usually love storms," Willow said, letting go and brushing a strand of dark hair behind her ear. "A reminder of Mother Nature's power. But today… it's hard to enjoy anything after what happened at the pub."

"I couldn't agree more," Ellie replied, following her to the counter. "I didn't see you there last night."

"You know me. I'm not a pub person." Willow's smile turned wistful as she moved behind the counter, straightening jars of dried herbs. "Or a séance person, for that matter. There are easier ways to contact the dead." She placed a hand over her heart, letting it rest there. "So, how are you? I heard about what you found in the shop. I've popped by a few times, but I haven't seen you in there."

"I've been a little... busy," Ellie admitted. "I'm actually here because of what happened last night. Or at least, something that might be connected to it." She hesitated, glancing around at the walls lined with jars of dried herbs and bundles of sage, their earthy scents mingling in the air. A row of leather-bound books with faded spines caught her eye, their titles almost illegible. "I keep hearing about a book. *The Real Ghosts of Wiltshire?*"

Willow's face brightened as she led Ellie to the 'Local History' shelves. Her ring-cluttered fingers skimmed the spines until she tugged out a thick, well-worn paperback.

"I remember when this was just an idea," Willow said, stepping back, her arms wrapping around herself. "Our father worked at the old book-printing factory. This was their one and only venture into self-publishing." A small smile flickered. "Our dad dug through boxes of photographs to come up with ghost pictures. That's me on this page," she added, flipping to an image of a young girl in front of textured glass doors. A faint woman's face hovered in the glare of the flash. "I'm the little girl, and that's my gran. She died two weeks after this picture, but Dad fudged the date for the cash prize."

"And they didn't fact-check?"

Willow chuckled. "No, and the factory shut down the next year. This book was their last-ditch effort to stay afloat. Dad became a mechanic after that, but he loved showing this book off at parties—proof he'd made it into

The Plot Thickens

print. You're the first person who's asked for it since I opened, and I've only ever kept one copy in stock." She handed it to Ellie with a faint smile. "Take it. Free of charge."

"Oh, I can't—" Ellie started, pulling out her phone to insist on paying, but a text flashed on the screen.

She smiled despite herself.

> DANIEL
>
> At The Giggling Goat if you're around for breakfast? My treat.

Willow's knowing glance didn't go unnoticed. "Daniel's a sweet man, and he respects you."

"He does?" Ellie asked, glancing up.

"Has he asked you to speak at the assembly?"

Ellie's smile faltered. "I... I don't think I can. I'm scared," she admitted, her voice trembling. She'd never had to hide her feelings from Willow. "Scared I didn't know Luke well enough to say anything. And scared I'll cry my way through it."

"I cried through my first one, but I needed to honour him." Willow placed a comforting hand on her arm. "Maybe if someone had broken down at one of Luke's assemblies, he might have realised it was best to slow down before taking that bend so fast." Her gaze softened. "You did know Luke. Who he was then. The young man he'll always be in our memories."

Ellie's throat tightened, and without thinking, she hugged Willow again.

"You know, Daniel consulted me before he asked you," Willow revealed, her hand moving in soothing circles on Ellie's back. "I encouraged him. I thought—no, I *knew*—it would be good for you." She stepped back, her hand resting on Ellie's shoulder. "You still have time to decide. Think about it, okay? For me?"

"I will," Ellie said, and this time, she meant it. "Thank you, Willow. For the book… and the chat. And the hug. I needed that."

"Any time." She winked. "And if you're around later, I'll see you at the café for lunch. But judging by how you rushed in here, I'd say you'll be busy."

Holding up the book, Ellie said, "I think I might be."

***

Spirits lifted, Ellie ducked out of the rain and into The Giggling Goat café, the book tucked securely in her jacket. In the far corner, with his back turned, Daniel was already seated, dunking soldiers into eggs. Ellie tried to slip past the cluster of post-school-drop-off mums gossiping with Oliver at the counter, but he wasn't about to let her go unnoticed.

"Oi!" he called, darting out from behind the counter to block her path. "I sent you off to talk to my mother last night, and you and Gran snuck off without saying goodbye."

"And what about you?" Ellie volleyed back,

mimicking his stance, one hand on her hip. "You were nowhere to be seen during the séance."

"If you're about to accuse me of murder, I have a firm alibi." He lowered his voice, biting back a cheeky smile. "You'll *never* guess who I went on a date with."

He paused.

"Are you expecting me to guess?" she asked.

His grin stretched from ear to ear. "Big ears! Your cute builder, Joey."

"He's not *my* builder," Ellie corrected, though a smile tugged at her lips. "You went on a *date* with him?"

"Well, more of a quick conversation outside the pub, but I'm calling it a date if anyone asks. I was surprised to find him on *my* dating app, but stranger things have happened." His lip bite turned into a playful purse. "Unfortunately, he did keep asking about you once I mentioned you were my sister. He definitely fancies *you*." He jabbed a finger in the middle of her chest. "But if you let him down gently, *I* can marry him, adopt two Cavalier King Charles Spaniels, and live happily ever after in a cottage surrounded by strawberry plants."

"You've really thought this through."

"I've thought of nothing else since he first came in for a bacon and egg sandwich last week," he said with a faraway sigh. "Do you believe in love at first sight?"

"These days, I don't know what I believe in."

"That answers my next question. You're still playing Agatha Christie."

"No comment," she said, tucking her arms tight

against the book hidden under her jacket. "But did you see anything outside the pub?"

"Other than Joey's dreamy smile? No. The lights cut off, and we heard the commotion. He said he had somewhere to be, so I resisted following him like a lovesick puppy and came back in to find you all scrambling around." He smirked but added, "You don't think he's the killer? He did leave at *just* the right moment."

"Joey?" Ellie laughed. "Pull the other one."

"Anyway, back to my strawberry cottage—"

"As much as I'd love that for you," Ellie interrupted before her brother drifted off again, "dating isn't my top priority right now."

"Oh, yeah?" Oliver arched a brow in Daniel's direction. "You're clearly not here to talk to me today, but I won't take offence on the grounds that I *love* love." He narrowed his eyes at her, scrutinising her face. "You look like our father when you're tired."

"Thanks."

"Anytime!"

Oliver returned to his waiting crowd at the counter, leaving Ellie to do what she'd wanted to since stepping inside. She slid into the chair across from Daniel, and his face lit up at the sight of her.

"Hi," he said shyly, pushing up his glasses. "Sorry, I ordered. You didn't respond, so I thought you might still be in bed." He leaned in, his tone playful. "You were late at least once a week from sleeping in as a kid."

The Plot Thickens

"Apparently, I've got my mother's sleeping habits and my father's face when I'm tired."

"You don't look tired," he said quickly, though he took a moment to study her. "Maybe a little, but you still look like you." A sweet smile lifted his rosy cheeks as he pushed the plate towards her. "I don't mind sharing if you want a dunk?" He paused, suddenly flustered. "The soldiers in the egg, I mean."

Ellie giggled, charmed by his awkwardness. "I've already eaten, but thanks. How was your nan after last night?"

"Disappointed," he admitted. "She was hoping Tina Turner would come back to thank her for buying all her records."

Oliver appeared again, setting a steaming cup of tea in front of Ellie, a teasing glint in his eyes. "Your nan has taste, but I don't think Tina's been gone long enough to come back via a Ouija board. If there are rules to that stuff, that is." He crouched between them. "Speaking of things that aren't tasteful, I just heard *another* rumour about you, sweet sister. And I know this one can't be true."

He glanced at the women at the counter, and Ellie noticed they were sneaking glances her way.

"Nothing is going on between you and Jack, is there?" Oliver asked, and Ellie rolled her eyes, a sufficient response for his hands to go up in surrender. "Once again, I'm just the messenger," he said. "Everyone knows Cassie is off her rocker. You wouldn't be the first woman she's gone to war with over him. And no offence to him, but you can do better." He darted a look at Daniel before fixing his love-sick eyes on her. "You will speak to Joey, won't you?"

"If I promise to, will you set those ladies straight?"

"What do you take me for?" He ruffled her hair on his way up. "I already have. Enjoy your date."

"It's not a…" Ellie stopped herself, glancing at Daniel as Oliver weaved his way back to the counter.

Was it a date? Daniel had invited her for breakfast. But breakfast was just breakfast. With the book tucked in her jacket and people gossiping about a fake affair with a man she'd barely spoken to, she couldn't make heads or tails of anything.

"I didn't believe it, by the way," Daniel said quietly. "The milkman told my nan this morning, but I said that didn't sound like the Ellie I knew."

"Thank you," she sighed, wrapping her hands around the warm mug, grateful to know someone was in her corner as a lie spread like wildfire about her. She pulled the book out and laid it on the table. "I don't think I can do much to stop Cassie from believing what she believes. Right now, I just want to look through this."

Daniel tilted his head to read the title. "*The Real Ghosts of Wiltshire?* Thought you'd had your fill of ghost stories after last night."

"Ghost pictures," Ellie corrected, opening the book on the table. "They say a picture is worth a thousand words. I hope that's true because this book barely has a word in it."

She flicked through the pages, scanning the grainy photos like the one Willow had shown her. Old snapshots of apparitions that weren't quite there—faces in windows, shapes in the dark, and blurry dust orbs floating in the glare of the flash. Most were the result of double exposure or smudged lenses. But as she reached the middle of the book, her hand slowed. These photographs, credited to 1994 but with the look of 1894, were different—they could almost pass as authentic.

The pages were filled with ghostly figures drifting through familiar Meadowfield landmarks. A spectral man hefting a barrel outside The Drowsy Duck looked strikingly like a young, translucent Harold. Spirits lingered in St. Mary's churchyard, their hazy forms echoing the eerie slides Joey had unearthed in the bookshop's attic. One image showed a woman in a vintage dress, perched on the war memorial, captured from a distance as if the photographer had been reluctant to get too close.

"They're... convincing," Daniel said, taking the words from Ellie's mouth. He leaned closer, adjusting his glasses. "My gran has postcards of these. The full set. Someone must have been selling them, but I can't figure out why."

"Tradition," Ellie said, her eyes still on the photographs. "Same techniques the Victorians used—from creation to sale." She glanced up. "And it's working all over again. You saw how many people were expecting John Partridge to float up from the cellar last night, all while paying through the nose for drinks."

"Good point," he admitted, pushing up his glasses. "My nan was one of them. She said she could feel the spirits in her bones. When I was a kid, she'd bring out those old postcards after one too many glasses of sherry. I think she wanted to give me a fright, and it worked—at first. But once I saw the pictures, all I wanted to do was figure out how they could exist. That led me to the library, and when I learned the history—"

"You couldn't believe the lie," Ellie finished, meeting his smile with her own. "Then you understand why I'm stuck in the middle of all this. History has so much to say about this case, but right now, I'm no closer than asking for a spirit to knock on the table three times." She pulled the book closer, frowning. "These pictures are only numbered. No titles, no credits."

"Check the index at the back."

Ellie flipped to the back, her finger trailing down a long list of names until she reached the credits for the middle pages. Her stomach turned as the answer came into view.

"I don't know whose name I was expecting to see," Ellie said, swallowing hard, "but it wasn't Tim Baker's."

"He was into photography, wasn't he?" Daniel reminded her.

Before Ellie could reply, the café door creaked open, and Amber swept in, her candy-floss pink hair catching

The Plot Thickens

the light. Ellie waved her over, and from the relief on Amber's face, it seemed she'd been looking for her. Daniel, engrossed in the book, didn't seem to mind Amber joining their table.

"I heard what happened at the pub," Amber said, pulling out a chair and sitting beside Ellie. "Glad I didn't go. The whole thing sounded too weird for me."

"It ended up that way," Ellie admitted, noticing Amber's gaze flick to the book. "You've seen it before?"

Amber nodded. "My Auntie Carol refused to have a copy in the house when I was a kid. She said it was bad luck."

"My gran said almost the same thing," Ellie said with a wry smile. "But... the ghost pictures are credited to Tim Baker. I know you never met him, but from what I've heard, I wouldn't have thought he'd be behind these photos."

Amber frowned. "He wasn't perfect—Auntie Carol didn't idolise him after he died. She used to complain he didn't visit enough after he moved out. And when he did, he'd get snappy if she asked too many questions about his love life. Her attic was stuffed with boxes of old camera equipment he'd been hoarding since he was a kid. But..."

"But?" Ellie prompted when Amber hesitated.

"Auntie Carol swore, till the day she died, that Tim *wouldn't* have taken those pictures," Amber said with a shrug. "And the day he died, he went home in a rush. Carol said he was digging through something in the attic but didn't have time to talk about it. She said it seemed important, though."

Ellie's stomach knotted. So similar to George. Had Tim found incriminating evidence in his attic too? And if he had, had that led to his death? History really was repeating itself.

"There's something," Daniel said, clearing his throat as he turned the book around. "This wasn't published until 1995. Tim's photographs were published posthumously, so maybe it wasn't his intention at all."

"But the postcards were circulating before the séance?" Ellie asked.

"1994," Amber confirmed. "They come through my shop from time to time. They sell for as much as old football cards. Collectors still love them."

"Do you know who created them?" Ellie asked.

Amber shook her head, rummaging through her oversized bag. "No, but from what I've heard, a lot of the original trading happened at The Drowsy Duck. I'm glad I caught you—I have something..." She paused, still digging.

Before Ellie could ask what, Sylvia floated into the café, her lips drawn into a dramatic frown.

"Terrible turn of events at the hospital!" Sylvia announced, joining their table. "I was doing my usual cheese rounds on the wards this morning and saw George. The poor man still hasn't woken up. But just as I was leaving, all the doctors rushed down the corridor like something out of a film. I thought they were going

The Plot Thickens

to George, but no—they were heading to Meredith's room."

"M-Meredith?" Daniel stammered, his face pale. "Is she alright?"

Sylvia shook her head as though scared to say more. "It's beyond tragic. But perhaps it's for the best if they go together. George was miserable without her, and I don't think he'll last much longer. It might be kinder this way."

Oliver's voice cut through from behind the counter, sharp and steady. "Are you a doctor now too, Sylvia? There are enough wild rumours flying around without you adding to them."

Sylvia offered a tight smile but said nothing more, turning her attention to Daniel and his untouched breakfast. Ellie's mind was racing. George hadn't woken up, and now Meredith's condition was worsening. Whatever answers the book held, they needed them—fast.

Amber broke the silence, still rummaging. "Oh, and I heard a rumour you're having a thing with Jack?" she said, half teasing, half serious. "He's a proper weirdo."

Ellie laughed, shaking her head. "*Where* is this coming from? That is not true, I—"

"You don't have to explain yourself," Daniel interrupted, his voice calm but firm. "Not for something someone else made up."

"Daniel's right, you know," Sylvia added with a playful wink. "I'll have to work doubly hard setting the record straight. It's only spreading like wildfire because it's so unbelievable. You and Jack Campbell? Come on now."

Ellie's relief grew as Amber finally pulled a yellowed envelope from her bag, steering the conversation away from Jack. She handed it over, the rushed handwriting on the front—addressed to 'Carol'—tugging at Ellie's memory. The scrawled loops looked unmistakably familiar, the same hurried penmanship on the VHS tape box in the museum archive.

"It was in Auntie Carol's things after she died, still sealed," Amber explained. "I told my mum what you found in the shop, and she thought you should have it. She could never bring herself to open it, and she didn't know why Carol didn't either."

"What is it?" Sylvia asked, practically salivating.

Ellie noticed Amber give a subtle shake of her head—too private to share in the middle of The Giggling Goat. Ellie slipped the envelope into *The Real Ghosts of Wiltshire* before tucking the book into her backpack.

"So, Sylvia," Amber said, her tone deliberately lighter, "what new cheese have you got in stock this week?"

That was all it took. Sylvia's face lit up like the Christmas tree on the green, and she launched into an enthusiastic spiel about her latest cheddar discovery, complete with stories of its origins and flavour profiles.

"Sorry for gate-crashing your breakfast," Ellie said to Daniel, leaning across the table. "How about dinner later? My treat?"

The Plot Thickens

"Disco prep at the school tonight, but it's fine, I—" Daniel began, only to knock his plate as he waved her off. The runny egg slid straight into his lap. "Oh, for crying out—" He laughed, grabbing a napkin to clean up the mess. "Nan's always said I had two left hands and two left feet." He nodded towards the door. "I can feel you're itching to run off somewhere." He dabbed at this lap, his eyes fixed on her as he said, "Just... be careful?"

"I always am," she said, the words leaving a faint chill as she realised how much they echoed George's final warning to her.

Chapter 15
The Excavation

Torn between visiting the photography studio above the gift shop or heading to the pub, Ellie decided Harold and Tilly were the lesser of two evils. Besides, Harold's convenient alibi of smoking outside during the séance still didn't sit right with her.

Passing the bookshop, Ellie noticed the lights were on. Curious if her gran had already dropped off Christina's bag, she cupped her hands to the foggy window for a better look. Inside, she spotted Zara from the gift shop, her arms braced awkwardly around Joey, who was struggling to stand. Zara's face was flushed with effort, and Joey looked pale, his movements unsteady. Something was clearly wrong.

Ellie burst through the door. "What happened?" She rushed to Joey's other side, catching him as he swayed. "Joey..."

"I'm *fine!*" he insisted, flashing a dopey smile that barely masked his pain.

"He is *not* fine," Zara snapped, clearly exasperated. "I have been trying to call an ambulance, but this man refuses to sit still. I was on my way to work when I saw him staggering around in here. I thought he was drunk, but—"

"Boxes of books fell on me, that's all," he interrupted, his words slightly slurred. "I've been through worse."

"How'd that happen?" Ellie reached for the back of his head and drew back sharply when he winced. Blood dotted her fingertips.

Zara sighed, shifting Joey's weight fully onto Ellie before striding off to call an ambulance.

"Please, don't fight me," Ellie insisted, dragging him to a chair by the fireplace. "You need to sit down and tell me what happened."

"I was upstairs, pulling up more floorboards to see if I could find anything else, and I must've bumped the boxes. Next thing I know, I'm buried, and things are blurry…" His grip tightened on the chair arms as he tried to sit up straight. "You know Handy Steve has a reupholstering tutorial on his channel."

Ellie couldn't help but laugh. "I yearn for the days when mould and Handy Steve were the biggest dramas in my life."

"There is mould. *So much.* In the cellar," Joey whispered, like a child confessing a secret. "I didn't want to say with everything going on… but don't worry,

I'll fix it all. You'll see..." He blinked slowly. "So, when are you going to let me take you out for that drink, anyway?"

Zara returned just in time. "The ambulance is on its way."

"I'm fi—"

"*Wait* here." Ellie dashed upstairs where books were scattered across the floor. She crouched to retrieve the ones that had fallen into the cavity where Joey had been working, sifting through the mess. The space under the floorboards was empty.

She traced his path through the books to where he must have dragged himself free—nowhere near the boxes, which were still by the door. Joey might be clumsy, but he'd need to have hit the boxes with serious force to knock them over. Someone could have pushed them onto him and slipped out unnoticed.

She hurried back downstairs as a paramedic rushed in, their voices raised as they tried to reason with Joey's protests.

"Did you see anything?" Ellie asked, pulling Zara aside.

Zara hesitated, watching the paramedics tend to Joey. "It has been raining on and off all morning, so I did not think anything of it, but someone was sprinting away from South Street with their hood up just before I found him."

"Which direction?"

"Towards the pond. Should I call the police?" Zara

searched Ellie's face for an explanation. "What's going on, Ellie?"

"Call them. And I don't know, Zara, but I'm trying to find out." She was halfway to the door when she turned back. "How have your upstairs neighbours been?"

Zara sighed in relief. "Your talk with them really helped. I haven't heard any more music since that day. It is almost like they are not there."

Ellie bit back the urge to suggest they might be hiding and stepped outside, heading for The Drowsy Duck. Before she could check if the hooded figure had run inside, Auntie Penny appeared, hurrying towards her with Duchess, both in matching orange raincoats.

"There's been an emergency!" Penny thrust the lead into Ellie's hands and spun to leave. "Your mother has been stolen from!"

"I'm in the middle of an *actual* emergency," Ellie protested.

"It's just for a few hours," Penny called over her shoulder, already rounding the corner towards Carolyn's cottage. "You're a star, Ellie!"

Ellie sighed, glancing down at Duchess. The little dog, snug in her rain hood, wagged her tail, unfazed by the chaos. Ellie crouched to scratch her ears, glancing at the paramedics as they coaxed Joey into the waiting ambulance. A small crowd of shopkeepers and early morning browsers had gathered on the street to watch. Everything was hitting far too close to home.

She shook herself and stood, considering whether

The Plot Thickens

The Drowsy Duck might allow dogs. But Duchess pulled towards the village green as rain began to fall again—and Ellie had left her umbrella at home. Typical.

Duchess the Third sniffed at the new Christmas tree, and while she did, movement by the war memorial caught Ellie's eye. Last night before the séance, crowds had gathered, but only one figure lingered now. Charles Blackwood was crouched at the old stone cross, listening for something.

"Good morning," Ellie said as she redirected Duchess.

Charles straightened as he turned. "Is it?" He beckoned her closer. "Can you hear that?"

As the rain softened, a faint, distorted moan reached her ears. Brushing aside the mud at the base of the memorial as Duchess dug for the source of the noise, Ellie uncovered a plastic sandwich pouch. Inside was a speaker and portable battery pack—a ghost in a bag.

"Who'd do this?" Charles asked.

"The same person who faked the photographs?" Ellie replied, examining the bag. "And perhaps that is the same person that pushed Tim... and George." She parted the items and there was something else. Another device. "A Dictaphone, and it's running."

"We're being recorded."

"Can this thing transmit?"

Charles pushed up his glasses as he took a closer look. "I'm not sure. We could take it to the museum? The police returned the archive box this morning. They must not have found anything, but you're welcome to have another look while we're there?"

Under the umbrella, they walked with Duchess back towards The Drowsy Duck. The pub was eerily quiet, and neither Harold nor Tilly were in sight.

The museum was eerily quiet, their footsteps the only sound as they reached the archive room at the back. A single lamp cast a faint yellow glow over the table where an open archive box waited, its contents meticulously organised in evidence bags.

Ellie was drawn to one photograph in particular: a group shot of the Ghost Watch team and the bar staff at The Drowsy Duck, dated 1994.

Familiar faces smiled back at her—Tim, now gone; George and Meredith, their health failing; Cassie and Jack, unmistakable in their punk-era defiance; and Harold and Tilly, lingering at the edges as though they didn't quite belong. Dr Christina's reflection lingered in the mirror behind the bar, the ghost behind the camera.

Ellie's chest tightened as she studied the frozen moment. So many lives entangled, so many secrets lingering just out of reach.

Someone in that picture had to be responsible.

While Duchess sniffed around the aisles, Ellie placed the plastic ghost in a bag on the table, pulling it open carefully. Charles stood beside her, his arms crossed, peering over her shoulder. Together, they examined the speaker and battery pack.

"Looks like a makeshift sound system," Ellie said, turning the speaker over in her hands. "Cheap, but functional, and could've been planted by anyone. There were reports of sounds at the memorial last time, and someone has gone to trouble to recreate the same conditions." She tapped the speaker in her palm. "But why fake ghostly sounds at the memorial in the first place?"

"To stir up more drama, maybe?" Charles suggested. "The séance, the graffiti, the attacks—it's all connected, isn't it?"

She nodded, placing the items back in the bag. Her fingers brushed against something sharp at the bottom. "What's this?"

She pulled out a crumpled scrap of paper, damp but legible. Written in thick black marker was a single word: 'Confess.'

Ellie and Charles exchanged a worried glance.

"Confess to what?" Charles whispered. "And who is this even for?"

"Whoever finds it?" Ellie mused, turning the Dictaphone around for any signs of a Wi-Fi symbol. "If this thing is being sent somewhere, they might know we've found it."

"Even if it could, it would need to be connected to the internet, so it would need to be someone who lives close by."

Through the wall, Ellie looked in the direction of the memorial, and then to the pub, with only the new Christmas tree and a large cottage separating the two. Her attention shifted to the 'Experiment 3' VHS tape. The handwriting on the label matched Dr Christina Marsh's letter. Ellie hesitated, then turned to Charles.

"Can I borrow this?" she asked.

"I'll need to sign it out," he said reluctantly. "And you'll have to return it for the archive."

"Of course. Thanks, Charles."

With a final glance at the archive, Ellie turned and headed for the door, Duchess trotting at her side. She thought ahead to her next move—find somewhere to play the tape. Behind her, the faint click of Charles locking the archive door echoed through the quiet museum. As she stepped out into the rain, the cool drops spattered against her face, grounding her.

On the corner by the pub, hugging the tape inside her jacket like a lifeline, a sudden blinding light flashed in her eyes, forcing her to squint. She raised a hand against the glare.

"Ellie!" her mother's upbeat, camera-ready voice cut through the rain. "*There* you are!"

A golf umbrella protected Carolyn's bouncy curls while Penny wrestled with the camera on her shoulder, its spotlight piercing through the drizzle.

Ellie held up her hand towards the lens. "Whatever it is, I don't—"

"We're about to shoot a cooking segment for the

The Plot Thickens

pilot!" Carolyn announced, a hint of pleading in her voice. "You know how *hopeless* I am in the kitchen. I need Penny's hands on deck, and I *had* to let our cameraman go."

Ellie paused, torn between the tangled threads of her investigation and this unexpected derailment. For a fleeting moment, she wished she could step into her mother's world—one where Jack was just a cameraman, not a suspect in a decades-old murder case. Her mother, after all, lived in her own version of Meadowfield, a world where she was always the star.

But a spark of an idea lit up.

"I'll help on one condition." Ellie thrust Duchess's lead into her mother's hands, quickly retrieving the tape from her jacket. "Do you still have that VHS player in your attic?"

"Of course!" Penny announced for her. "We were watching old *Heatherwood Haven* tapes last night, weren't we, Carolyn?"

"What have I told you about breaking the fourth wall?" Carolyn snapped, though her eyes were trained on the box in Ellie's hands. "If that's one of your granny's old home films, get ready for three hours of her narrating your boring school trips with her finger over the lens."

"I'm not sure what it is," Ellie admitted, ducking under the umbrella, clutching the tape for dear life. "But we're about to find out."

Chapter 16
Ghosts in the Attic

The old projector whirred to life in the attic above Carolyn's immaculate cottage, hooked to the clunky VHS player Ellie remembered from her childhood.

On the white sheet draped against the brick wall, a younger Carolyn appeared, her voice steady as she delivered a line on a studio set carefully crafted to resemble The Drowsy Duck. The wife of the man Carolyn's character was having an affair with raised a hand, ready to deliver a slap. Ellie couldn't help but wonder if Cassie's pint-throwing theatrics had inspired their choice of episode.

"They just don't make television like this anymore," Carolyn sighed. She tilted her head as the camera tracked her younger self moving through the pub, caught in the middle of the affair. "I *wish* someone would put the series on streaming. Imagine the new audience! They cancelled us before we could really make our mark."

"Wouldn't a reboot be fabulous?" Penny suggested, leaning against a stack of boxes overflowing with tinsel and baubles. "You'd have to star, of course."

But Ellie wasn't in the attic to indulge one of her mother's long, nostalgic rants about *Heatherwood Haven*'s untimely cancellation in 1979. Carolyn groaned as Ellie swapped the old soap for the archive tape.

"*Experiment 3?*" Penny read aloud. "What is that?"

"If you're trying to get back into television, Eleanor," Carolyn said, her eyelids fluttering, "and you've directed something without casting me, I'll be very—"

"I think this once belonged to Dr Christina Marsh," Ellie said as she rewound the tape. She pressed play. "Let's find out."

The film crackled with a hiss, static washing over the sheet before an image flickered to life—a bathroom cabinet with chipped paint, the mirror above it smudged and dim. Paper towels lay scattered on the counter. Ellie's stomach twisted. She knew this place. The men's bathroom at The Drowsy Duck.

A toilet flushed offscreen, and a cubicle door swung open. Tim Baker stepped out, and Ellie's breath caught. She'd only ever seen photographs of him—his floppy dark hair, his easy smile—but seeing him now, moving and alive, felt surreal. He adjusted the strap of a vintage camera around his neck, the one people always said he

The Plot Thickens

never went anywhere without—the one that was still missing.

Tim squinted at the lens and muttered, "Jack left it on again?" before the footage abruptly cut off.

The next shot burst to life in the pub itself, brimming with energy. Harold was behind the bar, recounting a story to a small crowd. "Had me by the throat, right up against the cellar wall!" he bellowed, a pint sloshing in his hand. "John Partridge himself! Swore he'd teach me a lesson!"

Ellie saw George, impossibly young, leaning against the wall with a pool cue. Christina Marsh was beside him, arms folded, smirking at Harold's dramatics.

Jack's voice broke in from behind the camera, sounding like he was narrating a nature documentary. "The sceptics in their natural habitat... being *boring*, but nothing new there..."

The lens swivelled to the bar, where Cassie and Meredith were huddled close, deep in conversation. Cassie looked different—lighter, freer. She was laughing, her head tipped back, the sound so genuine it reached through the years. Meredith, meanwhile, fiddled absently with her necklace, her smile small but present.

Jack zoomed in. "So... this séance." There was mocking in his voice. "Have we set a date to contact Johnny Boy yet?"

Cassie turned to the camera, rolling her eyes. "If you're not going to take this seriously, I would never have invited you. John Partridge is real. Isn't he, Meredith?"

Meredith nodded, though her attention was distant, her fingers tracing the curve of her pendant.

"So, Cassie, what are we going to do?" Jack prompted, his tone edging on teasing.

Cassie repositioned herself, turning her full attention to the camera. "We're going to prove everyone wrong. Ghosts are real. Right, Jack?"

"Right, Cass," he replied. Then, quieter, the camera dipping, he added, "Just try not to sound like a kid's TV presenter so much, yeah? If we want to get this onto the news, it has to feel real."

"It *is* real."

"But it has to *feel* it."

The footage cut again to a quieter, dimly lit scene. The lively chatter of the pub was gone, replaced by a hushed stillness. It was later in the night.

From behind the camera, someone put on a heavy Belgian accent and quipped, "Are your little *grey cells* hard at work, mon ami?"

The camera focused, revealing Tim Baker at a table, examining something closely under a bright desk lamp. It took Ellie a moment to place the setting: the photo studio.

Tim shook his head in disbelief. "This... this is incredible," he murmured, holding something up to the camera. Ellie leaned forward. It was one of the photographs from the book. The one of John Partridge in the cellar.

"I still can't believe how *real* it looks," Tim said, his

voice low, almost reverent. "And I *still* can't believe they just keep turning up."

Jack's laugh echoed from behind the camera. "For a sceptic, you sure sound like you want to believe."

Tim glanced up. "Someone's gone to a lot of trouble to make these look convincing. The techniques are—"

The footage cut, the screen snapping to black before flickering back to life. The room in the new scene was darker, the shapes harder to make out, their edges blurred as though the camera struggled with the lack of light.

In the attic, the projector whirred, loud against the sudden hush.

The video shifted, static crackling across the screen, before dissolving into grainy night vision. A pale green light picked out vague shapes—a table, a chair, and movement just beyond the camera's reach.

"This is rather boring, dear," Carolyn groaned, rummaging through her old *Heatherwood Haven* tapes to admire the faded covers. "If you're going to film your own show, at least try to make it entertaining."

"*Shh.*" Penny flapped her hands at Carolyn as the picture began to sharpen. "There's someone there—in the dark."

A gust of wind rattled the sagging roof slates above them, the attic air chilling around them. On the projector sheet, Tim appeared again, sitting alone in a chair in the middle of the pitch-black room. His head was bowed, his body unnervingly still.

"What is this?" Penny whispered, stepping back.

"Film noir?" Carolyn suggested breezily. "Eleanor?"

But Ellie ignored them, moving closer to the flickering projection. A figure emerged, circling Tim with a clipboard in hand. The figure's movements were calm, clinical, but as the static on the screen grew louder, Tim began thrashing in the chair. His panic was visceral, his struggle unmistakable.

Ellie's hand went up to her mouth. "He's *screaming*."

"There's no sound," Carolyn stated.

Ellie leaned in, her silhouette blending into the screen. The figure pacing around Tim was out of focus but undeniably familiar. As the static intensified, Tim's head snapped back, his mouth wide in a silent scream.

Then, the figure turned towards the camera. The image froze. Though blurry and grainy, the face was unmistakable. Dr Christina Marsh.

"Carolyn," Penny murmured, her voice trembling. "I don't like this."

"It's just a film, Penny," Carolyn replied softly, an unexpected gentleness in her tone. "It can't hurt you."

"But *she* was hurting *him*," Penny insisted. "What was she doing? It looked like... an experiment."

Ellie's mind raced, her questions piling up faster than she could form them. Why had this tape been gathering dust in the museum's archive for thirty years? And why had the police handed it back, as though it didn't matter?

* * *

The Plot Thickens

Ellie bolted from the attic, determined to escape their attempts to rope her into the cooking segment. There was only one place she needed to go. Though she'd been there just once, she remembered Sylvia's directions—even through the pavement-pounding rain.

George and Meredith Fenton's cottage loomed ahead, its overgrown garden wild and menacing. Ellie marched in, forgetting her earlier reservations of trespassing.

Granny Maggie and Christina Marsh sat by the fire in the sitting room, chatting over tea as if the horrors on that tape didn't exist.

Dripping wet and shivering to the bone, Ellie slammed the VHS onto the table with a crack that sliced through their conversation. Both women looked up, startled.

"That's your tape," Ellie said, her voice taut. "Explain what I just saw."

Maggie blinked, confusion and concern filling her face. Christina remained calm, her pale fingers curled around her teacup, her flat expression unreadable.

"Ellie, what are you—"

"Gran, *don't*," Ellie snapped, locking eyes with Christina's detached, glassy stare. "Don't pretend you don't know. *Experiment 3*?"

Maggie shifted uneasily in her seat, her hands fidgeting. Christina, unfazed, set her teacup down with deliberate precision, her icy gaze now fixed on Ellie.

"I don't know what you think you've seen, girl,"

Christina said, her voice sharp and measured, "but you're mistaken."

Ellie's chest tightened. "I know exactly what I saw. Tim was strapped to a chair, screaming. You were experimenting on him."

Christina's lips curved into something almost resembling a smile—cold, cruel, and utterly unfeeling. "What an imagination you have." Her calmness twisted Ellie's stomach. Words tangled on Ellie's tongue as she fought the primal urge to scream—just as Tim had on that tape. "What you saw was nothing Tim didn't ask for."

Maggie paled, her confusion deepening. She turned to Christina. "What is this, Tina? What is Ellie talking about?"

How quickly had the old doctor wormed her way into her gran's good books to be on a nickname basis? Ellie eyed the sagging bag Maggie had returned, tucked under the coffee table. Its contents spilled out in plain view—tissues and cough drops, nothing remotely incriminating or interesting.

Steadying her breathing, Ellie said, "I just saw footage of Tim from thirty years ago. He was terrified. And Dr Marsh was—"

"It's not what you think," Christina interrupted, her tone clipped and firm. She leaned forward, gripping her cane, which rested between her knees. Her voice softened slightly, almost as though offering an explanation, but her gaze remained hard. "Tim Baker desired proof of an afterlife—for conclusive evidence about the nature of life and death. I was the only one willing to help him."

Ellie's jaw tightened. "He was *screaming.*"

"Yes." Christina didn't flinch. "Tim knew the risks."

"T-Tina?" Maggie stammered as she stared at the VHS tape. "Is this true?"

Christina sighed, bracing herself on her cane as though the weight of memory had suddenly become too much. She pushed herself to her feet, looming over the tape.

"The truth mattered as little then as it does now," she said coldly. "We tried many things in that club—things others wouldn't dare attempt. Those experiments were part of it. I feel neither pride nor shame for what we did. My intentions were scientific. And Tim? He *asked* for my help. I didn't seek him out."

"Why wasn't there sound?" Ellie pushed. "What were you trying to hide?"

"I had my reasons." Christina jabbed her cane at the tape on the table, the sound sharp and final. "Take it. There's a reason I discarded that rubbish years ago. And now, you'll leave. I've said all I care to."

Ellie's pulse thundered as she stared at the tape, the words frozen in her throat. Maggie, wide-eyed and pale, looked as though she might crumble into her chair. Christina turned away, her cold dismissal like a slammed door.

Chapter 17
Flash, Bang...

As they trudged back to the village, the rain soaked them through, dripping from their hair and running in rivulets down their coats. Maggie didn't bother with the umbrella sticking out of her bag, seemingly too lost in thought to notice the downpour.

Ellie kept her gaze on the puddles forming along the winding lanes lined with familiar terraced cottages. Finally, she broke the silence, her voice barely above a whisper. "I don't know what's going on."

Maggie glanced at her but said nothing, waiting for her to continue.

"The pictures, the book, this tape..." Ellie trailed off, struggling to find the words. "And I found a ghost machine at the war memorial earlier." She shook her head, the weight of it all pressing against her chest. "It's just... it's all too much."

"You found the book."

Ellie nodded. "The pictures were credited to Tim Baker, but there was more footage on the tape, like something else had been taped over." She gulped, wishing the rest of the video had been focused on the old club having a jovial evening in the pub. "Tim was surprised by the images. Tim's mum didn't think he created them. Neither do I, but I still don't know what it all means." Stopping in her tracks, Ellie closed her eyes to the rain and held her face up to the sky. She opened them to a blanket of grey clouds, as murky as her thoughts. "Angela was right. I'm in over my head. I don't think I can do this anymore."

Maggie's arm slid around her shoulders, pulling her in close. For a moment, the two stood there in the downpour, neither saying anything. A car sped down the lane, splashing them as it went. They both laughed, exhaling a shared breath.

"Let's go to The Old Bell," Maggie whispered, nudging her arm. "Try to forget for an hour. Clear your mind."

Ellie was tempted by the thought of sitting in the warm pub, letting the morning's noise fade into the background, but she couldn't let herself sit down and fade away. Not when she had so many thoughts to untangle. She needed quiet and her pad, not a pint at the pub.

"I need to go to The Drowsy Duck, and the photo studio, and—"

The Plot Thickens

"Ellie." Maggie's grip tightened on her arm, pulling her further down the lane. "Take a breath. It's okay."

"It's *not* okay," Ellie insisted, her words tumbling out faster now. "Something else happened at the bookshop. Joey had a stack of boxes thrown on him. I think he's concussed, and he's probably at the hospital and we need to—"

Maggie ground to a halt. "*Thrown?*"

"It looks that way. The camera was stolen, and I think they came back for the projector. And who knows what else?" Ellie's hands were shivering now, though whether from cold or fear, she couldn't tell. "They're not afraid of people getting in their way. George, Joey... who's next? How can I just stop now?"

"Because you're shaking," Maggie said softly, her face twisted with concern. They emerged down the tight lane winding around the church, the village green ahead —the Christmas tree had already blown down in the wind. "Ten minutes to warm your bones through."

Despite herself, Ellie let her grandmother guide her across the boggy green towards The Old Bell. The familiar warmth wrapped around her as they stepped inside, and she let her gran guide her to the armchair by the fire.

The tape pressed against her chest under her jacket, Ellie couldn't shake the icy chill creeping through her, a lingering echo of Dr Christina Marsh's experiment. No amount of warmth would be enough to banish it.

* * *

A bright flash jolted Ellie awake. She blinked, stars swimming in her vision, the room around her slowly coming into focus. She squinted against the lingering glare, her heart racing as she tried to piece together where she was.

Two shapes loomed above her, merging and shifting until one came into focus: Jack, camera in hand, his face caught somewhere between sheepish and apologetic.

"Sorry, I didn't mean to startle you," he said, lowering the lens. "Forgot the flash was on. You just looked so peaceful—too honest a moment not to capture."

Ellie pushed herself upright, her head swimming as she took in her surroundings. She was still in The Old Bell, the fire crackling beside her, casting a warm, flickering glow. Night had fallen, and the rain had finally stopped, leaving the air with a faint, damp chill.

The pub hummed with the lively chatter of the evening crowd. At the bar, Oliver gestured animatedly as he regaled a group of drinkers with a tale. Sammy, the landlady, threw her head back in laughter, a hearty sound that carried over the clinking of glasses.

Ellie's gaze shifted to her gran, perched beside Oliver, sipping what looked like whisky. Her expression, more sour than ever, made it impossible to tell if she was enjoying herself or merely tolerating the company.

Ellie shifted, a coat she didn't recognise sliding from her shoulders as she straightened up. She blinked down at it, the faint scent of damp wool rising as she touched the fabric. Someone had draped it over her while she slept.

"What time is it?" she croaked, rubbing at her eyes.

"Just past eight," Jack replied, flicking through images on his viewfinder. "You've been out the whole time I've been here."

She wanted to be annoyed at losing so much time, but here was one of the people she needed to talk to, standing right in front of her. She took a steadying breath. "I need to ask you something."

"Want to step outside?" Jack patted his pocket. "I'm desperate for a smoke."

"No," Ellie said quickly, then hesitated. "Given the rumours about us, it's probably not wise to be seen leaving a pub alone together."

"Fair point." Jack scratched at his neck, leaving faint red lines. Ellie wondered if Cassie's wrong assumptions had been causing trouble for him. "This isn't about our chat in the beer garden, is it? Because I've been meaning to apologise for that."

"You have?"

"Yeah." He shrugged and, to Ellie's surprise, picked up the coat she'd been wrapped in and pulled it on. "I was stressed and out of order. Your mum had been pecking my head all night, and I—"

"I appreciate the apology, but no, it's not about that."

Ellie reached for her backpack, her heart skipping when it wasn't by her feet. She spotted it tucked under the chair. Inside was the book, with Amber's letter still hidden between its pages. She hadn't had time to break the seal. As she pulled out the book, the envelope slipped free. Jack caught it and handed it back without a word. She tucked it away and flipped through the book to the index.

"Haven't seen that in years," Jack said, almost amused.

"It's these pictures," Ellie said, opening the book to the glossy pages in the centre. "They were credited to Tim, but the book was published after he died. Do you know anything about that?"

"Yep." Jack brightened at the question, pulling a cigarette from his packet and tucking it behind his ear. "Those pictures turned up at the studio in unmarked envelopes. Tim loved them—he really admired the craftsmanship. After he passed, we thought it'd be a fitting tribute to include them under his name. Nobody ever came forward to claim them, so we assumed they were anonymous."

Ellie paused on the supposed photograph of John Partridge—the one she'd seen Tim holding before.

"These pictures," she continued, more to herself than Jack. "Everything seems to trace back to them."

"Does it?" Jack struck his lighter, the flint sparking weakly. "I've heard people saying George took his own life out of guilt for what he did to Meredith. Driving her around the bend, and all that."

Ellie frowned, scanning the pub. How many people believed that rumour? "I'm not so sure."

Jack nodded towards the door. "We never figured out where those pictures came from, but Harold's mum might be a good place to start. She used to make her living on the spiritualist circuit. If anyone knows how to fake pictures like that..."

Ellie blinked, surprised she hadn't made that connection herself. "Thanks for the tip."

Jack's phone buzzed. "Ah, that's me off. The old ball and chain wants me. See you around."

He headed into the night, presumably in search of Cassie. Ellie stood, her head still foggy, and wandered towards the bar. Maggie brightened when she saw her approach.

"You're awake," she said, holding out her drink. Ellie declined.

"What did *Jack* want?" Oliver asked.

"Apparently, I looked too peaceful not to photograph. Why didn't you wake me?"

"You did look peaceful," Oliver said, patting the empty stool beside him. "But people are going to talk if you two keep—"

"Not tonight," Ellie interrupted. Her patience was thin, and she wasn't in the mood for jokes. "Jack suggested I talk to Tilly about the fake pictures." She sighed, glancing at the closed door. "I should have asked him about the experiment."

"What experiment?" Oliver asked, leaning forward eagerly.

Before Ellie could answer, the pub doors swung open. She turned, hoping Jack had come back. Instead, Sylvia burst in, waving her arms to demand attention. Most people stared at her as if she'd gone mad, but Sylvia was never one to be deterred.

"Listen up, class," Maggie said with a slight slur, dragging out her words. "This might be important."

"Oh, it *is*!" Sylvia announced, buzzing with excitement. "For once, I've come bearing wonderful news. Some of you may have heard that I saw doctors rushing into Meredith Fenton's room this morning, and I feared the worst."

"I think you declared her dead," Oliver said, raising his glass. Ellie smirked at the reminder of how much she'd taken Sylvia's dramatics with a pinch of salt. "Please, do continue."

"Well, I may have jumped to the wrong conclusion, but I'm not afraid to admit when I'm mistaken." Sylvia bit back a smile, then announced triumphantly, "Meredith has come around! She regained consciousness and is already talking about her experiences on the other side. If only the timing of her husband's fall weren't so—"

Before Sylvia could veer into speculation about George's accident, Maggie shot off her stool. She darted for the door, abandoning her whisky.

"And she's off," Oliver said, finishing his drink. "Shall I—"

The Plot Thickens

As Ellie dashed for the door to follow her gran, Sylvia caught her arm. In a low voice, she said, "I know you and Charles Blackwood are quite friendly, so I thought you'd want to know—there was a break-in at the museum a few hours ago. Poor boy is rattled. He could use a friend."

"Thanks for telling me," Ellie replied, already stepping away.

Outside, she spotted Maggie hurrying up the lane. "If you're going home to call a taxi, it might be quicker to catch the bus."

"Meredith is awake!" Maggie cried, redirecting herself without slowing down. "She might know something to help us."

"Let's hope so."

Her gran fidgeted with her scarf, darting glances around the quiet village as if expecting trouble to leap from the shadows. Ellie, however, had her own worries. Something about Sylvia's second piece of news didn't sit right. Charles needed checking on, and she knew she couldn't wait.

"Won't take long," Ellie assured her gran at the bus stop, where the timetable pinned to the leaning wooden shelter confirmed the bus was running late.

Ellie looped back past the duck pond and The Drowsy Duck. Inside, Harold stood behind the bar, unusually subdued, pouring pints for a few regulars. At the far end, his mother, Tilly, was draping tinsel over the bar's mirror with forced cheer, determined to move on from the séance's shadows.

At the museum next door, the front door lay shattered, splintered wood framing the entrance like jagged teeth. Ellie could almost see someone bursting through it in a fit of desperation. The floorboards creaked beneath her feet, startling Charles, who spun around, clutching a broom handle like a weapon. His face was pale, his eyes wide.

"Oh, Charles." She crossed to him and gave him a quick hug. "Are you alright?"

"I'm fine. The door isn't, but I wasn't here when it happened." He ran a shaky hand through his hair. "I've been trying to figure out if anything's missing, but... everything seems to be here. Coins, medals—all accounted for."

"Not a snatch-and-grab, then?" Ellie asked, scanning the museum. She wouldn't know what was missing, but why go to so much effort? "Maybe they didn't find what they were looking for?"

"They were sloppy," he said. "They dropped something. The police took it. It was a receipt for a portable Bluetooth speaker and a battery pack."

Ellie's heart skipped. "The war memorial ghost machine."

"Seems to be. The police said I should lock up and go home, but I can't leave the museum like this."

Ellie pulled out her phone and typed a quick text message.

The Plot Thickens

> ELLIE
> Know anyone who can fix a door?

> SYLVIA
> Several! Consider it done!!

"You'll have a door before the end of the night," Ellie said, smiling as Charles let out a relieved sigh. "Sylvia's on the case."

Through the open doorway, Ellie spotted Maggie waving across the duck pond as headlights beamed at the road's end. Turning back, her gaze landed on the archive room door. It blended seamlessly into the museum displays, camouflaged within a WWII timeline.

"If they didn't take anything from here," she asked, nodding towards the door, "what about the archive room?"

"It was locked," Charles assured her, patting his pocket. "And there's only one key. I checked the 1994 box first, given what's been going on. Everything's there—except the tape."

"I have it," Ellie said, slinging her backpack around to her front and rummaging inside. Her stomach dropped as her hand came up empty. The tape wasn't there. She thought back to the pub—she'd tucked it into her jacket before dozing off by the fire. "I *had* it. It might've fallen out at The Old Bell."

"Or it's been stolen."

"There's a lot of that going on," Ellie muttered. "Like

someone is trying to clean up a mess they didn't mean to leave behind."

"Strange things are happening around this village, Ellie. I... I don't like it."

"No," she said, placing a steadying hand on his shoulder. "Me neither. But I'm doing everything I can to put things right. I'll find the tape—I'm sorry it's gone missing."

"Did you at least watch it?"

Ellie nodded, hesitating before speaking. She could tell Charles was waiting for her to share the contents. "Friend to friend, you don't want to know. Let's just say it doesn't paint Dr Christina Marsh in the best light."

"Then I'll take your word for it." Charles smiled shakily, taking in the damage with a deep inhale. "Now, go. What kind of friend would I be if I let you miss your bus?"

She squeezed his shoulder before jogging back past The Drowsy Duck to find her gran, who was stalling the bus driver. Ellie noticed Sylvia striding towards the museum from the corner of her eye. At least Charles wouldn't be alone.

They climbed aboard, and once settled near the front of the bus on their way to the hospital, Ellie filled her gran in on the museum's break-in.

"The incidents are getting closer together," Maggie said, her eyes fixed on the dark countryside blurring past the window. "But Charles is right—they're getting sloppy. They didn't find what they were looking for." She

The Plot Thickens

fell quiet as the bus jolted over a patch of potholes. "Do you think they were after the tape?"

"If they were, they might have it," Ellie admitted. "Either someone's taken it, or I've lost it. But when it comes to that archive... I've been visiting the museum since I was little, and I never once noticed the door. It's hidden in plain sight. You'd have to know what you were looking for, and it seems they didn't."

"Small mercies."

The bus hit another pothole, and silence stretched between them. Finally, Ellie spoke. "Whoever's behind this seems obsessed with cleaning up fragments of the past."

Maggie's hand tightened around Ellie's, her grip trembling. "As I've learned, the past can come back to haunt you if you don't clean up your mess." She paused, shrinking into her scarf. "What if Meredith doesn't want to see me?"

"She will," Ellie said, though she couldn't shake her own unease.

More than anything, she needed to know what Meadowfield's most ardent believer thought was going on.

Chapter 18
Vigil

After the bus dropped them off outside the hospital, they found George and Meredith's rooms. Maggie paced the corridor outside, her fingers twisting in knots. The doctors had put the married couple in rooms side by side in intensive care.

"I can't go in," Maggie said.

"Gran—"

"You go first," she cut in, stepping back. "I'll wait here."

Maggie stared out the window overlooking the car park. The view was ordinary, almost insultingly so, as if the world hadn't noticed what was unravelling inside. She'd forced herself this far, but Ellie could see the things her gran couldn't say aloud—what waited beyond the door was too much.

Inside George's room, Meredith was slumped over his bed, murmuring to herself as she rocked. Wires ran from his body to the machines that surrounded him, blinking and beeping in a language only the nurse beside him understood. Cocooned in her grief, Meredith had almost as many wires connected to machines at her side.

Ellie pressed her hand against the door. The sterile stillness told her she didn't belong, but leaving wasn't an option now.

"Meredith?" she said, stepping cautiously inside. "I'm Ellie. Maggie's granddaughter."

Meredith glanced up before returning her tired attention to George. Her hand trembled where it gripped his arm. Ellie couldn't bear to look at either of them for too long. Sylvia had been right—the scene was unbearably tragic. Ellie stayed close to the back wall.

"The detective said *you* might come," Meredith rasped, her voice cracking from disuse. "She warned me not to talk to you. Said you were interfering."

"You don't have to," Ellie said gently, moving closer. "But I am trying to help."

A faint twitch of Meredith's lips hinted at a smile. "The nurses said it's nearly Christmas. I always loved Christmas, but... that can't be true, can it? It was summer."

"Somehow," Ellie murmured, unsure of her response.

"Hmm." Meredith's tone shifted to something almost conversational. "Comes faster every year, doesn't it? George never liked Christmas. Or Halloween. Or Easter. He thought holidays were silly. *When you know where these traditions really come from...*" She mimicked the phrase in a weary, teacher-like voice. A sad chuckle escaped her. "I called him Scrooge. But he'd still eat mince pies, complain about the Christmas tree decorations not being in the right places, and he'd admit how much fun it all was every Boxing Day."

Her tired eyes glanced towards Ellie. "Were you there? At the séance? The detective said he fell... that he might have been *pushed*..."

Ellie pulled up a chair and sat beside Meredith. Beneath the harsh hospital lights, Meredith looked impossibly fragile—her skin stretched thin and translucent, her dark hair limp against hollow cheeks. Months in a coma had worn her down, yet her hand gripped George's arm with unwavering determination, as if her touch alone could bring him back.

"I think he was pushed," Ellie said softly, her sigh breaking the silence. "And I think the same person pushed Tim. Do you know anything about that?"

Meredith's grip slackened. "It was John Partridge..." she began, her voice wavering. "The detective told me about the words on the wall in your gran's bookshop." She hesitated, her breath quivering. "I *respected* Tim. I would *never*—" Her words broke off, her eyes clouding as though lost in an old memory. "They said it back then. Everyone did. Even if they didn't say it outright, I *saw* it in their eyes. People have always thought I was strange."

"There's nothing wrong with being a little strange," Ellie said gently.

"No, I suppose there isn't." Meredith's gaze drifted towards the window, her expression unreadable. "Your gran used to say something like that to me. Until..."

"Until the séance in 1994?" Ellie asked.

Meredith nodded.

"She said you were like sisters."

"We *were*."

"She misses you."

Meredith squeezed her eyes shut. "I can't think about that. I didn't mean to cause any harm."

Sensing she was close to a breakthrough, Ellie leaned forward, inching her chair closer. Her gaze settled on George's face—his mouth slack around the breathing tube. He looked nothing like her old history teacher now. She reached out and rested her hand on his arm beside Meredith's.

"George never fell out with Maggie," Meredith murmured, her voice distant. "We were like a family. All of us."

"The Ghost Watch?"

Meredith nodded. "Your gran never officially joined, but she was always there. There was..." She frowned, struggling to remember.

"Cassie and Jack, and Dr Christina?" Ellie prompted. "Harold and Tilly too."

Meredith nodded again. "They said my memory might be foggy for a while." She clenched her eyes shut once more. "We were like a family. We didn't always get along, but we had one thing in common."

The Plot Thickens

"The ghosts?"

"No." Meredith's brow furrowed as she tried to find the right words. "We were all searching—seeking. The ghosts brought us together." She swallowed hard. "I researched Tim's father because I wanted him to see... to *believe*. But Tim was right." Tears welled in her eyes, spilling down the network of lines on her cheeks. "He confronted me before the séance—he was so upset. He called me unethical, immoral... and I agreed. I didn't know how things got that far." She shook her head, her voice trembling. "But I didn't know what else to do. There was so much noise—pictures, strange phenomena, accusations that it was all staged. Meadowlings were losing faith. We *all* had to believe. Only then would the other side contact us." Her voice rose with weary passion. "I wasn't trying to hurt Tim, I only wanted the truth."

Ellie watched as Meredith unravelled, her words tying her in knots. The confused furrow in Meredith's brow suggested she wasn't blind to the contradictions.

"If everyone had someone like my brother guiding them," Meredith murmured, lowering her head, "they'd understand what I understand."

Ellie swallowed, her throat dry. "That's when it started for you—the near miss with the car?"

Meredith nodded, a distant smile softening her face. "I was a child. I didn't have many friends, and after my brother died, my parents hardly noticed me. I found a little red ball in the gutter, and I spent all afternoon kicking it against a wall. I didn't like football—it was just something to do." She swallowed. "I kicked too hard, and the ball bounced into the road. A car came out of nowhere. No headlights. It just... appeared. It should've hit me, but I saw a light. I *heard* Michael's voice. My brother told me to move, and when I didn't, he pulled me to the grassy bank. The car swerved and drove off. I was left there, his voice in my ear, telling me to be more careful, and that moment changed my life forever. George never believed me—not about Michael, not about any of it. We met in your grandmother's bookshop, reaching for the same book on the supernatural."

"Really?" Ellie asked, leaning closer.

"He thought he was so clever," Meredith said, stroking George's arm with her free hand. "Writing his thesis on why people believe in ghosts. But I wasn't trying to prove anything—I just wanted to read about people like me, people who'd seen what they couldn't explain." A weak smile lifted her cheeks. "We argued right there in the shop. Your gran had to shush us. She always played mediator."

"But you fell in love anyway?"

Meredith nodded. "He was different then. Curious, even if he didn't believe. He'd listen to my stories—and challenge them, but he *really* listened." Her voice cracked. "The Ghost Watch changed that. The more I tried to prove the hauntings were real, the more desperate he became to disprove them. It strained everything between us, but we never gave up. For better or worse, in sickness and health." She bowed her head, letting tears fall into her lap. "I always said we balanced each other out—wrong for each other in the right ways."

Ellie tilted her head at Meredith's words, the phrase catching her like a hook in her chest. *Wrong for each other in the right ways.* She thought of Luke—of their first meeting, when she'd known immediately they were opposites. He'd been impulsive, unpredictable, utterly infuriating—everything she wasn't. But he'd also been fearless where she doubted, hopeful where she fretted. They'd filled in each other's gaps. It hadn't been enough in the end, but for a while, it had felt like it might be.

"I had a fiancé once," Ellie said softly, her voice small but steady. "I was always so serious, and he was so silly." A faint smile crossed her lips, the memory warming her chest like a fading ember. "He could make me laugh about anything. Laugh like I'd never laughed before. We had nothing in common. I don't think it would have lasted, but... maybe one day, we could have been friends."

Meredith turned to her, their eyes meeting properly for the first time. "After I lost your gran, George was my only friend," she said, her voice thick with emotion. "I think I came back for him. The nurses told me he's been by my side every day, and now, I have to do the same for him. I know he loves me, and I love him. Despite everything—our differences, our flaws—I just want to tell him that. Wherever he is right now." Her expression fell, her tired eyes seeming to look through Ellie. "I've spent months on the edge of life and death, and do you know what I saw?"

Ellie shook her head. Their eyes met again, and Ellie wasn't sure she wanted to know.

"Nothing," Meredith said, her voice barely a whisper. "The last thing I remember is being in my garden. I saw a bright flash come from the bushes, and then... nothing. Blackness. They say I had a seizure... that it might have happened before, but I don't remember. But that doesn't make sense, does it?" She shook her head, her gaze shifting to George. A flicker of hope softened her expression. "It was *him*... Michael. He put me into that coma for a *reason*."

Ellie hesitated, biting back her doubts. This wasn't the time to challenge Meredith's belief. She was here for answers—about something specific—and they'd only brushed the surface of the séance.

"You said John Partridge pushed Tim," Ellie ventured, keeping her tone steady. "Did he push George too?"

Meredith's fingers whitened against George's arm, but she stayed silent, her eyes fixed on his face as though seeing something Ellie couldn't.

"The detective who came to see you—DS Cookson—said George called her to meet at the pub," Ellie continued.

"The evidence he found in the attic," Meredith interrupted, her voice tight. "I don't know anything about that. I rarely went up there—I didn't like the ladder."

The Plot Thickens

Ellie let that thread go. She wasn't getting anywhere with it.

"Did you know about Dr Christina's experiments?"

Meredith squirmed. "I... I don't want to talk about that."

But Ellie pressed on. "I saw the footage of Tim," she said, her voice firm now. "And I think someone tried to steal the archive box containing that film from the museum. I think the same person stole a Victorian camera hidden in my gran's bookshop. And I'm certain they tried to steal back a projector—injuring my friend in the process."

"Was the camera from 1862?" Meredith asked.

Ellie nodded. "George said he bought it for you. Out of love. Did you—"

"Fake those photographs?" Meredith chuckled softly, though it sounded hollow. "No. I always knew they were fake. I collected that kind of photography long before they started circulating in the village. It fascinated me, seeing how people imagined ghosts. Michael never came to me like that. It was more... in here." She patted her chest. "But I wanted to create my own image. I didn't have any pictures of Michael and me together. My parents weren't big on cameras, but I had some of his old school portraits. I just wanted to see us... together, the way I *felt* we were."

Ellie nodded, the sincerity in Meredith's words settling in her chest. "And George asked Tim for help?"

"Tim refused," Meredith said with a sigh. "He was

amused by the pictures at first, but he didn't like how people were getting carried away collecting those postcards. He knew I meant no harm, and when I told him the photograph would be for my private collection, he offered to sell George an authentic camera."

"How did it turn out?"

"We never got the chance," Meredith said, her eyes glazing over as she glanced towards the past. "The camera was only with us for a few days. Someone broke into our cottage and stole it before we could use it. They left the bag it came in—Tim had given us that—but the camera was gone." She shook her head slowly. "I think George put the bag in the attic. We didn't even know how to create those pictures. George said he'd research the double-exposure technique, but... Tim had too much integrity to show us how to fake them."

Meredith's frown deepened, her expression twisting into something darker.

Ellie leaned in. "But what?"

"Tim suggested we talk to Tilly," Meredith said, her hand slipping from George's arm. "He said she'd shown him some old tricks for photography. Apparently, her grandparents ran a roaring trade in that sort of thing when it first became fashionable. But..." She hesitated, bitterness creeping into her tone. "... I'd take anything Tilly says with a pinch of salt."

Ellie picked up on the venom in her voice, the way Meredith almost spat out Tilly's name.

"Why's that?" Ellie pressed.

"She's been fooling everyone for years," Meredith muttered. "A charlatan."

"Tilly told me she gave up that life when she was young."

"Liar," Meredith spat. "She's been offering private readings in the back room of the pub for years—for a fee, of course. I overheard her once, bragging to someone that she didn't have any *real* abilities. It was all tricks, and she knew she was conning people—she sounded proud of it. She gave me a reading for Michael once. Didn't tell me a single thing you couldn't have found in the papers."

Meredith turned back to George, her voice softening. "At least I believed. I might not have done things perfectly, but I believed... I... I'm sorry, but I can't talk about the past anymore."

Ellie nodded, recognising the moment to leave. "Then I'll let you two have some peace. There's someone else who wants to see you." She glanced at the door, where her gran lingered, biting her lip. "She comes in peace. I promise."

Meredith didn't respond, her gaze drifting back to George.

"He's with you, you know," Meredith said firmly. "Not too close, but he checks in."

Ellie didn't ask who 'he' was—she'd learned better than to get pulled into Meredith's ghost stories. Instead, she nodded. The thought didn't unsettle her; in fact, it felt strangely comforting.

"Yeah," Ellie said softly. "I hope so."

She stepped into the hallway, where Maggie waited with a cautious look that softened as Ellie approached.

"She's ready to see you," Ellie said quietly, glancing back at the room. "It might not be easy, but I think she's been waiting for this."

Maggie nodded, pressing her lips into a thin line. "She's not the only one."

Ellie lingered, watching Maggie step into the room. Her gran's careful movements betrayed the flood of emotions Ellie knew she was feeling. Meredith looked up at the sound of the door opening, her expression blank. But when Maggie raised her hand in a hesitant wave, something shifted.

Meredith stood, her chair scraping the floor. A moment later, they were in each other's arms, clutching tightly as decades of hurt melted into quiet, tearful murmurs.

Ellie slipped away, giving them the privacy they deserved. She paused at the edge of the hallway, glancing back once, hoping George might somehow see his wife and her old best friend reunited—even if only in spirit.

But there wasn't time to dwell. Not after where Meredith had pointed the finger.

Tilly knew how it was done. She'd been in the right place at the right time. And if she hadn't pushed Tim and George herself, her son might have.

Ellie stepped outside into the cool night air, but it did little to temper the fire building in her chest.

The Plot Thickens

Whatever Tilly was hiding, Ellie was going to uncover it.

* * *

She barely made it to the stop as the bus pulled up. The driver grinned as she climbed aboard.

"Lucky you—last bus of the night."

"I could use a bit of luck right now," Ellie replied before settling into a seat.

Her mind was already racing, piecing together what she knew: the camera, the break-in, the projector. Someone had gone to great lengths to rebury the past. The gentle hum of the engine vibrated beneath her as the village blurred past the windows, bathed in the soft glow of streetlights. Her thoughts tumbled over one another, threads of the mystery shifting, almost connecting.

Leaning her head against the cool glass of the window, Ellie let her thoughts drift. Without meaning to, her mind wandered back to Luke. She could almost picture him sitting beside her like they had as kids. His easy laughter, that crooked grin—memories that warmed her as much as they stung.

One memory stood out. A rainy afternoon. Luke had a broken foot, and the bus had been packed. They'd barely snagged seats when an elderly woman boarded. Without hesitation, Luke had stood, shifting his weight onto his good leg, grimacing as he offered her his seat.

The woman waved him off, grumbling that she didn't need it, but Luke insisted, smiling through the pain.

"I'm alright," he'd said, though Ellie knew he wasn't. His leg had been throbbing, but that was Luke—always putting others first.

A smile tugged at Ellie's lips, though the ache in her chest lingered. Would they still be friends if things had gone differently? She liked to think so. Maybe they'd still be side by side, dissecting life's mysteries together. But Luke was gone, and all she could do now was carry him with her, in quiet, private ways.

No matter what Willow and Daniel thought she could handle, she couldn't bring herself to talk about Luke in front of a roomful of people—not children, not adults, not anyone. Not now, not ever. She blinked back a tear as the bus slowed.

She pressed the stop button just past the duck pond, shaking off her reverie. There was no room for that tonight. Tilly Fletcher, the centenarian tucked away in the shadows at The Drowsy Duck, knew more than she was letting on. And Ellie wasn't about to walk in blind.

As she stepped off the bus, she pulled out her phone and started a new search: *What year was The Drowsy Duck in Meadowfield built?*

Chapter 19
The Centenarian's Sight

The Drowsy Duck sat eerily quiet. Harold had vanished, and the young barmaid was fixated on a video playing on her phone. The pub's calm made it easy to forget it had been a crime scene just a day earlier.

Holding her breath, Ellie snuck past the preoccupied barmaid and slipped behind the bar. She crept down the dim corridor, heading towards the back of the pub—the part she'd only ever glimpsed from afar. She had no idea what she'd find, but one thing was certain: she wasn't leaving without answers.

The back room was packed with dark wood furniture and crystal balls. The purple-papered walls were plastered with framed images of palms, spirits, and astrological charts.

By the window, Tilly stood stiff and unmoving, staring into the gloom. At the sound of a creaking floorboard, she spun around. She pulled her black shawl tight over her bony shoulders, staring at Ellie with a cold gaze ice.

"You have no business here," Tilly said, her voice sharp. "Your presence messes with my energies."

"Didn't you *see* me coming?" Ellie asked, undeterred by the theatrics.

"Leave now," Tilly warned, "and I won't call the police."

But Ellie refused to scare so easily. "Do you still offer private readings?" she asked, feigning confidence. "I want to... communicate with the *other* side. I'll pay." She fumbled for her phone. "Do you take contactless?"

Suspicion rippled across Tilly's face, but something in Ellie's words seemed to soften her resolve. A cold, faint smirk tugged at Tilly's lips, and Ellie caught the subtle shift—reluctance melting into curiosity. With a deliberate motion, Tilly gestured to a chair by a twisted table crowned with the largest crystal ball Ellie had ever seen. How many Meadowlings had fallen for the allure of smoke and mirrors, willingly parting with their coins?

Tilly worked silently, lighting stubby candles and sprinkling dried herbs into a shallow dish. She muttered under her breath, the words too low to catch, then blew gently on the herbs. A sharp, earthy scent filled the air, stinging Ellie's nose and making her eyes water.

The scene felt like something from a film. Ellie half-expected someone to yell, 'Action!' But the silence held, broken only by the faint rattle of the window as the wind pushed against it. Her muscles tightened. She took a steadying breath, reminding herself she wasn't here for superstition—she was here for the truth.

"I'm curious about the ancient graveyard," Ellie began, her voice low to match the room's hush. "Harold told me this place was built on top of one?"

"The old graveyard," Tilly began, her voice adopting the same theatrical flair Harold had used when telling the story, "has been here longer than anyone alive can recall. Saxon times, they say."

"Right," Ellie said, nodding—though she knew the truth. "Our village does have a lot of Saxon history."

"There was a warrior," Tilly continued, waving her hands over the crystal. "Aelfric. He was buried *here* with his sword. On moonless nights, you might still hear the clash of steel." Her accent shifted, taking on a haunting lilt, like Carolyn during the séance. "And there was a medieval lady, married to a cruel lord. She died giving him the heir he demanded. They say her spirit wanders this pub, searching in death for the love she was denied in life."

The candlelight trembled, casting shadows across Tilly's face. Ellie leaned closer, drawn in against her better judgment. It must have been the wind whistling through the old windowpanes—or so she told herself.

"Many were buried without proper rites," Tilly continued, her dark eyes locking onto Ellie's. "Forgotten by time, but the earth never forgets. When John Partridge built this pub, he disturbed their rest." Her voice dropped lower, chilling. "And they made sure John met his end."

Ellie suppressed a shiver. The stories felt disturbingly real, steeped in the kind of history Meadowfield was known for. The museum had coins and artefacts spanning centuries, after all. But even as she acknowledged the possibility, doubt lingered. These tales couldn't be proven—or disproven. She bit her tongue, careful not to give herself away, and leaned in, letting the eerie performance run its course.

"Who are you expecting to come through?" Tilly asked, her eyes narrowing as she peered into the crystal ball.

Ellie raised a brow. "Shouldn't you tell me that?"

Tilly shot her a withering look, then tipped her head back, rolling her eyes until only the whites were visible.

"Someone *is* coming through," she rasped, her voice distant, otherworldly. "A man... no, a boy... neither. He's on the cusp, caught between life stages, stuck between the living and the dead." She gasped sharply, her body tensing. "He's reaching out... reaching for you."

Ellie knew it was all a performance, but Tilly was unnervingly good at her craft. Determined to stay grounded, Ellie gripped the arms of her chair, yet doubt clawed at the edges of her mind.

"Luke... his crash... the accident," Tilly whispered, her eyelids fluttering. "He's reaching out, Ellie. He remembers. You wonder, don't you? Could it have been different?"

The Plot Thickens

Ellie's throat tightened, the words slicing through her defences.

"The guilt you carry... so heavy," Tilly continued. "He knows what you've been worrying about all these years—if you hadn't called off the wedding, would he still be alive?"

Ellie's chest ached, the sting of those words sharper than the wind slicing through the room. The lamps around her dimmed, and a chill crept up her spine as the wind blowing from a corner with no windows—cut through the air.

Forcing herself to move, Ellie walked to the source of the breeze. She pulled back the trembling curtain in the corner to reveal a small desk fan.

"Very good," Ellie said as Tilly's eyes opened. "But I've seen enough parlour tricks this past week to last a lifetime. How much do you charge for that performance?"

Tilly didn't try to defend herself as she shifted in her seat.

"What's the point of all this?" Ellie asked, returning to her chair. "The cold spots, the exploding bulbs, my mother's séance routine... it's all been passed down to you, hasn't it? From your Victorian grandparents and their travelling phantasmagoria shows."

"You don't know a thing," Tilly insisted, though her voice had lost its edge. "Now, if you don't mind, you need to leave—"

"I looked into this pub's history." Ellie leaned closer

to the glowing crystal ball, its distorted reflection warping her features. "There was no graveyard here. The Drowsy Duck was built in 1857—not exactly *ancient* history. Before that, it was a leather tannery. The roads outside date back to the Romans, and in medieval times, this was a village common and later a market square. No graveyards, no lost souls."

For a moment, silence hung heavy in the air.

"Well, well, well," Tilly said, amused. "Hark at you. Busy with your nose in the books, I see."

"A few minutes searching on Google," Ellie shot back. "Something I should've done when Harold first brought up the graveyard."

"Why ruin the fun?" Tilly reached around the crystal ball, her gnarled fingers wrapping around Ellie's wrists with a surprisingly firm grip. "So full of fire, so full of life..." she muttered, her gaze narrowing. "You remind me so much of myself at your age. How old are you, child?"

"Thirty," Ellie replied, gulping.

"Hmm. I still cared about right and wrong at that age." She released Ellie's wrist with a sigh, slumping back into her chair as though the last of her energy had drained away. "So long ago... That's about the age I closed the door on the spiritual realm. And now?" She gestured around the room, chuckling bitterly. "This is for bingo money. I let Harold keep whatever meagre profits this place makes. Not much money in pubs these days—a fact I wish I'd known when I left the family trade and married a tavern keeper."

Tilly's laugh faded, leaving the room steeped in a strange, weighted silence.

"Is that what all this was about?" Ellie asked. "Profit through the Ghost Ale?"

"Marketing," Tilly waved her hand. "And when you say, 'all this'...?"

"Tim's murder, George's attempted murder, all the running around trying to reclaim all the evidence left behind, like your grandparents' old projector and camera? and—"

"I'll stop you there, my dear," Tilly interrupted with a confident stare. "If I were you, I wouldn't get too carried away. I wasn't present when Tim Baker died, so I can't attest to Harold's involvement, though he assured me he had no part in that incident. I like to think we have a mostly honest relationship, but the reason I know my son wasn't responsible for George's fall is the same reason I know he isn't entirely honest with me." She pushed herself up from the chair and shuffled to the window, holding back the curtains to show the alley. "My son has two habits: smoking and thinking he can pull the wool over my eyes with breath spray."

"Harold told me he was smoking when George was pushed."

"And he was," she confirmed. "During the séance, when your mother was struggling through her readings and I was operating her spotlight, I saw him sneak out through the back for his usual cigarette in this alley. He hadn't come back by the time the lights cut out, which was never part of *our* performance. I abandoned the spotlight to check the fuses." She gestured to a wooden box partially hidden between a bookcase and a stand displaying a shrunken hand. "I smelled the usual cigarette smoke wafting in through this window."

"But you didn't see Harold?"

She laughed. "I heard him hacking his lungs up, and if there's one sound a mother knows, it's her child's cough. I heard George scream, and Harold came in through the back door."

"*After* the scream?"

She sighed. "If you're suggesting there is another way into the cellar, there is, and it would have taken far too long for him to get in that way, get to the top of the stairs, push George, go back into the cellar to run along the hidden passage and to the back door."

Ellie glanced at the fuse box again.

"Who in that little Ghost Watch group knew about the fuses?" Tilly asked before Ellie could, her voice calm but pointed. "I don't know. But I do know they weren't shy about treating this place like their private clubhouse. And as you've proven tonight, it's not hard to slip back here unnoticed."

Ellie nodded, unsure what to say. She wanted to trust Tilly, especially given the vulnerability in her tone, but the woman had admitted to duping people for bingo funds. Still, Ellie's instincts told her Tilly wasn't lying this time.

"Why did you walk away from your family's trade?" Ellie asked, shifting the conversation.

A sad smile softened Tilly's features. "When I finally escaped my parents' grasp, I met Harold's father. He was... just right for me in a way I didn't think I needed. We fell in love, and he made me realise it was okay to carve out my own path." She paused, her gaze distant. "Ironically, fooling people and telling them what they wanted to hear never sat right with me."

Ellie tilted her head, sceptical. "As sweet as that is, it all changed in 1994, didn't it? That's when the 'cold spots' started."

Tilly's expression sharpened. "We weren't the first to claim hauntings," she corrected. "There were stories about strange noises at the war memorial before we ever got involved. Like I said, it was marketing. And it worked —the pub's profits turned around. Things were finally looking up... until Tim's death."

The weight in her voice caught Ellie by surprise. For the first time, Tilly's sadness felt unguarded.

"We never meant for things to go that far," Tilly said quietly, her eyes shadowed with regret. "We liked Tim."

"And yet," Ellie replied, meeting her gaze, "you repeated them."

"The brewery is threatening to hand the pub over to someone else if we don't raise profits," Tilly admitted, her voice heavy. "I won't be around much longer, but

Harold..." She trailed off with a deep, pained sigh. "This place is all he has. His wife left him, he never had children, and he was always too... peculiar for the other kids. But he's always been a showman. We didn't cause any of this, Ellie, but yes, we exploited it."

Ellie nodded, studying Tilly. She wanted to believe her, and there was a rawness in Tilly's voice now that hadn't been there earlier. Still, the memory of the exaggerated eye rolls and crystal ball theatrics lingered. It would have looked convincing to someone less cynical.

"I found a device at the war memorial," Ellie said. "A speaker."

Tilly nodded. "Yes, that sounds right, but that's not my work."

"And the photographs?" Ellie pressed.

"What about them?"

"They were being traded here, in this pub," Ellie said, leaning forward. "You had the equipment, the know-how, and—"

"My dear," Tilly interrupted, holding up a hand, "I sold that equipment to Tim Baker when he was a teenager, years before his death. He had a passion for antiques and old photography techniques. I was happy to top up my bingo fund by selling off some junk I'd been hoarding in the attic."

"So, you told Tim how to create the ghost pictures with the projector?"

Tilly nodded, lowering the hand. "The boy took meticulous notes on the entire process."

The Plot Thickens

Ellie remembered the book in her backpack containing the ghostly photographs. Something about it had never felt right—not to her, not to Amber, not to Tim's mother. But if Tim had the knowledge, maybe he *had* forged the images himself.

"Do you think he created those photos?" Ellie asked. "They were credited to him in print."

Tilly shook her head. "If he did, he needed more practice. Those pictures might've been enough to fool Meadowlings and end up in that book, but they were amateurish. I was creating better ghost images as a child with a fraction of the tools." She huffed, frustration creeping into her tone. "I assure you, Eleanor Swan, the worst thing Harold and I are guilty of is shameless self-promotion. We're liars for the right fee, yes—but we're not murderers."

With that, Tilly returned to the table, her movements deliberate. She pressed a hidden button, and the dim lights brightened to full strength. Tilly's face was a map of creases, each line etched by decades of life. On any other day, Ellie might've asked her about those years—what she'd seen, what she remembered about every passing year. How had this woman, a living history book, been hiding all this time in the back room of the most infamous pub in Meadowfield?

But Ellie wasn't ready to drop the case.

Not yet.

"Why do you think Tim died?" Ellie asked.

Tilly's gaze drifted to the crystal ball, her expression

distant. She stared through it as if it were just a hunk of glass.

"I never intended to turn my back on my parents," Tilly said after a pause, her voice softer now. "But once they knew I wouldn't follow them into the spiritual world, they turned their backs on me. I started out with good intentions, but I've lost my integrity over the years—I'll admit that. It's easier than you think, in this world. But those who stand firm in their convictions... often become targets for those who want the truth buried."

Ellie's breath caught. "You think Tim found out who was behind everything and refused to back down?"

Tilly's gaze shifted to the bookshelf near the fuse box. "That printing company was offering cash for every photograph they printed. Over a dozen taken with my old equipment made their way into those pages." She exhaled heavily, pushing herself up from her seat but staying by the table. "It's time for me to prepare for the evening, but before I do... I know something that might stir the pot."

"Go on."

Tilly looked to the window, searching the dark alley. "About two hours ago, I was sitting by the wireless, listening to the radio, when I heard a commotion outside—someone kicking a door down, by the sound of it. I crossed the room to turn up the volume, and when I came back... a hooded figure was standing *there*, panting like he'd run a mile. He spoke to himself."

The Plot Thickens

Ellie's heart thudded in her chest as Tilly's dark eyes snapped back to her. She had to be talking about the museum's burglar.

"W-what did he say?" Ellie stammered, her throat tightening.

A faint smile played on Tilly's lips. "He said the most curious thing—that he was afraid *you* were going to kill him."

Ellie blinked, stunned. "Pardon?"

"*Ellie's going to kill me.* Those were his exact words." Tilly nodded surely. "And when he pulled down his hood to wipe the sweat from his youthful face, there was something *peculiar* about him." She raised her hands, using her index fingers to push her ears outward. "I've seen a lot in my years, but I've never seen a man with such enormous ears."

Ellie's stomach churned, dread twisting into rage as her mind raced.

"The man in the hood…" Ellie started, her voice tight. "… did he say anything else? Where he was going?"

Tilly shook her head, watching Ellie closely. "No. He didn't linger. He seemed afraid. Like he thought you were already on his heels. That's all I'll say tonight. Please…"

Ellie stood. "I'm leaving. Thank you, Tilly. You've been most informative."

"Good luck, Miss Swan," Tilly called after her. "Outlive me. I dare you."

Ellie bolted from the back room, her vision swimming as she stumbled down the corridor. The walls seemed to press in, the faint hum of the busying pub replaced by the thunder of her heartbeat. She braced herself against a stack of crisp boxes, struggling to steady her breath. But the anger was relentless, searing through her like wildfire.

"Ellie?" Harold's voice cut through her fury as he came thudding down the stairs. "You can't be back—"

Ignoring him, she straightened and pushed through the back door, not bothering to explain. She strode through the enclosed beer garden, the gate slamming shut behind her. As she reached South Street, she paused to catch her breath.

On the corner, the lights of Meadowfield Books glowed warmly. Through the window, she saw her gran, back from visiting Meredith. And Joey. The builder with the easy smile who'd reminded her of someone she couldn't put her finger on.

Ellie burst into the shop where Maggie and Joey were hunched over layout plans, pencils scratching, oblivious to her fury. Her stomach twisted at the sight. He'd been here all along, hiding in plain sight.

"You," Ellie said, her voice trembling despite herself. "Joey... I *trusted* you."

The Plot Thickens

"Ellie, what on earth—"

"Gran, get away from him," Ellie cried. "It's *him*. It's Joey. He broke into the museum. He was seen."

Maggie's smile faltered, her eyes darting between them. The colour drained from Joey's cheeks, and the look in his eyes told Ellie everything she needed to know. No denial came, and Maggie took a wary step back.

"Explain yourself, Joseph," Maggie stated, joining Ellie by the door. "Tell me Ellie has got things wrong."

"It's not what it looks like," he said, pleading with open palms. "Please... Maggie... Ellie... I wouldn't hurt you... I... I *can* explain."

Maggie looked as sick as Ellie felt. "I hope you can. Ellie, lock the door."

Ellie's hand hesitated on the latch, Joey's big brown eyes catching her off guard. He looked soft—he always had, like some cartoon character she couldn't help but root for. She couldn't stop thinking about how much Joey reminded her of Luke. She'd never let that thought bubble to the surface until now. The resemblance was messing with her head, but Luke would never have broken into a museum to try and steal evidence.

"It *was* you," Ellie said, her voice steadier now. "You kicked down the museum door. I don't think you found what you were looking for, but you left a receipt—for a speaker and a battery charger." She reached into her backpack and pulled out the plastic bag containing the device they'd unearthed at the war memorial. Tossing it onto the floorboards between them, she demanded, "Why, Joey? You weren't even born in 1994. You mentioned your grandad... was it him? Is this why you were pulling up the floorboards upstairs?"

"Ellie, I—"

"*No!*" she cut him off, her voice cracking. "I need to know why."

Maggie stepped in, resting a hand on Ellie's shoulder. "At least let the boy explain himself. And don't play dumb, Joey. I know you barely scraped by with that C in history, but don't act like you've never seen that thing before, whatever it is."

"I *haven't* seen it before!" Joey's voice cracked. "Not like that, at least. I've seen the parts, but I don't know what that is. And I was looking under the floorboards to *help* you, Ellie. I—" His words faltered as his eyes brimmed with tears he couldn't hold back. He turned away, groaning as he pressed his hands to his temples. He had a bandage patched against the back of his head from the boxes falling onto him. "This is why the nurse said I shouldn't be making big decisions—or operating machinery. But the money was too good, and I thought... I thought it would *help*. I'm not blaming anyone, but you're not paying me until you can, and I don't mind, but... my head hurts."

Ellie and Maggie exchanged bewildered glances.

"The money was too good from whom?" Maggie asked. "And don't lie, Joseph."

"I haven't lied!" Joey wiped his streaked face and

The Plot Thickens

turned back to them. "That old woman I met at the chippy last week," he muttered. "She reminded me of my nan, and it seemed harmless enough. She needed a speaker and a battery but couldn't find them in Meadowfield. She couldn't see very well, and since I was already heading to Marlborough for plaster mix, I thought..."

"Couldn't see?" Ellie pressed. "Was it Christina Marsh?"

"I don't know who that is," Joey muttered.

"Joey wasn't at the séance," Maggie reminded her. "Did she have a cane? Pearl handle at the top?"

"Yes!" Joey's eyes lit up with recognition. "That's her. I gave her my number after I bought those things for her. She called as I was being discharged from the hospital and told me this story about how the museum had stolen her belongings. She said she desperately needed them back and offered me five hundred quid to find some old tapes." He wiped his face with a trembling hand. "I'm... I'm sorry, Ellie. I didn't realise it was all connected, but I knew you'd be furious. I didn't mean to get caught up in this. I'm really, really sorry." He hesitated, then added softly, "You can hit me if you want. I deserve it."

Ellie's jaw tightened as she considered it, but after a moment, she sighed. "Joey, you're a big, concussed idiot. But I'm not going to hit you. What I need is for you to tell the police everything you just told me."

Maggie's voice was hesitant. "Are you sure that's wise?"

"Charles won't press charges once I explain the situation. Joey made a bad decision, but he's no more responsible for this than you or I."

"The way you barged in here," Maggie said. "I thought you were going to kill the lad."

"I wanted to," Ellie admitted. "I felt betrayed. But someone else needs to answer for their bad decisions first."

Maggie frowned. "Dr Marsh? I can't believe it. She seemed so nice. Why would she do this?"

Ellie's gaze hardened. "Maybe she wanted fame for publishing the pictures. Or maybe she needed the money. But the timing is too perfect. She was here when Tim died. Then she disappeared—only to 'return' when we found the graffiti on the wall, stirring everything up again. Nothing has been the same since."

"But Daniel gave her an alibi," Maggie pointed out. "During the séance, he swore she didn't move when the lights went out."

Ellie paused, chewing over the thought. Her eyes shifted to Joey, who shrank under her scrutiny. Dr Christina Marsh had no problem hiring people to do her dirty work.

"Gran, stay here and make sure Joey doesn't get it into his head to take on another job like this," Ellie said, unlocking the door. "I've got an appointment with a doctor."

The Plot Thickens

As Ellie left, a troubling thought crept in. Tilly's words echoed in her mind—about the strange sounds at the war memorial sparking everything the first time. A chill ran through her.

Had this all been one giant experiment for Doctor Christina Marsh's twisted amusement?

Chapter 20
The Doctor Will See You Now

Ellie slowed as she approached the Fenton residence, nothing between her and the icy wind. There was no denying Christmas was around the corner. Her mind felt caught in a rip current, tugging between Joey's tearful confession, Tilly's cryptic warnings, and the nagging sense that she was running out of time. She rubbed her temples as she walked, trying to knead the tension out of her skull.

She hadn't meant to scare Joey the way she had. His wide, pleading eyes had stuck with her, as much a mirror of his guilt as of her frustration. She hated how angry she'd been—not at him. Not really. It wasn't Joey's fault that she was chasing ghosts. Real ones, fake ones... it didn't matter anymore. They were leading her in circles.

She let out a breath and turned her attention back to the cottage. The light shifted softly behind the curtains, warm and welcoming as something played on the TV, but something about the stillness unsettled her. Ellie hesitated at the gate, her fingers brushing the latch. She felt silly, standing there like a nervous teenager. It was just Christina. Just another conversation, another question. But Ellie's instincts told her something was wrong.

As she reached for the door handle, a faint sound inside made her freeze. She strained to hear a muffled gurgling. Her heartbeat quickened. She edged towards the window and peeked through. The sitting room was dim, illuminated by the flickering light of an old *Columbo* episode. On-screen, the detective was mid-monologue, pausing with his signature, 'Just one more thing.'

Across the room, the glow fell on a hunched figure pressing a pillow over a shadowy form. Ellie burst through the door without thinking.

"*Stop!*" she shouted, her voice breaking with panic.

The attacker didn't flinch, their focus fixed on the pillow in their grip. Ellie snatched a framed photograph from a nearby shelf, and with a force she didn't know she had, she hurled it at the figure. The glass shattered, striking the side of their head. They recoiled with a grunt, dropping the pillow as the doctor beneath it gasped for air.

"Christina!" Ellie cried, rushing to her side.

The attacker staggered back, crashing into a coffee table with a sickening crack, their grunt revealing a man's voice.

The Plot Thickens

"Dr Marsh?" Ellie's arm wrapped around Christina's shoulders, her voice trembling. "It's me, Ellie. You need to get up."

Christina coughed, her hands clutching Ellie's arm. "I thought..." she whispered hoarsely, her eyes wide with fear. "I thought that was it."

"Not today," Ellie said firmly, her gaze darting to the attacker as they pulled themselves to their feet. "You've already died one too many times for my liking."

The man, masked and roughly Ellie's height, tried to loom over her, but his movements were unsteady. Even from across the room, Ellie caught the unmistakable stench of cigarettes and stale beer on his breath.

"You've made a huge mistake, Ellie," he growled, his Scottish accent sharp and unfamiliar.

Before Ellie could respond, Christina snatched her cane from where it had fallen and swung it with surprising speed. The cane struck the man squarely across the jaw, sending him stumbling into the wall.

"Out!" Ellie urged, half-dragging Christina towards the door. She grabbed the keys hanging by the frame, locking the Scottish man inside once they were outside. Fumbling with her phone, she called for the police.

"You... you saved my life," Christina said between shallow breaths. Her age showed now, her hands trembling against Ellie's for strength. "I'd already accepted my fate, but I've never wanted to live more than I do right now."

Ellie swallowed hard, her heart pounding. She

settled Christina on a large stone in Meredith's garden, looking back to the house for signs of movement.

"The police are on their way," Ellie said, settling beside her. "Whoever that was, they won't get far."

"Scottish," Christina croaked, rubbing at her throat. "I thought I'd know who this was... but I don't."

"Maybe they were hired. I came here because *you* paid Joey to break into the museum."

Christina continued rubbing at her neck, but she didn't deny the accusation.

"I... I only wanted my things back," she said quietly. "My old souvenirs. When you brought that tape, I wondered what else was still out there. There are more tapes—"

"More experiments?" Ellie pressed.

"Some, but most were home films we made."

"There was only one tape," Ellie said. "*Experiment 3.*"

Christina sighed. "I told you before, the experiments weren't what you think. But you'll never believe me, will you?"

Before Ellie could respond, the flashing lights of a police car swept over the street. PC Finn Walsh and another officer leapt out, and Ellie quickly explained the situation, directing them to the locked door.

Moments later, they returned, their expressions grim.

"It's empty," Finn said,shaking his head.

"A disappearing act," Christina said with a resigned sigh. "This is never going to end."

The Plot Thickens

"As frustrating as this is, you need to see a doctor."

Christina smiled faintly, the lines around her eyes deepening. "I prescribe myself a cup of tea. He... wasn't pushing that hard. Almost like he wasn't sure he wanted to go through with it. As if it was his first time."

Ellie stared at her, torn between anger and pity. The image of the attacker loomed in her mind—where had she recently heard a Scottish accent?

"Come inside," Christina said. "You've had as much of a fright as I have. We'll both feel better after a cuppa."

Ellie hesitated, glancing at the officers combing through the garden. She wasn't ready to let this go, not yet. But Christina's fragile figure leaning against the doorframe, her hands still trembling, softened something in her.

"Alright," Ellie said at last. "But only for a moment. Then I want answers."

Christina nodded, a shadow of relief crossing her face. "Answers," she murmured. "Yes. I suppose you deserve them."

Ellie and Christina sat in the back room of the cottage, sipping strong tea amidst the eclectic collection of Meredith's trinkets. Wind chimes tinkled softly in the breeze from the open window, and the warm textures of rugs and tapestries enveloped the space. It felt like stepping into a showroom for Willow's Apothecary.

"I hope I haven't got your builder friend into trouble," Christina began, setting her cup on its saucer. Her gaze rested on the peach gleam of a nearby salt lamp. "I'll take full responsibility."

"I'll tell Charles to send the invoice for the new door your way," Ellie replied, half-joking. Christina merely nodded as though the idea was entirely reasonable. "The experiments on those tapes—"

"How about we stop calling what Tim and I did *experiments*?" Christina interrupted, her tone sharp yet calm. "That's what we thought they were at the time, but now? They'd be seen more as intensive therapy sessions."

"He was screaming, Christina."

"Child, he was grieving for his father," Christina said firmly, her voice taking on a measured, almost clinical quality. "Everyone else turned it into something more. Meredith, mainly. She was the one who convinced Tim it was a good idea. She believed that intense trauma could weaken the veil between the living and the dead."

Ellie shifted in the beanbag. "Like her near-miss with that car?"

"Exactly." Christina exhaled as if relieved not to have to explain. "When someone has a brush with death, the mind bends around it. Meredith once described her experience—a sunny afternoon, she said, which was why she thought the bright light she saw couldn't have been from a car. A car she claimed she hadn't noticed until her ball rolled into the road. I took her account at face value until George showed me an old newspaper clipping about her claims. She told reporters her brother's ghost saved her in early November, at about four in the afternoon."

"Dark enough for headlights," Ellie said, "at that time of year."

"Precisely. But light enough for a child to pretend it was still daytime so she wouldn't have to go home to grieving parents." Christina shook her head, though Ellie suspected her disapproval was aimed more at Meredith's parents than at Meredith herself. "When I showed her the evidence, Meredith dismissed my theory outright. We decided no one could really know the truth. Childhood memories are unreliable. Perhaps the driver hadn't switched on their lights—cars didn't have automatic sensors then. Who's to say? For years, I was obsessed with changing people's minds about things I could disprove, but that session with Tim taught me something."

Ellie frowned. "I still don't understand what I saw."

"You saw a man finally releasing his pent-up grief," Christina said quietly. "Tim hadn't been able to cry—not even at his father's funeral. I told him stories I'd gathered from his family, little moments of love and kindness that showed what his father meant to him. That was all he needed to break. And in that moment, I realised something about myself." She lowered her head, tears spilling down her cheeks. "I finally understood why I'd been so driven to challenge people's beliefs. It was *my* father. No one ever believed what he was capable of."

Christina exhaled, letting go of something she'd been holding onto. "He was the life-of-the-party fisherman with a drinking problem. My mother worked in a salon where she could buy the thickest makeup to hide the bruises. After she died at forty-four from a heart attack brought on by years of stress, I spent years trying to make people see the truth about him. But I lost everything trying. When I vanished in 1999, it wasn't the first time I'd disappeared. I left my family behind years before that, and that's when little Tina became Dr Christina Marsh. It was when I turned to science."

Ellie's throat tightened as she pulled a tissue from a jewel-encrusted box nearby, handing it to Christina. She accepted it with a small squeeze of Ellie's fingers.

"The pain never truly leaves," Christina said, dabbing at her teary eyes. "It was fresh for Tim, and even though his rational mind knew better, he *wanted* to believe. He thought our session might give him clarity. I wasn't sure what would happen, but I gave him the space to feel, and I saw him change. After that, he stopped letting his grief consume him. That's when he started investigating those photographs that kept turning up at his studio."

Christina echoed Tilly's assessment.

"You think Tim worked out who was faking the pictures and was killed because of it?" Ellie asked.

Christina's lips tightened, her silence speaking volumes before she said, "It's a theory I've considered. But I couldn't prove it, and I couldn't disprove it either.

The Plot Thickens

As for the video, there was no sound because I wanted to respect Tim's privacy. I didn't want Meredith using it as ammunition. She was desperate to find anything to support her beliefs. I also know she took my notes about Tim's father. When I saw her séance script, it was clear she'd stolen them from me. She was determined to push Tim further—at the pub, no less, on top of that so-called ancient graveyard. She thought she could bring the dead back."

"But all she managed to create," Ellie said, sinking into the beanbag under the weight of the information, "were the perfect circumstances for murder."

Christina rose from her chair, brushing herself off. "For what it's worth, I don't believe Meredith or George could kill anyone. But that's only my opinion—anecdotal evidence. I've spent years reflecting on all of this. I was so lonely back then, trying to build a family from the Ghost Watch. And for the briefest of moments, we had one." A car door slammed outside. Christina sighed. "That'll be the detective."

But Ellie wasn't finished. "Why did you plant the device?"

Christina smiled faintly. "Which time?" She lingered by the door, sighing before continuing. "I wouldn't say I caused the hysteria of 1994, but I do believe my little device at the war memorial was the crack that broke the dam. The cold spots started a week later, and the unexplainable photographs cropped up the month after. I knew Meredith liked to meditate there in the afternoons, so I planted the device to see if she'd fall for it. It was a cruel trick, considering she and George were hosting me while I was between homes. But I couldn't take another day hearing her drone on about ghosts, spirits, orbs... I meant to fool her, then reveal the trick—show her how easily she could be misled." Any trace of a smile melted away. "And she did fall for it. They *all* did. But instead of coming clean, I stood back and watched. I became fascinated by how quickly the belief spread. By the time I wanted to stop it—when I started actively debunking everything—I was too much of a coward to admit to planting the device in the first place."

Ellie tilted her head. "Why didn't you just publish your evidence?"

Christina shrugged as if it were a trivial question. "They wouldn't have believed me. Besides, I was too busy playing pool with my new friends. I suppose I didn't want the fun to end."

She shuffled away with the careful gait of someone carrying years of regrets, leaving Ellie to her thoughts. Watching Christina go, she felt certain the doctor wasn't guilty of murder. And as her gaze drifted over Meredith's makeshift shrine to the paranormal, Ellie realised something else.

Meredith wasn't guilty either. Despite the rumours and the graffiti on the wall trying to immortalise the blame, Meredith's hunger for the supernatural didn't come from malice. It came from hope. So, who was the person exploiting that hope?

* * *

Detective Inspector Angela Cookson stepped into Ellie's path in the hallway. Expecting a confrontation, Ellie was surprised by Angela's unexpectedly gentle tone. "I heard you saved Christina from being suffocated," she said, folding her arms tightly. "Well done."

Ellie nodded, her heart still pounding from the adrenaline rush. Silently, she entered the living room and picked up the fallen picture frame. A crack ran through the glass, dividing George and Meredith on their wedding day—George rigid in his formal suit, Meredith glowing in her flowery gown. They were young, free, and gazing at each other as if nothing could stand in their way.

Ellie studied the photo and said, almost to herself, "She looked at him the same way in the hospital. Wrong for each other in all the right ways."

Angela sighed. "What are you talking about?"

Ellie set the frame back on the table. "Just something Meredith said."

"Do you know anything about the man who attacked Christina?" Angela asked, flipping open a pad. "Age? Description?"

"Medium height, dressed in black, average build," Ellie recalled. "He reeked of cigarette smoke and ale—

and had a Scottish accent." As she said it, a spark of memory flared. She hadn't heard a Scottish accent recently until saving Christina from her attacker, but she had heard about a man from Scotland. "The decorator's son."

"What?" Angela asked, puzzled.

"Do you remember dinner at my gran's before the séance? She mentioned contacting the old decorator about the graffiti in the bookshop. The company had shut down, but someone answered the phone. A Scottish man—she said it was the decorator's son."

Angela sighed, clearly unconvinced. "That's a bit of a leap, don't you think?"

Ellie nodded, but the thought stuck in her mind. It felt too coincidental to ignore.

"I was already on my way here to give Christina this." Angela reached into her coat and pulled out a brown envelope. "It's the package she handed over after George's fall—the evidence he found in the attic."

"What's inside?" Ellie asked.

"Old photography negatives," Angela said. "We found two sets of fingerprints on them. One belonged to George. The other... we're still working on it. And for what it's worth, it doesn't seem like Tim ever touched them."

"But they did come from his camera," Ellie said, her hands trembling as she pulled out the rust-coloured negatives. Squinting at them, she recognised the images from the book. "The camera Tim bought from Tilly when he was a teenager—the same one he sold to George. George bought it for Meredith so she could create pictures of her brother." She glanced up at the ceiling, imagining the dusty attic. "Meredith told me earlier that the camera bag was still in the attic. These must have been inside. George found them and pieced something together."

Angela snapped her pad shut, her patience thinning. "What are you wittering on about? Why does any of this matter?"

Ellie flicked through the negatives, her fingers trembling. "Because that camera was stolen from George and Meredith not long after they bought it from Tim. I doubt Tim knew it was being used to fake these ghost photographs—not when he sold it. But whoever stole it *needed* that camera for their ghost pictures. And after Tim's death, they got rid of it. They hid it in the bookshop. When we found it..." She paused, digging in her bag. Her voice dropped to a whisper. "Jack told me they submitted the photos under Tim's name to honour him. But this was never about honour."

"Ellie, for the love of—"

"The Scottish accent. The father..." Ellie's breath hitched as the pieces fell into place. "Oh, he *told* me about his father." She opened the book and flipped to the back page, where Tim Baker was credited for all the photographs. "Tim's name was never supposed to be there. But how could Jack put anyone else's name on these pictures after everything? It was always about this camera—and these photographs."

Angela's expression shifted as something clicked. "There's more. The chemical I mentioned?"

"The one splashed on Tim's clothes?" Ellie confirmed.

Angela nodded. "It was on these negatives. A rare developing liquid, only used in old photography."

"Then it's true," Ellie whispered, staring at the book in her hands. "Tim figured out who was behind these pictures, and they killed him to keep the truth hidden."

"But murder over some photographs?"

Ellie snapped the book shut. "Murder for glory. And money. Jack was in the bookshop when we found the camera. He acted like he'd never seen it before, but I had a feeling he had. Cassie too—she *told* me. So did George. And Jack."

"Told you *what?*"

Ellie met Angela's eyes. "That all Jack ever wanted was to live up to his father."

Angela froze. "Kenneth Campbell?"

"You've heard of him?"

Angela nodded slowly. "Everyone around here has. Maybe not someone your age, but Kenneth was a local legend. He took those riot photographs that made the national press. He never paid for a pint at the pub again."

Ellie squeezed her eyes shut, dredging up a memory. "Gran said the man on the phone with the Scottish accent told her that his father wasn't interested in

The Plot Thickens

running the decorating business. He had hobbies. Do you know what Kenneth did when he wasn't taking pictures?"

Angela's face lit up, her lips parting, but the words didn't come.

"Angela?" Ellie pushed.

The detective gulped. "He... he was a painter and decorator. Ken never took another photograph like those riot pictures. People said he died feeling like a failure—always chasing his glory years."

"Ken!" Ellie groaned, the missed connection glaring at her. "Gran said the man who ran the decorating company was called Ken. I think I've been researching the wrong local ghost stories." She shoved the book back into her bag. "He's been hiding behind the lens, showing off his accents. The first time I visited the studio, he spoke with an American accent. I heard him doing Poirot for Tim on that tape." She groaned louder, hating that she'd missed so much. "He was there when I woke up in the pub! He took a picture of me, and I had his coat draped over me, and the tape had gone. He was *right* there. We need to get to Tim's old studio."

"This is still my case," Angela snapped, marching towards the front door. "Those other fingerprints on the negatives? They didn't belong to a *man*."

Ellie followed, catching the door before it swung shut. Christina waved off paramedics draping a red blanket over her shoulders by an ambulance. Angela jumped into her car and slammed the door but hesitated before starting the engine. With a reluctant huff, she leaned over and shoved the passenger door open. Ellie climbed in without a word, and they sped towards South Street.

Angela broke the tense silence. "If there's anything else you're holding back, I'll still have you arrested for interfering."

Ellie's reply stuck in her throat as she spotted a thick plume of smoke rising above the village. Angela's eyes widened. She accelerated, grabbing the radio from the dashboard.

"Fire brigade attendance at Meadowfield village centre," Angela barked. "Possible fire in progress." She paused before adding, "It appears to be coming from South Street. Over."

The smoke loomed closer, thick against the night sky. Ellie gripped the edge of the seat, dread pooling in her chest. "Please don't be the bookshop."

Chapter 21
All The Wrong Ways

Ellie and Angela sprinted down the narrow back alley of South Street, thick smoke billowing orange against the night sky from behind one of the shops. Ellie's chest tightened with dread, but relief flooded her as they rounded the bend. The bookshop was further down the street—on the opposite side.

But her relief was short-lived—Tim Baker's Studio was the shop ablaze.

"*This* is where that old shoe shop used to be," Angela said between breaths. "Right under their studio."

"Which shoe shop?" Ellie asked, struggling to keep up.

"The old plastic bag you gave me the Victorian projector in. Zara's gift shop used to be *that* shoe shop." Angela shook her head, frustrated with herself. "I should have made the connection."

Zara watched in despair in the yard, her hair

wrapped in a silk scarf and her dressing gown drawn tight. Behind her, the door to her basement flat hung ajar, the faint sound of the ten o'clock news drifting out. Ellie caught a snippet about Meredith's recovery following George's fall.

"Where are the fire brigade?" Zara demanded, throwing her hands towards the crackling flames. "I smelled the smoke, and *who* do I see running out of the studio? Bonnie and Clyde!"

"Jack and Cassie?" Angela clarified, scanning the area.

"They have been blasting that dreadful music all night!" Zara exclaimed. "I have had enough! They treat me like a second-class citizen. I have made complaints, and still nothing changes! If you do not do something about them—"

"I promise we'll address it," Angela cut her off, her tone clipped, eyes fixed on the flames. "I'm sure I saw a fire extinguisher near the door last time I was here."

Without waiting for a response, Angela darted up the metal staircase, taking the steps two at a time. Ellie followed close behind, and she spotted the two planters near the door, their flowers wilted and lifeless. On a hunch, she rocked one back and saw the glint of a key hidden underneath.

"I found—" Ellie began, but Angela poised her elbow.

She thrust it through the window and the glass shattered with a crack, sending shards raining into the studio. Shielding her face, Angela reached through the jagged frame and unlocked the door from the inside.

Ellie tugged her paint-splattered jumper over her nose, her heart pounding as she searched the room. The smoke clawed at her throat, the heat of the flames licking against her skin. She noticed the extinguisher tucked under a shelf by the door. She grabbed it and held it at arm's length, unsure of herself.

"I've never used one," Ellie admitted, her voice wavering. "What do I—"

"Useless!" Angela snapped, snatching the extinguisher. "Get outside. *Now*."

Angela pulled the pin and squeezed the trigger. Instead of a burst of suffocating foam, a stream of colourful silly string erupted from the nozzle, melting into the flames. Ellie stared in disbelief as the fire responded with mocking pops and crackles, the sound almost gleeful.

"Is this a joke?" Ellie breathed. "We need to do something before this spreads across the whole street."

Angela stood frozen, still gripping the novelty extinguisher, and Ellie's stomach plummeted at the sight of what was burning. A heap of photography equipment lay engulfed in flames atop the large table. Among the wreckage, Ellie spotted the unmistakable outline of the 1862 camera they'd unearthed in the bookshop before it had been stolen for a second time. Its wooden frame burned brightest, disintegrating into ash before her eyes.

"There must be a tap in here—" Angela began, but a feral scream cut off her words.

The sound ripped through the studio like a war cry, raw and unhinged. Ellie spun around, bracing for Cassie's familiar charge. But it wasn't Cassie—it was Sylvia.

Eyes clenched shut, Sylvia dashed through the open door, a bucket clutched in her hands. With a wild swing, she hurled its contents over Ellie, Angela, and the fire. The freezing water drenched them all, eliciting a stifled squeak from Ellie as the flames sputtered and fizzled out.

Shivering, Ellie tugged her soaked jumper away from her skin and said, "So that's what it feels like to have a drink thrown at you."

"Oh, dear!" Sylvia opened her eyes, horrified. "What have I done?"

"You saved the day," Ellie reassured her.

Ellie moved closer, joining Angela at the smouldering table. Angela hunched over the smoke, using the tip of her pen to sift through the blackened debris, her movements deliberate and precise.

"It hasn't been burning for long," Ellie said.

Angela shot her a sharp look. "I told you to wait outside."

Ellie ignored her. "Looks like they built a campfire on their way out," she said, scanning the studio. The last time she'd been here, a young punk had been posing for a photoshoot while an older one sat at the table, casually eating chips. "They must feel the walls closing in."

The Plot Thickens

Angela didn't reply. She shifted the charred antique camera frame aside with her pen, her focus razor-sharp as though searching for something specific.

"What are you looking for?" Ellie asked, stepping closer. "I can help."

"*Enough*, Eleanor."

Before Ellie could respond, a faint creak echoed across the room. Both women turned as Zara pushed open a door on the far side of the studio. A rich red light spilled out, bathing the space in a sinister glow.

Zara gasped at what she saw inside, stumbling back into a bookcase. A cascade of books tumbled to the floor, and Sylvia grabbed Zara's arm just in time to stop her from losing her footing completely.

"Zara?" Sylvia whispered, steadying her. "It's just a red light. It can't hurt you."

"I *knew* it," Zara hissed, jabbing a trembling finger at the open door. "I told you these people were evil. I felt it in my bones!"

Angela ignored the commotion, still digging through the smoking pile. Ellie, however, moved towards the door, curiosity overriding her discomfort. She pushed it open further, revealing the source of the crimson light: the darkroom. She'd seen Cassie disappearing in there during her previous visit.

Photographs hung on washing lines crisscrossing the room, glistening from the developing solution. Ellie held her breath as she stepped closer. She assumed the lines were cluttered with multiple images, but she drew nearer—it was the same photograph, repeated over and over.

Her stomach churned as she reached out and plucked the nearest print from the line. The string snapped back, sending the remaining photographs fluttering, their wet surfaces gleaming in the red glow. The movement made them seem alive... taunting her, mocking them all.

She brought the print closer, her hands trembling. The image was blurred, warped by motion: a dark silhouette of a figure, jagged black lines jutting from its head like spikes. The camera's movement had smeared the figure's form, the lines stretching upward, distorting the composition.

A chill ran down Ellie's spine.

"What is it?" Sylvia whispered.

Ellie didn't answer. She couldn't bring herself to speak. She already knew.

Finally, the sound of approaching sirens broke the silence, their wails cutting through the night.

"It is a demon!" Zara declared, her voice trembling. "I *told* you..."

But Ellie wasn't listening. Her eyes were locked on the spiked silhouette repeated across the photographs. The jagged mohawk was unmistakable.

Her hands trembled with white-hot rage as she tore each picture from the line, the string snapping back and sending the others bouncing wildly. Tim Baker's studio. They'd done this here, of all places. His sign still hung outside, banging against the dead flower basket in the wind. How *dare* they.

She marched to the table and slammed the pile of pictures down next to Angela, who was holding something up by its strap with the tip of her pen. The object had been twisted and warped by the fire, its plastic body blackened and melted. But enough remained for Ellie to recognise what it must be.

"Tim Baker's missing camera," she whispered.

Angela nodded, sighing. "A vintage Zenit E from the 1960s. My dad had one of these when I was little. You've seen it before?"

"No, but do you remember your theory?" Ellie gulped, the pictures shaking in her hands. "Back at my gran's cottage, after dinner—you told me what your final shot would be if you had a camera around your neck when you were pushed to your death."

Angela hesitated, her face tightening. "I was half-joking."

"Tim Baker wasn't."

"What do you—" Angela's expression shifted, her eyes widening as Ellie spread the photographs across the scorched table. "Tim's final photograph."

Ellie nodded, unable to look away. "How did you know the camera would be in the fire?"

"A guess," Angela muttered. She pulled one of the pictures closer, studying the blurred, haunting image. "I showed Jack a picture of the camera model, and I didn't mention I knew it was Tim's. I pretended I was off-duty to gauge his reaction. He claimed he'd never seen one before. I thought maybe he'd forgotten what it looked like or that his memory was failing him... and then George was pushed, and I got a little sidetracked."

"Jack did the same to me with the antique camera," Ellie said, her voice tight. She couldn't bring herself to look at the twisted remains of the camera that had caused so much destruction. A thing of beauty, now ruined. But its legacy—the chaos and pain—still rippled through the village. "Jack has been lying about everything. We need to find him."

Angela spun to Zara. "Bonnie and Clyde? Did you see which way they went?"

"They were talking about going to the pub," Zara said, her gaze fixed on the photographs of the spiky-haired man. "For one last drink, Cassie said."

"This makes *no* sense," Sylvia exclaimed. "Why develop this incriminating image at all?"

The answer was clear to Ellie, but Angela voiced it first.

"Because he thinks there's no way he can be caught," Angela said, setting off at a run. "And for thirty years, he's proved himself right—"

She stopped mid-step as Dr Christina Marsh shuffled into the studio with PC Walsh's help.

"Have you ever heard the theory," Christina croaked, her voice rasping with effort, "that most murderers subconsciously desire to be caught? No recognition, no glory." Her fingers brushed her neck, as though the pillow from earlier still pressed down. "You're talking about Jack Campbell, aren't you?"

Angela's eyes narrowed. "What do you know?"

Christina let out a shaky breath, easing into a chair with Ellie's help. "When you left George's cottage, I remembered something about the Scottish accent… and how the man trying to strangle me didn't use it until Ellie arrived. He wasn't afraid of me recognising his voice because it was meant to be the last thing I ever heard." She paused, her words slow and deliberate. "I imagine he wanted me to figure it out, but it didn't click until I heard about the fire at Tim's studio. I… I haven't been here in so many years." She stared around the place as though she could see how it once was. "And Jack's is a voice I haven't heard in just as long—it took my memory a little while to catch up."

"What did he say to you?" Ellie asked, crouching by her side.

"That it was about time he cleaned up his mess," Christina whispered, her cloudy eyes briefly closing. "If you hadn't arrived when you did, I would have died thinking we weren't so different. He wanted me to realise that. I sent that naive boy to the museum to steal back my tapes, afraid they might hold something that could make me appear guilty. It took a cup of tea to stir my old mind, but then I remembered what I'd always thought of Jack."

She paused, exhaling shakily. "Years ago, I wrote a letter summarising the evidence I'd given to the police. Along with it, I included psychological assessments of each member of the group. I outlined who I thought were the most likely suspects, even though the police didn't agree with me."

Ellie's heart skipped. "Was that letter ever given to Tim's mother?" She tossed her backpack onto the table, fumbling with the zip.

Christina nodded. "It was. I told her it was my way of apologising, but before I could explain the contents, she slammed the door in my face. She said she didn't want an apology without an explanation. I posted the letter through her door, but I never knew if she read it."

"She didn't," Ellie said, pulling out the envelope and pressing it into Christina's hand. "Tim's cousin gave me this. It's still sealed."

Christina looked down at it, her trembling fingers moving to open it, but Angela snatched the envelope and slid it into an evidence bag. She shook her head at Ellie before she passed the bag to Finn. Angela left the studio, and Ellie wanted to follow, but she wanted to hear the doctor's assessments.

"What did you conclude about Jack?" Ellie pressed, her voice soft but insistent.

"The others were easier." Christina exhaled, the sound rattling deep in her chest. "Meredith was whimsical, imaginative, and vulnerable—her obsession with the paranormal was rooted in unresolved trauma and identity struggles. But I didn't believe she was malicious. George struggled with his rational worldview clashing with Meredith's beliefs. He feared losing control, but I never concluded he'd kill to protect that worldview." After a pause, she added, "I did also recognise that they were my friends, making me biased."

"They're not murderers," Ellie said, "and I don't care what that wall in the bookshop says—Meredith *didn't* kill Tim Baker." She'd never been more certain of anything. "And the others?"

"Harold and Tilly were greedy and they didn't try to hide it," Christina continued. "They eavesdropped on all our meetings, cooking up their marketing plans. I never cared at the time since it was as silly as everything else going on, but I did conclude that if Tim had thrown a spanner in the works, they could have pushed him to kill for self-preservation." Inhaling sharply, she took a moment to gather her thoughts before she said, "And then there was Cassie. Loyal but deeply anxious, screaming at the world before it screamed at her. We had a heart-to-heart over a game of pool once—a rare moment without Jack hovering over her like a shadow. She told me about her unloving family, how they'd kept her older siblings and given her away. I understood we weren't too different. She said she never felt love until Jack. He was her whole world. She desperately sought his approval, his validation..." Christina trailed off, her lips tightening. "And then there was Jack."

Ellie leaned closer, and she could have heard a pin drop in the silent studio.

"Jack left no impression at all." Christina shook her head, anger twisting her face. She might have been blinded by time, but she seemed to see it all so clearly now. "He was always behind his camera, documenting everything. Looking back, I think I understand why we rarely spoke."

Ellie swallowed the lump in her throat. "Jack avoided you because you were the *one* person who might have seen through him."

Christina nodded, her expression heavy with regret. "Yes. And I let it slip past me. I was so busy trying to play happy families with strangers that I didn't stop to question the gaps. If I hadn't been so focused on keeping the peace, I might have seen him for who he truly is."

Ellie rested her hands over Christina's. "This isn't your fault."

"Isn't it?" Christina replied, offering a sad, brittle smile. "My dear, I was there. I saw the signs. And, like with my father, I chose to look away until it was too late."

"Monsters," Zara whispered, her voice shaking as she knelt to gather the books she'd knocked over. "They have been above my shop this whole time. I told everyone they were trouble. The police, the council... but I—I could have done more."

"Oh, Zara!" Sylvia swept to her side to help with the books. "You couldn't have known. I always thought you were being harsh on Jack. He took the photographs for my shop's website, and I thought he was sweet. I should have sniffed him out as a murderer."

"Some people are very good at hiding in plain sight,"

The Plot Thickens

Christina murmured with a wag of her finger. "They only reveal their true selves through the cracks."

Ellie's mind spun, replaying every interaction she'd had with Jack. He'd hidden behind his camera during their first meeting in the bookshop. And in the studio, he'd casually eaten chips while talking about Tim being his best friend. He'd photographed her while she slept in the pub, draping his coat over her like some warped act of kindness. She could count only one moment where she might have glimpsed the real Jack—when he'd warned her to 'leave it alone' in the smoking area. Even then, Harold had seemed the harsher of the two.

"We saw what he wanted us to see," Ellie said quietly, helping Zara stack the books. She searched the titles, but the one she was looking for, the book containing Kenneth Campbell's famous photographs, wasn't there.

Of course, he wouldn't have left *that* book behind to perish in the fire.

"He inherited a sense of failure from his father," Ellie continued. "And he's been trying to make up for it ever since."

"My third husband was like that," Sylvia admitted, hugging herself. "He thought he had me wrapped around his finger, and he did—for a while. But I saw through him in the end."

Ellie thought of Cassie, her chest aching. "But what if you'd never seen through him? What if you'd stayed wrapped around his finger?"

"Then I imagine you would have led a miserable life," Christina concluded, her tone low and measured. "As did my mother. My only regret now is that I didn't do more to warn the girl away from him. Even then, I couldn't shake the feeling they were a poor match. Cassie believed in ghosts, whereas Jack constantly flip-flopped his opinions about the afterlife. I never understood why, but looking back, I imagine the times he claimed to believe were when Cassie was present, and other times... it didn't matter."

Heavy boots on the metal stairs broke the silence as the firefighters arrived. Ellie stepped back, leaving Sylvia and Zara to explain the situation.

Another fire needed extinguishing—the one that had been burning since 1994. And it might already be too late.

Ellie caught up to Angela at the top of South Street. The detective stood rigid, barking orders into her radio as she stared at the distant glow of The Drowsy Duck. Her voice cut through the night, demanding every available officer in Wiltshire converge on Meadowfield without question.

"Don't arrest Jack," Ellie said firmly.

"What?" Angela snapped, setting off again without pause. "I don't have time for this. Playtime is over."

But Ellie wasn't playing. She'd never been more serious—never surer.

"I'm asking you to trust me," Ellie said, hurrying to

The Plot Thickens

keep pace as they wound around the duck pond. "I know you don't like me, but—"

"This isn't about any of that," Angela barked, her strides lengthening. "This is about ending this case."

"And you will," Ellie assured her, nearly jogging to keep up. "But don't arrest Jack. Not first, at least. Arrest Cassie."

Angela stopped, turning on her heel. "Ellie, I won't—"

"Cassie needs to see what kind of man Jack is," Ellie pressed, her voice rising with urgency. "And so does everyone else." She took a steadying breath. "A ghost pushed Tim Baker to his death in 1994."

Angela's eyes narrowed. "A *ghost*? Do you honestly think that will hold up in court? It can't be proven. It can't be explained—"

"Except tonight, it *can*," Ellie interrupted, grabbing Angela's arm to stop her just shy of the pub's glow. The clacking of billiard balls and muffled laughter seeped into the crisp night air. Ellie's voice dropped. "Arrest Cassie first, and Meadowlings might finally see who has been haunting this town."

"*Ellie!*" The voice cut through the moment, sharp and familiar. Ellie turned to see Auntie Penny hurrying towards her, rounding the corner from the direction of Carolyn's cottage near the green. "There you are! I knew I could hear your voice. We've been texting and calling—"

Ellie pinched the bridge of her nose. "I've been a little busy, Auntie Penny."

"But there's been an emergency!" Penny insisted, grabbing Ellie's jumper. "A *huge* one!"

"It's *never* an emergency," Ellie said, trying to tug away. "Tell my mother she can fix her hair or find another camera person because we're about to—"

"This *is* about the cameraman!" Penny cut in, her voice rising. "And it *is* an emergency. We know who killed Tim Baker, and we have *proof*."

Ellie froze as Penny's eyes darted past her to Angela, who had returned to her radio to mutter in more commands.

"DS Cookson, you'll want to come too," Penny added, her unusually firm gaze urging them to follow her. "Carolyn won't be happy about you coming into the house, but you *must* see this."

Chapter 22
The Final Truth Bomb

Ten minutes later, the faint clink of glass bottles echoed behind the bar at The Drowsy Duck. Harold was restocking the shelves, his eyes fixed on the bell that would chime for last orders in another few hours. Despite the drama of the séance, the pub was still packed. Ellie's mother and aunt sat at a table, waiting for their cue.

Cassie and Jack occupied the pool table, playing a listless game with mechanical movements. Cassie lined up her shot, going through the motions, while Jack stood idle with a thousand-yard stare.

They should have run after setting the fire.

But Jack was too sure of himself.

Ellie stepped into his line of sight. His brows lifted, and he gave Cassie a nudge with his pool cue. He tried to look indifferent, but his eyes betrayed him—they darted for the exit with a flare of panic.

Cassie whirled around, ready to pounce. But this time, Ellie held her ground. She strode further into the pub as the door swung open behind her. DS Angela Cookson entered with her team of officers filing in behind her. The low murmur of conversation stilled as the officers formed a wall between the pool table and the door. Behind the bar, Harold froze with a bottle of vodka in hand, his face revealing the fear Jack and Cassie struggled to conceal.

Angela's voice cut cleanly through the silence. "Cassandra Winters?" she called. "You're under arrest for the murder of Tim Baker, the attempted murder of George Fenton, arson, and multiple counts of perverting the course of justice. You do not have to say anything, but—"

Cassie didn't let the detective finish. She flung her pool cue onto the table with a sharp clatter and bolted for the door. She crashed headlong into the waiting officers, thrashing as they pinned her against a table. Pints of beer toppled, smashing onto the floor.

"*Jack!*" Cassie screamed desperately. Frothy spittle splattered across the table as the cable tie handcuffs tightened around her wrists. "Jack, do *something!*"

Cassie twisted in the officers' grip, her body jerking as they hauled her upright. She craned her neck to look at Jack.

"Help me, Jack!"

But Jack didn't move.

The Plot Thickens

"Jack?" Cassie's voice wavered, breaking into a soft, pitiful plea. "Why won't you *do* something?"

The silence was unbearable, suffocating the room like an oppressive fog. It was Ellie who finally broke it. Clearing her throat, she strode to the pool table. She picked up a lone yellow ball from the corner and rolled it into a pocket. The ball rattled through the machine with a metallic clink, but Jack's gaze stayed fixed on her.

"He won't help you, Cassie," Ellie said, her voice steady, slicing through the air like a knife through butter. "He's happy to let you take the blame. Just like he was happy for Tim to take the fall for those fake ghost photos."

Reaching into her bag, Ellie pulled out the hefty *The Real Ghosts of Wiltshire* book and dropped it onto the pool table with a loud thud. She flipped it open to the middle pages, but Jack's eyes never left hers.

"You said those photos were mysteriously left on the studio doorstep," Ellie continued. "But if someone had proof of ghosts—real, *undeniable* proof—why wouldn't they claim the glory? Accept the applause? No one captures evidence of the impossible to then hide in the shadows."

Jack's silence was damning as his hardened stare faltered. He looked around for an escape that didn't exist.

"Did you ever care about the ghosts?" Ellie asked, tilting her head at the book. "Or was it a means to an end?

A way to get yourself into the history books?" She fixed him with an unwavering glare, her voice sharper now. "Did the money even matter, Jack? Or was it all about reclaiming your father's lost glory? You had the whole village in the palm of your hand with these pictures. But you didn't publish them under *your* name. That must've stung."

Still, he gave her nothing.

Ellie continued, "When I started looking into all this, I found an old article where you said you were a sceptic. That you'd only believe in ghosts if you saw convincing proof." She slid *The Real Ghosts of Wiltshire* across the green felt table to him, open to the infamous photo of the ghost in the cellar beneath the pub. "But these photos weren't left anonymously on the studio doorstep, were they? And Tim didn't make them. He had the skills and the equipment, yes—but he didn't want to *trick* people. That wasn't who he was." She shook her head, disgusted. "To claim this book was published to honour him? That's an insult to everything he stood for."

Jack's response was a deep, venomous hiss. "You know nothing."

Ellie leaned in, gripping the edge of the pool table. "Don't I? I know there were women's fingerprints on the original negatives. It won't take much to confirm they belong to Cassie. You've been trying to tidy up the mess you made—hiding evidence wherever you could—but there were things you couldn't cover up. Not in the walls, not under the floor."

She produced an envelope from her bag and

The Plot Thickens

scattered the negatives onto the book's open pages. Jack's hands darted to his thinning hair, raking through it before scratching at his neck, leaving deep red streaks in his stubble.

"You must have panicked when Tim sold that 1862 camera to George in 1994," Ellie continued. "Tim didn't know *you* were using it, but that's why you stole it. Though maybe you should've taken the bag too. You left the negatives behind, and they've been waiting in George's attic for thirty years. He must have connected the dots—you were who he was waiting to meet in the bathroom. He was a fair man. He wanted to give you the benefit of the doubt, and that's why you cut the lights and pushed him. Just like you did to Tim." Ellie exhaled a shaky breath, unable to look at him. She looked at the closed cellar door. "You pushed your best friend with such force that he flew down the steps to the cellar without hitting a single one. If only George had a camera around his neck..."

Ellie pulled out another photograph and placed it carefully on top of the negatives. Jack's eyes locked on it, transfixed, as though he were staring back at himself down the years.

"Tim Baker's final photograph," Ellie said, a disbelieving laugh escaping her lips. "It's almost poetic. You spent your whole life trying to capture an image that would make people remember you, only to become the subject of a picture that will outlive you. You wanted to be Jack Campbell, the photographer—not Jack

Campbell, the son of Kenneth Campbell. Ken. Scottish Ken. Part-time photographer, part-time painter and decorator. A man who never had to buy his own pint because even when he felt like a failure, people respected him. I bet you worked with him on the bookshop back in '94?" She paused, waiting, but Jack gave her nothing.

"Wrap it up, Ellie," Angela ordered from behind.

"Tim figured out what you were doing that night at the séance," Ellie pressed on. "Tim's cousin told me that he'd been digging in his mum's attic and something he found—or *didn't* find—made him storm out. That was the last time his mother saw him. She died not knowing what happened to her son." Her voice shrank, a knot in her chest. But she wasn't finished. Finding her voice, she said, "Did Tim realise his old projector and slides were gone? The ones he bought from Tilly as a teenager? The ones he no doubt told you, his best friend, about? The ones you buried in my bookshop—wrapped in a bag from the shoe shop that used to be under the studio—that you tried to steal back, injuring my friend, Joey, in the process?"

Tim folded his arms, his jaw clenched, but his defence still didn't materialise.

"You warned Tim about Meredith having her script, didn't you?" Ellie continued, ducking to meet his avoiding gaze. "Which must've made him want some distance. Did he go to the photo studio when he shouldn't have? Did he see your latest 'masterpiece' developing?" Still, Jack didn't respond. "He confronted you, and it got heated. You splashed him with developing solution, and then he stormed out—back to *this* pub. But you followed him. And you waited until the right moment to clean up your mess, just like when George confronted you. You pushed Tim to his death and snatched his camera from his body, and you kept it for all these years as a souvenir." Her lips curled into a snarl as she stared at the blurry spiked hair in the photograph. "Was tonight the first time you developed this picture? I bet you couldn't stand not knowing how it looked for all these years, the camera and the film reel hiding in the studio you took over from Tim." She shook her head and added, "You took everything from him."

Jack's lips twisted into a slow, unnerving smile. He leaned across the pool table, his eyes burrowing into Ellie with a fiery intensity that burned into her skin.

"You think you've got it all figured out, little Ellie Swan?" he murmured, his voice as sharp as a blade. "Good luck proving any of this beyond reasonable doubt. Like you said—my fingerprints aren't on the negatives or anything else. And this photograph? It proves *nothing*."

Ellie didn't flinch. She leaned in, her voice dropping to a matching whisper. "Don't you see how sloppy you've been?" Then, louder, she called over her shoulder, "Now's a good time to debut your pilot, Mother. I think the audience is ready for your reality show."

The lights cut out, plunging the pub into darkness. A projector beam glowed across the room, framing Ellie and Jack in a spotlight like they were on stage in a theatre show. Jack didn't turn around to see what was being shown, but Ellie's defiant gaze never left him.

The footage began, the familiar setting of the pub they stood in filling the screen. Harold and Tilly were behind the bar, speaking in hushed tones. Harold stacked dirty pint glasses into plastic crates while Tilly leaned in close.

"What should we do, Mother?" Harold asked, his voice low and nervous.

"The police will back off," Tilly replied. "But that Swan girl? She's trouble…"

The audience in the room barely had time to process the exchange before the focus of the footage shifted. From the left side of the frame, Cassie and Jack entered the pub, glancing around cautiously before stopping just out of view of the camera.

"It's obvious where this is going," Jack muttered on the tape, his voice cold. The clink of billiard balls sounded faintly in the background, suggesting the camera was hidden beneath the pool table. "Harold left out the smoke machine fluid again," Jack continued. "It's like he wants to get caught, but he's always been an idiot."

"He's back to faking cold spots?" Cassie's irritated voice rang out. "What's the point when he's got a *legend* like John Partridge roaming the place?" She snorted, sounding smug, as though she'd solved the mystery. "I bet his tricks are why John doesn't show himself to him. We're the lucky ones."

The Plot Thickens

There was a pause, followed by her Doc Martens scuffing against the floor as she moved closer to Jack's worn Vans.

"Not that all tricks are bad, though," Cassie said. "I managed to scare the hell out of that girl who came sniffing around the studio. Remembered the name of that dead husband of hers and brought him forward on the Ouija board, didn't I?"

"They didn't even get married," Jack shot back. "Her tight mother asked for a refund on the deposit."

Ellie and Carolyn exchanged uneasy glances, both uncomfortable with this old history being dragged into the open. But they weren't there for that. She turned back to the screen as the footage played on.

"I still can't believe you got a job with her mum," Cassie muttered.

"What did I tell you?" Jack's voice snapped like a whip, sudden and loud enough to make Cassie flinch. "I didn't make the connection. It's been over a decade, and it's not like she's been living around here."

Cassie's voice hardened, defensive now. "Why did she have to come back and mess things up anyway?"

Jack exhaled, the sound of a man trying to hold his temper in check. Ellie could almost picture him, head dropping, his thinning ponytail drooping with him.

"What did I tell you?" he repeated, slower, more deliberate, his voice colder now. "Nothing is messed up. I have *everything* under control."

Cassie muttered something under her breath, quieter

but no less bitter. "It's not like any channel will pick up the pilot anyway. Don't know why you're wasting your time."

"Well," Jack snapped, his voice dripping with disdain, "aren't you an idiot? Look what I found today." There was a metallic rattle, faint but distinct, as he unzipped something and slid it back into his pocket. "Old bat won't notice a few bits of missing jewellery. We'll need money for our new start."

Cassie's response was a grumble, a reluctant agreement.

"Aren't we?" Jack pressed, louder this time.

"Yes, Jack," she said, softening, stepping closer to lean on him. "Promise me it was John who pushed George."

Jack grunted. "I've *told* you. Stop asking. He pushed Tim, and then he pushed George. They annoyed him. Got it? What are you trying to suggest?"

"N-nothing."

Ellie's eyes darted across the pub to Cassie, who now stared at the floor, shifting under the weight of Ellie's silent scrutiny. Jack, too, was watching, his gaze dark and fixed, peering at Ellie from beneath his eyebrows. But she wasn't afraid of him.

In the video, Jack's voice softened into a smooth, almost hypnotic tone. "Everything's going to be perfect. I'll make sure of it. You've been so loyal, Cassie. And soon, we're going to have everything we've ever wanted. It's all going to be ours. *Trust* me. Stay by my side, like always. These past few years have been perfect—just you and me against the world. Think of how much we've sacrificed. How much we've gone through together..."

After a brief silence, Cassie finally spoke, her voice uncertain. "Do you promise it's over this time? That John will leave us alone?"

"Hey, what have I told you?" Jack replied with the tone of a parent soothing a child. "It's over. It's *all* over. John is gone, and we're going to find a place where nothing and no one can hurt us again." He let the words settle before continuing. "If you could move to any country...?"

"Spain," she answered instantly. Her voice softened as she continued, "When I was a kid at the children's home, one of the foster workers had a sister who worked as a travel agent. Every few months, she'd dump her out-of-date catalogues on us, like we should be grateful to see pictures of hotels we'd never visit. It made us sad about all the places we couldn't go." Cassie paused, her voice even smaller. "You always said you'd take me."

"Then Spain it is," Jack said. "We'll go, and we'll never come back here. You and me against the—"

His voice cut off abruptly. The camera lifted, swinging awkwardly to show his face as he squinted at the lens.

"How long has this been turned on?" Jack barked, his anger sparking like a struck match. "You *idiot*. It's wasting battery."

"I'm sorry," Cassie choked. "I might've bumped it. Just don't get—"

The footage cut to black, and the room fell into stunned silence. Ellie felt the truth blanket the pub as the onlookers absorbed what they'd witnessed—the proof she and Angela had watched unfold in her mother and auntie's attic before entering the pub.

"Cassie wanted to believe there was more out there," Ellie said, narrowing her eyes at Jack's cold face. "Something waiting on the other side. Something better than this life." Her voice faltered. "And she wanted to believe her boyfriend—the man who constantly corrected her, fed her lies, manipulated her—she wanted so desperately to *believe* you weren't a cold-blooded killer."

A heavy stillness fell over the pub as people shifted uncomfortably in their seats.

"*Well?*" Harold's gruff voice broke the silence from behind the bar. "Was it you, Jack?"

"Yes," Jack roared suddenly, his voice booming. His arms shot out wide, fists clenched. "The little swan is right. I killed Tim Baker. My name is Jack Campbell, and you will remember me."

Before the officers could close in to arrest him, Jack opened his fists, revealing small cloth sacks, his final trick. Ellie recognised them immediately—the smoke bombs Cassie had used with the young punk in the photoshoot.

Ellie wanted to scream, but it was too late. He hurled

one sack at his feet and the other across the room, where it exploded near the officers guarding Cassie.

Black smoke billowed into the air, and like the night of the séance, chaos erupted. Shouts and coughs filled the room as the smoke obscured everything. Ellie staggered, trying to clear her stinging eyes, her lungs burning with every breath. Through the haze, she darted around the pool table, waving her hands to clear her view. She couldn't let him escape.

A hand shot out of the smoke, gripping her arm with the force of a vice. She gasped as she was dragged away from the pool table, her eyes watering from the smoke. Somewhere behind them, she heard Angela and her mother shouting her name, their voices sharp with shared fear.

Ellie couldn't answer. Smoke choked her words, thick in her lungs. Her chest burned as someone dragged her through the haze.

Then, a blast of cold, damp air struck her face like a slap. And like Tim Baker and George Fenton before her, she stared helplessly down the stone steps into the dank cellar.

Chapter 23
Well, Well, Well...

Ellie's foot slipped, teetering on the edge of the cellar stairs. Jack's grip tightened around her arms, yanking her back before she could tumble into the darkness below. Her heart thundered in her chest as she clung to his arm, her fingers digging into him for balance.

His band t-shirt stared back at her—the one he'd worn when they first met. *Anthrax* in silver text, though some of the silver had flaked away. She could almost picture George's fingers clawing at it for grip before he fell. The nurse had mentioned silver under his fingernails—a clue Ellie had let slip through her fingers.

"It would sound quite tidy, wouldn't it?" Jack mused, his voice a low rumble dripping with malice. "I killed you all by pushing you down the stairs. Maybe it's good that you stopped me from suffocating that old bat?"

Ellie's shoes scrambled for purchase, her toes

brushing the edge of the top step. Jack yanked the door shut behind them, sealing them in the suffocating darkness.

"Why bother to try and kill Christina?" Ellie asked, glancing over her shoulder to the cellar. If she was going to fall to her death, she wanted the whole truth. "Was it something to do with that tape you stole from me?"

"I recognised her handwriting poking out of your jacket in the pub," he muttered, his breath hot with cigarettes and beer like it had been at the cottage. "She was always borrowing my old tapes, but she'd never tell me what for. I couldn't risk what she might have captured."

Her feet finally found solid ground, but before she could wrench herself free, a loud banging erupted on the other side of the door.

"Jack!" Cassie called, muffled by the smoke. "I got away. Are you in there?"

His grin widened, stretching into something twisted and cruel. The pit in Ellie's stomach deepened. Cassie was still on his side, and Jack knew it. Clearing away the fog was going to take more than the truth.

"*Jack?*" Cassie's voice came again, rising with urgency. "Jack!"

He drew in a slow, deliberate breath, weighing his options. Then, he threw open the door and yanked Cassie inside.

For a fleeting moment, the three of them stood in the darkness together on the top step, the disorder of the smoke-filled pub muffled beyond the thick door. Cassie gasped, but before she could scream, Jack's hand clamped over her mouth, his fingers pressing hard.

"Let's make sure we're not disturbed," he said sternly. He reached for the door, sliding a heavy metal bar across with a loud scrape, locking them in. "That's better."

Cassie raised her bound hands. "My hands."

Jack sighed as if inconvenienced by the detail. With a swift motion, he pulled something from his pocket—a Stanley knife—and sliced the cable tie securing her wrists. Cassie rubbed at the red marks, exhaling a long breath.

Cassie didn't speak or glance at Jack as she grabbed Ellie by the arm, her grip tighter than Jack's. She half-dragged, half-shoved Ellie down the uneven stone steps. Her fingers pulsed into Ellie's flesh as though trying to communicate something.

When she reached the bottom, after everything—after piecing together the truth about the two men who hadn't made it out of this place in one piece—she wanted to collapse and kiss the icy floor. She wasn't dead. Not yet.

The bottom door slammed shut, the rattling of chains and the heavy clunk of locks echoing in the confined space.

"That should slow them down for a while," Jack declared. "We need to find another way out."

"It's over, Jack," Ellie said firmly.

But Jack ignored her as though she wasn't there. He began pacing the dimly lit cellar, muttering under his breath.

"Don't just stand there!" he snapped at Cassie. "Look for a way out. This is a pub—there's always another door in and out of these places."

Cassie didn't move. She stood frozen, her expression unreadable, her body locked in place.

"*Hello?*" Jack waved a hand in front of her face. When she didn't respond, he rolled his eyes and turned away. "You can't do anything right, can you?"

Leaving Cassie in her daze, Jack started pressing his hands along the damp stone walls, his fingers searching for some hidden latch or trick brick, his frustration growing.

"Need a hand?" Ellie asked, keeping her tone deliberately casual. "I've heard there's an old well in here somewhere, but that might have been Harold playing one of his tricks."

Jack's jaw tightened, his body stiffening at her remark. Ellie knew she was provoking him, but she couldn't stop now.

"When did your story start to feel out of control, Jack?" Ellie asked, her voice steady. "Was it when you killed Tim? Or was it earlier—back in the '80s, when you were just a boy, living in the shadow of your father's success?"

"*Shut. Up.*"

"You're the son of a man who made the history

The Plot Thickens

books," Ellie pressed, ignoring the warning. "That's *your* ghost. The ghost that possessed you, that drove you to all of this. It wasn't John Partridge—it was Ken. You could have been inspired by him—"

"Turn up at the right protest at the right moment, you mean?" Jack interrupted, his voice dripping with disdain. "He got *lucky*. And history will remember him. My father's name will be attached to that moment forever. *Immortality*." His sneer deepened. "He didn't deserve it. He was just... some guy."

"Is that the story you tell yourself now?" Ellie pushed. "The story that justifies all of this? Do you think *you* deserve it? Even after everything you've done?"

Jack's fists clenched at his sides, his voice a low, guttural growl. "I did what I *had* to. To *survive*."

Ellie looked at Cassie, who had wandered to the wall and pressed her hands against the damp stone, only to stop there, motionless. Jack, consumed by his frantic escape plan, hadn't noticed.

"Wake up, Cassie," Ellie said softly, taking a cautious step towards her. "Jack wanted to live forever, but you... you just didn't want to live alone, did you? Do you even remember how you got here? That teenage girl who thought this man was her whole world?"

Cassie's vacant stare dropped to her hands, then rose to meet Ellie's. Her expression was terrifyingly hollow, caught in a loop she couldn't escape. There was no bravado, no mask. Cassie looked like a cornered animal, unsure of what was real or who to trust. It was disturbingly familiar—Ellie had felt the same way since this nightmare began, ever since she'd peeled back that wallpaper to find the black words scrawled beneath.

Cassie's movements changed as she sped up her search, and Jack didn't notice.

"Find something to tie her up!" he barked over his shoulder, not even sparing his girlfriend a glance. His phone was in his hand, his thumbs flying over the screen as he muttered to himself. "We can take some pictures of Ellie to spook them upstairs—use them for leverage. I should've paid more attention to Harold's rambling. He must've mentioned another way out of this bloody cellar."

"I... I don't know what to do..." Cassie's voice was quieter this time, barely more than a whisper.

With a sudden, guttural scream, Jack doubled over, his frustration boiling. Grabbing a crate, he smashed it against the floor, the sound of splintering wood echoing off the cold stone walls.

Amid the chaos, Cassie moved. She retrieved a small metal canister, her hands trembling as she aimed and sprayed its contents over Jack. The liquid splashed across him, soaking him from head to toe. The scent was sharp and unmistakable. Cassie let the empty canister clatter to the floor. Her fingers dipped into her pocket, emerging with a small box of matches.

Jack's stunned gaze lifted from his soaked clothes to Cassie's face, his disbelief hardening into a volatile mix of fury and fear.

The Plot Thickens

"What did you throw on me?" he demanded, his voice low and wary. He glanced down at the liquid darkening his shirt. "Answer me, Cassie. Answer me *now*!" His voice rose, his desperation spilling out. "Answer me! *Speak*! Why won't you—"

"Lighter fluid," Cassie interrupted, her voice ice-cold. She slid a single match from the box, flicking her thumb against its tip but not striking it. "Harold sneaks down here for a ciggie sometimes when he thinks no one's looking."

"Cassie..." Jack's voice shifted, warning and pleading in equal measure. He held his hands out, palms up, as though soothing her. "Don't you dare. I love you... we can fix this."

"*Stop* talking," she snapped. "I don't want to hear your voice anymore."

"You wouldn't."

"I... I don't know what I'd do," she said blankly, staring at the unlit match. "I never thought things would get this far."

"But I *love* you, Cassie," Jack pressed, his tone desperate. "Don't let Ellie poison you against me. She's nobody. She means nothing. She's jealous of what we have."

Cassie didn't falter, her eyes hard and unyielding. "George and Meredith love each other," she said quietly. "You never wanted me to like them. You didn't want me getting close to Dr Marsh either—said they were bad influences. And then there was Tim." Tears began to slide down her cheeks. "You *knew* I fancied him. It was silly—something that would've passed—but you couldn't let it, could you?"

Jack's lips parted, a protest forming, but Cassie lifted the match higher, daring him to speak. His mouth snapped shut, his jaw clenching so tightly it looked painful.

"Instead of letting it pass," Cassie continued, her voice gaining strength with every word, "you told Tim you felt betrayed by him like *he'd* done something wrong. And all because I had a stupid crush. He never even looked at me like that, but you twisted it. Just like you twisted things with Ellie. You told me she was throwing herself at you, and I believed you." She turned to Ellie with an imploring gaze. "Did you? Try to kiss him in the photo studio when I was in the darkroom?"

The question stunned Ellie. She blinked, taken aback, her voice caught in her throat. She shook her head, unable to form the words to defend herself.

"Who tries to kiss a man shovelling chips into his mouth?" Cassie said in a small voice. "I can't *believe* I fell for it again. Did any of those women you told me about ever try it on with you?"

"I don't think so," Ellie said, her throat dry. "I think it was a way to keep you controlled. To keep you jealous... keep you *wanting* him."

Cassie turned back to Jack, stepping closer, her movements deliberate, the match trembling but still raised. "You made Tim win back your friendship after

The Plot Thickens

that. And then we were both too scared to even talk to each other. But that's exactly what you wanted. That was my punishment. All because I fancied him—for no other reason than he was sweet to me. *Actually* sweet. Not pretending, like you."

Jack scrambled for the right words to lull Cassie back into her dream life—but none were left.

"*That's* when the ghost photographs started showing up," Cassie said, her voice stronger now. "After you overheard Meredith talking about seeing a ghost in the graveyard that night. It was the same day you found that flyer for the book. I was with you—I *saw* it all. I'd never seen you so excited."

"Cass—"

"You craved fame, and I *helped* you," she cried. "You used Tim's reputation and studio, and you stole his old equipment. Tim always felt like he owed you because of me. I don't even think he liked you." Her face twisted. "You used him. And you used me. *I* went back and stole that camera from George. *I* hid everything in the bookshop."

"And *I* told *you* to get *rid* of it!" Jack roared, stamping his foot. The wooden trapdoor beneath him groaned, but he didn't notice. "But you had to complicate things, didn't you? Leaving your little trail of evidence, and I've been cleaning up *your* mess ever since!"

"*My* mess?" Cassie snorted, her laugh bitter. "You sprayed that wall to blame Meredith. *Insurance*, you called it. Something to confuse people in the future. But why would you need insurance if John was really behind the murders? John didn't do anything, did he?"

Jack's jaw tightened.

"John Partridge died from tuberculosis in a hospital months after he built and opened this place," Ellie said, another result of her earlier searching on the bus. "But that doesn't make for much of a ghost story, does it?"

"*Shut up*," Jack hissed at Ellie, extending a finger in her direction. He stepped off the wood door back onto the damp slate. "None of this would've happened if it weren't for *you*! For thirty years, everything worked—until Meadowfield Books decided it needed redecorating! You just had to strip it all back, didn't you? Couldn't slap on a new coat of paint? No one would've noticed!"

"Some cracks can't be smoothed over," Ellie said. "That's why this is all happening now. You knew we'd find the message. You knew interest in the case would start up again. And even then, you thought you could cover your tracks."

Cassie dropped the matches and sunk to the ground, too exhausted to follow through with her attempts to stand up to Jack. How many times had she given up like this? The sight broke Ellie's heart.

Ellie closed her eyes, trying to centre herself, to push past the cold grip of fear. A whisper from her memory, long buried, rose to the surface: *You've got this, Ellie. Don't worry.*

The Plot Thickens

A sudden flash of light filled her mind—another memory—and her eyes snapped open.

"That's why this is happening now," Ellie repeated, meeting Jack's cold stare. "Meredith saw a bright light. That's the last thing she remembers. You dazzled her with the flash from your camera, just like you did to me in the pub when I was asleep."

Jack's lips twisted into a dark grin. "Meredith did the rest," he replied, his tone almost casual. "I was going to try and frame it to look like suicide from the guilt, but I cut my losses and left her to it."

"Left her to *die*," Ellie cried, unable to contain herself. "You didn't want her around to defend herself. And you tried to twist my mind against George, too."

Jack laughed, the sound bouncing off the damp stone walls. "It was all too easy... and it always has been. There are always people like you, Ellie. And Cassie. And Meredith. And every other idiot in this village, so desperate to believe in something. Anything. Ghosts, the truth..." His grin widened, his eyes alight with twisted amusement. "Those people? They fade away, hoping and praying. But *you* know that history remembers the bold."

From his pocket, Jack pulled out the knife he'd used to cut Cassie's bindings. He wiped the rusted blade on his soaked shirt. Ellie glanced at the matches on the floor by Cassie, but she couldn't stoop to that.

"I heard George isn't doing so well," Jack continued,

his voice dripping with mock concern. "Soon, he'll die and become my second *official* victim. Which means you two get to be numbers three and four." He paused, pointing the blade to himself, his grin spreading. "I did consider a murder-suicide, but I think I'd rather stick around for the trial. It always looked fun on TV. And maybe I'll have time to swing by the hospital to finish off Meredith properly and hopefully find Christina along the way. A clean sweep, making me the last surviving member of the Ghost Club massacre. Let's hope they hire a decent courtroom sketch artist..." He chuckled, twirling the knife on his fingertip. "*If* they catch me, that is."

Ellie's heart thudded in her chest as her eyes darted sideways, catching the faintest motion in the corner of her vision. Was it Cassie? No, she hadn't moved. Her gaze returned to Jack, who was now utterly lost in his twisted fantasy.

"You know," he continued, taking another step closer to Ellie, "I've thought a lot about how I'll pose when I walk in and out of court. I need to look strong. Defiant. The press loves that, don't they? The pictures will live forever. I'll wear a suit. Do people still wear ties these days? Maybe I'll skip the tie. Or—*wait!*" His eyes lit up with manic excitement. "Forget the suit. How about a tuxedo? With a cape. Red lining. A little on the nose, but it'll photograph like nothing else."

There it was again—movement creeping towards Jack. A dark shadow. Ellie's heart pounded as she struggled to focus on him, resisting the urge to dart her eyes. Despite knowing the truth, her mind conjured the image of John Partridge, returning to claim his final victim. She glanced again, her eyes flicking back and forth.

This time, Jack noticed. He didn't whip around or panic. Instead, he rolled his eyes, irritated. Holding the rusted blade in front of him, he checked his teeth in the dull reflection—stained yellow from years of cigarettes—then pointed the knife back at Ellie.

"I'd say it's not personal," he said, his voice dropping to a low rumble, "but if I'm being honest, I've wanted to kill you since the moment we met. I told you, didn't I? I *knew* you were trouble."

The movement behind him grew closer now—a figure emerging in the dim light. Ellie's breath hitched. That familiar voice whispered again in her mind: *Keep him talking, Ellie. Just try*.

"This cape," Ellie blurted, swallowing her fear. "Collar or no collar?"

Jack's lips quirked into a smug smile. "Oh, collar," he said, gesturing to his neck. "Something grand. Nobody ever takes it there, do they? I'll find someone to make it. Serial killers are practically celebrities these days, aren't they?"

"You could get a book deal," Ellie offered.

"Now we're talking!" His wicked grin stretched from ear to ear. "You could launch it at the bookshop. You're welcome, by the way. *Our* stories are forever now linked. Sure, you'll just be a footnote, but it's always going to be *your* bookshop that *I* chose." He sighed, fanning a mock yawn. "Do you honestly think I'll fall for the oldest trick in the book? Something's behind me, in a locked cellar? I turn and look, and in that split second, you pull out whatever you've got clutched in your palm to try to overpower me?"

Ellie opened her hand, revealing nothing but the reddened imprint where she'd been digging her nails into her skin.

Jack chuckled darkly. "Want to know a little secret?" He leaned in, his voice dipping into a conspiratorial whisper. "It's a little twisted."

"Surprise me."

"I'm most excited to kill you," he said with a giddy, almost childlike giggle. "The girl who figured it all out. Not the police, just... *you*. Some local girl from a bookshop. You're the perfect ending to our story." He sighed. "You know, in another life, you and me—"

"In *no* life," Ellie cut in, her voice as sharp as the blade between them. "You and Cassie might have been right for each other in all the wrong ways, but you and me?" She let out a sharp laugh, taking him by surprise. "I'd rather die."

"Ask, and you shall receive," Jack replied, his grin widening as he moved closer, the knife held steadily before him. The distance between them shrank. "Any last words?" he asked, tilting his head. "I'll make sure to quote you accurately in my book. Leave your last words after the beep." He held the knife out like an answering machine.

She said nothing, and he stopped just short of lunging distance, his expression gleeful.

"C'mon! You're not saving them for your dead fiancé, are you?" His voice lowered into a vicious sneer. "Newsflash: there's no other side. *This* is it."

"I do have something to say," Ellie said, drawing a deep breath as the moment pressed down on her. She leaned in, locking eyes with Jack. "You probably should have killed me while you had the chance."

Jack blinked, his confidence wavering. "Disappointing," he muttered with another pretend yawn. "You had one last chance to make your mark, and you threw it away. But you know what? I'm feeling generous. You only commit your second murder once, so... I'll give you a second take." He waved the knife like a prop in a pantomime. "I've never stabbed anyone before. It'll make my kills inconsistent, but..." He gestured to the cold stone walls of the cellar. "At least all the victims will be in the same location. That's something for the books."

Ellie choked on her breath, realising Jack was about to turn and see the figure moving in the shadows behind him. She now knew exactly what—or who—was behind the black shawl stretched high, creeping closer.

Jack pretended to rewind the knife, holding it out, daring her to say something memorable. Ellie's heartbeat pounded in her ears, but she forced herself to smile sweetly.

"You're not going to stab me," she said.

"And you're *not* understanding," Jack whined, his voice rising, high-pitched and strained. "Imagine this written down—you're not going to stab me—then I stab you. Pathetic. Get it? Try again. Third time's a charm, right?" He gritted his teeth. "Get this wrong, and it'll be the difference between an open and a closed coffin."

Ellie's smile widened, slow and deliberate. "Turn around."

Jack's laugh bubbled out as he hunched over, brandishing the knife. "They'll never believe this when I tell them," he said, shaking his head. "And I thought *I* was the crazy one!" He straightened, shouting now. "I'm getting tired of repeating myself—"

"Then don't!"

The voice rang out from the shadows, low and commanding—neither Ellie's, Jack's, nor Cassie's.

A black shawl wrapped itself around Jack's front with sudden force. His knife clattered to the ground as he struggled, his wide-eyed look of confusion lasting only a moment before he was yanked backwards into the darkness.

"Give it some welly, Harold!" Tilly's voice called out as Jack disappeared through the trapdoor.

Ellie rushed to Cassie's side, finding her curled in a tight ball, her eyes distant and unfocused. Maybe, Ellie thought, Cassie wasn't in the cellar at all. Maybe she was in Spain, seeing what all the fuss was about, far away from the horrors of this night.

The Plot Thickens

"What a tiresome man," Tilly declared, shuffling across the room as she flipped on the lights. She planted her hands on her hips with a satisfied grin. "Are you alright, dears?"

"We will be," Ellie said, resting a hand on Cassie's trembling shoulder. "How did you—"

"John Partridge did one good thing," Tilly said, kicking the door. "He built a tunnel to the well left behind from the old tannery." She jerked her head upstairs as she unlocked the chains sealing the bottom door. "The police are still up there arguing about red tape and experts. Typical."

Ellie stared at the trapdoor Harold had warned her about on her first visit to the pub. At the time, she'd thought he was trying to scare her. But the pub landlord had unknowingly saved her life. She peered through the open door into the tunnel below, where Harold and Jack grappled, the pair slipping and splashing in the pooled water.

Ellie dropped through the opening, scrambling to help Harold. Jack thrashed violently, his strength fuelled by desperation, fighting until the bitter end.

"Where does the tunnel lead?" Ellie shouted over the commotion, her breath ragged as she tried to hold Jack down. "He can't get away!"

"The other side of Meadowfield Manor," Harold grunted, his arms locked around Jack's shoulders. "Stop squirming, you chicken!"

Jack's struggles intensified, and he broke free,

scrambling to his feet. He bolted down the dark tunnel at full speed, laughing at his sliminess.

"Ellie, stop!" Harold cried as she took off after him. "The well!"

But Jack reached the well first. He cried, his voice echoing along the tunnel as Ellie caught up. There he was, clinging to the edge, his fingers digging into the slippery cobbles. But his expression wasn't one of fear. Instead, his lips curled into a taunting grin, twisted and sinister.

"Go on," he rasped. "*Do it.* One little nudge of your shoe, and you'll give my story the ending it needs. It *had* to be you. It all makes sense—"

He didn't reach out for help, and Ellie didn't offer it. They both knew how this moment would end.

"If you're not going to do what's right," Jack continued, his grin widening, "then tell people you pushed me. You'll forever be the woman who slayed me."

Ellie's eyes stayed locked on his, calm and steady. She took a deliberate step back. She crouched, bringing herself to his eye level.

"I don't need that kind of glory, Jack," she said softly. "I got my prize—I saw the life you stole return to Cassie's eyes. Only a flicker, but she'll never believe another word you say again."

Jack's grin vanished. For a brief moment, Ellie saw the pure terror in his eyes before his fingers slipped. His body jerked into the dark, scrambling for purchase one last time, but it was too late. He made no sound as he fell,

The Plot Thickens

and the silence stretched until a dull thud echoed from the bottom of the well.

"If he's lucky, he made it," Harold said, pulling Ellie back from the edge. "And if we're lucky..." He hesitated, then shook his head. "On second thought, I hope he does make it. At least until he's off the property. This cellar is at full capacity with ghosts, and the only spirits we'll be serving from now on are—"

"Oh, give it a *rest*, Harold!" Tilly interrupted, her soft steps padding down the tunnel as she approached. "Enough with the ghost stories."

"Yes, Mother."

Tilly shuffled to the edge of the well, peering into the darkness and squinting as if she could see to the bottom.

"He's not dead," she said with certainty.

"A feeling?" Ellie asked.

Tilly tapped her hearing aid, which let out a faint whistle. "No... the pathetic whimpers of a man who won't admit how much pain he's in." She paused, tilting her head. "I'd guess several broken bones. Hardly justice for Tim, but it's a start."

"Seal it up!" Jack's scream echoed faintly from the depths. "Leave me here to die!"

"Yesterday, I might have," Tilly replied, tugging Ellie's sleeve gently. "Today? A little swan reminded me I used to have integrity. We'll call you an ambulance, Jack, and see how much you enjoy your fame from behind bars."

As they walked away, Jack's sobs echoed behind them.

Tilly was right.

Pathetic.

"Now then," Tilly said lightly as they walked, "I'd like to say I didn't see this coming, but would you believe me if I foresaw a similar outcome—minus the well, of course—from the first moment we met?"

"How?" Ellie asked.

Tilly held back a knowing smile. "Youngsters like yourself always think they're doing a brilliant job hiding their thoughts. But even a polite girl like you wouldn't have humoured my son as much as you did during that first meeting if the truth didn't matter. I could see it—you were desperate not to let us see how much the past meant to you. Nothing was going to get in your way."

She glanced back at the well's opening as Harold hurried to catch up.

"Keep an eye on your future for me, will you?" Tilly added. "You don't want to tunnel in a direction you never intended. Believe me, it's a difficult place to return from."

"I will," Ellie promised.

"Do you mean it?"

Ellie smiled, looping her arm through Tilly's. "I promise. And you too."

"At my age?" Tilly laughed. "Sure, why not?"

"You're not one-hundred-and-one, are you?"

Tilly laughed again. "How did you know?"

"A feeling," Ellie said, glancing back at Harold. "That, and your son is far too young."

"Did you hear *that*, Mother? I'm young!"

"Oh, do be quiet, Harold. You're fifty-six!"

"Yes, Mother."

They reached the ladder, looking up to see Angela peering down at them, her torch in hand, her frown softening with visible relief. Ellie offered an apologetic smile, and the detective's expression cracked just long enough to show a shred of warmth.

Somewhere above, Ellie heard her mother shriek her name, putting on what was undoubtedly the performance of her lifetime.

"Now," Tilly declared, clapping her hands together. "Enough talk of cheap phantasmagoria! This is long past my bedtime."

Chapter 24
The Future Awaits

After the fire brigade used a ladder to pull Jack from the well, the police escorted him and Cassie away in separate cars. Their flashing lights disappeared around the corner, taking the pair out of Meadowfield for good.

Ellie stood outside the pub, the crisp night air cooling her skin. It wasn't the dramatic getaway they'd planned, but it was the ending they'd earned. Cassie, though an accomplice, might still have a chance. Ellie hoped the judge reviewing Cassie's case would show some leniency. Everyone deserved a shot at life beyond bars. Jack, on the other hand? He could've stayed at the bottom of that well.

Ellie's mother and Auntie Penny hovered nearby, clucking with concern as they patted her arms and fussed over her coat. Was she warm enough? Had she had enough water? Their fretting was almost amusing, a soothing counterpoint to the chaos she'd left behind in the cellar.

In the distance, faint music drifted from Meadowfield Primary School—the winter disco.

"*My* niece!" Auntie Penny's voice rang out, her grin wide and unapologetic, as though the day's drama hadn't happened. "I always knew you were a star, Ellie. Look at you soar!"

"*My* footage," Carolyn announced, adjusting her silk scarf with an air of pride. "Without it, Jack Campbell would never have been arrested. Though I'm not sure what it means for the pilot." She chewed her lip, as if that were the night's most pressing issue. "It is rather unfocused."

"You've had your hands full," Ellie said gently. "Of all of us, you spent a week with a murderer."

"I did, didn't I? And I had to fire him for rifling through my jewellery box. I knew it felt lighter, but Penny said it was all in my head."

"It usually is," Penny said.

"Hmm." Carolyn wrinkled her nose in disgust, but her mood shifted instantly as an idea sparked. "Ellie! You're brilliant. First, the reality show. Now this! *My Week with a Murderer*. It's perfect. We've already filmed half of it!"

"Channel 4 would buy it," Penny chimed in, nodding. "Or Channel 5, at least!"

"That's... not what I meant," Ellie tried to interject.

"No, no, don't worry. I'll give you half credit! We'll

talk later." Carolyn was already rushing towards her cottage, waving for Penny to follow. "There's no time to lose!"

Across the road, DS Angela Cookson stood in quiet conversation with Granny Maggie. From what Ellie could gather, the detective was recounting the night's events to Maggie, who'd spent it unaware at the hospital after returning to visit Meredith again.

Her gaze drifted towards the pond, where Dr Christina Marsh sat on a mossy rock, clutching the envelope she had once tried to give Tim's mother. Christina stared at the water, her fingers lightly tracing its edges.

Ellie approached quietly and crouched beside her. "Will you open it?"

Christina hesitated. Her grip on the envelope tightened, but then she shook her head. Slowly, her fingers loosened, and the letter fluttered from her hands into the water. Christina peered up at the starry sky as ink bled through the paper.

"I don't need souvenirs," she said softly. "I only ever wanted to bring truth to the madness."

"And now you have," Ellie replied.

Christina grumbled, her cane digging into the moss. "Hmm. Not enough. I checked what I found on that device Joey buried at the war memorial—just local gossip, like last time. I wasted my focus on the wrong lead."

"Time to let go," Ellie said, watching the ripples spread across the pond as the letter floated away.

Christina's expression softened, and she exhaled deeply. "Yes. Time to let go."

They sat in silence for a while, the distant thump of disco music blending with the hum of a TV crew setting up nearby. Ellie shifted uncomfortably. The last thing she wanted was to get caught in a news segment. Her thoughts drifted back to the cellar—to the moment Jack's knife hovered inches from her, and to the voice she'd heard.

"Down there," she murmured, almost to herself. "I heard someone. Someone I couldn't have. Luke."

"You remember what I said about near-death experiences?" Christina replied with a kind smile. "The mind bends. It plays tricks."

Ellie nodded but couldn't shake the feeling lingering in her chest. Christina sighed and leaned on her cane as she shifted to her feet.

"Who am I to say what's waiting for us on the other side?" Christina concluded, her gaze drifting back to the stars she couldn't see. "The more I learn, the less I know. And at my age, I'm content not knowing what awaits me. I'll find out soon enough." She reached out and patted Ellie's shoulder. "Thank you. You did what I couldn't."

Ellie reached up to touch the doctor's hand. "I did what I had to." She wrapped Christina in a quick hug. "Take care of yourself."

They parted ways, Christina walking slowly towards

the shadows of the pub, and Ellie following the faint pull of music in the distance. Maggie stepped into her path, raising a hand.

"You don't have to explain," Maggie said, her voice low but steady. "Thank you, Ellie. And I'm sorry."

Ellie met her grandmother's gaze and smiled. "Don't be sorry, Gran. Be happy. It's over. The truth about Tim Baker is finally out. That has to be enough now."

Maggie hesitated, her voice trembling. "Yes. It does."

Ellie draped an arm around Maggie's shoulders, tilting her so they faced the bookshop on the corner of the street. Resting her head against her grandmother's, Ellie exhaled the stress that had built up since she'd uncovered that graffiti—she was glad it was over.

"And tomorrow," Ellie said quietly, "we keep going. Meadowfield Books needs us."

Maggie nodded. "Yes, it does." She paused, seeming to sense Ellie's restless energy. "But you're slipping off somewhere, aren't you?"

Ellie grinned, stepping back to kiss her gran's cheek. "To my future. I hope."

Before Maggie could respond, Ellie turned and ran, her steps light and quick as the faint music grew louder.

* * *

Ellie pushed open the heavy school doors, greeted by Noddy Holder's iconic yell, *'It's Christmas!'* The assembly hall buzzed with life, the winter disco in full swing. Smoke from the fog machine curled under the coloured lights, filling the air with the faint, plastic scent of Harold's infamous cold spot machine. She laughed to herself—if she hadn't uncovered his trick in the middle of a murder investigation, she might have been more impressed.

The swirling smoke wrapped around her as she stepped inside, leaving the chaos of the pub and the horrors of the cellar far behind. For the first time in days, she felt like she could breathe again. This world—loud, warm, and filled with laughter—was untouched by the darkness she had fought to escape.

She found Daniel in the crowd. He stood at the centre of a circle of children, leading them through a series of dance moves. The kids followed his lead with shrieks of laughter as he twirled in slow motion, fanning the smoke around him in dramatic spirals like some theatrical magician.

Ellie leaned against the wall, a smile tugging at her lips. The Daniel she remembered from childhood would never have danced like this. He'd have been perched awkwardly on the edge of the room with the other wallflowers—quiet, reserved, invisible. She'd have been beside him, nose buried in a book, trying to pretend the music didn't exist. But things had changed. Watching him now, vibrant and at ease, filled her with a quiet sense of pride—and something more she couldn't quite name.

Then he noticed her. His movements faltered, and a blush crept into his cheeks, as familiar as the boy she once knew. After muttering something to the children, he excused himself and weaved towards her through the smoke.

"Hey," Daniel said, adjusting his glasses, his voice soft but curious. "I didn't expect to see you here. Something wrong?"

"I was just admiring your moves," she said, shrugging. "And I wanted to see you."

His shoulders relaxed as he stepped closer. Ellie leaned against him, resting her head on his crisp white shirt. His warmth chased away the lingering chill from the cellar, and she could hear his heart quicken as she nestled closer. A tentative hand rested on her back before wrapping around her fully.

The opening notes of *Last Christmas* by Wham! drifted through the room, the melody tugging at something unspoken between them. Daniel hesitated before he slid his arms around her completely, holding her tight. They began to sway on the spot, the song weaving around them like a cocoon.

"I think we're dancing," he said, his voice barely above a whisper.

Ellie smiled against his chest. "I think we are."

They moved together until the song faded, the moment stretching in quiet comfort. Ellie pulled back slightly, her thoughts swirling.

"Daniel..." she began, unsure how to ask what she wanted to know. What was this between them? But as she looked up at him, his steady gaze anchoring her, she realised this was enough tonight. His arms around her felt like home. After everything, he was the one person she wanted to be around.

Daniel broke the silence, his tone teasing. "This isn't about my nan, is it? Has she said something again?"

Ellie laughed, the sound light and genuine. "No, it's not your nan."

Before she could overthink it, she rose onto her toes and kissed him. The world fell away for a moment—until the eruption of whistles and exaggerated *oooohs* from the kids broke the spell. Ellie pulled back, cheeks burning, and saw Daniel's face was just as red.

"Was that..." He blinked, his shyness breaking through. "Was that our first kiss?"

"I think so?"

His hopeful smile was impossible to miss. "Will there be more?"

"I hope so."

"Me too." He took her hand, glancing towards the kids, who were still giggling and whispering behind them. With a playful tug, he nodded towards the edge of the hall. "C'mon. I think I've earned a break."

As they walked out of the disco, the sound of *Santa Claus Is Coming to Town* faded into the background. Ellie didn't mind the curious eyes following their every move. Let them look, she thought. For the first time in what felt like forever, she didn't feel out of place.

In the hallway, she stopped. Against the wall stood a life-sized cardboard cut-out of Luke in his football kit, half-obscured by wisps of smoke from the fog machine. His dopey grin, the familiar flop of his hair—it was as though he had stepped out of her memories and into the room.

"Sorry," Daniel said quickly. "It's for the assembly. To make it feel more... real."

"It's alright." She stepped closer to the cut-out, her gaze tracing its edges. "It's nice to see him, actually." Her lips curved into a small smile as she turned back to Daniel, squeezing his hand. "I'll talk at the assembly," she said with quiet determination. "Public speaking... it's not as scary as I thought."

Chapter 25
But So Did Ellie

The following day, The Drowsy Duck buzzed with life. Sylvia had spread the word, turning the pub into a live exhibition of exposed truths. Harold demonstrated the tricks behind the cold spots, while Tilly wowed the crowd with light and table illusions, showcasing the surprising uses of pumps and pressurised air. Against the wall, a looping video of Jack and Cassie at the pool table played silently.

"So, *are* ghosts real?" Oliver asked, leaning against the bar.

Ellie sighed, her patience worn thin. "I never want to hear that question again. I don't know. I don't care."

"That's disappointing."

"Did you think Meadowfield would become the epicentre of an afterlife revolution?" Meredith's voice interrupted dryly as Joey wheeled her in. "I wanted to come down and... support the truth." Her hesitant glance towards Maggie softened. "If I'm welcome?"

Maggie, on the verge of tears, nodded quickly. "You always have been. I shouldn't have made you think otherwise."

"And I shouldn't have expected you to stretch so far," Meredith said, closing her eyes as if gathering strength. "I'll always believe it was my brother, but maybe, just maybe, it was headlights." Her steady, calm gaze met Maggie's. "But one thing's clear—a real, living person killed Tim Baker. George will be glad to know. He woke up this morning. Though before I tell him, I might ask why he's been neglecting my garden."

They laughed, and as Meredith and Maggie left for a long-overdue conversation, Joey lingered, hands stuffed in his pockets. He shifted nervously before facing Ellie.

"I, uh... I wanted to apologise again," he mumbled, avoiding her eyes. "You know, for all the museum stuff."

"It's fine, Joey," Ellie said again. "You're forgiven. We all make mistakes when we're not ourselves. In the grand scheme of things, it's not important. Jack could've done much worse than pushing boxes on you."

"You're right," Joey said, though his nerves didn't fade. "Actually, I've been meaning to ask... would you fancy—"

Ellie's smile froze. She stopped him gently. "Oh, Joey, I'm flattered, but I don't think we're—"

"I was going to ask if you fancied coming on a double

The Plot Thickens

date?" Joey interrupted, his words tumbling out. "With me and Oliver?"

Ellie blinked. "Oh."

"It's not official," Joey added quickly. "I said I'd ask you first, you know, with him being your brother and us being friends—"

Ellie hugged him. "I wouldn't mind at all."

"So," Oliver said, appearing between them, his hands going around their shoulders, "are you buying me that drink, Joey, or do I need to flutter my lashes?"

Joey grinned and led Oliver to The Old Bell, leaving Ellie at The Drowsy Duck. She slid onto the stool next to Angela, who was nursing her wine.

"You know," Angela said, glancing around, "I've never spent this much time in this pub before. It's still rough around the edges, but... without the Ouija boards and exploding lightbulbs, it's just a dump. A dump with cheap drinks."

"For now," Harold called from behind the bar. "This place is going up-market! We'll get profits up the old-fashioned way—higher prices."

"And a coat of paint wouldn't hurt," Angela added, sipping her wine. "Oh, and no more funny business in the cellar."

Harold gave an exaggerated nod. "Of course. After today, that is. Mother is giving tours down there now—five quid each. Want the Meadowling discount?"

Angela waved him off. "I'll pass."

"I've seen enough," Ellie said.

Harold moved on to serve others, leaving Ellie and Angela alone.

"How's Cassie?" Ellie asked.

"Coming to her senses. She confessed to throwing a brick through the bookshop window and ripping out your notes. Seems like she did a lot of Jack's dirty work, but she didn't commit murder." She sipped her wine, swilling it around before swallowing. "I want to believe that she didn't know about him being behind the murders... but... how could she not?"

Ellie wasn't sure, but it was out of her hands now. "I hope she finds peace," Ellie said instead. "And Jack? What about him?"

"Alive." Angela took another sip. "They had to scrape him up, but he'll live. Fractured pelvis, arm, leg—a silver lining, if you ask me." She toasted her glass. "Off the record, of course."

* * *

Later, Ellie walked to Luke's bench, the sky painted like milk in tea as the sun set. She sat, gazing at the school and the church. For the first time since the message, she felt her own sense of peace.

Jack's biggest distraction from the truth, a declaration that he'd witnessed Meredith murdering Tim, had almost worked.

"You saw it all," Ellie said to herself as she opened *A*

Christmas Carol by Charles Dickens in her lap. "But so did I."

Chapter 26
Managing Expectations

The Driving Safety Assembly was in full swing, and to Ellie's surprise, speaking to a room full of children was easier than she'd expected. The kids were curious, open, and on her side. The teachers, standing along the edges, listened just as intently. It had been explained that Ellie was close to Luke, but she wasn't there to revisit the details of his motorbike accident.

"I want to tell you things about him you might not know," she began, watching the cross-legged children lean in closer. "You know his name, I'm sure, and what happened to him that awful day outside the school." Her eyes flicked towards the bench outside but didn't linger. Turning back to the hall, she smiled. "The things I want to share might not seem important, but they're the little details that make us who we are. They make us human. And if you listen carefully, you might leave here today feeling like you know more about Luke than you did before. That's how we keep the people we love alive."

At the back of the hall, Willow stood with the teachers, smiling warmly. George, Meredith, and Maggie were there too, their silent support grounding Ellie.

"Luke grew up not far from here," she said. "He loved football, Oasis, and his family." She glanced at Willow, who nodded encouragingly. "He hated history homework, was allergic to peanuts, and broke his big toe when he was six." Her lips quirked into a soft smile. "That's who Luke was. A Meadowling, a friend, a son, a brother, a boyfriend…"

Her voice wavered. Words that had come so easily moments ago now felt out of reach. She paused, searching for what to say next. Her eyes drifted to the side, catching a glimpse of the cardboard cut-out of Luke in her peripheral vision.

"Luke was here," she said, her voice steadying. "And now, he isn't. And that makes me sad." Her tone grew more serious. "But every story has something to teach us, even the ones that end in tragedy."

And even the bad ones, she thought.

As the deputy headteacher stepped forward to thank her, Ellie caught Daniel's eye. He gave her a thumbs-up and a heartfelt smile—a small but genuine gesture that seemed to fill the hall with quiet reassurance.

As Ellie looked out over the sea of soft, innocent faces, she couldn't help but wonder: how many would grow up to be footballers like Luke? How many would

The Plot Thickens

buy a motorbike? Was there another Cassie or Jack sitting among them?

That last thought tugged at her. Looking back on Jack, the signs had been there from the very start. Dr Christina Marsh had been right—Ellie had fallen into the trap of ignoring them.

She shook her head, turning away from the hall. No. She wasn't going to go there. There was no way to know.

In the foyer, teachers lingered in quiet conversation while children played outside on the playground. George, still recovering from surgery and seated in a wheelchair, rolled up to Ellie. His handshake was firm.

"You should be proud," he said.

Ellie glanced at the cardboard cutout of Luke and smiled softly. "I'm proud of him."

George smiled back. "I taught Luke in high school, you know. Funny thing—he liked history, even if he wasn't very good at the work. But he had an interest." He paused, his expression thoughtful. "Truth be told, I never thought you and Luke were right for each other. Typical teenagers, thinking they'd found *the one*." He glanced at Meredith, who was giggling with Maggie like a schoolgirl. His face softened. "But what do I know?"

"You know a lot, Mr Fenton," Ellie replied, patting his arm. "How are you doing?"

"I'll be back on my feet in a few months," he said

with a sigh. "But more importantly, I have my wife back—in more ways than one."

Maggie appeared at Ellie's side, her eyes bright. "I'm proud of you," she said warmly. Ellie loved seeing her gran like this—smiling, socialising, and hiding her limp, though there was a noticeable spring in her step.

"Thank you for bringing Meredith back to me," Maggie added.

"I didn't do that," Ellie said.

Maggie gave her a firm look. "You did. You crossed to the other side with evidence as your guiding light and brought her back."

"I just followed the trail."

"And you did it splendidly," Maggie said, squeezing her arm.

"A few more steps, and I might have followed it through a trapdoor."

"Then you're starting to understand life, dear granddaughter—timing. Knowing when to stop, when to start, when to leave, and when to stay. Not that anyone figures it out completely. But sometimes, when you take the wrong step, life gives you a second chance to set things right." She checked her watch and asked, "So, what now?"

"All I want to do is what we should've been doing all along—getting on with the decorating," Ellie said, kissing her gran on the cheek. "I'll meet you at the bookshop."

* * *

The Plot Thickens

Ellie met Charles at the museum, where he carefully sorted her notes and the evidence that had led to Jack's arrest into the archives. He labelled the folder: *The Campbell Files—1994–2024*.

"It's strange," Charles said, setting the folder into place. "Someone will sift through this someday. And stranger still that despite all these records, Ellie Swan's name is nowhere in any of it... nor did it come up in the limited press coverage."

"Just the way I wanted it," Ellie replied. After a pause, she added, "Though I didn't pull it off alone. Sylvia called in one of her many media contacts. Turns out, having a busybody reputation makes her the perfect guardian angel. I never wanted my name linked to Jack Campbell again."

Charles nodded, though his curiosity lingered. Tilly had been right—young people didn't hide their feelings well.

"What really happened in that cellar, Ellie?" he asked in a cautious whisper. "People are saying the wildest things."

"Of course they are," Ellie said, crossing her arms.

"I heard he was... performing? Tap dancing? Doing magic tricks?" Charles pressed, half-serious. "And that he fell fifty feet down a well and somehow survived?"

Ellie studied him for a moment, weighing her words, then nodded. "Not as far from the truth as you'd think."

* * *

Ellie turned the corner to Meadowfield Books as it began to snow, bracing for another day of fixing, scrubbing, and quietly fretting about the future. But she froze mid-step. The bookshop was full.

Not with builders or curious passers-by but with actual customers. Arms full of books, they chatted excitedly as they queued by the counter.

The sight was surreal. Books lay spread across sheets on the exposed floorboards, their covers gleaming under the afternoon sun streaming through the dusty windows. Behind the counter, Maggie stood like a seasoned shopkeeper, phone in hand to take card payments. She smiled and nodded at customers, radiating energy as though this had been the plan all along. Meredith stood beside her, carefully bagging books.

"Ellie! Isn't this marvellous?" Maggie's cheeks were flushed with excitement, her enthusiasm infectious.

Ellie blinked. "Gran... what's going on?"

"People kept showing up to see the wall," Maggie explained, gesturing towards the graffiti still splashed across the exposed bricks. "Joey—bless him—suggested we throw down some books and see what happened." She gestured to the bustling shop. "And look at this! We've sold nearly enough to pay him back already. He thinks we'll be ready for a *proper* opening come New Year!"

Ellie let the words sink in, hope fizzing in her chest. "New Year," she echoed, glancing around the bustling shop. "I hope he's right."

The Plot Thickens

Maggie gave her a knowing look. "Of course he is. This is what happens when a shop is loved, Ellie—it gives back."

As the last queuing customer left with a stack of books and Meredith headed home to George, Maggie turned to Ellie, her eyes glinting mischievously. A few customers still browsed the makeshift spread, but Maggie pivoted and slipped her hand into her pocket.

"Guess what's in here," Maggie teased.

Ellie sighed, already smiling. "No more mysteries, Gran."

"Fair point." Maggie pulled out a small badge and handed it to her. "It's a manager badge. You don't have to wear it—it's more symbolic."

Ellie turned the badge over in her hand, its weight unexpected. Words failed her.

"I know I'm stuck in my ways," Maggie said with a chuckle. "And I'm so stuck that I won't change that. But it's not going to be my way anymore. It's your way now. Remember what I've always told you—it's called Meadowfield Books because it's for the people of Meadowfield. It's not about us. You're the next generation, Ellie. I've had my time."

Ellie looked up, her throat tight. "I still want your input, Gran. I like your ideas."

"And I'll keep giving them," Maggie said warmly. She tapped the badge. "But this lets us both know where the book ends. With you. From my mother to my sister to me, and now to you. In my attempts to turn back the clock, I've been haunting this place. You do what you think is best, and I'll be here to support you."

Ellie hesitated. "What if I don't know what's best?"

"You *will*." Maggie's eyes softened. "You know I wouldn't pass the baton to just anyone. No one else qualifies. This is what you do—details, history, books. Just take it one decision at a time."

Ellie took a deep breath and clipped the badge onto her shirt—a seal of approval, a quiet pact with the shop and its legacy.

"I've put stars next to the wallpapers I like, but the choice is yours." Maggie pulled out a catalogue and gestured towards the graffiti wall. "Well, away you go."

The hum of the kettle filled the air as Maggie disappeared into the back room.

Ellie surveyed the shop—its chaotic charm, its hopeful future. She pulled out her phone, flipping to a page in the catalogue. A sepia-toned mural of rolling countryside caught her eye, a scene reminiscent of Meadowfield's hills. She lined up the camera to snap a picture, but a notification slid down the screen: a job alert from a film production company looking for people 'in her field.'

Ellie stared at the notification for a moment. Then, without hesitation, she long-pressed the app until it shivered. The delete button winked at her like an old friend. She tapped it and sent it to the cloud—it wasn't needed, for now.

"Fancy the next episode of Handy Steve later?"

The Plot Thickens

Maggie's voice interrupted as she bustled back in with two steaming mugs of tea. "I want to know if his lawyer agrees it's unrealistic for his ex-wife to demand visitation for the cat while also filing a restraining order. At least Steve got custody of Mr Bean."

"Restraining order?" Ellie raised an eyebrow. "He hasn't mentioned that yet."

"Ah!" Maggie bit her lip, handing over the tea. "I *might* have skipped ahead. And I almost wish I hadn't, but we'll get there. First, we've got his thoughts on complementary neutrals for the retail space. I think I understood some of the words I just said."

Ellie smiled. "We'll figure it out together." She reached into her bag, pulling out a postcard. "This came this morning. From Dad." The postcard depicted the Scottish Highlands, and Ellie handed it over. "He says he'll be home next year."

Maggie glanced at it, her interest mild. "Your father's always been a man of few words."

"Well, he added a couple more," Ellie said, tapping the postscript. "Why does he want to know if he's still welcome at your cottage? And why does he want me to ask without you realising what I'm asking?"

Maggie looked up, amused. "I'd say you've already failed that brief, dear."

"No more secrets, Gran," Ellie said, folding her arms. "What's going on?"

"I'm not surprised he wants to know," she sighed. "Before your father left, he took my savings from the biscuit tin in the kitchen. It wasn't much—just a couple of hundred—"

"That's not the point," Ellie cut in, disbelief in her voice. "Dad *stole* from you?"

Maggie shrugged, brushing off the question with a smile. "Tell him to come. We'll clear the air."

"He didn't leave a return address."

"That..." Maggie chuckled, shaking her head. "... that sounds like your father. I suppose we'll see him next year. But for now—where were we? Oh, yes—Handy Steve." She winked conspiratorially. "I'm sorry for skipping ahead—"

"Spoilers, Gran."

"Oh, we never cared about spoilers in my day!" Maggie threw up her hands in mock defeat. "All I'll say is, you'll never guess where it's going."

Ellie shook her head as she opened her pad. A fresh list of ideas stared back at her, brimming with possibilities. She glanced around the shop again, watching a few late customers browsing the makeshift displays. For the first time, the weight of responsibility didn't feel so daunting. As the snow fluttered past the window, she flipped to the end of the list and hovered with her pen over 'Open the shop!'

"Close enough," she said, ticking it off before closing the book.

Meadowfield Books wasn't just surviving. It was alive.

The Plot Thickens

* * *

Thank you for visiting Meadowfield again! If you want to support the series and me, the best way is to let people know what you thought of the book...

And it only takes a minute to leave a rating/review!

* * *

Return to Meadowfield with Ellie Swan in...

THE FATAL FIRST EDITION

**COMING SPRING 2025
PRE-ORDER NOW**

Thank you for reading!

DON'T FORGET TO RATE AND REVIEW ON AMAZON

Reviews are more important than ever, so show your support for the series by rating and reviewing the book on Amazon! Reviews are **CRUCIAL** for the longevity of any series, and they're the best way to let authors know you want more! They help us reach more people! I appreciate any feedback, no matter how long or short. It's a great way of letting other cozy mystery fans know what you thought about the book.

Being an independent author means this is my livelihood, and *every review* really does make a **huge difference**. Reviews are the best way to support me so I can continue doing what I love, which is bringing you, the readers, more fun cozy adventures!

WANT TO BE KEPT UP TO DATE WITH AGATHA FROST RELEASES? *SIGN UP THE FREE NEWSLETTER!*

www.AgathaFrost.com

You can also follow **Agatha Frost** across social media. Search 'Agatha Frost' on:

Facebook
Twitter
Goodreads
Instagram

Also by Agatha Frost

Meadowfield Mysteries (NEW!)

3. The Fatal First Edition
2. The Plot Thickens
1. The Last Draft

Peridale Cafe

33. Cruffins and Confessions (coming soon)
32. Lemon Drizzle and Loathing
31. Sangria and Secrets
30. Mince Pies and Madness
29. Pumpkins and Peril
28. Eton Mess and Enemies
27. Banana Bread and Betrayal
26. Carrot Cake and Concern
25. Marshmallows and Memories
24. Popcorn and Panic
23. Raspberry Lemonade and Ruin
22. Scones and Scandal
21. Profiteroles and Poison
20. Cocktails and Cowardice

19. Brownies and Bloodshed
18. Cheesecake and Confusion
17. Vegetables and Vengeance
16. Red Velvet and Revenge
15. Wedding Cake and Woes
14. Champagne and Catastrophes
13. Ice Cream and Incidents
12. Blueberry Muffins and Misfortune
11. Cupcakes and Casualties
10. Gingerbread and Ghosts
9. Birthday Cake and Bodies
8. Fruit Cake and Fear
7. Macarons and Mayhem
6. Espresso and Evil
5. Shortbread and Sorrow
4. Chocolate Cake and Chaos
3. Doughnuts and Deception
2. Lemonade and Lies
1. Pancakes and Corpses

Claire's Candles

1. Vanilla Bean Vengeance
2. Black Cherry Betrayal
3. Coconut Milk Casualty

4. Rose Petal Revenge
5. Fresh Linen Fraud
6. Toffee Apple Torment
7. Candy Cane Conspiracies
8. Wildflower Worries
9. Frosted Plum Fears
10. Double Espresso Deception
11. Spiced Orange Suspicion

Other

The Agatha Frost Winter Anthology

Peridale Cafe Book 1-10

Peridale Cafe Book 11-20

Claire's Candles Book 1-3

Printed in Great Britain
by Amazon